# Readers love th[illegible] series by R. Cooper

## *Some Kind of Magic*

"There's glitter and wings and magic… it's a wonderful thing!"

—The Blogger Girls

## *A Boy and His Dragon*

"This is one of the loveliest romances that I have read…"

—Gay Book Reviews

## *A Beginner's Guide to Wooing Your Mate*

"…this book was friggin BRILLIANT!! I absolutely loved it to pieces and I could not put it down."

—Love Bytes

## *Little Wolf*

"This has been bar none the most emotionally satisfying book I've read this year!!"

—Coffee Time Romance & More

## *The Firebird and Other Stories*

"My words are no match for the exquisite language of *The Firebird and Other Stories*."

—Inked Rainbow Reviews

## *A Dandelion for Tulip*

"This is an absolutely gorgeous love story…"

—The Novel Approach

By R. Cooper

Animal Magnetism (Dreamspinner Anthology)
Dancing Lessons
Let There Be Light
Medium, Sweet, Extra Shot of Geek
Play It Again, Charlie
A Wealth of Unsaid Words
Wicklow's Odyssey
Winner Takes It All
The Winter Prince

BEING(S) IN LOVE
Some Kind of Magic
A Boy and His Dragon
A Beginner's Guide to Wooing Your Mate
Little Wolf
The Firebird and Other Stories
A Dandelion for Tulip
Treasure for Treasure

Published by Dreamspinner Press
www.dreamspinnerpress.com

# Treasure for Treasure

R. Cooper

Published by
DREAMSPINNER PRESS

5032 Capital Circle SW, Suite 2, PMB# 279, Tallahassee, FL 32305-7886 USA
www.dreamspinnerpress.com

This is a work of fiction. Names, characters, places, and incidents either are the product of author imagination or are used fictitiously, and any resemblance to actual persons, living or dead, business establishments, events, or locales is entirely coincidental.



ISBN: 978-1-63477-887-9
Digital ISBN: 978-1-63477-888-6
Library of Congress Control Number: 2016913580
Published December 2016
v. 1.0

Printed in the United States of America
♾
This paper meets the requirements of
ANSI/NISO Z39.48-1992 (Permanence of Paper).

To the anonymous person who asked me for more dragons.
And to the rest of my readers, for daring me to keep going.
Treasure, all of you.

JOE COULDN'T hear anything but the occasional drag of his shoelace on the pavement and the distant crash of the tide. When the waves were silent, he caught the sound of his own choked, uneven breathing. He jammed his hands into his pockets and clenched them tight. He focused on the cracks in the old sidewalk and the soft bump of his backpack against his back as he walked. His feet were cold. Everlasting was chilly at night, even at the tail end of May. It didn't help that one of his sneakers had a hole and he'd forgotten his coat.

He told himself to ignore the temperature, although no one was around to see him shiver. The town didn't have much of a nightlife—a few bars, the corporate coffee shop open until ten, the occasional fancy gathering in one of the big houses overlooking the bay. Anyone looking for a good time had to drive down the highway to one of the bigger towns or all the way to the city, although that was supposed to change soon. His mom had said something about summer tourism increasing, probably to suggest he get a part-time job before he moved to the city for school.

He didn't mind. Anything to get out.

He crossed an empty intersection, heading vaguely toward the harbor and the bay. He could walk along the sand for hours, and did sometimes when his mom was working and he had nothing else to do. Everything would taste of salt and lightning, and the wind would be wild. The view was best when the fog and clouds were rolling in and the sea and the sky were gray at the same time.

That view was one of the few things he'd miss about this shitty town. The city was farther inland and down where the waters were warmer. The coastline would be different, and so would the mountains and the trees.

On his way down Old Main Street, he passed historic homes—well-maintained Victorians that were the town's second claim to fame. If he stayed on this street, he could walk for hours and not encounter a single person, just more old houses and then eventually trees, acres and acres of the variety of redwoods that had given the town its name back in the days of the Gold Rush. If he went back the way he'd come, he'd pass through the streets where the regular people lived, the normal, good, respectable, mostly white people and their kids.

He'd hear them first, though. Grad night parties were probably as loud as their other parties.

He kept to his current path, passing silently under pretty streetlamps and disregarding traffic signals since they had no traffic to worry about. The city was going to be a change. He'd be one in a crowd there, not just one.

He swung his backpack to his other shoulder to check his phone. He had several unopened texts. He ignored them to look at the time.

Twelve o'clock on grad night. He imagined most of the kids were good and drunk by now, gathered around a fire pit in someone's backyard to share beer. Their grad night parties were probably like their other parties, which he heard about the following Monday in snatches of conversation as he walked through the hall. Mostly he overheard a lot about them throwing up or making out in the shadows at the edge of the firelight, semipublic groping. Because dating someone wasn't nearly as important as everyone else knowing about it and approving. Like being invited to those parties in the first place—it wasn't about fun; it was about the show. It had to look right.

Joe scrubbed at his cold cheeks and wiped his eyes, then turned toward the harbor. The sea would be black this time of night, but he would have had to borrow his mom's car to go to the trees. The presence of the redwoods would be too much right now. He wanted noise. It might keep him from doing something stupid.

His phone buzzed in his pants pocket—another text—but he ignored it and took a right, toward the park in the town square. Sometimes there were transients down by the harbor, and some of the workers at the factories drank there after hours, but other than that, Everlasting wasn't dangerous. People hurt each other like they probably did everywhere, and some of them were good at it, but nobody did anything illegal, not really. Because of the town's first claim to fame.

Joe came to an abrupt stop at the entrance to the square and tipped his head back to stare at the statue of the town's most famous founder. Dìzhèn the dragon stared back at him with knowing bronze eyes. Dìzhèn was beautiful, or at least her sculpture was. But Joe knew, deep down, that she must have been. All dragons were. They moved with careless grace, and spoke in elegant, clipped words, and they shined in the light like jewels.

Even with distant streetlamps to let him see, Joe could tell she was just like them—her family, her descendants, here to watch over the town.

He snorted at the thought and stepped closer to the statue's giant brick base. He didn't care about the turn of the century design of the rest of the park, with its hedges and wrought iron fences curled protectively around small trees. He focused on Dìzhèn, the reason people wanted to come to this town.

Everlasting was famous because it had been chosen by a dragon. That was supposed to mean something.

Everyone knew the fantastic story of the dragon who had conquered a town—or at least bought one, and kept it. He was supposed to draw inspiration from it, or feel flattered; he'd never been sure which. Part of him did like the story, because he knew the humans at the time must have hated Dìzhèn with a burning passion for being everything they weren't. They had probably glared at her with jealous hatred in their blue eyes, and spent their every waking moments either pretending she didn't exist or trying to make her life miserable. She had triumphed over them, but it must have hurt to be the only one of her kind in a hostile land.

But he looked at her and couldn't imagine her making stupid mistakes. If she had, she'd probably burned all the evidence, or hexed it with her magic, or whatever it was dragons did.

Joe didn't have magic that he knew of, although that didn't stop people at school from saying he did. But he hadn't spelled anyone. He hadn't done anything.

He clenched his hands in his jeans pockets again, then raised one hand to wipe at his nose. He hadn't done anything but say yes, because he was stupid like that. He should have known he would be the one to get in trouble. He should have been smarter, not dumb and pathetic enough to think attention meant he was special.

His phone buzzed again.

Joe wondered if it was another apology, each one full of more and more typos as Russ got drunker and drunker at whatever party he and his girlfriend had gone to. Jock party, cheerleader party, honor student party, rich kids party. It could have been anywhere in the right part of town. Russ and Mads were wealthy and white and popular and going to proper four-year schools in the fall, and not the nearest junior college like Joe.

# 4

Russ was going to miss him. That was the last text Joe had read. He would have smashed his phone, but no way would he have been able to replace it. As it was, he'd kissed his mom on her cheek before she'd headed to her shift, and then he'd grabbed his backpack and started walking.

He'd been wandering through town for hours and didn't know why. Russ didn't even know where Joe lived, and he sure as hell wouldn't have shown up there anyway. Wrong part of town, even if his girlfriend would have let him go.

Not his girlfriend, just a friend, he claimed. An ex, he'd added after that. But she was crazy, so he had to be careful. But Joe made him want to be brave, made him want to try things, made him *want*.

A trace of heat shot through Joe's skin and made his mouth go dry. He immediately felt sick. The memory of getting fucked in Russ's house while his parents weren't home shouldn't make him horny. Joe wasn't at any party. He was compliments about his mouth and a text in class asking for a blowjob. He was slick kisses in Russ's shiny car and then private excuses and text apologies and watching Russ turn away from him in the halls.

He frowned as he studied the sinuous curve of the dragon's body, the shine on her scales so bright he could still see it in the dark. He listened to arriving texts he wasn't going to answer, and stared at her. His stomach was twisting so much he could feel bile in his throat. The cold had him shivering. His phone wouldn't stop. Russ must be wasted, or maybe he wasn't and this was all some hilarious joke to everyone at that party.

They thought he was magic, that he must have made Russ do it, because otherwise why would Russ want him. Poor and Native or poor and Mexican, it didn't matter which they thought was worse. It mattered what Russ thought, and it turned out that no matter what he'd said, he felt the same as everyone else. He hadn't seen anything in Joe but an ass and a mouth and probably Joe's stupid hope that someone like Russ would like him.

His whole life in this town, in the same schools with the same group of kids, and still Joe hadn't learned he wasn't one of them.

He'd remember it now.

Joe had a can of spray paint in his backpack and a fever in his blood. He wouldn't face a dragon's wrath if he did anything. There weren't any dragons here anymore. They hadn't chosen anything.

He pulled the can of paint from his backpack and turned to look at Dìzhèn's face. His eyes went to hers, and stayed there.

Lightning shot down his back and then a hot flush ran under his skin. His cheeks felt like they'd been scalded.

Dìzhèn's eyes gleamed at him in the dark, but Joe glared stubbornly back at her. His phone stopped buzzing, and he wanted to smile even though his eyes were dry and stinging. No more drunk texts. No more offers to meet down by the harbor or while parents were away for the weekend. No more front seat hand jobs and sucking Russ off in the bathroom. No more wanting to bring Russ home but hoping he'd never have to show him their crappy apartment.

No more silent treatment at school the next day, or being ignored in class, or thinking about anyone making out with anyone more socially acceptable in front of their respectable, decent friends.

Joe squared his shoulders and looked at Dìzhèn and waited.

Dragons were supposed to be able to see the worth in something. She must have seen something in this town, in these people, all those years ago, but Joe couldn't imagine what. What right did she have to judge, to choose, anyway? What right did any of them have?

He stuck his chin out and considered her. She might have accomplished a lot, but what had the rest of the dragons done? They weren't even here anymore. Not one golden figure remained in their mansion in the hills.

The wind picked up. The stirring trees sent a shadow across Dìzhèn's face that turned her lips up at the corner, gave her lines of laughter around her eyes.

Joe startled backward and dropped the can of paint. It rolled along the pavement, obnoxious and loud, and he chased after it with sudden panic. When he finally grabbed it and spun back toward Dìzhèn, the shadow had passed.

He stared at unmoving bronze for several minutes, until his phone buzzed again and made him jump.

He turned it off with a furious snarl, his face hot with how stupid he was, and then shoved the can of paint into his bag. There was no dragon magic, and no one was going to choose anything. There was just Joe and a hunk of bronze that wasn't nearly bright enough.

He turned his back on it and walked through the empty park in the direction of the trees.

# CHAPTER 1

THE STATUE of Dìzhèn watched over the park in the center of the town. Raised high on a square brick base, Zarrin's illustrious ancestor twinkled in the pale winter sunlight. The imposing bronze figure, dressed in a nineteenth-century men's suit and hat and standing on two legs, looked similar to any statue in any other small town, at least so Zarrin understood from television. But unlike most founding citizens of that era, this one had Chinese features. She also had a large dragon coiled around her feet, made of the same gleaming metal.

The tourists who came to Everlasting for the quaint restored houses, or the coastal views, or to hike or hunt in the nearby mountains, probably thought the dragon was ornamental. The artists who had cast the statue might have thought so too. Out of necessity, Dìzhèn had hidden from most humans and left much of her public business in the hands of her human secretary. When Dìzhèn had needed to venture out into the world, she had chosen a human form, a *male* human form to make her business easier. It hadn't been until sometime after the First World War that the truth came out that Dìzhèn had been both female and dragon. That was her elegant, powerful form curled around the feet of the standing figure.

She had come to this country with all her treasure and made a home for herself and her grown children. She bought the land the loggers of the time had nearly destroyed, poured money into the fisheries and the ships in the harbor, and built the grand house her descendants still owned, all at a time when beings were hidden, the Chinese were unwelcome in white communities, and women were considered weaker.

She was true dragon.

Zarrin liked to imagine she would have been fond of him, if only for what little they had in common besides blood. He also had a male form when shifted into a human, although he had figured out his preference for his male body early in life, and lived it whether or not he was in the public eye.

But deep down he knew that though he might watch over her legacy, her town and the guarded nature preserve a few miles away, Dìzhèn had been a hundred times the dragon he was.

He nodded respectfully at her as he did every day and then left his Vespa parked in her shadow, with his helmet balanced on the seat.

The post office was across the street from the park in the center of town. At midmorning, traffic was light, but Zarrin adjusted his messenger bag as he waited at the light, and wound his cherry-red scarf tighter around his neck.

He wasn't cold, exactly, but his human body never seemed as warm as it could be. His matching gloves kept the chill from his fingers, but though he pulled his white knitted cap down over his ears, his skin tingled at the damp winter air. The cap was a gift from Bernard, his former housekeeper. Zarrin loved it, but was ashamed to admit he might need earmuffs as well before winter was over. This winter was colder than usual already, or perhaps it seemed that way now that Zarrin spent so much time in town as a human.

He hurried on his way once the light indicated he could safely cross the street, and he dashed past the silent, staring human holding the door open for him. He was eager for news. Bernard, a thirtyish elf, had been with Zarrin's family for ten years, but had decided at the end of summer that it was time he visit his family and possibly think about finding a home of his own.

The house was quiet without him. Zarrin thought he had done well, though. He bought his very own groceries now, in his daily trips to town, and picked up the mail, and rode his shiny Vespa down the winding roads every day without incident. He'd told Bernard so in his last letter before anxiously inquiring about what Bernard was up to. It was difficult to keep a watchful eye on one's treasure when it was so far away.

But the mailbox was empty when he unlocked it. Bernard was probably too busy to respond. He never had enjoyed being distracted when he had a task to do. Elves were like that, he had often told Zarrin and then usually banished him to the stool in the corner of the kitchen, to keep him out of the way while Bernard cooked.

Zarrin closed the mailbox and pocketed his key before heading back out into the cold. Puddles in the street from last night's rain made him pause to worriedly consider the storm drains and whether or not they might be blocked. He had no idea whom to approach if that was the case, but it felt like something a responsible dragon should monitor.

He was getting better at this, he decided, and resolved to check again tomorrow for a letter from Bernard, and in his answering letter to ask Bernard about the town's drainage. Bernard had been with his family for years, he'd probably know what Zarrin's parents or grandparents would do to keep their town running smoothly.

Presumably someone in City Hall would also know, but Zarrin wasn't quite ready to approach that building yet. Perhaps, once he learned more, the council would approach him. Zarrin was the only Xu left, or at least, the only member of his family currently occupying the house and the land. He would do his best to uphold the legacy and keep the town safe. They would see that. The humans might have forgotten in the time his family had been away and the year Zarrin had been left to the house and the Preserve and Bernard's care, but they would remember soon.

He smiled as he continued down the sidewalk across the street from the park. He could see the bay, in between buildings and over roofs. Far ahead was the silhouette of one of the city's older, prouder buildings, although of course it didn't rival his family's home. Next to him were a number of shops and boutiques that catered to tourists and locals alike, their windows lined with decorative white lights in preparation for the holiday season.

With summer tourism over, the streets were much less crowded. That was one of the reasons Zarrin had decided to venture down from the house. He paused in front of a particularly fantastic window display, then turned, which caused someone to bump into him.

"Could you watch where you're going, assho…." A muscular blond human teenager trailed off in the middle of his sentence and then swallowed audibly. "Never mind. My fault." He spun on his heel and headed in the other direction.

Zarrin had yet to get the knack of humans, but he was certain he would in time. He was dragon, after all. Not much of a dragon, but still dragon. It couldn't be fear of him that kept them from speaking. The locals at least would know his family was here to protect them. There had to be some other reason for their silence. Maybe it was his breath. Maybe it *was* offensive to humans and he should take up smoking to disguise his fiery breath as many dragons did. He didn't like the taste of tobacco, but he might be able to find something sweet. Possibly he could try those mints that came in the tins they sold at the coffee shop.

Zarrin went back to considering the display in the window. The sign above him indicated the shop sold antiques and curiosities. The interior certainly appeared to be cluttered with glass lamps and books and sconces and things. But the window display had all the curiosities. He saw wooden carvings of bears and eagles, and ships in bottles, but it was one framed painting among an arrangement of them that caught his eye.

A small painting, deliberately unfinished, with penciled lines at the edges leading to the multitude of colors at the center. Everyone, even a dragon, was small among the redwoods. Anyone standing in the cold, damp groves, looking up toward the hint of sky above, knew they were nothing compared to those ancient trees. The massive redwoods lived for thousands of years. They were among the oldest living things on earth, and even towered over giants.

Zarrin knew the view, knew the feeling of admiring the trees but being alone among them and yet comforted to see them standing. He hadn't realized others might feel the same.

He put his hand to the glass, already itching to hold the painting, and then tore himself away from the window to enter the shop.

The old man behind the counter looked up from his book and stood there with his mouth agape as Zarrin came inside.

Zarrin approached him with haste.

"The painting in the window, the unfinished one with the redwoods, I like it." He couldn't help how his hands curled into a grabbing motion at the words. His heart raced to imagine holding the painting. He didn't know where he would put it yet, but he'd find a place.

The old human closed his mouth with a snap. For a moment, his gaze followed the curling trails of smoke in the air around Zarrin, and then he blinked. "Painting?"

"In the window," Zarrin reminded him. "The small one. The one with the mist and the sense of cold. I would like to have it."

That made the old man blink again, a few times. Then he blurted, "Of course!" in what Zarrin privately thought was an overly loud voice, and came out from behind the counter. Zarrin twisted to watch him while reaching into his bag for his debit card. He knew the card was in there someplace, and it was much easier to keep track of than cash. Zarrin always seemed to lose cash.

He held it out when the man returned, but kept his eyes on the artwork that was soon to be his. The man froze again, which was enough to make Zarrin raise his head and try to focus on him, but then the man pushed the painting at him and took a step back.

"Don't… don't worry about it." The man was behind the counter again before Zarrin could respond. "It's my treat."

Zarrin was already clutching the painting to his chest, but he paused. He always paid at the grocery store, and at the coffee shop. Giving money for goods was part of what it meant to be a good and generous benefactor. Also, Bernard had said that not paying for things was stealing.

He held out his card again. "I didn't ask for a gift," he corrected, to make certain this was clear, and frowned when the man hesitated before accepting the card. The old man lowered his gaze, focusing on the task of running the card and then tearing off a tiny piece of paper.

"My receipt." Zarrin nodded sagely as he received it and his card. Receipts were a part of paying for things. Some people used them to keep track of their money. Even Bernard did. So Zarrin tucked it away in his messenger bag and gave a contented sigh. "Thank you for my lovely painting." He held it out, generously, for the man to see one last time, and then he put it in his bag, with a murmured, "Mine."

He smiled as he went back out the door, leaving the old man quiet behind him, and was so pleased he could almost forget that once again he had failed to get a human to really speak with him. He didn't think his breath was that bad, but he stopped at the crosswalk and discreetly exhaled into his gloved palm.

Smoke scent, like clean-burning dry timber, shouldn't drive anyone away. But he could try the mints. He could even ask about them. He'd use them for his dragon breath and also to start a conversation. "Are these good?" he imagined himself asking, and liked the sound of it. That was simple, friendly. That should get a response.

He crossed the street and made a beeline for Everlasting Cuppa, the independent coffee shop in town and the local favorite. Situated between a deli and an ice cream parlor that served flavors like rosemary orange and candied violet, Everlasting Cuppa looked almost like a pub from the nineteenth century. The building itself was old, down to the glass in most of the windows. Someone—Zarrin didn't dare try to guess who—had strung up white lights in all those windows sometime since his visit yesterday.

The effect was so pretty Zarrin felt a curl of warm need in his chest. *Mine*, he thought, with a satisfied puff of air, although his family did not own the coffee shop. All the same, this was his place, as surely as the stand of rocks by the twisting bend of Fool's Creek and the nest of pillows in the center of his bed. He felt it in his bones, in the magma-hot pit of fire behind his ribs.

Nonetheless, because he also felt a thousand fluttering tremors in his stomach, he paused outside the door to yank his hat from his head and tried to smooth down the dark mess of his hair. He glimpsed himself in the crosshatched glass window of the top half of the shop's front door—not-tall, not-imposing, shining gold—and lifted his chin as his father might have done. Dignity was what people admired in dragons, not wide, burnished bronze eyes and bitten, chapped lips.

He licked his lips nervously one last time despite that, then braced himself and stepped inside.

He took a second to glance at the tables and stuffed chairs arranged around the central stone fireplace, and shivered at the change in temperature. The fireplace heated much of the main room, with help from the heating system and the collection of coffee brewers behind the counter.

Zarrin shoved his hat into his bag and came farther inside. He should have stared at the board above the counter like many of the other people in line were doing, but his attention immediately went to the man standing behind the cash register.

The quakes in Zarrin's stomach multiplied. The heat in the shop must be even greater at the front counter, because even on the coldest days, Joe and his coworker wore T-shirts under their aprons. It was possible they wore more clothes earlier in the morning, but Zarrin had yet to witness that. He came into town every day after a sunrise walk through the Preserve, and arrived at the shop usually as Joe or the other human was attempting to clean up from the morning rush.

Today, however, there was a line, and both men were in front of the coffee and espresso machines.

Zarrin's mouth was unaccountably dry. Joe leaned over the register to wiggle one of the old, loose wires that made it run, and cracked a brief smile for something his coworker called out. When he'd fixed the wire, he straightened up again to take the next person's order. He flashed a smile for them as well. Zarrin could always tell when Joe was fond of a customer. He'd tilt his head toward them while they talked, even if he was doing something else, like pouring milk or tapping the register buttons. Some of the customers leaned toward him as well, with more than polite interest, but then, Joe was very handsome.

He had black hair that reached his earlobes, although he tied it back in a lazy sort of stubby ponytail most of the time, and blew away the strands that fell into his face while he worked. His hands were clean, sometimes smudged with coffee grounds or crushed bits of loose-leaf tea, his fingernails smooth and short. He wasn't overly muscular, but there wasn't much flesh to spare on him, and jeans revealed enough of his thighs and ass for Zarrin to know Joe was someone who walked or hiked often.

He moved with the confidence of someone who had known this place a very long time, and yet Zarrin didn't think he was older than twenty-five or twenty-six. He had high cheekbones and what Bernard might have called a stubborn jaw, and beautiful black tattoos inked into his skin like scrimshaw, drawings of musical notes and patterns like the weave of a basket at his upper arm and on the side of his neck. His eyes were as dark as his hair, and his lips were full, and when he stood up, he was taller than Zarrin by four inches.

He wore a black shirt and jeans with his scarlet work apron, and with his brown skin, it made him seem very serious, which he was. But he was well, and smiling, and working hard, and the tremors in Zarrin's stomach vanished.

*Treasure.*

He took a last swipe at his hair before stepping closer to the end of the line and waiting to order.

Much too far away from Zarrin, Joe stopped. For the space of a heartbeat, his hands were motionless and his attention seemed fixed on the countertop. Then he handed the customer their change and called out to the next one. His smile had disappeared.

Zarrin reached for his debit card. Then he thought it might be too early to have the card out and put it back. He glanced over toward the fire in the fireplace, aware of the prickle of sweat beneath his clothes.

The woman in line ahead of him seemed to feel it too. She reached up to tug at her long pink scarf, only to visibly pause when she noticed Zarrin behind her. She gave him a tight smile, almost as if she was nervous, and waved him forward. "I'm in no hurry," she murmured, before casting her eyes in a different direction.

Zarrin swung his head from her to Joe, now even closer. That was kind of her. Clearly she must understand his need to be near Joe. He nodded his appreciation, because it wouldn't do to embarrass her for her generosity, and took her place in line.

Something must have upset Joe, perhaps his last customer, who kept interrupting Joe's current customer. Joe scowled, fierce and furious, and had nothing at all to say to the warmly dressed young man trying to start up a conversation with him.

Zarrin didn't recognize the man. Perhaps he wasn't local, despite his mention of the high school. But as he had already paid for and received his drink, Zarrin saw no good reason for him to linger at the counter.

He cleared his throat before speaking to make certain he was heard. "Once you have ordered and paid, you are free to find a seat in the other room." Zarrin stared without blinking at the human as he and the other humans nearby turned around.

Joe looked to Zarrin too, frowning even harder. Zarrin wanted to ask what had upset him, but obviously it was not his place.

He considered the stranger. He was about Joe's age, with pale brown hair and light skin. He was tall as well as structurally handsome. But he didn't make Joe smile, and he was in Zarrin's way.

"That is, unless you care to leave now." The puff of smoke that followed the words wasn't entirely intentional, but Zarrin forgave himself. Another dragon might have done worse, even if Joe wasn't their treasure to defend.

The human's face paled even further when he saw Zarrin, and then he left the counter without another word to Joe.

Zarrin narrowed his eyes until the man was seated at a table far away.

He got out his debit card and held it tight in his hand as he again faced the counter. He had purchased a painting, a beautiful painting. And he had defended Joe from someone who had bothered him. Today was a good day. It was going to be *the* day, he knew it. Today he would get Joe to speak to him, to smile at him. Today Zarrin would be dragon enough to captivate the handsomest human he had ever seen.

He kept from dancing restlessly from foot to foot by continually reminding himself of the long line of powerful dragons he came from, and how it wouldn't do to have the humans in his care think he was weak and foolish.

But Joe was so close, and today, Zarrin was going to really talk to him.

Joe finished handing a tiny paper cup of hot chocolate to a little human child with brightly beaded braids of hair sticking out from the bottom of her winter hat, then accepted paper bills from the girl's father. When the man and the girl walked away, Joe popped open the register, made the change, and then stuck that in the tip jar.

Zarrin raised his gaze from Joe's hands and then froze in awkward, delighted excitement when their eyes met.

Joe's eyes were a deep, warm brown. They locked onto Zarrin, and for a moment, Zarrin thought of how humans over the centuries had claimed it was to be studied by a dragon, how insignificant they had felt as the dragons considered them.

Then Joe's attention dipped down to Zarrin's hands as Zarrin rested them on the counter. He blinked, maybe at the sight of the red gloves Zarrin had forgotten to remove.

Zarrin quickly crossed his arms so he could tuck his hands out of sight. He leaned closer to the register, and the warmth of the coffee machines, and the fragrant display of teas, and Joe. He licked his lower lip and breathed through his mouth to capture the myriad of scents until he found the exhaustion and irritation and odd notes of salty-spice of Joe's emotions. Zarrin couldn't decipher them, but he found them fascinating.

Joe's gaze flicked to Zarrin's mouth, then up to his eyes. Zarrin held himself still while his fire raged and made the air around him thick. He trembled as he waited. He thought of telling Joe about his morning, and the sunrise and his painting, and the gleam of Dìzhèn's bronze. Joe sat in the park sometimes, and stared across to Dìzhèn's statue. He must admire her greatness. Joe saw art in everything. He talked about it with some of the customers—the sky over the bay before a storm, the curl of steam above a mug of tea, the soaring crescendos in the classical music on the coffee shop's sound system.

Zarrin kept his arms crossed and his chin up, as dignified as he could be, and felt the heat behind his ribs flare when Joe drew his eyebrows together.

Then, with barely a pause, the frown disappeared and Joe's expression went blank. "What can I get you?"

The politeness in his low voice made Zarrin drop his arms. He returned to leaning against the counter as he stared into the hot coffee and caramel of Joe's eyes, searching for some hint that Joe remembered him.

How could he not remember him? Zarrin was here every day! He was dragon! Zarrin was not the most beautiful, or the fiercest of dragons, but he was the child of the family that protected this town. They all must know him.

He opened his mouth, then closed it so nothing like a whine would escape. He swallowed his protest and glanced around, as if the teas or the wide eyes of Joe's coworker, Martin, could help him.

Joe was human, and had such an ordinary name. "Joe" was a name without power, and yet Zarrin had noticed the splendor of him from the start. It had been too much to expect Joe might do the same, and instantly see something in Zarrin worth having. But to be remembered, to be spoken to in more than that same hated question every day, Zarrin had hoped for at least that.

He lowered his chin, then recalled himself and lifted it. "A latte." He always ordered a latte. From his first visit here after Bernard had left, he had ordered a latte. He didn't understand the appeal of a latte, but he ordered them, because people in coffee shops ordered things like that and appeared to love them.

Lattes had too much milk as well as a bitter aftertaste. But he ordered them, and paid for them, and drank them. That had to count for something.

"What?" Joe's voice seemed lower somehow, almost warm with concern, and Zarrin's heart beat a touch faster until he realized he must have whispered his answer.

"A… latte," Zarrin tried again, horrified at the hint of a stammer. His skin felt unnaturally hot, especially his face, and he jerked his head up high so Joe wouldn't think he was blushing and embarrassed. "A medium latte."

He was *dragon*. He was *mighty*. He was the protector of this town, and he wanted nothing in return except for a few words, or simply for Joe to remember his order.

"Medium latte," Joe said, angling his head toward Martin without taking his eyes from Zarrin. His gaze tracked Zarrin's restless hands, his quick swallows, the dart of Zarrin's tongue over his lips once again. Then they returned to Zarrin's eyes.

Martin pushed forward a paper cup full of foamy, hot milk without a word, as if he'd had it ready.

Zarrin took a long, long breath. He shoved a hand into his pocket and wrapped it tight around the heavy coin he'd brought with him. Then he reached out with his other hand to give Joe his debit card.

Joe took it, used it, and gave it back. He didn't speak, but he glanced up, almost carefully. When he found Zarrin continuing to stare at him, he tensed.

The trail of gray smoke between them was a visible indication of Zarrin's despair and confusion as he tried to think of what he was doing wrong, and then Joe reached behind him and plucked a plastic lid from a dispenser so he could fit it over the top of Zarrin's latte.

He sealed it tight, then pushed the cup toward Zarrin.

He'd never done that before.

Zarrin straightened up and heard a multitude of startled gasps behind him as a trickle of white smoke escaped him. Martin made a croaking noise.

Joe raised his head. "Was there something else?" he asked, with only a little pause as he studied the disappearing wisps of white. Something similar to wonder lit his expression, but then when Zarrin remained frozen, his frown returned. "There are people waiting."

Zarrin twisted reflexively at his harsh tone and caught the wary look the woman in pink was giving him. Behind her, another line had formed, as if the bell over the entrance had been chiming while Zarrin stared at Joe, and Zarrin hadn't noticed.

He turned back to Joe. "I…. This is adequate." He heard himself stammer again, and shivered at what his father would think of him for acting this way. It was no wonder Joe was disappointed, that he would echo the word, "Adequate," with a snort.

Zarrin yanked his hand from his pocket and dropped the coin into the tip jar, something that got only slightly easier with time. Then he picked up his card, and his latte, and inclined his head.

"Thank you." Thanking people was important too. Bernard had insisted. Zarrin sent one last glance Joe's way, trying to discern anything to tell him what he was doing wrong, but Joe was already helping the next customer with deliberate attention.

Zarrin heaved a smoky breath that reminded him he'd failed to buy a tin of mints, but he took his latte with him as he went slowly to the door.

Someone held it open for him, and in return, Zarrin handed them his latte before he went outside.

He stared out toward the bay for a while, then pulled his hat back over his ears when the cold got to be too much. His pocket felt empty without the coin, but it was for the best. A dragon showed his appreciation for treasure *with* treasure. Sooner or later, Joe would comment on the friendly gesture.

More than friendly, if Zarrin had his way, but as he had learned today, it was too early to get his hopes up. But if he could get handsome, wonderful Joe to smile at him, and speak with him, then someday he could get everyone to. As it was, Joe had put the lid on his drink for him. That was new. It could mean good things, and not merely that Joe was impatient for Zarrin to get out of the line.

Zarrin shoved his hands in his pockets as he headed back toward his scooter. He had work to do today. Dinner to prepare, and another walk through the Preserve to make sure all was well.

But he couldn't look up at Dìzhèn as he traded his hat for his helmet and secured his bag for the ride home. She would likely have agreed, as most dragons did, that Zarrin was too soft. She would have roared and shaken the earth to remind the town of her power. She would have impressed Joe with gold and the other shiny things humans admired. At the very least, she would have spoken more than a few whispered words to him.

Or perhaps Joe would not have been afraid of her. Joe might be one of the brave ones, the ones who sought out dragons and challenged them. Any culture that knew dragons also knew tales of the ones sent to conquer or appease them. The ones who spoke truth to power and reminded the dragons that treasure was meant to be *treasured.*

Zarrin put a hand to his chest, where he felt a hollowness much like his empty pocket. He had no errands left in town, no reason not to return home.

It wouldn't be so bad, he argued with himself as he started his Vespa and began his slow journey toward his family's house. He took side streets instead of the main road out of town, avoiding people heading toward the freeway. Stunted redwood trees began to appear in patches of land between houses. He passed an old pink mansion, much, much smaller than his family's home, though of roughly the same time.

The next Victorian he passed was black-and-white, and advertised itself as a bed-and-breakfast. There would be more of those along the coast, but he headed inland.

The redwoods were taller the farther he went from the sea—and humans. The road grew darker and colder, the sky blocked by countless trees. By nightfall the coastal fog would leave everything dripping with condensation, and anyone foolish enough to be out in the woods would be shivering. Water slowly falling from high branches to the earth below would tap out a soft melody, accompanied by the rustle of leaves in the wind and a chorus of frogs and scattering animals.

A small part of the ache in his chest eased at the sight of so many ancient giants, long-lived enough to remind him to be patient. They survived as no other trees did, in the chilly, wet fog, and yet when the sun broke through their canopy, the forest floor beneath them was alive with green ferns and rich ochre-colored earth tangled with black roots to complement their coppery bark.

*Treasure.*

He would skip dinner preparations and put away his new painting before heading straight into the Preserve his family maintained. He would watch over the trees and protect them from careless campers with unattended fires, and the humans who hunted both the animals and the sought-after redwood.

The thought warmed him as he passed the signs warning trespassers away from the Preserve. The first sign was large and direct, bold black words across a white background: Xu Family Preserve. Private Property. No Trespassing. The second sign was smaller, more discreet: Entrance Permitted by Invitation Only. It rested near the gate at the start of the driveway leading to his home. Farther down the hill was an abandoned railroad track, where a small, private train had once brought Dìzhèn's visitors halfway from town. A carriage had taken them the rest of the way. Her son, in the 1920s, had sent a car down for his guests. After that, better roads had led to the train being donated to a museum in town and guests chauffeured up in cars.

The gate, as well as the wall surrounding the mansion, were as old as the house itself. Historians who snuck pictures of it lauded its fusion of Victorian aesthetics and Imperial Chinese design. They said the same of the house itself.

Zarrin continued up through the open gate and around the circular driveway to the side of the house, where he parked his scooter in the detached garage next to the covered Silver Ghost and red Speedster. He left his helmet with it as he came back out to face the house.

Three stories, not including the attic space and servants' quarters or the basement. The indoor garden was its own building, although without anyone to maintain it, the plants had grown into a jungle. The small pool, quite large by twenties standards, had been drained years before since neither Zarrin nor his sister cared to use it and there was no one to clean it.

Bernard hadn't considered it part of his duties, and Zarrin couldn't blame him. Keeping the house clean was a job in itself.

Zarrin was going to have to hire someone soon. But since that would involve telling his parents Bernard had left, he'd avoided it.

It had been months since he'd last spoken to any member of his family, which helped when keeping a secret. But sooner or later, they would find out.

He looked up to the highest point in the house, the tower decorated with Victorian latticework on its many pagoda-style tiers. No smoke rose from any of the chimneys. The house would be cold. Zarrin alone was not strong enough to heat more than a few rooms. It wasn't his magic protecting it.

He clasped his gloved hands together to ward off the chill as he went up the steps and into the house.

He would talk to Joe and get other humans to talk to him. He would understand them, and then he would find help, much as Dìzhèn had found her secretary.

Tomorrow, he decided, as his footsteps carried through the house. Tomorrow there might be a letter from Bernard, and Zarrin could write back and ask him what he was doing wrong and how best to approach pretty humans who frowned. And he would buy a tin of mints.

Tomorrow he would make Dìzhèn proud.

JOE ROLLED out of bed and reached for his phone in the same motion. The alarm gave one more ring before he silenced it. Once he was up and safely on his feet, he allowed himself a minute to stare into the predawn darkness of his apartment and mourn the sleep he was missing.

Then a violent shiver tore through him as his body became aware of how cold it was. He lurched forward toward the bathroom and hissed the second he stepped onto the tiled floor. He pissed in the dark, sleepily surprised by how much the temperature had dropped. He'd gone to bed bundled up under a pile of secondhand quilts. With the heat on, his loose sleep pants should have been enough.

He washed his hands and face, cursing softly at the chilled water, and didn't bother to shower. He'd want to clean up after work when he came home with coffee grounds under his nails, not before it.

When he was done, he went to the kitchen and flipped on the light. He got a drink from the sink, then left the mug next to the cups full of water and paintbrushes that lined the counter.

The cold water made him shiver more, but it also helped wake him up. He was much more motivated to get ready for work if it involved putting on warm clothes. He only had to take a few steps to get to the battered chest of drawers, since the living room served as his bedroom. He'd turned the bedroom into his studio shortly after he'd moved in, because it had better lighting.

He chose a sleeveless T-shirt to go beneath his gray henley, then slipped on a pair of jeans and a thick pair of socks. The heating vent was ice-cold, which meant he'd have to call the landlord that afternoon after work, because that did not seem like a temporary problem.

He muttered to himself about that as he put on his comfortable, and more importantly, *warm* boots and then grabbed his coat from the back of a chair. He threw it on and zipped it up, but left his gloves in his coat pocket. He'd be inside the coffee shop in a minute, and the work would only get his gloves dirty.

He didn't bother with breakfast either, just reached for a band for his hair from the bowl by the door. The bowl also held his keys and loose change from the tip jar he hadn't exchanged for bills yet.

He tied back his hair, only to pause as he reached for his keys. The improbable sensation of warmth against his fingertips made him look down, but he already knew what he'd see.

At the bottom of the bowl were fourteen heavy, textured coins, discolored with age and yet glinting in the small bit of light. Two more sat on a table in his studio. They were all different, with uneven edges worn down over time—over centuries—with stamped images and languages from a variety of countries on their faces.

Most were silver, but they all were warm to the touch, as if steady exposure to heat and magic at the same time had somehow given the coins a hint of life.

He had never taken them to any of the antique shops in town or looked them up on one of the library's computers, but he knew they were real and likely worth a lot for the value of the metal alone.

He held one between his thumb and forefinger. The coin was probably silver through and through, and yet it felt nearly as warm as the two in his studio. Joe had no attachment to gold, despite living in a cramped apartment and working in a coffee shop. Gold caused a sickness in some people and led them to do cruel things. The yellow metal was garishly bright and too soft to be useful for anything other than jewelry.

But the bronzed, faded warmth in the other two coins had caught his attention and held it. Old gold, darkened with age and history, made him think of treasure chests, and silly childhood games of playing pirate.

The fact that these coins, until very recently, had most likely been piled inside an *actual* treasure chest made him grunt and finally let go. He forcefully grabbed his keys and his phone, then headed out and locked up behind him, although the only things in his apartment worth stealing were those coins and some of his art supplies.

The wet air sweeping in from the bay immediately hit him, and he shuddered as he turned and dashed down the wooden steps to the alley below. A few yards down the alley was the back door to Everlasting Cuppa, convenient for the person opening up on a frigid winter morning in the dark, which had been Joe for as long as he'd worked there.

Joe flipped on the lights and cranked up the heater, then went in to turn on all the machines without taking off his coat. He swept past the now-empty tip jar and scowled into the shadows of the shop because there was no one there to bug him about his sour mood.

*Dragons*, he thought, with a huffed breath, and brought all the chairs down from on top of the tables, where the closing crew had put them so they could mop the floor. He shook with cold, a far cry from how hot he'd be in a few hours.

He went to the back office to get out the money for the register and unexpectedly flinched at the echoing clang of the safe door as it opened. By eleven, he would be surrounded by the murmurs of contented families and the clacking keyboards of frustrated students, too-loud phone conversations and giggling teenagers. For now, it was as if no one else in the entire town was awake, aside from Joe, the pastry delivery guy, and a deputy or two. But they were outside, and he was in here, with the hum of the machines and the distant meowing of the cat in the alley for company.

He yanked the money envelopes out of the safe and then counted out the day's starting total at the register.

This morning the change seemed thin and cold. The nickels were too light. The dimes weren't bright enough. His fingertips passed right over them.

The very rich had no idea about the value of anything. To them, five dollars a day on coffee was nothing. Ancient coins made of precious metals might as well have been pennies. But that was the way of rich people. Even if the coin had no value to them, they were going to want it back the moment they noticed it was gone. It had to be an accident the coins had wound up in the tip jar in the first place. The dragon had probably meant to reach for change in the piles and piles of gold in its hoard and grabbed the old coins instead.

It wasn't as if Joe had earned those tips. He knew damn well he hadn't. And he didn't need the dragon's pity any more than he needed his intervention with people Joe didn't want to see.

He closed the cash drawer on the register with more force than necessary, then went to the back door, with only a brief stop at the storage fridge. The cold morning air hit him all over again as he stepped outside.

# Treasure for Treasure

# 23

The alley cat, a gray thing, neither sleek nor fluffy, was skulking somewhere near the dumpster. Joe set out the plastic bowl he'd started thinking of as the cat's bowl, and poured in a bit of milk. Milk wasn't good for adult cats, but he didn't have anything else, and it was better than whatever garbage the cat had been eating. Milk probably went well with mice too, and hopefully the rats that sometimes snuck up from the harbor.

The shadowy space beside the dumpster regarded him for another moment, and then the alley cat poked its head out.

No amount of coaxing was going to make the cat come any closer, not even to sniff Joe's hand, so Joe stood up.

"Don't expect this tomorrow," Joe warned in a soft voice that would have made his mother laugh at him. He went inside, under the cat's suspicious and impatient stare, where he put the milk away and washed his hands.

He should have turned on the music first. The shop was far too quiet this morning. Everything seemed to echo, every noise standing out against the silence. He was tired enough to drift for a moment in the sound of splashing water and the momentary warmth in his fingers.

The sudden knock at the back door made him flinch, his heart leaping despite knowing it was just Martin.

Martin stared blearily at him from the other side of the door, holding the boxes of today's pastries. They must have been delivered while Martin had waited to be let in. There was no sign of the cat, but the milk was gone. Martin was going to have something to say about that later, when he was warm again and more awake. Joe would ignore it as usual.

For now, he took the boxes of baked goods so Martin could close the door and take off his layered sweatshirts. Then he set the boxes on the counter to test the machines. He thought he could do this in his sleep. If it hadn't been so cold, he would have thought he *was* sleeping.

The realization did not improve his mood. This wasn't a bad job. It paid the bills his artwork only sometimes helped pay. He got free food and coffee, lots of conversation, and coworkers who didn't leave him to do most of the work by himself.

The brewers were warm enough. He started the first batch of coffees—dark roast, blend of the day, and decaf—then pulled shots in the espresso machine to get it going. Martin came up behind him and started setting out fresh pastries on the covered platters in the small but crowded section of the counter on the other side of the register. He handed over one of yesterday's, and Joe ate it as he wrote today's blend on the chalkboard above the brew station. Then he went to the back to remove his coat, clean up, check on the milk supply in the big fridge. When he returned, Martin was holding a ceramic cup under the stream of brewing coffee.

He handed it over with a grin, then got one for himself. Martin was nice for a middle-class white kid who spent most of his time outside of work stoned out of his mind. More importantly, although he'd gone to the same middle and high schools as Joe, he was from a later year, so Joe didn't have to hear him talk about the supposed "good times."

"You're in a mood," Martin observed, but sleepily. He wouldn't really wake up for about another hour.

"I didn't ask for a rich patron." Joe glared at his coffee as he poured in a splash of milk to cool it so he could drink it immediately.

Martin rubbed at his eye for a few moments, then bobbed his head. "Okay. Yeah. Is this about the guy who wouldn't shut up until the dragon stepped in, or is this about the coins again?" He cracked a yawn when Joe glowered in his direction. "You could handle that other guy. So it's got to be the coins, right? I wish I had your problem, but we both know those coins are not for me."

"It's been over two weeks since he started with them." Joe avoided the implied question and drank his coffee as he switched on the sound system. Shostakovich was playing, sweeping and tragic and Russian. "He should have noticed by now… unless he's doing it on purpose. I don't know what he thinks he's going to gain by giving me those, but—"

"Chill. Please." Martin swept past him to go out the front door to get the stack of newspapers and stick them in the rack near the fireplace. He left the door unlocked behind him, but it was nearly opening time anyway. He put a few logs on, then wasted two matches trying to light them before giving up. "I know—" Martin paused to lower his voice for two words. "*—the dragon* and his family own the town, but—"

"They don't own the town, they just think they do," Joe pointed out. They gave money to the library and the restoration projects, and owned over 50 percent of the stock of the fishing companies that employed much of the town, and had successfully protected about ninety acres of ancient redwood groves for over a hundred years. They might as well have owned the town. But none of them visited here. None of them even lived here anymore, except one.

"Yeah, but Zarrin doesn't actually own you," Martin countered, then stopped. "Huh," he remarked thoughtfully, and shivered a little as he turned on the neon Open sign as well as the decorative strands of lights around the windows.

"What?" Joe narrowed his eyes at Martin and didn't acknowledge the first customer walking in. It was only Ridley, anyway, retired and never in the mood for conversation. Joe had Ridley's black coffee waiting for him before he'd reached the counter. "He can't even wait in line. He cuts ahead. Like he has the right. Like it's *owed* to him. He doesn't get to tell people to leave. This place isn't his."

"Okay." Martin waved Joe off, then brought him his apron.

Joe slipped it over his head as he continued. "He buys expensive drinks he doesn't finish. He handed his off yesterday without taking a single sip. I don't even think he likes them. It's wasteful."

Martin turned away to eat another stale pastry. He coughed a bit.

"If someone says they own something, if they're going to claim it as theirs, they should know the value of it. See the beauty in it. Not drop it in a tip jar for their 'adequate' latte." Joe knotted the apron strings at his back with enough force to ensure they'd stay tied through the morning rush.

"It would be easier if you had his drink ready for him." Martin ran a hand through his buzzed hair, then seemed to realize he'd now have to wash his hands. He sighed and went to the back, where he called out, "If you did that, he'd just leave. Easy. You wouldn't even have to exchange words."

That was true. Joe wouldn't have to hear a single syllable from that quiet, smoky voice, or lean forward to catch the soft replies and feel the most incredible heat rising from golden skin. No, not skin, *scales*, the shade of old gold at the base of Zarrin's throat, and then darker, hotter bronze down the back of his neck. They looked like they were beneath the surface, as if they would feel like regular skin under his fingertips. Zarrin's lips were nearly the same color. All of him seemed gilded, which made it all the more ridiculous that Joe should give him anything without making him ask for it.

Joe finished his coffee in one swallow. "Enough in his life is easy," he rasped, and then went to start a triple shot cappuccino for Helene, the early morning jogger walking through the door.

"Good morning," she sang out. Helene wasn't just active first thing in the morning, she was chipper. She also didn't do anything but jog and spend her partner's money and visit the shop several times a day. Despite that, she was pleasant and tipped regularly, and she would actually say hi to Joe if she saw him somewhere else in town. A lot of people, especially the newer residents, didn't seem to recognize their servers outside of the context of the coffee shop. Or, if they did, they pretended they didn't.

Joe had been called José by those people more than a few times. He usually replied by getting their name wrong in return.

Helene pulled a five from her pocket and chatted to Martin while Joe finished her drink and brought it over. Maybe because she'd come to this town as an adult, with money, she and her partner were out and proud the way almost no one had been when Joe was younger. She always got her cappuccino in a ceramic cup and skimmed through the newspaper while she drank it. She brought her cup and saucer to the counter when she was done too.

Joe was actually pretty fond of her, as far as customers went, which was why he was taken aback when she abruptly turned to him with her dark eyebrows raised. "So?"

"So?" he repeated blankly, and caught Martin's careful warning headshake.

"So, the dragon." Helene made a comically devious face, as if she and Joe were exchanging secrets. "Has he revealed what he wants yet?"

"He doesn't really talk much." Martin tried to cut her off—or keep Joe from snapping at her.

"He doesn't talk to anyone." Helene ignored him, still peering at Joe. "I saw him considering broccoli in the grocery store and then again in the aisle with all the cleaning products, and there was no one with him."

Joe put aside the confusing image of Zarrin comparing various cleaning products in order to focus on the rest of this conversation.

"You're not the first person to say that," he finally replied, because what else was there to say? Any of them were welcome to walk up to Zarrin and introduce themselves and ask what he wanted. But of course, no one was going to do that. Even the mayor, even the other business owners, wouldn't dare.

"That's because it's driving everyone crazy!" Helene gestured wildly for a moment, then shook her head. "The dragons were all but gone, with just the youngest up in that house, and now he's here, *with us*. What the heck does he want? Holly thinks he's looking for a bride."

Helene uttered *that* incredible statement about her partner and then gave Joe a significant look. So did Martin.

Joe opened his mouth, then closed it tight. Whatever sort of fairy tale the town had been dreaming up didn't matter to him. Yes, there were tons of tales in every culture about magical creatures taking humans for their own. In a lot of the stories, it was an honor and not a horror. Some humans even chose that fate. But the stories were just that: stories. This wasn't Cinderella, and Zarrin was no Prince Charming. Zarrin was a brat, soft-spoken maybe, but still a brat. And anyway, the whole idea was ridiculous.

Like Joe was going to let some dragon have him to make the town less nervous about their dragon overlords. He didn't care what Zarrin's hair did when he pulled off his knit beanie, or how often Zarrin licked his lips while looking at him. This town hadn't done anything for Joe to make him want to sacrifice himself for them.

Being poor, and brown, and gay in a small-town school system meant Joe had been a popular target for kids in his class with something to prove. The high school principal had condescendingly told him that junior college was the best he could ever hope for and that art was a waste of time as a major for someone like him. More than once a customer expressed surprise that someone behind the counter at a coffee shop would know anything about music or current events. His mother had worked at the care facility for fifteen years, and some of the staff still treated her like a servant and not the nursing assistant she'd worked hard to become.

Helene saw him as a person, and Joe liked a lot of the people who came in to get coffee and talk with him, but he wasn't going to take one for their team either.

"Pretty sure if the dragon wanted something, he'd say so," Joe finally answered, then took a step back. "Also fairly sure it's none of my business. Whatever he wants, he'll get. If you really want to know, ask him. Make him tell you. Make him work for something for a change."

Despite being four years older than Martin, Joe felt like a teenager for the look he got. It didn't help that his mother probably would have given him the same disbelieving stare.

Joe had lived in Everlasting his entire life, except for the years he'd moved to the city to attend the JC, and everything in this town was a reminder of the dragons in their big house out by the Preserve—the Preserve that they also owned. Acres and acres of untouched old-growth forest they wouldn't allow anyone to see.

Joe had a vivid memory of being in a pageant in sixth grade, something stupid and false about the state's history meant to honor the dragons' recent donation to their school. The dragons had surprised everyone by attending, sitting in the front row of the auditorium, looking bored while every kid recited their lines.

He remembered being surprised that the father had hooded eyes, that the mother had dark skin and hair. The sister was about his age, but of course she hadn't attended the local school. Neither had Zarrin, but Joe had been fascinated by him anyway. He'd been a kindergartener's age then, maybe four or five, this tiny, funny-looking creature in clothes that had never seen a speck of dirt. Joe could recall the exact moment he'd noticed that baby dragon had brown skin too, paler but still enough like Joe's for him to notice, although Zarrin's had also been flecked with gold. The lights in the auditorium had bounced off his scales as he'd slipped out of his mother's arms three times in an attempt to run up onto the stage and join in the play.

Joe had wanted him to make it, so that small dragon could come closer and Joe could ask him about his skin and his eyes and if Zarrin got dumb questions all the time from the kids at his school, the way Joe did. Until that moment, he hadn't known dragons could be like him.

But of course they weren't like him, or even any of the white kids in the school. The dragons might pretend to get along, but they answered to no one. In the middle of the performance, the dragons had left without apology, taking a squirming Zarrin with them. They hadn't been seen together in Everlasting since, although for years their cars with their drivers would roll through town on their way to their big house.

There were a lot of theories floating round now about why Zarrin was walking among them, but searching for a bride was a new one, and Joe had a sinking feeling he'd be hearing it again. Arguing wouldn't do him any good, although he would anyway, only to get shushed and told not to speak of them like that—they might hear. *Dragons have magic, you know.* That's what everyone said. They might not know what kind of magic, but they knew it was there. Most campers and hikers who entered the Preserve, whether accidentally or on purpose, tended to immediately hurry out again, citing an uneasy feeling, as if they were being hunted. There were stories of humans who had tried to cross the previous dragons in business deals and wound up penniless.

And then, of course, there were the earthquakes. But it was easy to discount those as normal phenomenon, since aside from a few minor tremors that had been felt in the rest of the state, Everlasting had been remarkably quake-free for a long time now.

If the dragons were a source of some power that allegedly protected the town, as well as the origin of the earthquakes, then it was no wonder everything had gone quiet. The dragons, save one, had left, proving exactly how much they cared about what was "theirs."

Plenty of trappers and hunters had been prowling through town all summer, and Joe doubted they'd felt any invisible boundary keeping them off the Preserve.

The truth was the dragons didn't care about this place anymore, if they ever really had. They were only interested in getting either awe or fear from the humans around them—and Joe was never going to give them that. Joe had spent most of his life with people attempting to make him feel subhuman for one reason or another—being of Wiyot and Mexican descent, being gay, being uneducated but outspoken about the things that mattered—and no one, not even a rich, well-connected dragon with magic in his eyes, was going to get admiration or obedience from him. Whatever Zarrin's reasons for being in Everlasting after all this time, he could wait in line and pay full price for his coffee like anyone else.

Joe's ancestors had never worshiped dragons the way many other cultures had done before so many gods turned out to be damaged and easily hurt and not gods at all. He knew nothing personally of shifters, and fairies tended not to go too far north into the cold climates. What he did know of beings mostly involved his years in the city and the fairies and elves who had brightly introduced themselves to him.

Their expressions had been similar to the look on Zarrin's face when he first walked up to the counter to order a latte, although that was a comparison Joe hadn't made at the time. He didn't like making it now. If there was anything to make him stop and reconsider his actions, it was the idea that he'd taken someone's joy from them when they didn't deserve to be hurt. Luckily, every time he'd hesitated and wondered if he'd gone too far with a dragon who hadn't been that rude to him, Zarrin would casually intimidate people without any sign he was sorry about it.

*"That is, unless you care to leave now."*

Zarrin wasn't normally that direct. People got out of his way without him having to say anything.

Joe found it easier to feel anger when he thought of the people stepping out of line to let Zarrin go first than when he remembered Zarrin raising his voice as he suggested Roger Delamitri go take a seat in the other room. Roger hadn't stopped talking since the moment he'd noticed Joe at the register. Joe had been half a second from describing to him exactly how different their high school experiences had been and why he didn't want to speak about them, ever, with anyone, much less Roger, when Zarrin had interrupted. Zarrin had probably been tired of the sound of his voice.

Zarrin's feelings and motivations were not Joe's problem, Joe reminded himself as he got out a carton of milk for Martin and replaced him in front of the register. Zarrin was an adult, with the security of millions of dollars, a mansion, and magic in his every scale. He wasn't weak, or soft, and he didn't need to be protected. Nothing Joe could do would ever really hurt him, because ultimately Joe didn't mean anything to him.

The thought was not as comforting as it should have been.

Joe frowned so deeply that Mrs. Pickering, who ran the Laundromat he used, went silent in the middle of giving her order, and he had to shake his head and smile before she'd continue.

BY THE time the chairs around the empty fireplace were full of people contentedly sipping their coffees and the morning crowds had dwindled to a trickle, Joe had calmed down enough to blame his bad mood on waking up to unexpected freezing temperatures and the surprise of finding comfort and warmth in coins that by all rights should have been ice-cold.

He was not, as Martin seemed to be implying with his raised eyebrows, obsessed with Everlasting's remaining dragon.

Around ten thirty, with two cups of coffee in him and the breathing room to start cleaning up, he took a moment to wipe down the counter and restock the milk. A customer would have been nice. Several would have been more than welcome, and not just because of tips. He kept moving because the caffeine had his heart racing, and he did his best to seem impassive when Martin made a comment about the time.

Martin also expectantly put a medium paper cup down right next to the espresso machine.

Annoyed beyond reason at the smug look directed at him from a pothead, Joe left the counter to go finally light a fire in the fireplace. He had one blazing prettily in no time, then closed the screen. He removed his henley at the blast of heat and had retied his apron strings by the time he was back at the counter.

The chiming bell over the door made him raise his head, but then he quickly turned away and pretended to flick a crumb off the edge of the cash register. The rush of blood in his ears momentarily deafened him. His recently bared arms tingled with goose bumps as if he were cold, when he knew he wasn't.

He imagined most humans experienced this when a dragon entered a room. Dragons were supposed to be able to measure a person's worth simply by looking at them. To be studied by a dragon was to be judged, and to be chosen by one was an honor in many cultures—if the person was strong enough, or special enough, to handle it.

The first time Zarrin had come to the shop, it felt as though the world stopped, as if everyone there held their breath the second they realized who was among them. Joe had gone so still that the opening register drawer hit him in the stomach.

He should have been over it now, should have been as unconcerned as Martin wiping down the steam wands on the espresso machine.

But shine drew his attention no matter what direction he looked. Not a brilliant shine, more something like the haze around a fire, and the polished brass of the screen over their fireplace. Zarrin was gold, but a version of the metal that had been worn smooth by countless hands. *Old gold*, Joe thought once again, and wondered for the fiftieth time if Zarrin's skin would feel like one of the coins Zarrin had briefly held in his hand. He had an idea it would. He also had an idea that Zarrin would let him find out if he wanted.

That did not make him the dragon's bride. He didn't care what the story was.

The space behind the counter was suddenly almost unbearably hot, and yet Zarrin was by the door. Anyway, although Zarrin's presence sometimes raised the shop's temperature, it had never been like that. It felt like standing too close to boiling water, sticky with steam and parched with thirst.

Joe swallowed before risking a glance up.

Zarrin's gaze was on him, gleaming and interested. His skin was a deep tan all over, except for the golden sheen of scales at the back of his neck, not visible today since Zarrin had bundled up in a long red scarf. The ends fell to his chest, which was hidden from view by a black coat. He'd forgotten his gloves and was rubbing his hands together to warm them.

Joe expelled a breath at the sight, wanting to be exasperated at the rich idiot who'd forgotten something as practical as gloves, but also struggling not to ask why a dragon would need them in the first place.

Zarrin's darkly golden fingernails were short and bitten—something else Joe had to hold his tongue not to ask about. Zarrin's nerves, if he had them, were not Joe's business. The upward tilt to Zarrin's chin made that more than clear. In fact, the only thing keeping the bottom half of Zarrin's face from being swallowed up by his huge scarf was the arrogant angle of his head.

That childishly resentful thought kept Joe still for another moment, and then Zarrin began to move toward the counter, and Joe had to grasp the corner of the register to stay where he was.

Zarrin didn't walk as much as slink. His feet didn't make a sound. He didn't call out a greeting. He fixed his gaze on Joe and approached him as if Martin wasn't even there. Martin was likely fine with that.

The longer Joe waited to look back, the greater the odds that Zarrin would lower his head and widen his eyes and, for the briefest moment, appear hurt and helpless and almost human. That made Joe warmer than all the clinging tendrils of smoke curling into the air between them, because in that second when Zarrin wasn't posturing, Joe could remember the little boy kicking his legs back and forth while his parents hissed at him to behave.

Zarrin reached across the counter and closed his hand around one of the cutesy tins of mints the owner had recently decided to sell the way their corporate competitor did. His fingers slipped and he dropped it, then caught it again with a gasp that made Joe snap his head up to stare at him.

Black hair at uneven lengths, as if inexpertly cut with household scissors, fell across Zarrin's eyes, which because of their shape and his dark eyelashes seemed to have a vaguely feline look about them. His nose, like the rest of his face, was somehow delicate, although that could have been the way he moved. Joe had seen smaller, slighter men who didn't give that overall impression of softness. But Zarrin held himself like someone accustomed to comfort and ease, which he was.

Yet his expression was startled, as if Joe wasn't supposed to have seen him drop the mints. Then Zarrin's lips parted, and Joe's attention fell to the hint of tongue.

Zarrin wet his lips a lot. Joe assumed he was thirsty, and that was why he came in to the shop in the first place. In the winter cold, it was no wonder his lips were chapped. Joe would have loved to pretend he hadn't noticed that or thought about Zarrin's mouth, but he wasn't in the habit of lying to himself. Zarrin had a wide, pretty mouth, and a tongue Joe had seen more times than he could count, and a habit of gazing at Joe as if he wanted to drag Joe to the nearest bed and keep him there. Of course Joe had thought about it.

He'd also thought about Zarrin's skin and his lean, graceful lines and the burnished tips of his fingers that never seemed like claws. He had thought, many times, of challenging Zarrin to do something about the ridiculous gifts of coins and the smoldering gazes. He'd imagined Zarrin beneath him, hot and weak and panting, Zarrin wrapped around him in his crappy bed, sliding into him, sucking Zarrin's cock on the stairs to his apartment, as if they couldn't even make it through the door.

Zarrin continued to stare at him, startled and hungry. Then the mints slipped from his hand again and fell noisily to the countertop. He snatched them up and clutched the tin to his chest before he turned his head toward the tea display. He did that a lot too, despite how he never requested tea.

Normally Joe would have suggested a tea blend if a customer had shown that much interest. He also would have greeted the customer by now, or, in the case of a regular with a standing order, have it waiting for them. Maybe if Zarrin would have greeted him in return, the way the rest of the customers did, he would have done it. But Zarrin said nothing. He licked his lips again and regally regarded the teas. Apparently he was finished ogling Joe for the day and was back to standing silently in front of Joe while being waited on.

Joe could finally move now that Zarrin wasn't staring at him as if he wanted to devour him. There was nothing like being ignored to remind him why Zarrin was not to be trusted. He sure as hell wasn't for sleeping with either, no matter how interesting or beautiful he was. This wasn't high school, and Joe wasn't anyone's secret anything.

He braced himself, then heard the words fall from his mouth in a calm, almost bland tone. "What would you like?"

Behind him, in a fearful voice, Martin whispered, "Here we go again."

Zarrin's attention swung to Joe and stayed there. He raised his chin to something beyond its usual imperious angle. Then he blinked rapidly a few times, and the injured sound he made was almost as soft as the curve of his parted lips.

The quick beat of Joe's heart and the shiver that ran down his spine were both familiar and startling. Zarrin's little huff was hot, like trickles of steam. Then Zarrin leaned forward.

"I place the same order every day," he whispered, his soft hurt and outrage at odds with the ripples of ancient metal beneath his skin.

Joe's mouth went dry, and his hands twitched, actually twitched, with the need to capture that on paper, on canvas, on anything he could. Zarrin was so beautiful. Handsome, sexy, attractive—all the usual words applied too—but more than that, he was beautiful. He was inhuman and shimmering and so *interesting*, catlike and demanding and then suddenly small and needy. No one in Everlasting was like him. No one in the city had come close.

Joe wanted to rub his thumb over Zarrin's pulse point as though it was an old coin. He wanted him in his tiny apartment, where he could stroke his back until the confused note in his voice went away. The idea sent a pang straight through him. He wasn't here to comfort Zarrin or to kiss him or to soothe his stung ego.

But his stomach flipped when Zarrin's voice trembled. "You… don't remember?"

Joe was absolutely certain Zarrin was used to being waited on, although the family's housekeeper hadn't been seen in town for some time. Zarrin didn't need anyone else fawning all over him.

Despite that, Joe had to glance away before he spoke. He'd worked with the public long enough to know how to be rude without being direct.

"I take a lot of orders every day," he answered honestly, and felt the force of the glare his mother would have given him if she'd been there. Although she had raised him to speak the truth, so she should have expected this.

Zarrin made that small huffing sound again and sent a stream of hotter smoke into the air. The scent was like a wood fire, and the hint of an extinguished match. Then he straightened, with a move so sharp Joe imagined the flick of a tail behind him.

A tail, because Zarrin was a dragon.

The thought repeated in Joe's head as though he was reminding himself of something he'd momentarily forgotten. Zarrin was a dragon, a dragon who could roast him, eat him, or at the very least, buy this shop and fire him.

But Zarrin slapped his debit card on the counter and then crossed his arms. "A latte," he barked to the air over Joe's shoulder. "Medium." He curled his fingers into the sleeves of his coat. "That's the only thing I've ever ordered."

Martin slid the latte forward with embarrassing swiftness. He'd obviously had it ready, again, and wasn't being shy about it.

Zarrin slowly lowered his gaze to the paper cup and then brought it up to consider the two of them. His bottom lip trembled.

Joe's face warmed with a blush. There was no way Zarrin was close to tears. He knew that, because Joe couldn't mean that much to him. Even on Zarrin's worst days, Joe couldn't be anything more than the vexing human who made him ask for things.

He knew that. But he reached for a lid and stuck it on Zarrin's drink anyway. He put a jacket on the cup as well, although Zarrin was hardly going to think the temperature was too hot. Then he nudged it closer to Zarrin. He resolutely did not glance at Martin, and the second he raised his head, Zarrin looked away.

"I would also like these mints." Zarrin slipped the tin into his pocket and kept his hand there. He mumbled something under his breath that sounded like "Mine," although Joe must have heard wrong.

"Mints," Joe repeated, somewhat blankly.

"Yesss." Zarrin drew out the word and shot Joe a significant look. "Mints."

"Just sell him the mints, man," Martin stage-whispered from behind him.

Joe frowned slightly, more in confusion this time than anything else. Maybe dragons were serious about their peppermint drops.

He belatedly entered the amount into the register and swiped Zarrin's card. He didn't know why he paused before he handed it back, but Zarrin took it without a glance. The careless way he dealt with money should have been irritating, but at the moment, Joe was more curious about Zarrin's hesitation.

"I'll use them next time," Zarrin offered in his smoky, husky voice before finally looking at Joe again. He stared into Joe's face and seemed to hold his breath. When Joe didn't say anything, something flickered in Zarrin's expression and made it dim. "Thank you," he added, and for once the regal way he inclined his head at them barely registered.

Joe didn't get a chance to be irked at being treated like a dutiful servant, or to wonder about the mints, or Zarrin's subdued softness. Zarrin pulled his hand from his pocket and dropped something heavy into the tip jar.

Then he closed both hands around his latte and held it to his chest.

"You're welcome," Joe answered gruffly, and nearly flipped off Martin, who let out a strangled cough. He was probably torn between fear and amusement.

The gentle, startled parting of Zarrin's lips sent another pang straight through Joe's chest. The warm shine of his eyes made it hard to breathe.

Then something moved behind Zarrin, and Joe abruptly focused on the line of people that had formed while Joe had been helping him. Despite the wait, not a single one had voiced a complaint. Most of them weren't even daring to look directly at Zarrin. The only person Joe could see who was openly considering the dragon in the room was four-year-old Hazel, sitting on her knees in her chair by the fireplace. Kids didn't understand things like the power of money, or danger, or being rude.

The humans in line, however, every single one of them born and raised in his town, understood their relationship to the dragon family only too well.

Zarrin tilted his head at them in gracious acknowledgment, the Sun King gazing upon the common masses. It instantly brought the scowl back to Joe's face. Not that Zarrin saw. He was gliding toward the door so silently he might as well have been walking on clouds.

Joe watched him go and then shivered at the rush of air that came through the open door. The wind stung his cheeks, and he must have been still for too long, because he was cold again.

He turned to Martin.

Martin picked the coin out of the tip jar and held it up to the light. The bronze circle had a square missing from the middle and characters that could have been Chinese on each side. He solemnly handed it to Joe.

Joe held it in his palm. It was warm, as if Zarrin had held it close to him before giving it away.

He dropped it back into the tip jar and then firmly greeted the next, patiently waiting customer.

Zarrin didn't know the value of the thing, Joe silently reminded himself one last time. Although whether he did or not didn't really matter. Joe already knew he'd be taking it home, where it would rest in his studio with the other two.

# CHAPTER 2

ZARRIN BRACED himself before he entered Everlasting Cuppa. He still had no word from Bernard, and no advice to go on, but he thought of Dìzhèn as he stuffed his hat in his pocket and smoothed his hair. Dìzhèn had not given up, and so he would not either.

Yesterday had been both disheartening and promising. Martin had remembered Zarrin, at least. Zarrin wasn't certain if he should try befriending the other human before he got in Joe's good graces.

A dragon needed to curry no human's favor. The very idea would have been humiliating to his parents and his grandparents. And yet Zarrin had to try. Joe saw beauty in the world. Surely he would see beauty in Zarrin too, something worth speaking to. And then Zarrin would learn what it was he was doing wrong with the rest of the humans, and he would do better. They would approach him with their concerns, and he would answer them, and he could rest at last, knowing his treasure was cared for.

If they had forgotten the way things were supposed to be, it seemed impolite to say so. It was better to remind them of his presence by walking among them and doing as they did.

Another latte it was, then. He would even drink it today.

Zarrin froze briefly to see the coffee shop nearly empty and Joe by himself behind the front counter. Then he skipped forward so quickly he almost tripped. Fortunately none of the townspeople saw their dragon behaving so foolishly.

Zarrin stopped just short of bumping into the counter as he stared hungrily at the line of Joe's back and the bared skin of his shoulders.

The ink patterns in Joe's skin tormented him. He didn't know why, only that thinking of them got him hot and bothered—as Bernard used to refer to lustful feelings. He wanted to touch all of Joe, but especially the mysteries beneath his skin. That they would forever remain out of his reach increased his longing for them. Even if someday Joe might allow Zarrin near him, the tattoos would always be Joe's alone.

He parted his lips, just a little, to inhale steam and coffee and the subtly shifting currents of Joe's emotions, and then made himself pull back from the counter. He reached into his pocket for the tin of mints and popped two into his mouth before he hid the tin away again.

The cold crunch of them was startling, then gone.

He cleared his throat politely and then with more force before he could think of his father's view on timidity. Joe immediately went still and then tensed before he turned around.

Zarrin glanced into his eyes and then dropped his gaze to the counter. He was a weak dragon, with only so much bravery in him.

"The mints are quite good. They feel very cold, which I did not expect. But then their taste is sweet, which I prefer." Speaking was remarkably easier if he wasn't looking at his treasure. "Please inform the owner I will be buying more of them."

Silence answered that, so Zarrin dared another look at Joe, who hadn't moved.

The minty taste was already fading. Zarrin fiddled with the tin as he pulled it out once more and then sent it flying toward the register as he tried to open it. He snatched it back quickly and put three in his mouth before he stowed it away again.

Joe made a small sound.

Zarrin crunched them into pieces and then swallowed them. The icy sensation on his tongue was so strange, like eating snow, and yet tingly.

"Bernard—my housekeeper, recommended this shop to me before he left." Zarrin wanted to rub his face whenever he thought of Bernard. It made his eyes itch, as though he was going to cry, and he refused to cry in front of Joe. "He has been gone for a while now. I don't hear from him as much as I'd like to. It's… it's difficult without him." He clutched at the air for the treasure he could not hold, then released a loud breath.

"Bernard." Joe surprised him by speaking, and saying that name of all things. His voice was flat. "Your housekeeper." Zarrin raised his head in time to see Joe glance toward the back of the shop. Then he looked at Zarrin again. "Bernard was a good customer. Please inform him he ought to come by again."

Joe's tone was strange. So was his expression. He stared meaningfully at Zarrin, so Zarrin regarded him seriously in return. After a while, he bobbed his head in agreement.

"I will. He hasn't written to me in some time. I checked the post office again today. I'm sure it won't be much longer." Zarrin stuffed his hands into his pockets so more of his anxiety wouldn't show. "He's very smart and capable. I'm certain he's fine without me, having the adventures he spoke of."

Zarrin realized he was probably saying too much and forced himself to pause and to make his voice less soft and wistful. "But I will relay your message."

"Relay my message?" Joe repeated, then tossed his head. He hadn't moved from the espresso machine. Of course he had not. Just as he had not begun to prepare Zarrin's drink.

Zarrin bit down on his lip, then recalled himself enough to stop. He lifted his chin, although once again his gaze fell to the counter. "I… I would like a latte. Medium size." He didn't think he could take that same blank question from Joe about what he would like. Not today. Not after this much progress.

He waited, unsure if he should say more, and fixed his attention openly on Joe as Joe faced the machine and began to prepare his drink. He could take his time with so few customers in the shop, and seemed to be doing just that. He steamed some fresh milk first and then let the foam settle while he pulled a shot of the dark espresso. His hand hovered over the squeeze bottle of caramel for a moment, but then he moved on to grab a paper cup.

Caramel in a latte might make it palatable, but Zarrin was so close to getting Joe to remember his order it didn't seem wise to change it.

Joe's hands were sure as they prepared everything. Zarrin would have paid simply to see that, although he had enough sense to keep that to himself. Joe hadn't frowned yet. This was good.

Joe gave him a lid again, as well as the tiny paper slip that fit around the cup for some purpose Zarrin didn't understand. Then Joe took a small brown packet and a thin wooden stirring stick and placed them on the counter next to the finished latte. He stared down at the register and cleared his throat. "Anything else?"

Zarrin considered the unusual gifts from his treasure and clucked his tongue as he stuck them into his pocket. "Mine," he told them quietly and then stared innocently at Joe when Joe's gaze went from his pocket to his face.

"You don't have to take the sugar," Joe told him in the gruff voice he used sometimes. Zarrin didn't know what that tone meant, but he knew Joe directed it at him quite frequently. Yet he didn't smell of anger. He never really did, even when his scowls were fiercest. At least, not anger like Zarrin's father or mother smelled of it. Joe's scents were more fluid, like water or air. They tingled like the mint sometimes, but mostly they were salty and electric.

"I don't have to do anything," Zarrin responded, and clucked his tongue again.

Joe drew his eyebrows together sharply. "Of course you don't." His tone was much more than gruff this time.

Zarrin huffed at him, with all the traces of cooling mint vanished from the hot cloud of smoke that left him.

"Exactly," he insisted, with a nod. Joe should understand. Zarrin didn't have to do anything. He chose to come here. The coffee shop was naturally welcome to feel honored.

But Joe continued to regard him with that unhappy line between his beautiful eyes.

Zarrin wet his lips in nervous indecision. Then he ventured a question. "Martin isn't here?"

Something heavy fell to the floor out of sight in the back of the coffee shop. Joe's shoulders hitched up higher with tension, and his frown did not lessen. "Martin?" he asked, his tone aggrieved or confused, Zarrin couldn't tell which. He glared at Zarrin so intensely Zarrin nearly took a faltering step away. "Martin is in the back. Would you rather he made your drink?"

"What?" Zarrin cocked his head to the side. "Did I say I did?"

"No." Joe practically grunted it. But he reached for the latte as though he was going to take it back, so Zarrin grabbed it and held it to his chest. Joe went on talking anyway. "Some customers are like that. It's not a big deal if you don't want me… if you don't want me to make your latte."

Zarrin spoke over Joe's low, furious voice that seemed to imply it *was* a big deal. "A latte is a latte." Honestly, Zarrin doubted the taste could be that different depending on who made it. They both prepared them the same.

He tossed his head when Joe got quiet. Humans were so perplexing. "It's good that he's here. You aren't all alone." Zarrin curled his fingers around the heat from the paper cup. "Being alone is much harder."

He felt Joe's gaze on him, but meeting it was difficult when he had no distractions save the music coming from distant speakers. He didn't want to let go of the cup and risk Joe taking it away, so he moved it from one hand to the other as he reached into his bag for his debit card, which he pushed across the counter.

Joe took the card with a forceful, irritated sort of gesture and swiped it with much the same attitude. "I—" He started to say something, then cut himself off.

"Yes?" Zarrin leaned closer with interest. His pulse raced to think of how much they were speaking together. Granted, he still couldn't read Joe's moods, but he didn't think Joe wanted him to. Joe was someone who kept his treasures to himself. Zarrin could understand that. It made his gift of a sugar packet all the more surprising.

"I can handle being alone." Joe held out the card. His jaw was clenched. It made him appear stubborn.

Zarrin took the card and tried not to visibly react to the thrill of their fingers touching. But there was fire in his skin, racing along his nerves. He drew in a quick breath and wondered if it was his wishful thinking that Joe did the same.

"Can you?" Zarrin's parents would have been startled at how out of breath he was, how carefully excited. He blinked the haze of heat and wonder from his eyes and did his best to seem as thoughtful and serious as Joe. "How?"

"How do I handle being alone?" Joe asked in an uncertain voice. He glanced around at the machines and the tea display before giving a shrug. "I'm used to it. I just do my work."

"Do your work?" Zarrin repeated.

"Yes. Work." Joe put a lot of emphasis on that word. He seemed to direct it both at Zarrin and at the hidden, Employees Only area of the shop. But his intense gaze was for Zarrin alone. "And I should get back to it, unless you need something else."

Zarrin held tightly to his latte. Somehow he did not think even Bernard would have known what to say with Joe's attention so firmly fixed on him. He could not tell if he had annoyed Joe or even registered to him. He could tell nothing except that his scent was prickly and warm, and that his attention only flickered away when Zarrin licked his upper lip in an attempt to catch more and know him better.

"Yes." Zarrin disgraced his every ancestor and living relative by starting to pick at his cup lid, but it was that or bite his fingernails. "I won't keep you from your work. You're very good at it."

"You could say I'm adequate." Joe's tone was too level, if there was such a thing.

Zarrin peeked up at him and noted with some dismay that Joe's blank expression had returned. He didn't understand. They'd been better this time. They had talked about more than the latte. But he shook his head.

"More than adequate," he whispered, and felt a twisting panic in his stomach for what he was saying and how he was saying it. That was no way to woo a human treasure. He doubted it was even how humans would make friends.

He reached into his coat for his tip money and hurriedly put it in the jar.

Martin appeared in the doorway from the back as Zarrin started to make his escape, so Zarrin nodded to him and didn't know what to make of the startled wave Martin gave in reply.

He was too warm and foolish. This was not how it was supposed to go.

That was the difference, he supposed, between having humans as treasure to be protected and actually speaking with them. He didn't understand how Dìzhèn had done it and earned the love of her secretary. But she had been much older, and much greater, than he would ever be.

He hurried to his scooter so he could get home, and gulped down his latte without regard for the stinging temperature.

Perhaps his family was right and it was better to stay away from humans. Zarrin was not what they wanted when they imagined dragons as their rulers and protectors.

He was beginning to think Bernard and the story lines on television had been very wrong. For over a month now, Zarrin had been doing his best, and he had nothing to show for it but a packet of sugar.

WHEN ZARRIN got home, he immediately went upstairs to his suite of rooms, where he placed the sugar and the stirrer stick on his dresser next to his favorite stones from the river. He had never gotten sugar or the stick to stir it into his milk before, but Joe had never been the one to make his latte before either.

Joe was intense as he worked. Zarrin had expected no less. Joe was a human who was nothing if not focused. If Zarrin had asked for his latte in a clear glass as some customers did, he had no doubt Joe's would have had lovely contrasting layers of white and deep brown. He suspected, from how Joe spoke of the music in the shop, and the quality of work in his tattoos, that Joe was a perfectionist.

He also had an interest in the world that stood out, even with his gruff words and occasional frowns. That had been good. He had asked questions. Zarrin could sympathize with that; there were a lot of things he also wanted to understand. It was difficult to be patient when no one would explain.

The paper of the sugar packet was not remarkable. Neither was the sugar itself. Zarrin could have taken his own from the table with all the milks and sweeteners already on it if he'd wanted some. He'd never considered it, but he thought Joe was telling him he ought to.

The thought made him sigh. Joe had noticed Zarrin didn't care for the lattes. And Zarrin thought he'd been so discreet.

He wished Joe were less beautiful, perhaps *slightly* less observant of everything around him. These feelings wouldn't be as painful if Zarrin didn't know how amazing Joe was.

Zarrin left the sugar on his dresser and turned toward the two twitching, expectant cats watching him. "Come on, little ones. Your treats are in the kitchen."

They twisted between his feet as he went downstairs, both of them purring enough that Bernard would have called them motorboats. Zarrin clucked at them as he fed them each one treat that the stuttering girl at the pet store had assured him would help keep their teeth clean.

Then he washed his hands and got food for himself. He hadn't lingered long in town today. He had time to do some chores and have a snack before his show came on. Then he'd be out in the Preserve, guarding the trees. He'd detected traces of humans at the western edge of the Preserve yesterday, and although their scent had already been fading, he'd also noticed hints of the oily steel he had come to associate with guns. If he found that again today, the trespassers would have to be dealt with.

Work was good for being alone, according to Joe, and Zarrin was inclined to agree. Being alone was harder than he'd expected, although he found being by himself in Dìzhèn's mansion easier than being alone in his family's city townhouse. He did miss Bernard. Bernard was cranky but honest, and his mutterings as he cooked and cleaned had been pleasant to hear in such an empty house.

Zarrin piled up his laundry and carried it upstairs, along with a plate of pizza rolls he'd cooked in the microwave. The cheese ones were his favorite. And the microwave's timer meant he couldn't possibly burn them.

The two cats trailed after him as he went, impatient for him to sit down. Zarrin set his laundry next to him on the bed and then curled up with pillows and the wall at his back to face his TV. He turned it on while he ate his tiny, strange pizzas with searing-hot cheese in the center. The cats immediately sat on either side of him, kneading his legs with prickly claws.

Fogg was nearly full-grown now, according to the Internet, though still somewhat undersized, as he had been when Zarrin found him in a side street near the harbor. He had one good eye and one discolored and sightless from an infection when he'd been a kitten. A good chunk of his right ear was missing as well, although Fogg didn't seem to notice.

Captain Nemo was orange and wicked. She was very arrogant for a cat abandoned in a box outside a grocery store. Bernard had rescued her and brought her home for Zarrin to care for. Zarrin had done his best, although she was not a frightened rabbit or a lost fawn.

He glanced over at the thought, but Peter, the snowshoe hare, seemed content inside his cage. Most of his fur had grown back from where the vet had shaved it off in order to tend to his injured leg. That meant he was nearly well, and Zarrin would have to release him soon. He didn't like that part.

He finished his lunch and pushed the thought away in order to focus on his soap opera. The fact that it began with Blake's story line didn't help distract him from his upset, confused feelings when he thought of today. Blake was a boring lump. What kind of werewolf was too stupid to recognize his own mate right away? Magic or no magic, he should have known. Zarrin had known Joe was precious the moment he'd first seen him, and that fact had become more true the more he knew of Joe.

*Diedre's Secret* was not real life. But all the same, the trials of one clueless werewolf were of no interest to him. The fairy actor recently brought on, however, was fascinating. Not for his acting. If it was true that fairies couldn't lie, it showed in the fairy's acting skills. His story line wasn't very exciting either, something about a lost baby and a secret wedding.

What Zarrin was curious about was the bursts of glitter from the fairy whenever the actor playing *Diedre's Secret*'s favorite villain appeared. The fairy, very obviously, loved that human, and yet the show was choosing to ignore it. So was the human, as far as Zarrin could tell.

He let out a long, sad breath as he settled in to watch, and the cats tried to climb into his lap.

Or Zarrin was wrong about the fairy. What did Zarrin know of love, anyway? He couldn't even make friends.

Martin had waved, he immediately reminded himself. And Joe had given him sugar. He had *noticed* Zarrin. For a moment, that thought made Zarrin so warm the cats flopped onto his lap and began to purr in happiness.

Joe had noticed him, and spoken with him, and been strange but not rude or mean. That was a far cry from friendship, and yet Zarrin felt the way he did when he found a fossil or an artifact buried in the damp earth beneath the trees. If he was patient and careful, the small, fragile thing in his palm would not break, and he would be allowed to treasure it.

He flushed even hotter for that thought alone. Obviously, Joe was not his treasure in that sense, or ever likely to be. But he couldn't help imagining it. Joe here, among everything he cherished and valued. Joe in his bed with him. Only the cats rolling around on his lap prevented him from dwelling on the thought so he could idly stroke himself while he considered it.

To be honest, Zarrin wasn't certain what he would do with Joe in his bed, what Joe would allow. His lack of experience with humans meant he had only movies and his knowledge of human pornography to draw from. They seemed to like the same things dragons did, although

Zarrin's experience there was also limited to the things he'd done with the dragons his parents had set him up with when he'd been a teenager. Many dragons now were concerned about the weakening of their bloodlines and their reputations. Trying to make connections between their offspring was not uncommon, and Zarrin had done his best to do as they wanted, but despite enjoying the dates and some of the sex that had followed, his heart hadn't been in it.

He wasn't the ideal match for any dragon determined to pair up with someone powerful. Not even Dìzhèn's legacy could make up for Zarrin's shortcomings. Dragons his age found him nice enough, but he was not what they wanted. Humans might feel the same. Those who sought out the dragons had sought out strong dragons, fearless dragons, large and terrifyingly potent rulers who had made the ground tremble.

A dragon's boy, so the saying went, despite also meaning girls, had to be equally as strong as the creature in his bed.

He didn't know what Joe might want—if Joe would ever want him at all. He imagined, breathlessly, with a soft gasp, that he would like to press Joe to the mattress and keep him there. The details beyond that were fuzzy, because no one was going to ask for that sort of strength from Zarrin. But he'd like to kiss Joe's mouth and put his hands to his shoulders. He wanted to slide their bodies together and feel Joe's cock against him.

Making Joe laugh and smile in bed with him would be good too. Joe had a warm smile. Not nearly as pleasant as his laugh, but still good. He wanted Joe to smile at him and choose to be in his bed, to be with him, as Dìzhèn's secretary had chosen her.

Zarrin sank down into the pillows and crossed his arms. He should try to talk to other humans. That was what Bernard had said last time. But he had! He spoke to others at the store when he bought food, and he greeted the postal workers and had wished a good afternoon to the employees of the deli when he'd gone in there. It wasn't his fault none of them were as interesting as Joe. They would barely look him in the eye, no matter how polite he was or how much he thanked them.

Joe was the sole human in Everlasting who saw him. Zarrin would have tipped him with all the gold in the family vaults just for that. Although he was starting to suspect gold didn't please Joe. That wouldn't do.

Show, and stupid Blake, forgotten, Zarrin closed his eyes while he tried to think of what treasure would finally make Joe smile.

# CHAPTER 3

ABOUT THE only good thing about working an afternoon shift was not stumbling over someone's garbage in the alley at five thirty in the morning. Joe had tripped over a box of abandoned books the day before and was still feeling unforgiving about it. More so whenever he considered the books *in* the box.

English had never been his subject, and he was not inclined to worship the so-called classics of Western lit, but there was something inherently wrong with seeing antique, hardbound copies of any book left in a dirty alley.

Martin had surprised him by agreeing and then claiming the fragile copy of *Nicholas Nickleby* for himself. Which would have been cute, if he hadn't then made Dickens puns for the rest of the day. He'd been calling for Joe to "Suck his Dickens" when Zarrin had walked in, and Joe still wasn't sure who had the better reaction, Martin for blushing and protesting that he was just kidding or Zarrin for turning to Joe with sharp, hot interest.

Joe's mouth went slightly dry when he thought of that look. Zarrin hadn't done anything about it, like always. He'd moved forward in that delicate, sinuous way of his, placed both hands on the counter, then quietly requested his drink.

Joe had chosen to focus on Martin rather than the curiosity in Zarrin's expression.

"Stop expressing your latent desire for me through humor," he'd deadpanned, simply to see the straight guy panic in Martin's face. Martin had turned as scarlet as his apron, so Joe had laughed. He'd earned it after an entire shift of that joke.

His laugh wasn't anything special. But he still didn't know what to do about how Zarrin had stared at him.

In a way, it was better that Joe had agreed to work Jessie's shift so she could go to the wedding shower or whatever she'd been invited to. His whole internal clock was thrown off, but at least he wouldn't have to face Zarrin today. Everything would have been a hell of a lot easier if Zarrin had secretly propositioned him like a closeted high school quarterback, or expressed an interest in Joe's artwork while Joe was a student in his class only to lose interest after a few private office hours, or sat on his lap with no warning like that one pushy fairy at the community college. If Zarrin expected something for the silver and gold he kept leaving in the tip jar, then Joe could have dealt with it already.

Joe shoved his hands into his coat pockets and jaywalked across the street toward the park. He'd been up late working the night before, but despite his efforts, he hadn't been able to sleep in. He'd taken the books to the library to donate them, to the gaping surprise of the new lady behind the counter, who had then demanded to know if they were stolen.

In a calmer mood, he could admit a guy in ratty jeans and the secondhand winter coat probably didn't look like someone with antique books to give away, regardless of skin color. At the time, he'd scowled at her, then taken the books to the assisted living facility where his mom worked. They'd appreciated the books much more.

He'd even had time to go into one of the shops in town that sold his paintings on consignment and collect a check. Since it wasn't tourist season, the check had been a nice surprise, and he'd treated himself to a burrito from the place by the organic grocery store. He would eat alone, but that was nothing new. Anyway, lots of working people ate their lunches by themselves in the park. It was so much better than sharing a table with strangers or sitting at a table with pigeons and seagulls for company.

But once he got to the park and sat down, he realized he'd chosen the bench directly across from the statue of Dìzhèn.

The dragon was beautifully made. The sculpted bronze must have been enchanted, because it gleamed even when the sky was overcast.

It also seemed to mock him, but it always had. Joe wasn't, as Martin liked to insist, *obsessed* with Everlasting's remaining dragon. He simply couldn't escape reminders of him. From the gilt edges of the copy of *Journey to the Center of the Earth* now beneath his bowl of coins and keys, to the statue in front of him.

Joe kept his eye on Dìzhèn as he ate. In the right mood, he could admire Zarrin's ancestor. The land Dìzhèn had purchased hadn't belonged to her any more than the white loggers and factory owners who had stolen it before her. But Joe appreciated what it must have taken for a Chinese immigrant—and a secret being, and a woman—to claim and hold so much in those days. And to be honest, he kind of enjoyed thinking about all those pompous-ass, rich white timber barons being scared shitless by someone they'd looked down on.

Dìzhèn must have been something, because the town was still under her influence. The revelation, sometime in the twenties, that the family who owned about 70 percent of the town and surrounding area were actually dragons had added to their mystique. There was no rooting them out now, although the family had long since left Everlasting behind.

Except for Zarrin, who could have been left behind as well, for all Joe knew.

Not that it was his business. The dragons of Everlasting had all the riches and power dragons might want. Unless they were finally admitting they didn't give a crap about the town or opening up the Preserve to the public, Joe didn't care what they did. Zarrin's chapped lips and nervously chewed fingernails were not his concern.

Dìzhèn's bronze glinted mockingly at him.

Joe narrowed his eyes at it, beautifully constructed piece of art or not, and finished his burrito with one final, resentful bite. He left the dragon to loom over the park and headed to Cuppa.

If Zarrin wasn't happy here, he had the resources to leave. That was what money meant, more than anything else. It meant breathing room and choices. Joe had worked and scraped up the money to move near the city to go to the junior college for art classes, killing himself to study masters he mostly didn't like and to learn techniques he could teach himself.

He'd also found that life too far from the ocean was stifling. He needed the salty dampness of the bay and the rising heights of the redwoods to feel like he was home.

Zarrin probably just enjoyed living in a place where he was well-known, or maybe he wasn't the studious type. He was the age of most college students, with the money to buy his way into any school in the country. If he'd wanted to, he'd be gone.

Joe stepped into the shop and shivered when the temperature wasn't all that different from outside. A glance at the fireplace reminded him that neither Martin nor Jessie could get a fire going if their lives depended on it.

"This place is almost as cold as my apartment," he announced as he went behind the counter to the back to remove his outer layers.

Jessie was texting someone while restocking the milk, which meant she wasn't doing either task well, but the afternoons were slow, so it didn't really matter. Joe put on his apron and walked back out front, only to be confronted by a grinning Martin.

"You had better not be stoned while at work." Joe shook his head at him with way more fondness than he meant to show.

Martin's grin was starting to seem suspicious. Joe emptied the tip jar for him and Jessie and handed over the money to start his shift fresh. No heavy old coins fell out.

"Did you know he's worried he has bad breath?" Martin began without saying hello or even saying who he was talking about. Nonetheless, Joe knew.

Joe hadn't been in a physical fight since middle school when Andy Pritchard had made fun of him for his raggedy sneakers, but for a second, he was honestly tempted to punch Martin right in his smug smile.

"He talked to you?" Joe stopped himself so he could lower his voice to something less embarrassingly hurt. He tipped his chin up the way Zarrin always did. "His Majesty condescended to speak with you?" he rephrased calmly and turned away to make himself a coconut milk latte. He felt like having something more than a simple coffee. Zarrin had asked about Martin the other day. Joe shouldn't feel so surprised that Zarrin had talked with him.

"I knew it. I knew you'd be pissed." Martin was definitely high. That was Jessie's influence. Joe felt like their babysitter half the time, which was stupid, because he was only a few years older than them. Not that he wanted them to offer him weed while at work, but being around a party all the time without being a part of it was similar to his entire school experience. Jessie and Martin were younger, so they couldn't be expected to know that, and he didn't tell them, because it was stupid that it would still have the power to hurt him.

"Why would I be pissed?" Joe drank his coconut milk latte from a glass and cleaned up so he could avoid Martin's bloodshot yet knowing eyes.

"He's kind of scary!" Jessie chimed in from the back.

"Joe or Zarrin?" Martin shouted in answer, probably unaware of how loud he was.

"Where's Gina?" Joe asked after the coworker who would be closing with him, but was ignored by two potheads.

"Both, I guess." Martin nodded seriously, answering his own question. "Different, though. Like…." He trailed off, lost in thought or just lost, so Joe went over to light a fire in the fireplace. The small evening crowd might enjoy it. The dimmer light in the evening combined with the fire and the white window lights was sort of cozy and romantic, according to some customers.

Joe had no idea. He didn't get asked out on dates. He got offers for hookups, and fairies in his lap, and ancient, priceless coins in his tip jar to drive him crazy.

He returned to the counter in time to hear Jessie say, "I want him to like me, you know?"

He stopped dead. "She wants Zarrin to like her?" He regretted the question the second he heard himself ask it.

"He did like her." Martin nodded again, very slowly. "Like, not at first. But then, like, yeah. But not, you know, how he likes you. Like, the dragon *likes* you." Martin was close to making no sense, yet Joe understood every word.

Martin went on, cheerfully oblivious and still too loud. "Jessie means she wants *you* to like her. She thinks you hate her."

Joe stared at Martin for what felt like a long time before he sighed and turned toward the back. "I don't hate you, Jessie. But stop getting high at work. It makes my job harder."

"Shit. Really?" she called out in surprise, as if this had never occurred to her. Joe pointed accusingly at Martin.

"Okay. Not at work," Martin agreed sleepily. Then his grin returned. "It only even happened because he was asking about smoking. He said he could smell the… hey. Did you know he's worried about his breath?"

Of all the things Joe could have imagined happening today, this conversation was not on the list. "Zarrin spoke with you two, and it was about weed and his breath?"

"The whole town is scared of that guy, and he's worried about his breath offending you." Jessie joined them. Her cheeks were flushed, and her green eyes were half-closed, but she'd curled her hair for the shower. She was pretty, like the American vision of the girl next door, if the girl next door reeked of weed. Joe could understand why she might have caught Zarrin's eye.

"Yeah. He bought more mints. Says he doesn't like cigarettes. *Dragon breath*!" Martin suddenly started laughing. "I just got it!"

Jessie let out a breathy giggle.

"That's great," Joe announced over their laughter. "You can help him tomorrow, then, since he likes you so much."

They had no customers, so he left the two of them to crack themselves up and went in the back to straighten up.

He got about five minutes of peace before Martin followed him to the office.

"So, like, Jessie has heard us talk about him, but she's never actually been face-to-face with him," he began without preamble. "And I forgot that Zarrin wouldn't know you were on a different schedule and would come in at his usual time to see you."

Joe tried to interrupt. "He doesn't—"

"Yeah. He does. He's not here on the weekends when you're gone." Martin slumped into the desk chair opposite him. "So she was surprised, I guess. Because I heard her blurt out, 'Holy shit! You're the dragon!' and the whole place went silent. Like in a movie. Like pins dropping, or whatever that expression is. Like they were waiting to see if they had to bolt to the door before he rained down fire and earthquakes, or whatever."

Joe did not look up from the scrap of paper he was sketching on. "So he didn't roast her. That's decent of him." It was, actually, in a sense. Everlasting had tons of urban legends about what the dragons did to those who offended them. Roasted victims featured heavily in the tales of Dìzhèn, in particular. He told himself he wasn't curious, then gave in because Martin was too stoned to remember this conversation anyway. "What did he do?"

"He went all 'Yes, I am' in this *voice*. Like...," Martin mused, "like if a mountain could talk."

"No more smoking for you, ever." Joe continued to sketch, although he knew precisely what Martin meant. Zarrin spoke softly most of the time, but every once in a while, he had a *presence*. Usually it was just before he'd be surrounded by rising wisps of gray smoke, like a young volcano asserting itself as it grew.

"He asked about you." Martin leaned over to try to peer at Joe's sketch. "He is hot to stand next to. Did you know that? I never noticed before."

"You never got close before." Joe grunted, then paused. "The books?"

That was something else that had occurred to him after being accused of stealing by the librarian. This town had a lot of old Victorian mansions full of antiques, but only one still occupied by its original owners and with a habit of visiting Cuppa.

"Didn't say a word about them. Maybe it wasn't him." Martin sat back. "The dragon likes you. Deal with it. For a guy, I mean, I'm not into that, but if I was, like you are, he'd probably be pretty hot, right? So... wait—he's *hot*!" Martin lost himself in another round of giggles.

Joe thought about that edition of Jules Verne in his house and wondered how much it was worth. Not as much as the coins, probably, but still Joe's rent at least. And someone, he had no proof of who, had all but thrown it away. Rich people didn't value anything. Even if the books were a gift, which they shouldn't be, they shouldn't have been left outside in that alley. There was nothing in that alley but puddles and garbage and a scared, pissed-off cat.

He raised his head. "Did you feed the cat this morning?"

"Yes, Joseph." Martin started to twirl in the chair. Joe spared a thought for Jessie out there by herself, then shook his head and refused to get up to go help her. Nope. He was already doing her a favor.

He sighed a second later. "Is Gina out there with Jessie?"

He continued his sketch when Martin assured him Jessie wasn't alone. Martin went quiet. Joe couldn't tell if he'd passed out, and he didn't feel like looking. Zarrin's decisions didn't affect him. If Zarrin wanted to bring him old books or talk to Jessie of all people, about mints of all things, that was his business.

Joe paused to stare at his messy sketch. Zarrin had commented on the mints when he'd bought them and also the day after, after eating a handful. Then he'd stuck them in his pocket.

"He's really worried about his breath? What *I* think about his breath?" he asked and finally glanced over at Martin.

Martin was asleep, head down, the rest of him slumped to one side of the chair.

He probably wouldn't have had more answers anyway, only smartass comments about why Joe wouldn't admit he was as curious about Zarrin as everyone else in town.

Dìzhèn's grown children had left town after her death, and their children did not visit Everlasting. No dragon had regularly walked among them, not in anyone's lifetime. Zarrin seemed to be making a point of it, and every local was holding their breath to find out why. Zarrin *had* to want something more than Joe.

Joe considered his sketch. A pencil would have been a better choice than pen, or, even better than silvery gray graphite, something in soft gold or bronze. He wondered if Jessie had an eyeliner pencil he could try. That would be a strange medium, but it might do to get the sheen he needed. But black was perfect for the shape of the eyes, and the dramatic color of the long lashes, and the wide, endlessly dark pupils.

A dragon, more Asian in form than European, was in a circle, curled with its arms around a treasure Joe hadn't drawn. The dragon itself was a graceful serpent, tempting and light, and yet settled onto its invisible pile. Its hoard, some said.

But a hoard of gleaming treasure didn't suit this dragon. Zarrin seemed willing enough to give up his coins and his valuables. He'd probably forget to take his debit card with him if Joe wasn't sure to hand it to him. Whatever Zarrin was after, it wasn't money, not like that.

Joe darted another look to Martin, still peacefully sleeping away the rest of his shift.

The other dragons, off in the big city, he could have drawn from memory. The father in a suit, the mother in a coat that looked warm and expensive. He thought Zarrin's sister was a lawyer for the family. They already sat on piles of gold in their city mansion. They had the town at their feet, and the Preserve behind them.

Zarrin clutched at the strap of his messenger bag, and fumbled for his mints while speaking softly. But his gaze was hungry. This dragon might be small and quiet, but he was not meek. Joe flicked the pen over the dragon's claws, ensuring they were visible, a clear message that this dragon intended to hang on to its treasures, whatever they might be.

After another moment, Joe outlined a tin of mints under one scaled but feline paw. Under the other, he drew a packet of sugar. He made smoke rising from the delicate, nervous face, and regretted that he hadn't drawn it in a regal posture that seemed to defy its fearful attitude.

He was being ridiculous. He had no idea what a dragon really looked like in their true form. Even the statue of Dìzhèn was highly stylized for all that its expression seemed particularly bold and clever. Zarrin would probably be similar to his ancestor, and yet, his mother's side of the family were from somewhere else, Turkey or somewhere around the middle of Asia. Zarrin would take after those kinds of dragons too, whatever they looked like.

But Joe stared at his dragon and couldn't throw it out. Before he could stop himself, he titled it "Mine" and signed the bottom.

He could never show it anywhere in town. They'd think he was mocking the dragons by implying they'd collect small bits of nothing.

All the same, he held it in his hands for a while longer before Jessie called him out to the front. He went, stopping long enough to tuck the sketch into his coat. Maybe he'd try again with his best pencils. Zarrin was uniquely beautiful. Any artist would want to capture him on paper. That big mansion was probably filled with portraits of every dragon who had once lived there, Zarrin included. A few sketches were nothing in the long run. Joe might not even bother.

But he moved faster with the excitement of inspiration in him.

HE DIDN'T regret it the next morning, but it did take him longer than usual to wake up. Thankfully, Martin was there to pick up the slack and only gave him a little shit for looking so tired.

Evidently one glance at Joe's messy appearance and vague smile had made Martin assume Joe had gotten laid. That in itself would have been hilarious if Martin hadn't followed it up with, "Was it the dragon?"

The numerous sketches taped to his studio wall had prevented Joe from telling Martin to shut up. In a sense, it had been Zarrin, and the act of creation always felt good, like a release of every thought and emotion Joe had been keeping to himself. He hadn't been fucked, but he was exhausted and in no mood to argue about anything, which was almost the same thing.

Not a single figure Joe had drawn last night would be marketable in this town, and he didn't care, although the paper cost good money and he'd used quality pencils. He had no intention of showing those drawings anywhere. The sketches, like all his work, were for him, and for others only if he wanted them to be.

He said none of that to Martin. Martin was unreasonably smug already, as if he remembered some of the day before, despite however much he'd smoked.

For the first few hours, Joe was content to leave Martin on the register and ignore nearly everyone as he made the drinks. He responded when Martin tossed a request at him or when a regular would chat while waiting on their espresso, but ignored the conversations about the lighting of the town's tree in a few weeks and if it would snow by then. A few inches of quickly melting snow were all they ever got—hardly a scenic white Christmas.

Up until fairly recently, the dragons had been the ones to donate the large pine tree the town used. From what he understood, each Xu dragon would stay around Everlasting for a while, some longer than others, but they all eventually left. While here, some of them had attended the tree lighting, although Joe seriously doubted any of them celebrated Christmas. If they did, they wouldn't have done it with pine trees and carols and other Western or Eurocentric traditions.

From the way everyone paused in the middle of these discussions, he could tell they expected him to know if Zarrin was going, or, at the very least, they wanted him to ask. By the tail end of the morning rush, he was tense and frowning and Martin kept huffing at him in disappointment.

"It's plain insulting." Mr. Marcus, who co-owned the oil change place close to the highway, complained about the situation to the people standing in line behind him. "That boy knows we're terrified, and he doesn't care enough to tell us what he's planning."

"That boy." The knowing tone from Addison made Joe briefly turn to look at her. She had a disapproving frown on her face. "That *boy*, my foot. I've lived here a long time, and my memory is sharp."

"Beings aren't like us. You know they aren't." Alice Reyes, at least as old as Addison, but probably slightly older, spoke up from behind her. "They're less nosy, for one thing. Anyway, that *boy* hasn't done us any harm, one way or the other. Leave him be. As long as the factories are running, none of them owe us anything."

Addison made a hurt sound but faced the counter to avoid Alice's sharp, dark eyes.

Joe studied Alice for another few seconds, all wrapped up in her thickest winter clothes to go in for her shift as a smoke spotter out in the woods. She'd want her two thermoses filled with coffee.

Alice met his gaze with a brief, businesslike nod. Joe couldn't think of what to say to her, or even why he wanted to, so he nodded and then went back to preparing drinks.

His mother had raised him to respect his elders, although he'd learned early that a lot of older people didn't feel the need to respect him or his mother in return. But if he were ever going to assume a woman was wise simply from the lines on her face, it would be Alice Reyes.

Addison, however, had frown lines that said more about frustration than knowledge.

"Insulting." Mr. Marcus took his drink but didn't move from the counter right away. "I feel like we're all being studied, and they sent him to do it. He's a surveyor. He's here to report back to them all. They're probably going to sell the land. Close everything. Leave us to wither and die."

"They don't let go of things. Not ever once has that family given away anything without a reason." Addison had a steely voice, which was surprising for a bookkeeper who wore soft skirts and cardigans. "Mark my words, that one is here to try to take something. You had better be careful, Martin. Joseph too, from what I hear."

"That will be $4.25," Martin responded politely, too chipper to be believable. Joe smiled to himself as the door chimed with another customer and Martin asked Alice if she wanted her usual.

"Not a single one can be trusted, and no one in this town is going to tell them no," Addison went on, oblivious to Martin's attempt to shut down the conversation. Joe twisted around to hand over her latte and get her out of there faster, only to freeze when he saw Zarrin at the end of the line.

Zarrin had his head tilted toward Addison and was obviously listening.

He hadn't taken off his hat, Joe noticed, but removed his gloves while he stood there, and put them away in one pocket before reaching into the other for his tin of mints.

Joe turned back to fiddle with the espresso machine, although he had no drinks to make unless he felt like making a medium latte.

"There won't be any lighting of trees or donations to the firehouse this time. You had best be careful," Addison warned, sounding as paranoid as those survivalist types convinced the government had a secret army of trolls and werewolves who weren't afraid of any guns, yet stockpiled them anyway.

"Hey, Zarrin," Martin called out so loudly Joe flinched, and the noise from the other room stopped completely.

For a moment or two, there were only the quiet strains of Chopin coming through the speakers and Addison's frightened breathing, and then Zarrin said, "Good morning, Martin." His smoky voice carried across the distance. "And Joe."

The sound of his name, heavy with whatever Zarrin felt for him, made Joe turn toward the register to find those golden eyes—and everyone else's—on him. Mr. Marcus's whole attitude was confused. Addison was petrified. Alice coughed and told Martin to keep the change.

Zarrin's eyes were nothing like Joe had drawn. He'd gotten the shape right, but not the expression. Zarrin might claim small things as his, but he didn't regard them with covetous interest and heat. A portrait of him as he looked at Joe would be a very different thing, if Joe could catch the moment before Zarrin would suddenly redirect his gaze and lift his chin to say something arrogant.

Zarrin glanced toward Alice as she left, then focused on Addison. Joe turned to reach for the milk, his stomach twisting and his nerves electrified.

"Excuse me," Addison whispered, barely audible, and then the chimes above the door rang out twice. Mr. Marcus might have made himself scarce as well.

The regulars in the other room were beginning to talk again, although they were more muted now than they'd been a few minutes ago.

Zarrin was subdued too. "I imagine they must be very busy."

"Yeah," Martin agreed, way too awkwardly for Zarrin not to pick up on it. "You want a latte? Medium, right?" he asked as if he didn't know, as if Joe wasn't standing there with a pitcher of milk in his hand already.

If Martin ever got his shit together, he might make a decent diplomat.

"Yes." The *s* was ever so slightly more sibilant today than usual. Joe wondered if Zarrin was excited about something or agitated to have found himself under discussion.

Although what did he expect? He'd descended into town by himself after nearly a decade with no dragon attention. Of course people were talking. Addison was probably right, not that Joe wanted to agree with her. He started steaming milk to distract himself.

"Listen, I have to run to the bathroom," Martin went on, not giving Joe a chance to pretend to ignore anything. "I'll be right back, though." He nudged Joe hard in the side on his way to the door. "Joe will take care of you."

Joe twisted to scowl at him, but Martin was already gone.

"I…." Zarrin's hesitation drifted across to him like wisps of white smoke. Joe could feel that on his bare skin, soothing where he thought it should have stung. But then it was magic. Deep inside Zarrin was a fire that didn't burn him, that wouldn't burn him. He was indestructible in a way that other beings weren't. Yet he hesitated. "You weren't here yesterday."

"Traded shifts with Jessie," Joe grunted, although Zarrin would know that already. Martin was likely listening from the other side of the doorway. "She had to go to something."

"So she said." A drumming sound followed that, like Zarrin running his fingers along the countertop. "She talks quite a lot."

"I thought you liked that," Joe said, when he should have stayed quiet.

"I did," Zarrin answered earnestly. "She and I had things in common, to my surprise."

"You into getting high?" Joe snapped, too fast and too sharp, because he was an idiot. He finished Zarrin's drink and spent a couple of seconds putting a lid on it. "She's sweet," he added, kinder, and turned around.

Zarrin blinked at him. "She's afraid you don't like her." He flicked a wary look up to Joe's face, then swung around to study the tea. "But she mentioned you are an artist. That's why you appreciate beauty."

"What?" Joe had no clue what part of that to address first. He set down the latte and stared at Zarrin as he tried to memorize the tea selection.

"Well, of course." Zarrin's tone rose to arrogance again. He clucked his tongue. "I could see you were gifted with far more than the ability to make and serve coffee."

"It pays the bills." Joe narrowed his eyes. "There's no shame in putting food on the table, even if it's by making and serving coffee."

Zarrin turned toward him, his mouth moving as if he was silently repeating Joe's words. The line between his eyes indicated he didn't understand a thing Joe had just said. "If you made bad coffee, I wouldn't come here," he said slowly, as though Joe were being stupid.

The unsteady, almost painfully anxious feeling in Joe's gut disappeared, or at least became easier to deal with. He reached back to snag a sugar packet, which he threw down onto the countertop in front of Zarrin.

Instead of taking it as the challenge it was, Zarrin closed both hands around the packet and slipped it into his pocket. He raised his head with a smile so wide and warm Joe was caught off guard. He had a feeling he leaned forward, but couldn't stop himself.

"As an artist, I thought you would like to see something I bought the other day." Zarrin opened his messenger bag, then paused. "It's mine, but I wanted to share it with you." He kept his eyes on the bag as he spoke, then quickly tugged out something square, wrapped in brown paper.

He pushed it carefully and reverently onto the counter and heaved a breath before he unwrapped it. He clenched his hands around the edges of the frame, as if he didn't want to let go.

Joe stared down at Zarrin's hands on the frame of his painting in stunned silence.

The small pictures of the redwoods were popular with tourists, although Joe didn't paint them for that reason. That was his land, or his people's once, as much as land could belong to anyone. He supposed it was why he was tied to this town. Things had changed a lot since his school days, with lots of new businesses, new money, new people. But he stayed. This was his home, and the trees that had given the town its name, the ancient, everlasting redwoods, were a part of him as much as the bay.

He'd gone hiking the day before he'd painted that one. He hiked a lot on his days off, although he was as careful as anyone else when it came to the Preserve. As an angry teenager, he'd vandalized the first sign along the road warning away trespassers, but that was the farthest he'd gone. It had never gotten any response anyway. The graffiti could still be there, for all he knew. The price the town paid for knowing the ninety-nine acres of untouched forest were protected was never being allowed to see them, or to walk among trees that had been alive before Columbus had landed.

The Preserve called to him sometimes, when he was out in the trees, but he knew better than to risk the wrath of the dragons. He'd come close the day that had inspired that painting, though, very close. Then he'd stopped and raised his gaze to what he could see of the sky.

"Look at the canopy," Zarrin commanded in his softest voice. "Doesn't it have majesty? It's so lovely and untouchable that it creates an ache in my heart. The trees themselves are above us, greater than us. We should be nothing to them, but then they gave the artist this, this *moment*." He glanced up, and Joe met his gaze in shock. His skin felt brushed by flame. The hollow place in his chest lit up for the briefest second, lightning in a black cloud. Zarrin's voice only grew softer. "This moment where we are staring up, and the trees seem to be gazing down, eternal and everlasting. Somehow Dìzhèn understood them, and tied them to her. I could never hold such power, and yet I feel… better when I am among the tallest of the redwoods, though they should make me feel small and weak. There is a connection, and this painting has it. Amid the trees, we are lonely, but we also feel hope."

Those eyes were begging Joe for something, and he had no idea what. He couldn't speak. He parted his lips and tasted smoke.

He realized he was pressed against the counter, listening silently as Zarrin described his own painting to him.

"You saw all of that?" emerged from his dry mouth, while his cheeks itched with heat.

“Yes.” Satisfaction laced Zarrin’s voice, a rumble Joe felt in his bones. No one spoke about his work like that. No one contacted him about it. He was lucky when someone bought it.

“You really like it?” Staring into Zarrin’s eyes didn’t give him anything except what Zarrin had already told him, but Joe couldn’t look away.

“It’s *mine*,” Zarrin whispered proudly, and Joe realized Zarrin still hadn’t let go of the frame.

He dragged his attention back to his painting. “You think it’s lonely?” he murmured, trying to forget that dragons were supposed to know things. They could look into souls and see worth. “Hopeful? I’m not… I don’t—”

“It’s safe to hope when you’re around the trees. The trees don’t judge,” Zarrin answered somberly, then patted one corner of the frame, near the bottom.

The painting’s title was the date Joe had gone hiking, a series of numbers written in a nearly indecipherable scrawl at the bottom next to his signature, Joseph Andres, which was also practically illegible. There was no sign of the Local Artist tag the shop owners loved to put on things like this to sell them to tourists.

Joe looked back at Zarrin, who was still wide-eyed and warm.

“What do you think of it?” Zarrin couldn’t possibly know it was Joe’s if he was asking that.

“I didn’t know anyone else felt that way,” Joe offered quietly. “About the trees, I mean.”

“So you like it?” Zarrin exhaled the words with a pained sigh. But his eyes were bright. “I chose well?”

“I love it.” Joe wished he had the ability to frown, to demand to know if Zarrin was playing with him. “Of course I do.”

Zarrin gave a half smile, bittersweet, and then took a deep, deep breath. A moment later, he released the painting and stepped back. He briefly squeezed his eyes shut before opening them to stare at Joe in wonder.

“It’s more difficult than I anticipated.” Zarrin clenched and unclenched his hands. “But I can do it.”

“What?” Once a painting was sold, Joe never expected to see it again. He glanced from it to Zarrin. “Do what?”

"It is—was mine." Zarrin raised his head to a lofty angle. "I would like to share it with you. To *give* it to you."

Some part of Joe's mind, the part that never forgot he was talking to a dragon, wanted him to run away from the force beneath Zarrin's words. The stupid, furious rest of him made him stay.

He tore his attention from the painting that had moved Zarrin, *his* painting that Zarrin had chosen and was now trying to give away. "You can't just give me a painting," he insisted, the way he hadn't for any of the old coins in the tip jar. "I thought you liked it." He should lower his voice, but that wasn't happening. "You chose it," he added. "You bought it."

Zarrin appeared startled. "I do. I did." He considered Joe in obvious bewilderment. "Does it matter that I bought it? The money was nothing."

"Nothing," Joe echoed flatly. Someone—Martin—swore behind him, but Joe didn't turn around. "It's not 'nothing.' It meant something to the artist who made it."

"I don't understand." Zarrin was hesitant for another second. Then he crossed his arms. "But you liked it. You don't… want it? You truly don't?"

"That isn't the point." Joe told himself firmly he didn't care that Zarrin's expression was hurt. Zarrin's feelings were not his responsibility. "You should value the things you have."

Just like that, the little volcano before him rose up.

Zarrin narrowed his eyes and straightened his shoulders. Someone in the other room made a small noise of panic. Joe felt sweat trickle down his spine.

Gray smoke, the kind so hot it made men shiver, began to curl in the air above the counter.

"Are you implying I don't value my treasure?" Zarrin's voice trembled as he gestured at the painting. "I *chose* to share this with you!"

Joe took a step back in surprise. "I didn't…." Whatever he'd been going to say trailed away in the face of Zarrin's strange insistence. He looked toward Martin. Then he clenched his jaw and looked danger in the face. He lowered his voice. "And what did you expect in return for it?"

The volcano puffed out of existence, with one last burst of light smoke.

Zarrin seemed absolutely lost. "Expect?"

His confusion took some of Joe's tension, although he continued to stare at Zarrin as if he was an alien.

In a way, he was. Zarrin didn't know this town, didn't know the people, probably didn't know humans at all. Zarrin had no designs on him, not like that, because if he had, Joe wouldn't have to explain this to him.

Zarrin hadn't any plans for Joe. He was just rich and sheltered, and possibly thought Joe was attractive. He hadn't seen anything special or of interest in Joe. Zarrin was playing generous benefactor. That was all.

Instead of this riling Joe up further, the anger rushed out of him. Joe had an ache where he'd felt a flutter a few minutes before.

"Rich people giving poor people like me expensive gifts usually have a reason," he explained. "So I thought you did." His face was stinging again.

"Is sixty dollars expensive?" Zarrin blinked a few times. "Keeping track of those things is tricky."

Joe sucked in a sharp breath.

"I meant no offense." Zarrin made a strange gesture—his hands out, his head down—that it took Joe a moment to recognize as apologetic. It looked like something from a movie. Zarrin had probably never had to say he was sorry before. "Was I wrong to offer this to you?"

"*Joe*," Martin warned. He was right to do it. Just because Joe had snapped at a dragon didn't mean Martin needed to experience the dragon's wrath. But Martin also didn't know that was Joe's painting on the counter between them.

Joe's voice was rough when he spoke. "It wouldn't be right. I can't take it." Somehow it was his job to explain the world to Zarrin, and for some reason, he was doing it as gently as he was able. Maybe it was because Zarrin liked his painting enough to buy it. "*You* should enjoy it. It…. Trust me. It meant a lot to that artist that someone bought their work."

"It did?" The interest and amazement in Zarrin's face was the reason Joe was being careful. He could admit that, if only to himself. Zarrin was pleased by Joe's explanation, and responding to that made Joe less hollow. Zarrin crept closer once again. "Even if I don't know the value of it?"

"You don't know the value of *dollars*," Joe corrected him gruffly. "But you *like* the painting. You chose it because you responded to it. This one was from the curiosity shop, right?" He didn't wait for an answer. "Out of all the works there, you chose this one. So… you should keep it. It's yours."

Zarrin's lips parted. His eyes had fires behind them. "*Mine*."

Joe cleared his throat and stepped to the register. He kept his gaze firmly on the buttons because Zarrin was still talking about the painting. "Four dollars for the latte."

Martin swung around to his other side to consider the artwork under discussion. "Pretty trees. Reminds me of the time my friends and I dared each other to sneak onto the Pre… into the state park without a camping permit. Yeah. I don't go out there anymore, though."

Zarrin didn't reach for his debit card or acknowledge Martin. He continued to stare at Joe. Joe could *feel* him staring. "Compared to what I've spent on coffee, sixty dollars was not a lot. Is that what you meant? Yet so small an amount will make that artist smile? This painting in my collection will give the artist satisfaction? I didn't think of that when I bought it. I never thought my feelings would matter."

Zarrin had seen loneliness in that painting, and it made his chest ache, so he had bought it. Then he'd brought it in here to show it off.

It occurred to Joe that Zarrin might not have anyone else to show it off to. But he couldn't look at him. "Bet you have a big art collection, up there in that mansion." And he'd chosen Joe's work to add to it. There was no reason to feel disappointed.

"Yes," Zarrin agreed, nearly hissing. "Almost as beautiful as the Preserve itself."

That got Joe to raise his head, his anger revived like a spark to gunpowder. "I wouldn't know. No one is allowed out there." He waited another second, and then when Zarrin frowned, he repeated himself. "Four dollars."

Zarrin pursed his lips stubbornly, but then found his card and held it out. Joe swiped it and gave it back. He watched Zarrin put it away, then reach into his coat pocket.

"Don't." It would be an insult to get a coin Zarrin didn't know the value of after something like this. He waved his hand over the painting. "This was good for today."

"But you don't get to keep it." Zarrin shook his head. "It's still mine."

*Mine*, Joe thought, and wondered where his painting rated next to a tin of mints. He focused on folding the brown paper around the painting. He might never see it again, but at least he knew the person who had it appreciated it.

"I like seeing people enjoy art," he explained quietly and then pushed the painting toward Zarrin.

"I've made an artist very happy," Zarrin told him, almost childlike with wonder at the idea. "I've given someone that. But I wouldn't have known." He let out a long, pleased sigh before blinking up at Joe with his eyes shining like a kid's vision of pirate treasure. "You gave me *hope*." Then his expression unexpectedly went solemn.

Joe watched intently as Zarrin curled his hands around the edges of the frame as he had done before and then tucked the small painting into his bag. "Mine," he murmured over it, and then rested his hand on the strap. He peeked up at Joe. "There *is* a lot of artwork at the house."

For a second, Joe thought Zarrin was waiting, although he didn't know for what. So he nodded. "I'm sure there is."

Zarrin stared at him for a bit longer, then came forward to wrap one hand delicately around the latte he probably wouldn't drink. "This has been good," he announced, as Joe felt more than a little lost. To be honest, Joe was so lost he wanted to go to the back and stare at a piece of paper until he could make something make sense. "This was good." Zarrin inclined his head to Martin and then grinned brightly as he turned around.

He appeared as startled to notice the people congregating behind him as Joe was.

"Were all of you waiting to order?" Zarrin asked, managing to sound confused and imperious at the same time. Maybe it was the way he waved them toward the counter.

He sipped his latte, made a small moue of dislike, then smiled again as he sailed out the door.

Joe waited until he was out of sight before putting his hands on the counter and hanging his head while he caught his breath.

"What was that?" Martin demanded, an anxious shadow next to him.

Joe flexed his hands over the empty counter, which was, improbably, warm to the touch. He let out a pained breath.

"It was mine."

THE URGE to draw chased him for the rest of his shift, but once he was across the alley in his apartment, he didn't think he could be still long enough to start anything new. He stripped off his coat and went to his studio. He breathed in the scent of paint and ran his fingers over his case of pencils.

They spoke to him sometimes. He'd felt the pull before he'd known what art was, and spelled out his hopes and fears with dollar-store watercolors and poster paints. He'd gone to every museum close enough for him to afford to visit, checked out every book on technique in the two closest libraries, and spent every spare cent he had on paper and razor blades and sandpaper for sharpening his pencils.

He knew what he wanted to create before he ever sat down with paper, or canvas, and yet when he looked later, what he'd made was never what he expected.

Carving or sculpture had never been his medium. His hands had always passed over wood and stone. He didn't understand why they would stop for the metal of old coins now. Metal was not stripes of black spray paint slashed across a sign he hated, or graphite or charcoal for the gray lines of frustration. The coins were perfect as they were. He wasn't going to melt them down to make something new.

He wasn't going to make anything, not today, although he felt the need to try.

Joe stared unhappily at the stack of sketches at his table. It hadn't seemed like so many last night, but today it was an excess. Too many drawings, none of them right.

The coins winked at him in the light from the windows. Magic coins or not, Joe hadn't decided. He knew that if he mixed his own paint, he could paint their exact shade, but hours upon hours had proved he couldn't capture the color of Zarrin's eyes. He also knew that shouldn't matter.

He wasn't sixteen and secretly wishing a football player would notice him. He wasn't ten and staring too hard at creatures that would never acknowledge he existed, or seventeen and glaring at a piece of bronze. He didn't need to be chosen. He had chosen himself, and he was honest enough to know when he had failed.

The painting of the trees had been good, but these drawings weren't. He'd gotten Zarrin wrong.

He snatched one of them and flipped it over to the blank side of the paper. This paper was thin and cheap, but that wasn't important with his fingers already curling around a pencil.

He bent over the table and made four lines, a small square. At the edges of the square he drew two slender hands with short nails bitten to the quick with nerves and fear. He hated that he saw that and couldn't pretend he hadn't. The hands were untouched by the cold. No hints of a flush from the chill, or mottled blue veins. He didn't understand how Zarrin could need gloves when everything about him was heat.

Joe shivered, vaguely aware of the temperature in his apartment and the fact that his arms were bare, but he didn't stop. The hands were important, the sweep of the thumbs, strength that had never once been evident until Zarrin had gripped the frame of the painting.

Joe stopped. That was it. He resumed the sketch, slowly filling in the hint of muscle, and the sinews of Zarrin's wrists.

Martin had never seen Joe's artwork before, and in his way, he'd been complimentary. But he didn't see loneliness or hope. He hadn't held the painting tight while softly, shyly, offering it to Joe.

Joe didn't know what to do with that. The stories about this in town would be worse now. People would have heard, or Martin would get high and mention it to someone. Zarrin shouldn't do things like this. He gave away coins, and lattes, and paintings, and probably books. He gave these things to anyone, not just Joe, despite what people thought. They didn't mean anything, and if they did, he should do something about it, say what he wanted.

Joe forced himself to put down the pencil to consider Zarrin's hands. A flush spread through him, slow and hot, because those were Zarrin's hands at the moment Zarrin had said the painting was his.

Would Zarrin see that too, if he were to look at this sketch? He'd seen more than trees. He might notice the desire in Joe's depiction of his hands. With desire came longing. If Zarrin knew that, he might realize what he'd done to Joe by fiercely claiming his painting.

Joe pushed away from the table and went to his living room and bedroom. He kicked at the heating vent in irritation at the cold, then walked into the bathroom. He turned on the shower with a vicious twist of the knob and then yanked his milk-stained shirt over his head. His hair band went next, tossed into the sink. When his shoes and jeans were gone, he stepped into the water and ducked his head under the hot spray.

Zarrin didn't expect anything for his gifts.

Joe cranked the temperature of the water up higher, hotter, until steam curled between his legs and then rose up to caress his shoulder blades.

This wasn't the first time he'd done this, but it was the only time he closed his eyes and really pictured it—if Zarrin had wanted him enough to do something about it, to openly want him as much as he'd wanted that painting.

Zarrin gazed hungrily at his tattoos. He stared at Joe's body when he thought Joe couldn't see. He swept to the front of the line as if it was his *right*, and Joe hated it every time he did it, hated how he nodded oh so graciously at those who got out of his way and assumed Joe would remember his drink without prompting. He gave away what he wanted. Joe shouldn't desire this. There shouldn't be longing, not anymore.

Joe let out a loud breath with his face almost pressed to the tile wall of the shower. He hadn't even touched himself and he was hard. Zarrin had claimed his art. That shouldn't do this to him. But one word and he was burning up, the water close to scalding on his skin, the steam like a whisper at the back of his neck.

"Mine," he said aloud, with his lips wet, and slid a hand down to his cock.

# CHAPTER 4

ZARRIN HAD woken to snow, more than the usual dusting at the higher elevations. At least an inch of snow covered the road. It might have melted already if the sun had come out from the clouds, but the sky was light gray and snowflakes drifted down a few times as Zarrin drove into town.

He had rushed out of the house without his knit cap and without his breakfast. He'd stopped only long enough to choose a nice warm sweater and to make sure the animals were fed.

Cold weather was unpleasant in a human body, and yet he had to admit to a secret love of the first snowfall of the year. Everlasting never got much, but for a few hours, ice and snow would sparkle along rooftops and windowsills. Most importantly, this year Zarrin saw it in person and not through the window of a car as he was taken to or from the highway on his way to the airport.

He parked his Vespa beneath Dìzhèn in all her splendor, then hurried to the post office, where to his delight, he had a letter from Bernard waiting for him. He made it as far as the sidewalk outside before he tore it open.

Zarrin read it quickly, then began to walk as he reread the lines.

*Dear Golden Boy,*

*Buy the broccoli next time. How many times do I have to tell you that cheese and bread are not a complete diet? And when are you going to learn to e-mail like the rest of us?*

*That was a joke, all right? The old-fashioned way works too, and the trips into town will do you some good. I'm glad to hear the recommended coffee shop had exactly what you were looking for. I had a feeling it would when I first went in there. Perfect, right? I bet if I had wings, that one would shine like the sun to me. But I got sense enough of his rightness. It's obscured, like he's squirreled it away out of sight, but it's still there. Same feeling that told me it was time for me to go, and for you to be on your own. It's an elf thing, like the sensation of a job well done. But I'm thinking about you all the time. If you ever decide to leave your trees, you're always welcome with me—the little beasts too, if they behave. But I have a feeling you're fine right where you are.*

*Although buy some vegetables and actually eat them. I have a new job and might respond slowly next time, but I will ask again about your diet.*

*Love,*

*Bernard*

*P.S. Remember that humans have strange, fragile minds and far too many feelings. You have to treat them delicately. Always patience with humans—or murder, if you can get away with it.*

*P.P.S. That was another joke, Golden Boy. They prosecute dragons for roasting people now.*

Zarrin let out a scoffing laugh at the last comment and started the letter over again. Bernard, with his elf senses, had a way of seeing right to the heart of matters. His letters weren't long because they didn't need to be. He'd found a job; that was good. One less thing for Zarrin to worry about.

But Zarrin bit at his thumbnail as he skipped through the lines regarding the coffee shop. He noted his hands were freezing. He must have forgotten his gloves as well in his rush this morning, but he was more preoccupied with what Bernard was hinting at.

How had Bernard known what he was looking for? Zarrin hadn't dared to even confess to Bernard the glimpses of hope he'd seen over the years. Zarrin had known for what felt like his entire life that what he was looking for was in Everlasting, until those years when it had been gone. He hated those years without even the knowledge that his treasure was alive and well. That was why he'd tolerated his parents' attempts to find him a suitable dragon mate. But none of them had lasted long, and Zarrin, a failure, had returned to the family home. He'd had only the trees and Bernard to love, and then Bernard had left him too, after first suggesting that Zarrin go get coffee in town.

Bernard had known. Zarrin clutched the letter to his chest and closed his eyes.

A car honked loudly to his left, and he gave a start. He looked in time to see the wet puddle of icy slush he'd just stepped into, and then his feet slipped in the water. He hit the edge of the sidewalk as he fell, not without pain, although shame made him push himself to his feet before the throbbing in his side even registered.

He locked eyes with the driver of the car he had crossed in front of—carelessly, it appeared. He had forgotten to wait at the crosswalk. The driver was a human man with a horrified expression. He must have thought he would hit Zarrin.

Zarrin forced himself to straighten up and get out of the street. He peered down at the letter, safely dry, although the envelope was wet with snow, and then tucked them both away in the dry side of his coat. The other side of his pretty coat was a mess of mud and frigid water, although some of it was already turning to steam.

He was so flushed it was no surprise. He glanced around, to the terrified driver and then to the people in his immediate area. A mother holding hands with her small child turned away, pulling her child with her. An old man walking his dog raised his gaze to the sky, as if he was studying the clouds. A younger man in a hunter's plaid hat covered his mouth with one hand, then quickly walked in the opposite direction.

They would not even look at him. That was what a disappointment Zarrin was to them. Bernard had advised patience, and after yesterday, with the painting and Joe, Zarrin had thought he was doing well. But perhaps the humans were right not to trust him with their protection.

He stared sadly down at the stains on his pants, and resisted the urge to rub his side where the throbbing was getting sharp and hot. Without another look at the car or its driver, he continued toward the coffee shop. Moving wasn't agony, and the chill of melted snow sticking to his skin would go away. He would not disgrace his family anymore with complaints or tears. Even his shivers would fade in time.

He swept a hand through his hair to try to pat it down and then brushed off what remnants of snow he could, despite how it froze his very human fingers. His red scarf was soaked at the ends.

Perhaps he shouldn't get his latte today. He didn't want to risk Joe thinking he was the sort of fool who couldn't even cross the street on his own.

But it was Friday. Joe didn't work the weekends, and if Zarrin didn't go in today, then he would have to go three unacceptable days without seeing Joe.

His body gave a strong shudder at the thought, or perhaps at the uncomfortable sting of damp cold against his skin. The warmth of the coffee shop decided him.

He hurried on, avoiding the gazes of the humans as much as they were avoiding his, until he nearly bumped into someone walking into Everlasting Cuppa at the same time as him. He moved from foot to foot while waiting for the human to open the door, and snorted in annoyance when the human looked at him and went utterly still. Zarrin waved him onward simply to get inside faster, and shook his head when the human skirted around him to head for the bathroom.

The line was unusually long. Zarrin *was* earlier than usual. The shop might always be this busy at this time of the morning. Or perhaps the snowfall had sent everyone in here in search of a warm beverage and a place by the fire.

Except there was no fire. As happened from time to time, someone had forgotten to light it. Joe and Martin certainly looked busy enough to have forgotten.

Zarrin sniffled and wiped melted snowflakes from his cheeks. Joe was moving with concise, graceful movements to prepare drinks and brew more coffee, all while nodding along to whatever an older woman with skin like his was saying. The fresh coffee must have been for her. She had two large containers for it, and they must have run out. She didn't seem to mind waiting, and Joe didn't appear to mind her there. He was smiling distractedly as he never did for Zarrin.

Zarrin sniffled again, his eyes getting hot despite his best efforts. He was such a weak dragon, unable to please his humans, raw with humiliation at a fall in the snow that would never have happened to his sister.

The snow he'd gotten in his hair was dripping down his neck and then vanishing into steam as he blushed, but the damp trails it left behind felt every touch of the cold air in the coffee shop. Either Joe and Martin had forgotten to turn the heater on as well, or Zarrin was covered in more snow than he'd thought.

It would be some time before he would be able to order, and he doubted he would be able to talk with Joe. So many people were in the other room that the music was drowned out by the chiming of the register and the hum of conversation.

He pulled the dry part of his scarf closer to his neck and then stopped at the crude, angry words being spoken by the couple directly in front of him.

"Fuck. This line needs to move faster. I want to get my coffee before the dragon shows up."

The woman was probably young, from the way she talked, no older than Joe, certainly. Her black lace leggings added to the impression of youth. She had also covered herself in a cloud of flowery perfume.

Zarrin studied the twin braids in her short brown hair, then flicked a look to her friend as she answered.

"Why are you even worried? He's hardly going to notice you." The friend wore a short skirt with no leggings. Even with her thick college sweatshirt, she should have been shivering. Zarrin studied her in confusion while the first girl made a rough, amused sound, not quite a full laugh.

"Right? He's only got eyes for that one." She nodded toward the counter. "I hate being home for break so early. No one else is around yet, and the only remotely acceptably hot guy is the queermo at the coffee shop. The other one is too skinny."

*Queermo*, Zarrin repeated silently. From the tone, he knew the word was not complimentary. He also didn't think Martin was too skinny and thought Joe was far more than "acceptably hot."

"*Queermo*, really?" her friend demanded, as if agreeing, but then sighed. "He has always been hot, though."

"Touch him and die. That's what my mom says," the first girl answered, then lowered her voice. "Of course, she always said that about him. Not the kind you bring home, even if there wasn't a dragon sniffing around his gay ass. Who knew dragons could be as bad as fairies."

Her friend offered another mild protest. "Fairies aren't so bad."

"They are the worst," the first girl scoffed. "I wouldn't be surprised if they spread disease, even if they can't catch it."

"Mads, you know that's not true." Her friend had a soft voice. Zarrin studied her, because he could not look at her friend without a strong, overwhelming surge of heat in his chest. He slowly became aware that his hands were curled into fists in his pockets. The line moved, bringing them closer to Joe. These two belonged nowhere near him.

"Whatever." The one with the braids tossed her head. "I just want my coffee before I have to wait to get it because the dragon is too good to stand in line. Nobody's going to tell him no and risk ending up his dinner."

Zarrin startled, and closed one hand tight around his empty tin of mints. The fire in his middle flared ever hotter, but he opened his mouth to protest that he had no intention to do anything violent. Everyone knew that. They must. A dragon protected its treasure.

"He's not going to kill you, Mads," her friend pointed out. "These days they just sue you or destroy your business. Fire your parents, maybe. I don't know."

"God, this line is taking forever. Joe up there is probably doing it on purpose to get back at me. *Some people* can't let go of things." The first girl twirled one braid around a finger.

"High school was a long time ago." The friend was far too reasonable to associate with someone who covered her bitterness with flower perfume. Zarrin tilted his head toward her, curious about their relationship to Joe, who must have attended the town's small high school with them. "I doubt he still cares about what a bitch you were."

"He shouldn't have been such a slut."

The tin crumpled in Zarrin's palm, giving in to heat and pressure. His every breath was full of smoke.

"Maybe if your boyfriend hadn't… you know what? Never mind." The friend had apparently had enough. "Just lower your voice. Or be quiet, before he hears you, or someone else hears you, and then the dragon will find out."

"He turned Russ gay," Mads hissed. "Russ swore to me."

The door opened behind Zarrin, then quickly closed without anyone coming inside. He felt the shock of cold air on his burning skin, but did not shiver.

The line moved forward again. Both girls moved with it. "*Finally*. Bet he doesn't keep his dragon boyfriend waiting like this. Do you think they, you know, when he's a dragon-dragon?" The friend shook her head, but that barely slowed Mads down. "What's he going to do? Say no? I bet if he did, the dragon would roast him too. It's almost enough to make me feel sorry for him. Joe might not have managed college, but even he's not so stupid that he'd piss off one of them."

"One of them?" Zarrin growled, his head up as they both turned toward him.

The friend's mouth fell open. Mads jumped back with a small scream that silenced everyone in close proximity and made many others turn to see what was going on. Zarrin could sense their attention as well as the silence spreading to the far reaches of the other room and behind the counter, but he kept his gaze on the one called Mads.

"I—*we*—were just messing around." She smacked her friend's arm, but her friend remained speechless.

Zarrin huffed, sending dark smoke into their faces. Somewhere in the other room, a chair scraped backward against the floor. Zarrin took his eyes off this girl, whom he did not like, and would remember, to glance over the other room, searching for the cause of the disturbance.

Every eye was on him. Every human was frozen in the middle of some act, stirring coffee, holding a book open for their child, answering their phone. All of them were transfixed, and for a long moment, he didn't understand why.

Then he noticed the deathly tight grip one of them had on his young child's coat.

They were afraid—*afraid* of *Zarrin*, and not the malicious, blue-eyed creature in front of him, who spoke out of hurt and created more pain to make herself feel better. The only hope he saw in her was the presence of the friend who somehow hadn't sickened of her yet.

"I'm sorry," the friend whispered suddenly, drawing his gaze to her. Zarrin stared into her frightened face and scowled. The humans behind her took several hurried steps backward.

They weren't wishing he was a stronger dragon, someone fierce and proud to protect them. They weren't lamenting his fall in the snow or his failure to win his treasure under the eyes of the entire town. They were wishing he wasn't a dragon. They were afraid of him.

All this time, all these weeks of making an effort to connect with them, and they thought he was here to hurt them. They did not see Zarrin; they saw dragon, and they feared it.

*It*. He was an it. One of *them*.

When he looked at the humans again, their gazes fell to the floor. They always had, but he'd thought they were uncertain. He'd never imagined they believed he would harm them. The town was his treasure, but they thought he was cruel, a petty tyrant who'd destroy them for standing in front of him in a line.

The times he had moved quickly to the front of the queue, the things Joe had said, had new meaning. Zarrin swallowed the ball of fire in his throat. Joe had thought it too. He'd thought Zarrin was here to take from them. He'd thought…. Joe had thought Zarrin was… a monster.

The girls took advantage of his distraction to flee without ordering their coffee, but Zarrin didn't move.

Joe's eyes stayed on him. He was frowning. Of course he was; he thought the worst of Zarrin. He had from the start, and Zarrin had confirmed that by taking the free things he'd been offered. He'd only wanted to know him, to know all of them. They should know the dragons hadn't forgotten them.

The smoke around him faded, turned to wisps of white before it was gone. Zarrin shivered, cold again at the wind coming through the door as a few more humans fled from him and his imagined wrath.

A dragon like Dìzhèn might have shown them wrath. Those two girls at least had earned some, Mads for her cruelty, and her friend for allowing it to be voiced without any real objections. But they were accepted, and he was not.

Zarrin's eyes were painfully dry and then prickling with tears he had to blink away.

He should never have come among the humans. He should have stayed in the Preserve and guarded the trees and the deer, the only things he was fit to protect, defective dragon that he was.

That was it, then. He was not meant for treasure or humans. He would go home and pile his blankets into a proper nest and remain there until spring, and by then all of his foolish thoughts about this town, about Joe, would be forgotten. Perhaps he would leave like all the other dragons in his family had done, although he did not want to.

He sniffled again.

"Are you cold?" A small voice, a child's voice, caught his attention.

Zarrin looked down to see a tiny human gazing up at him, ignoring how her father caught up to her a second too late to tug her back by the sleeve of her puffy coat. He darted a look up and smiled apologetically at Zarrin even as he pulled his daughter toward him with frantic concern.

"Hazel," he addressed his daughter in a lower voice, still smiling nervously. "Get back here. Please don't bother the dr—the nice man."

*Please don't bother the dragon*, Zarrin finished the thought and lifted his head high. He was here to be bothered. That was the point.

He remembered Bernard and his warning and took his eyes off the father to focus on the girl.

She went still, as if some part of her knew it was no time to play around when a dragon was studying you.

"Am I cold?" Zarrin repeated her question. He wasn't certain anyone had ever asked him that before. But he held her gaze as he nodded. "I'm frozen, little one."

He spoke as softly as he would to a startled doe. He had no need to raise his voice. The shop was so quiet he could hear the faint static beneath the music on the radio.

The tiny human stared at him. He recognized the beads in her braided hair. She liked hot chocolate, and Joe always smiled for her. "I'm cold too," she remarked, while inching away from her father's hands. "Can you make fire?"

A cup clattered into a saucer at one of the tables.

"Hazel!" her father scolded in a hush. "Don't be rude. We don't ask dra—strangers to do things for us like that."

Being an unfeeling, cruel dragon, it was easy to ignore him. Zarrin lowered his head to better let her study him, which she was, quite boldly. Her tiny nose was running.

"Yes," he answered finally. "I can make fire. All dragons can make fire. Unless you were asking if I can make a fire for you, little one. Is that what you were asking?"

"No," her father immediately replied. "Of course she wasn't."

Hazel nodded.

Zarrin nodded back to show he understood. "Dragons care for what is theirs. You had only to ask. I've been waiting for someone to ask. In all the stories—do you know the stories about dragons?"

When she slowly shook her head, Zarrin had to take a moment to breathe carefully in and out. Then he continued, letting everyone in the shop hear him. "In the stories of dragons, humans were terrified of us, and sent their heroes to speak for them. They sent their brave ones." Her gaze didn't leave his. "Are you a brave one?"

Hazel tilted her head, maybe confused by the question. Then she wiped her nose on her hand and answered, "I can get to the top of the jungle gym."

Zarrin had no idea what a jungle gym was, but getting to the top of anything was important. He nodded again to show his respect. "My sister is like you." Bold in a way Zarrin wasn't. He couldn't help a glance toward Joe. Joe, at least, could meet his eye. Zarrin let out a small, sad exhale and then turned back to Hazel. "The brave ones should be rewarded."

Hazel's father was trying to save his daughter from trouble. "You really don't have to—"

Zarrin moved around him without letting him finish. He clenched his jaw as a few humans took more cautious steps away, but he didn't acknowledge them. He wove his way around tables full of wide-eyed people, and took silent note of those who leaned away from him and those who didn't.

At the fireplace, he came to a stop. He'd never been close to it before and took a moment to study the screen in front of it. It appeared to be heavy, he supposed to discourage customers from touching it. He swiped it aside easily, to the gasping surprise of a woman he vaguely recognized as a regular customer.

Then he bent down, took a deep breath, and exhaled a stream of flame over the three logs someone had placed on the grate.

Something in the area of the espresso machines tumbled to the floor and broke.

Zarrin took another breath and then roasted the logs again until he was sure they were on fire and all the horrible fury that had risen in him at the words of those girls was gone.

They'd forgotten about dragons. Now they would remember.

When the logs were crackling, Zarrin replaced the screen and stood for a moment in front of the warm fire he had made. He gave them this, and they would still fear him. They might fear him *more*. Joe might, even his brave one, the treasure Bernard had spotted.

Zarrin curled his hands in front of him when he felt a sudden pain in his chest. To them he was a monster, but he knew he was a weakling of a dragon, because he could not make himself look to see the fear on Joe's face.

He licked his mouth for the scent traces of tea and coffee he wouldn't smell ever again, listened for the gentle rise of the classical music Joe preferred, and then turned to go back through the hushed, watching crowd.

He stopped at the door, and wished there weren't so many eyes on him, because giving up treasure, even the possibility of treasure, was no easy thing. He glanced to Hazel to acknowledge that her request had been answered, but his gaze drifted up to Joe despite himself.

Joe stared at Zarrin as if he'd never seen him before. Zarrin felt it in his heart, above the simmering heat of his spent fire. Those girls had been right about one thing only; he might have hurt them if they had said another word against Joe. He would have been tempted. No one would harm Joe, the way no one would ever harm this town.

He looked at Joe's face, at his eyes that saw too much, the hair falling down over his ears, and the black lines of music at his throat. Remarkable, but not Zarrin's.

Zarrin was out the door in the next moment.

# CHAPTER 5

JOE SPENT the weekend painting fire.

He painted until he ran out of yellows and reds, then switched to blues and greens and elusive hints of purple. He painted to understand the chemistry of dragonfire, the living color and unnatural heat of it. He didn't draw a single thing. His pencils remained untouched for two solid days as he used every warm hue in his possession to depict dragonfire and still came up short.

He ignored his phone buzzing with texts from Martin and the friend from college he'd thought about driving down to see. Dirty laundry didn't cross his mind, or replacing the food he ate. Everlasting would be full of rumors and wild stories. Everyone who had witnessed that fire was as electrified as he was, but he didn't want to talk to any of them about it. He put it on canvas and paper and then when those ran out, part of the wall.

He surrounded himself with flames that didn't burn. Dragonfire was more than a regular fire, although it had burned through the logs in the fireplace like any other flame. The colors were different. Chemically, that was probably significant, but Joe didn't know enough to analyze anything. Zarrin could direct fire wherever he wanted. Zarrin in human form could do that, which meant Zarrin in dragon form would be a creature to be reckoned with.

Dragons had magic. Joe hadn't realized exactly what that meant when he'd been confronted with Zarrin's golden, alien seductiveness. He saw the dragon, the ever-present smoke. He'd witnessed Zarrin push aside the heavy fireplace screen as though it weighed nothing. Because Zarrin wasn't human. He was a dragon who chose to *look* human. He possessed magic and used it every day, probably without conscious thought.

He was that powerful, and he'd stood in the back of that line with mud all over his clothes and listened to whatever venom Mads had been undoubtedly saying until the air around them had been thick with sulfurous smoke and Mads had screamed. Then he'd glanced around the shop until his gaze had landed on Joe.

Zarrin had been angry. Joe had recognized the dark cloud around him even if he'd never seen it so black. Much later in the day, after leaving work and coming home, Joe had realized he'd known the girls Zarrin had been speaking with. Mads and Tami, two friends who had held on to high school tighter than anyone should. Of course they'd pissed Zarrin off. Mads in particular was good at spouting ignorant bullshit. Tami was good at letting her.

But the look in Zarrin's eyes after that was what had finally driven Joe to leave his studio and do something, anything other than think about Zarrin.

He went to his mother's to stare at her TV while she was at work, since he didn't have one. Then he went home and to bed.

MONDAY, EVEN Martin was subdued as they went through their morning routine. He had no comments on all the rumors he'd heard over the weekend about the fire.

The shop was busier than usual, which left them little time to talk about anything. Joe stayed at the register and watched how every single customer walked through the door and scanned the place for signs of a dragon. When they didn't find one, their expressions were a mix of relief and disappointment.

They were afraid, but fascinated too. Joe would have been furious, but he understood those feelings well.

Not that it mattered. Joe glanced at the clock more than once, but the end of his shift came and went without an appearance from Zarrin. No antique coins were dropped into his tip jar. No hungry eyes followed him as he worked, only to dart away when Joe faced him.

Martin was surprisingly upset about it. He checked the tip jar twice and then gave Joe a tentative pat on the back on his way out.

Joe shook his head at him and went home to get his laundry and take it to the Laundromat. One of Zarrin's coins ended up in his pocket with all the quarters. He stroked it with his thumb while the dryer in front of him rumbled and shook.

TUESDAY, HAZEL and her father came in, with Hazel leading the way. She didn't seem afraid. But she had no reason to; she had spoken with a dragon and lived to tell the tale.

She took her hot chocolate and curled up as close to the fireplace as she could get without her dad warning her about burns.

"She called it dragonfire," Martin whispered to Joe. No one had corrected her to tell her that fire had gone out days ago and that teenage gothy amateur magic users had stormed in after the fire had gone out on Friday and demanded the ashes.

Joe had sent the teens off with a few select words and then collected the hot ashes in a tea canister. He didn't know shit about magic, but he knew that if ash from a dragon fire was powerful, it didn't belong with teenagers. Teenagers did nothing but make bad decisions and wish for things they shouldn't.

If anything, the ash belonged to Hazel. She was the only one in town to ask Zarrin a direct question.

And Zarrin had answered her. He'd never spoken like that before, regal but gentle, called her "little one" and "brave one" and then done what she'd asked. He'd been furious a minute before, but not a bit of that had shown when he'd talked softly to a four-year-old.

Joe scrubbed the counters and thought about that while the morning came and went with no Zarrin. He wondered if using fire took a lot out of a dragon, or if that had been a mere hint of what Zarrin was capable of. He made a list of the paints he wanted to buy, although he didn't have the money yet, unless he sold one of those coins. He considered what it meant that Zarrin had said Joe had given him hope.

*Dragons care for what is theirs*, he'd said, when seconds before he'd been wide-eyed with hurt and shock.

Joe doodled a picture of Hazel on a napkin. Then, after work, he went to the library, to get glared at by his nemesis behind the circulation desk while he prowled around picking out and then rejecting books on local history. He wanted to know why the dragons would tie themselves to the land, and say they cared for it, then leave. But history books probably wouldn't have had answers anyway.

BY WEDNESDAY, he couldn't stop frowning.

"I'm telling you, the dragon came down here to judge us, and he didn't like what he saw." Addison never knew when to shut up. Joe let Martin deal with her. "I don't blame him. Who lets their child run free around a dragon anyway? She's lucky he didn't charbroil her."

"You don't walk up to the rich and powerful and demand things." Forrester, who hadn't been the most openly motivated student in school, wasn't any more motivated now that he was a sheriff's deputy. He was in uniform and on duty, but had been leaning against the table full of milks and sugars for half an hour. "You don't even pull them over unless you want to get a lecture from the sheriff. Enough lectures might even get you fired someday."

"The justice system in action," Joe remarked, not bothering to be quiet. Forrester stared at him, so Joe crossed his arms across his chest and stared back, wondering how many lectures Forrester had gotten so far, and how many more he'd risk.

"You don't," Forrester insisted, as if he would *never* hand out tickets to asshole wealthy drivers, when he *did*, because Joe heard them complain about it. "People were just getting used to seeing the youngest Xu in town, and now he's gone again. They want someone to—"

He stopped there, but Helene in the other room continued for him, speaking up to be heard. "They want someone to go up to the house and ask him what he wants."

"He's been waiting for someone to ask," Joe answered. His face began to get uncomfortably warm. But that was what Zarrin had said—he'd been waiting for someone to seek him out like a brave one in a story. "He said he was. And you're all wrong. He wasn't mad at Hazel. He was kind with her. She asked, so he answered."

He realized his tone had softened when Martin turned around to stare incredulously at him.

Joe straightened his shoulders. "He wasn't angry with Hazel. He was angry about something else before then." Joe had been busy, but he'd seen the glimmer of Zarrin's scales in the light and the tendrils of black escaping him as he'd stood there.

His heart beat faster at the sudden flash of memory of the second before the girls had screamed and the entire place had turned to stare at Zarrin. Golden scales shining through the dark mist, Zarrin focused on the girls as intently as a snake watching mice.

Joe had no love for Mads, or any of the kids from his class, but he didn't want her murdered in front of him either. He had no proof Zarrin had intended violence, but he'd known then that all his comparisons to volcanoes had been right. Zarrin was dangerous and inhuman.

But the look in his eyes afterward….

Joe inhaled sharply. "Whatever pissed him off, it wasn't Hazel," he argued again, before hesitating. "And that's not why he left. I… I don't know why he left, but it wasn't because of Hazel. She was brave and approached him, and he liked it."

"So someone else should approach him," Helene suggested while bringing her cup and saucer back to the counter. "And if our local constabulary won't"—she didn't even glance in Forrester's direction—"then someone the dragon likes. Someone who isn't afraid of him either."

Zarrin had breathed fire. Just because Joe had been able to look at him afterward didn't mean Joe hadn't been afraid.

"That isn't why people want me to go up there," Joe answered, with pointed honesty that made Helene look away.

Addison wrinkled her nose.

Joe turned to Addison and narrowed his eyes. He looked her slowly up and down while she stood there in mute shock. "Are you disgusted at me or him? Not that it matters what you think." Her flush took over her whole face. Joe continued to frown at her. "You have a problem with the dragons, take it up with the dragons, or shut up about it."

He'd been braver—if angrier—than her at seventeen.

"He's waiting for you to ask," Joe reminded her, because Zarrin had said those exact words in a tone to haunt Joe's nights. He turned his back on Addison to vent some steam from the wands on the espresso machine. The furious hissing noises were soothing.

"Angry or not, something upset the dragon." Forrester spoke up again. "Nothing here for him, no one up at the house, he might leave. And he's probably the last of them who'd bother. He's already lasted longer than most of the others." He sounded as though he was warning someone.

Joe frowned harder as he twisted to watch Forrester go out the door. Helene gave Joe an apologetic look, and then she left too.

Addison wasn't worth more of his time, so Joe returned to cleaning the machine. From here, he couldn't see the clock on the register.

Martin came up next to him and put the medium paper cup he'd gotten down earlier back into the stack. "If you don't want people to ask you about him, maybe don't act like you know him so well," he advised, and leaned against Joe's arm. Joe stiffened, and then Martin moved over to the coffee brewers to prepare a new pot.

Joe glared at him and pretended his face wasn't stinging. "I told them what he said."

"Joseph, you're the only one who even *noticed* what he said." Martin, the asshole, didn't even turn to look at him. "Everyone else was shitting themselves, myself included."

"I was scared. Of course I was. But I…." Joe trailed off and shook his head to clear it. "That doesn't mean anything."

"It might to him, though." Martin was quiet as he replaced a coffee filter. "And to us. We're all a little embarrassed at ourselves for losing it like we did, right, Addison?"

Joe looked at her. He'd forgotten she was there.

She gave them both one final glance and then took off in a huff for the other room, where, if it had been cold enough, she would have been happy to sit in the warmth of dragonfire.

Joe returned to wiping down the espresso machine and let Martin's last remark go unanswered.

JOE WANTED to paint, but didn't sell any of the coins for supplies. He hiked along the beach after work until his legs were jelly and his face and hands were frozen, then walked to his apartment through the rain the snow had turned into. The heater was attempting to work. The landlord promised repairs over the weekend. Since he couldn't sleep anyway, Joe let it go.

He hadn't done any work in a few days, which bothered him. But it wasn't why he got out of bed earlier than usual and opened up the shop on Thursday before he remembered it was Thanksgiving. Martin wouldn't be coming in. No one else would. The shop would be open a few hours for the people buying coffee to go on their way to their relatives' houses. Joe had volunteered to work because he didn't give a shit about Thanksgiving, and he saw his mom all the time.

He lit the fire in the fireplace, set the coffee to brewing, and then straightened in surprise when the first person in was Alice Reyes. She was more bundled up than usual, which made sense when he noticed the snowflakes on her shoulders. It must have started to snow again in the time he'd been inside.

He thought of the alley cat, but nothing he did had ever gotten that cat to trust him with more than its breakfast. It was probably going to freeze.

"You scowling for a new reason or the same reason?" Alice set her two thermoses onto the counter.

Since the coffee was still brewing, Joe didn't move. "It's my right to scowl."

Alice nodded. She was fairly scowly herself in the mornings. Joe got up to grab a mug and hold it under the stream of brewing coffee. When it was halfway full, he pushed it toward her. He got one for himself to avoid dealing with her surprise at the gift.

He got himself a tiny bit of milk too, and offered her some, though she preferred her coffee black. "You're working today?"

"Snow or rain, someone has to watch out for traces of smoke." As a smoke spotter, Alice sat in a cabin on stilts in one of the hills and basically kept an eye out for illegal campfires or lightning strikes, although the redwoods were so damp around here, fires were rare. The job didn't pay much, but it was mostly tough old retirees out there anyway, working their twenty-four hour shifts alone. "In fact, if it's cold, anyone out there at this time will definitely have a campfire. A big fire's not likely at this time of year, but since it'll just be me out there today, I have to go."

"In about half an hour, I'm going to get a bunch of grouchy people in here on the way to visit their families," Joe commiserated with her. "But I get to go home afterward. I might see my mom. She'll be tired, so I'll bring her some Chinese if Daniel's place is open tonight. It was last year."

Alice inclined her head in a serious sort of way, then stuck her hip against the counter. "That's it? Afternoon off, and that's it?"

"Not my holiday," Joe said shortly, and she nodded again.

"Yes, but I didn't think you were the type to bullshit. But that's your business. None of mine." She held up her hands innocently before pushing her thermoses forward. "Fill 'em up. Long day for me."

Joe squinted at her. The caffeine hadn't hit him yet, and he really needed it. "I'm not bullshitting anything."

"The dragonfire." Alice didn't mess around. "It's something, isn't it?"

Joe froze with his cup halfway to his mouth. "Yeah." His voice was husky. "When did you see it?"

"He melts traps when he finds them." Alice took a sip of her coffee, though it was hot enough to make her cough and then blow on it. "I've seen it a few times."

"He melts…?" Joe couldn't finish, too distracted by the idea of Zarrin melting illegal poaching traps. Little Zarrin with his soft voice. Joe had seen him turn into something dangerous, and yet he couldn't picture it. Zarrin in his knitted hat and his scarf and his gloves, out in the woods hunting trappers? "*Zarrin* melts animal traps?"

Alice nodded gravely. "And not just on the Preserve. He wanders into the state park all the time, and we mostly let it go, because he's doing worthy work out there."

Joe stared at her, then took a long, steadying drink of his coffee.

"It's easier than calling in the wardens, since he's already on-site, so to speak." Alice politely pretended not to notice Joe staring at her. "And most illegal trappers get the message when they find their traps turned into useless chunks of metal. They leave on their own."

"Zarrin?" Joe didn't know why he couldn't believe it; he'd seen the fire with his own eyes. He considered what the melting point of steel might be, then refocused on Alice. "Small Zarrin? Who wears a thick winter coat in October?"

She shrugged. "He's the only dragon out there, so when we peer through our binoculars and see one prowling, we assume it's him." She abruptly glanced away before giving another shrug, this one more self-conscious. "I grew up in this town, and I still never thought I'd see one of the dragons as… themselves."

"You've seen him?" Joe's voice went embarrassingly high. Luckily Alice wasn't likely to care or comment.

"He's out there most days, in the Preserve and out of it. He keeps an eye on things. Blends in fairly well, despite the shine on those scales." She paused to blow on her coffee. "Though the snow will put an end to that, make him stand out like a cardinal in December—not that he's being hunted. But I guess that doesn't matter now."

"Doesn't matter?" Joe belatedly picked up a thermos. He had a hundred questions about what Zarrin looked like as a dragon and no way to ask them. He nearly dropped the thermos twice and only had to walk two feet to the brewers. "What do you mean? Did he stop going out there?"

"The dragon. Zarrin. Hasn't been seen in a while." Alice grunted. "Nobody's caught sight of him since last week." Joe looked over at her in alarm, and she squinted. "What day was it again, when the girl asked him to light the fire?"

Joe didn't answer that, since she clearly knew already. He narrowed his attention to her thermos, watching it fill up with coffee like he'd never seen anything more exciting. Meanwhile his mind raced with images of Zarrin, already gone.

If Zarrin had left, taken his little red scooter and gone in the middle of the night, who in town would have noticed? He had every reason to go, like Forrester had said. There was nothing for Zarrin here. No family, no friends.

He abruptly remembered Zarrin asking how Joe dealt with being alone, and stopped.

The splash of overflowing coffee brought him back to the moment, and Joe swore and set down the thermos. He wiped up his mess with a towel and ignored his stinging hand. Burns were common enough in the shop, and this one wasn't a big deal.

"So he's gone?" He cleaned up the thermos too, then reached for the second one.

"Didn't say that." Alice sipped at her coffee like that cat outside drank from its bowl. Joe recovered enough to frown, and she either didn't see or pretended not to. "Smoke's coming from the chimney of the house. Well, one of the chimneys. That house has a few. Someone's there. Maybe not your boy, but—"

"He's not my boy," Joe protested. "And no one else lives there. The housekeeper is gone. He said so."

"Hmm." Alice made the noise into her cup of coffee.

"There's no one else," Joe continued, his voice strangely rough. Only Zarrin and the elf housekeeper lived up there, and according to Zarrin the elf was gone. He didn't know how dragon families worked, but he'd guess they didn't usually leave their twenty or twenty-one-year-old by himself in an antique mansion while the rest of them lived together in the city. None of that made sense, which Joe would have thought about before if he hadn't been so pissed off about the coins and Zarrin watching him like that, as if… Joe was worth the price of those coins. More than that, maybe. As if Joe had value the coins didn't.

"Shit," Joe said out loud and glanced at Alice. She was watching him, her aged face calm and unconcerned, which he highly doubted. She was making a point about this to him. She must have waited to get him alone to talk about it.

Zarrin had no one. He hadn't come into town to observe them and report back, or to find people to worship him. He'd come into town because he was lonely. He had walked around every single day completing errands he hadn't needed to do, had ordered drinks he didn't even like, because he was lonely, because he'd wanted to talk to people.

Joe put the lid on Alice's second thermos automatically. Whatever Zarrin's motive for tipping Joe like he had, he hadn't done or said anything inappropriate. He'd only waited, as if hoping Joe would say something friendly. Or remember his drink order.

"Shit," Joe said again.

Zarrin held the power of *fire*, and he'd been standing at the back of the line. He had warmed everyone in the coffee shop despite their fear of him, and made a little girl happy, and then left, because he terrified them.

Joe had seen him realize it. He had witnessed Zarrin's awareness that every human around him was afraid of him. Joe just hadn't known that's what it was at the time.

And now Zarrin was gone. From the shop, from town, even from the Preserve. As suddenly as Zarrin had begun to appear around town, he had disappeared from it.

"You know." Alice set out the right amount of money for the coffee on the counter. "The fact that hunting the deer is legal with a permit has never stopped him from roaring to frighten the hunters away. He is very protective of those deer. Thinks they're his, I imagine."

"Deer?" Joe's eyes were burning. He forced himself to blink.

"Strangest thing. Deer will freeze in front of a car. Bolt at the slightest crackle of leaves. But they'll drink from the river next to a dragon, with no concern at all—unless it's the time for rut, of course. He just confused them then." Alice wasn't moving from the counter.

The dragons were supposed to watch over everything. That was the myth, one of the things tourists loved to talk about. Joe had always assumed that meant with their money, or threatening to devour any criminals. He hadn't imagined Zarrin as a beast of legend, and never thought Zarrin would be the defender of the small and furry.

"Zarrin protects the deer?" Joe was going to blame being this slow on not getting his caffeine earlier, but he had been this slow for weeks. "So he can keep them all to himself?"

"Well, he's not eating them." Alice huffed a bit as if this idea amused her. "You know what I think?" She leaned over the counter, so Joe did too. "I think if one of those deer could talk, it would be his only friend in the world. Now, it's not my affair why it's just him in that mansion Dìzhèn built. Addison Bernes, who never got the chance to understand love, might have some theories, but anyone with sense would ignore them. I can't tell you why he came here again, or if he'll leave like the rest. I can't tell you if he's a good person, or any fun at parties, or if he wants to do things to you that we didn't talk about in my day—at least not in public."

"Alice!" Joe reared back.

Alice rolled her eyes and took hold of her coffee. "All I can tell you is, that boy came here every day for weeks without a problem. And now he's gone."

"And like the rest of the town, you want me to go see if that's for good and try to 'convince' him to stay?" Joe wondered sarcastically. "Funny how the thing—*one* of the things—they shunned me for in school is now what they want to save them."

"I don't want you to do anything." Alice's gaze was steady. "I just thought you should know. Anyway, I'm not going to wish you a happy holiday. I'll wish you a good half a day off."

"Thanks," Joe growled, still caught up in his annoyance at being the town's offering to the dragon. But Alice was already heading for the door. The bell chimed as she slipped out into the faintly swirling snowfall.

Joe exhaled shakily and stood there feeling stupid and wound up on caffeine. People should start streaming in soon, but for now, he was alone with the snow and the silence. He hadn't even turned on the radio.

He had no responsibility whatsoever for Zarrin's happiness or the well-being of the town. Most of what he'd thought about Zarrin from the beginning was still true: he was rich, he was powerful, and the fire proved he could take care of himself.

But, if the ancient coins in his tip jar weren't an ostentatious display of wealth, or the absentminded gesture of someone with too much money, or an attempt to buy Joe, as Martin had joked, then they were something else—an offering, quite possibly, of peace or friendship or goodwill.

Nobody who spoke quietly and respectfully to children, or saved deer, or brought in a painting simply for something to *talk about* was out to hurt anyone.

Joe had the horrible feeling Zarrin had wanted to be *liked*, and Joe had helped take that away from him.

HE MANAGED not to think about it any more until the coffee shop cleared out around eleven and he realized he had the rest of the day free, with nothing to do to distract him. Everything was closed, and his mother wasn't off work yet. He couldn't paint.

A hike would have been his usual activity with unexpected free time. There were dozens of trails in the state park, many of which would be easy even with a dusting of snow. But as he cleaned up the shop and ate pastries he would have had to throw out otherwise, he knew he wasn't going to go anywhere near the park today.

He turned off the lights and locked up and then stood in the alley, feeling foolish although there was no one to see him. Everyone was inside celebrating their holiday. The town was quiet. Even the cat was gone or hiding.

He hesitated for one more moment, then let himself back into the shop and marched to the espresso machine.

He wasn't a brave one, but he owed Zarrin something. Zarrin had shared Joe's painting with him and didn't know it. This was the least Joe could do.

And it was all he was going to do. He wasn't an offering or an envoy, he thought firmly as he took the latte with him around the block to where he parked his old car. He'd wrapped the paper cup in napkins to help it retain heat, but only a few minutes in his freezing car as it warmed up made that a waste of time.

He grimaced but finally got his car defrosted enough to drive, not that he could go fast in the slush.

By the time he was out of town, he already regretted everything. Just because his mother had raised him to be a decent human being didn't mean he should be risking death, either on these roads or at the hands of a dragon, simply to deliver an ice-cold latte.

But he wasn't one for bullshit, exactly as Alice had said. If he were, he would have stayed at the junior college, or never left town in the first place and kept on being Russ Monroe's secret shame.

The reminder of his last year of high school felt appropriate as he drove past the sign announcing he was entering dragon property. He didn't see a trace of spray paint on it. Someone had either cleaned it up or replaced it to get rid of his stupid teen vandalism.

He was surprised how little he minded it being gone, but his anger then had never really been about the dragons anyway. He didn't like their careless treatment of something they claimed to own, but they hadn't been the ones making him miserable. They would have had to notice him to do that.

All the same, he slowed after the sign was out of sight in his rearview mirror. He'd never been beyond the first sign. Very few had, as far as he knew, even in Alice's lifetime.

His heart began to beat faster.

He turned on his headlights, so he couldn't be accused of sneaking up on anyone, and crept farther into the hills. The road seemed unnecessarily winding, but it was old and took its time with the incline as older cars must have had to do.

His mouth went dry when he saw the second sign, informing him he should have been invited here. It didn't say what would happen to him if he hadn't been. There weren't any reports of trespassers being set afire or gobbled up as a snack by hungry dragons. There were, however, always those campers and hikers who went missing.

Which made it madness that he kept going, until a house appeared in the middle of the trees, a beautiful house he needed to see up close. It didn't loom over anything, despite its size. The house—Dìzhèn's house—was a castle in a clearing.

Joe stopped at the end of the driveway to stare at the tiered towers, the elaborately painted windowsills and balconies. His hand itched with the urge to sketch. He generally didn't care much about architecture, but he recognized a work of art when he saw one. He couldn't snap pictures, not even with his phone. It would have been like taking something without permission, but he wanted to remember enough that he could draw it later.

He saw the surrounding outbuildings and the gate and then the trail of smoke rising from one chimney. Lights were on inside as well, on the first and second floor but not the third.

His car was running. Joe didn't know about dragon hearing, or magic, but his presence was already obvious, and no one had charged out to roast him.

He took a few minutes to breathe and study the unusual lines of the house, and then when he'd delayed it as much as he reasonably could, he continued up the long driveway.

Nothing happened when he passed through the gate, not even the weird sensation of touching a spell he'd felt a few times when passing a magic supply store in the city. It didn't mean no magic was being worked, only that it hadn't struck Joe dead.

"Small favors," he murmured as he parked several yards from the entrance to the house. He took the latte with him, although not the napkins, and carried it to the foot of the stairs leading to the front door.

He wasn't an expert, but the glasswork in the front door looked like Tiffany to him, probably over a hundred years old and as forgotten as the rest of this amazing house. What the fuck was he doing here? Alice Reyes might be right about Zarrin, but Joe must have lost his mind. He stared at the latte, definitely too cold to taste good, then squared his shoulders and headed up the stairs. He'd made it this far.

He rang the doorbell and snapped his head up when a blast of wind swept across the porch. His coat and henley weren't close to warm enough to be out in this. He shivered and listened to the sound of the ringing doorbell carrying through the house.

There was still a faint echo when the door swung open. Joe jerked back, because he hadn't seen any motion through the glass. Then he caught his breath to see a woman staring at him from the doorway.

His first thought, after realizing it wasn't Zarrin and that Zarrin wasn't visible behind her, was that she was either métis or light-skinned. He studied her in surprise and confusion, until she flashed a grin and said, "Tansi," and then paused as if waiting for him to answer.

Joe didn't know which language she was speaking. Not that it mattered, since he didn't speak anything but English. But his cheeks stung as he glanced away. Then she said, "*Oh,*" in this sorry, polite tone that wasn't pity, but it might as well have been.

Joe looked back at her. His ignorance was all over him, no point in trying to hide it. But instead of clucking her tongue or shaking her head or laughing, she studied him. Her gaze was curious and then appreciative, and she winked when he met her eyes.

He scowled. She responded to that by leaning against the doorjamb as if she hadn't a care in the world.

She was taller than Joe, with widely spaced eyes and dramatic cheekbones, and her hair was in a long, loose braid over her shoulder. But what caught his attention was the sweater she was wearing. It was red and probably cashmere, and it was too small for her. Zarrin could have fit into it perfectly.

Joe squeezed the paper cup until he felt it dimple under his fingers, then forced himself to relax. He wasn't in high school anymore. He didn't sit next to boys who chose not to acknowledge him in the full light of day in front of their friends. He didn't allow confused popular kids with girlfriends to make eyes at him.

"Sorry." He ground out the word, the lie, the complete bullshit, as Alice might have said.

"Who are you?" The woman stopped him as he was starting to turn around.

"Who are you?" he asked in return, without looking at her.

"To strangers? I'm Marie Greenleaf." She said that like it meant something, and it must have. Something about it was familiar. Joe couldn't remember what, but when he shot her a glance, she shrugged. "But I suppose you're not exactly a stranger. You're a surprise, to say the least. And you smell sort of… itchy. Hmm."

"Are you speaking in riddles on purpose?" Joe faced her again.

"Greenleaf means nothing to you?" She sighed a little. "Ah well. I can't blame you. And I am a long way from home. Your face was familiar enough to get me excited and a bit homesick. Sorry for that before."

For a moment, her voice sounded aged and very tired. Her eyes were like that too, interesting enough to draw, if he was inclined, because otherwise she didn't seem much older than him. But he wasn't inclined.

"Joseph Andres," he introduced himself anyway, and wanted to throw away the stupid latte so he could put his gloves on and then leave.

Marie's expression lit up. "Joseph, huh?" She flashed those teeth again in a sharp smile. Her eyes seemed to get lighter as they swept over him. Joe got those kinds of looks a lot, but usually not from women wearing Zarrin's clothes.

"What else would it be?" he answered, with his chin in the air.

Her smile got wider. "*Joe* maybe," she suggested. "Do people call you Joe?"

"Sometimes." He watched her carefully when she took a step out of the doorway. Her feet were wrapped in two pairs of men's socks.

She leaned in his direction and took a deep breath. Then she raised her head and did it again. Joe had seen Zarrin do that. "Is that a latte?" she asked, sniffing the air. "Did you bring a latte from town? Hmm, and with sugar in your pocket."

Joe had an astonished second to realize she could *smell* the sugar packet in his coat pocket, and then he remembered talk from some of his mother's older relatives about what *Greenleaf* meant.

She was wolf.

His heart rate kicked up. She could probably hear it, and he couldn't do anything about it but stand and stare at her. There was a werewolf in Zarrin's house.

He remembered her teeth and the strange light in her eyes and then being sniffed. Whatever he smelled like now kept the smile on her face.

"Boy comes calling with sugar in his pocket." She seemed very pleased about something. "Well, well."

Joe's mouth was too dry to speak. He had to swallow and try again. "Is Zarrin here?" He didn't like her grin or how she kept sniffing the air around him. She was of a line that went to the first wolf, courageous and loyal and ferocious. She was a hunter, more than equal to a dragon. Joe was a barista. Standing on this porch in the cold was about as humiliating as being a dumb kid trying to stare down a statue. He held out the cup and wished he was anywhere else in the world. "Just give him this, all right? Or don't. It's cold now anyway."

Marie clapped her hands together excitedly, more like a cheerleader than a bloodthirsty predator. "This is the most adorable thing I've ever seen," she exclaimed. Joe stiffened, but she came forward in her socks and her sweater and took the cup from him. She sniffed the lid too, which was nosy. "You didn't drink any. You brought him a latte all the way from town." Even when she was happy she seemed deadly. "This is a good gift. You did well."

"I didn't *do* anything," Joe practically snarled at her. Maybe he *was* a brave one. Or maybe he was freezing, but his face was hot with embarrassment and he wanted to leave.

"Did you want me to give him the sugar too?" Marie held out her hand and the sleeve of the sweater rose higher with the motion. White slashes of scar tissue marred the smooth skin on the inside of her arm, long vicious tears with jagged ends.

She startled when she saw he'd noticed, and tugged the sweater down. "It's healed," she explained, awkward for the first time. "Careless of me, but I've been a little careless lately, and I was so distracted by the magicky fire scent that I didn't notice the trap until I'd stepped in it."

"You stepped in an animal trap?" Joe swept a furious look out into the trees. "Here?" Trapping was already illegal, but a trapper who had accidentally harmed a shifter was going to be in serious trouble. Joe didn't know if that was a job for Fish and Game or the police, but either way, they were lucky she'd been able to shift back and free herself and heal. "Are you all right?"

She tilted her head to one side to study him. "I am now."

Joe looked behind her to the house. What he could see of the interior seemed like the lap of nineteenth century luxury. He could feel heat emanating in waves from the open door. Zarrin might be in there somewhere, listening to all this or oblivious to it.

"Right," he answered shortly, then took his gaze from the house.

"Any message to go with the drink, Joseph?" Marie was sweetness itself.

Joe gave her a brief, narrow look. "I didn't come calling. I'm not asking for anything."

She blinked a few times, then smiled slyly. "So, no message, then? Not even any sugar?"

Werewolf or not, Joe raised his head to glare at her for a moment, then turned and stalked down the stairs toward his car. Next to the antique grandeur of the house, his car looked as out of place as it was possible to be.

He half expected the sound of her laughter to follow him, but he only heard the wind, and when he looked back at the mansion through his windshield, the door was closed.

He glanced up to the many windows, bright with internal light and heat. They seemed to watch him with knowing amusement, like the statue of Dìzhèn in the park, but of course they weren't, any more than the statue did. He wasn't anything to them.

He started the car on that thought and didn't look back until the first warning sign was behind him.

# CHAPTER 6

MARIE WAS tall and beautiful and fiercely different. No one in Everlasting was quite like her, except possibly Joe. But not merely for their shared ethnicity; Marie met the gaze of everyone on the street who looked at her, and raised an eyebrow if they stared too long.

If she felt fear, Zarrin saw no sign of it, only defiance.

She was also as kind as Joe, although it showed in different ways. For example, if she smelled Zarrin's anxiety at being out in town again, she politely ignored it.

But she linked their arms together after he'd led her across the street from the park, and pressed herself against his side as if she knew. She liked touching people and claimed it was werewolf instinct, but this much touching was new.

Unless they were on his bed watching *Diedre's Secret* together. Then, she was also prone to snuggling. Zarrin was getting used to that, although he didn't really mind. His family was not the sort to lay about watching television and cuddling, and Bernard had always been doing something. Anyway, it wouldn't have occurred to Zarrin to ask him to snuggle.

Marie had gone right past asking, to sniffing the air in his bedroom and then hopping onto the bed uninvited to stare at the TV with him, the same way she had taken a long look around the intersection as they had waited at the crosswalk, and then decided she needed to hold his arm.

"They're afraid of me," he confided to her in a whisper he knew she'd hear.

She nodded as she continued studying the various buildings and making him stop at all the shop windows. Zarrin had no interest in shopping today but stayed with her out of respect for her wishes.

"Of course they are. Humans are always afraid of us." Marie tugged him closer, with zero respect for the dignity of a dragon. "They're afraid of themselves too, as well as each other. Tiny bundles of fear most of the time."

"But I'm here to help them." Zarrin shook his head. "Or, I was. They don't seem to want me." His lower lip did not tremble. His voice did not quiver. But she knew anyway. Werewolves were incredible with scent. He'd been aware of that, but he'd never met one before her.

"Don't pretend dragons aren't capable of violence, Zarrin. That's the worst thing you can do, because it's a lie. You are, and they know you are." Marie put her chin on the top of his head, which made him wrinkle his nose and caused a human behind them to gasp as if shocked. "Well, okay." Marie relented. "Maybe *you* are a powderpuff, but you're still powerful—a powerful powderpuff."

"Powderpuff?" Zarrin echoed, utterly offended, although he was as weak a dragon as had ever held a hoard.

Marie clucked her tongue and dragged him back to the sidewalk. Zarrin consented to be dragged, although he did raise his chin to make it seem as though it was his idea.

"Zarrin, if you weren't a being, the situation might be different. But you are. And you're a *dragon*, which means you have strength, and magic, and fire. More than all that, you have *money*." Marie met his gaze. "Believe me, I'm not one to defend these people, but you have to understand how they see you. Yes, you can set the world on fire. But more likely in today's world, you can crush them with lawyers and layoffs and… whatever else it is that rich people do to the regular people they don't care about."

"My sister is a lawyer," Zarrin volunteered. "She's clever and sharp, and my grandmother is very proud of her."

"There you go." Marie waved a hand. "Human instincts scream *danger* at the sight of a dragon, and then their actual thinking brain reminds them that you're sort of their boss."

"But I'm not involved in the business," Zarrin protested. Marie made a sound similar to the ones Bernard made when Zarrin said things like that. It meant Zarrin wasn't a part of the business, but he could have been, and he still earned money from it.

He thought about this as they waited at another crosswalk and were covertly watched by everyone in the vicinity. "Joe said something about rich people too. He said they *expect* things in return when they give something."

"Oh, did he?" Marie's hooting laugh was loud and distracting, but Zarrin thought it was the way her eyes caught the light and turned gold that made the man in the business suit next to them cross himself and back away. "*Joe*." Marie had repeated the name that way since the very first time Zarrin had mentioned Joe to her. "You know, all your talk about him did not lead me to think he'd show up at your door, and with a gift of his own no less."

"I didn't either," Zarrin confessed, and wished he hadn't put on gloves, because he couldn't bite his fingernails with them on. He ducked his head to conceal his smile when he imagined Joe at his house. He shouldn't smile. He hadn't been home when Joe had shown up. Zarrin hadn't even drunk the latte, since he didn't care for them and it had been cold anyway, but he would have kept it if not for the worry over souring milk and bad smells.

One human, at least, was not afraid of him. And that human was the person Zarrin most loved to think about. It was both wonderful and terrifying.

He could have spent days lying in bed, daydreaming about it and what to do next, but then Marie had asked to be shown "the town you own" and then also requested coffee from his *nichimoose*—a word she still hadn't translated for him.

"What do you think the latte meant?" Zarrin asked her, for the tenth time that morning alone. "You're sure he didn't say anything else?"

"He barely spoke." Marie lifted her head to sniff the air and then began to lead them with confidence toward the coffee shop despite never having been there before. Zarrin's stomach dropped alarmingly when he realized how close they were. He was going to see Joe again.

He unhooked their arms and hurried toward Everlasting Cuppa. He should never have stayed away.

He made it through the door ahead of her and stopped at the back of the line to stare at Joe in absolute contentment.

Joe was busy working, adding espresso beans to the machine while asking people waiting in line if they wanted their usual orders. His gaze skipped to where Zarrin stood, and he stopped moving long enough for espresso beans to tumble from the top of the grinder.

Martin laughed at him for overpouring and then turned to help sweep the mess from the counter. But he stopped when he too saw Zarrin. He said something to Joe out of the side of his mouth and then gave Zarrin a small wave that made many of the people in line twist around to see whom he'd waved at.

They all seemed stunned, but no one was scrambling away in fear. Zarrin should have cared about that and what it might mean, but he was busy staring at Joe. Joe must have had a hectic morning, because he was wearing a shirt with long sleeves and a loose collar and not his usual T-shirt. But even with his skin covered up, Zarrin could have stared at him for hours.

Treasure was working hard, and obviously well, and Zarrin wanted to take him from this place and pull his hair free and pet him while they lay together in his bed. He would kiss that stubborn mouth, and run his hands beneath the gray fabric of Joe's shirt, and settle between his legs. Joe had such firm thighs, surely he wouldn't mind if Zarrin claimed them and lived between them and lifted them up when he—

"Zarrin," Marie hissed, and Zarrin turned to her in astonishment. She raised her eyebrows at him. "You're lucky everyone else in this room can only guess what you're thinking," she warned him in a whisper. Then she tapped her nose. "I can smell it."

"I want to keep him safe," Zarrin explained, with dignity.

Marie snorted. "You want to *keep* him. Like a fairy does. Hmm, I wonder about him and fairies. This town doesn't have any, does it?"

"Too cold." Zarrin's hands became fists as he thought about fairies in this town. They were smart enough to see the qualities in Joe that these humans often overlooked. "Fairies do not get to have him."

"If you don't want anyone else near your mate, Zarrin, I suggest you do something about it." Marie said this as though Zarrin was as bold as she was, as though he had any idea what he was doing.

Anyway, he had tried to get closer to Joe, and it hadn't worked. He huffed at her and then turned toward the counter. Joe was ringing someone up, but his attention didn't seem to be on his work.

"Hmm. He's kind of delicate, your painted human. Sensitive." Marie spoke into Zarrin's ear. She continued before Zarrin could protest that Joe was strong, and tell her all about his muscles. "Everyone is watching, and you're not doing anything but staring at him. You're making him tense."

Zarrin shivered at the ticklish sensation of her breath on his neck. "What else should I do?" he asked earnestly, and hated that he had to. "You think I'm a failure too?"

The human directly in front of them swung around at the words and then blinked a few times. He focused on Marie, then Zarrin. His mouth was hanging open.

"You've all seen me try," Zarrin explained to him, furious and embarrassed. "What else am I to do?" He raised his gaze to Joe once again and found Joe looking back at him. Then Joe glanced at Marie. A moment later, he frowned and said something to Martin.

Martin darted an unhappy look Zarrin's way. Joe didn't look at Zarrin again.

Zarrin felt his excitement from the morning leave him. "He came all the way out to bring a drink to me," he whined softly, shaming himself. "I don't understand."

"You sheltered thing." Marie patted his shoulder and ignored how Zarrin stiffened to remind her he needed advice, not pity. She gestured vaguely toward the counter. "How do dragons do this, then?"

Zarrin considered the equally puzzled human man in front of him. "Do what?" he asked him. The man finally closed his mouth.

"I'm going to say *date*," Marie answered, sounding amused now. "Although that word hardly applies here, for so many reasons."

Zarrin didn't see the relevance, but responded anyway. "Dating is not usual. However, if a pairing with another dragon is desired by the parents for the purposes of children, we meet somewhere our parents would arrange it, to see if we like each other. Love isn't expected, although it happens. Mostly our parents want us to get to know other dragons, so that if we choose to have hatchlings one day, the option is there…." He trailed off when the human's mouth fell open again, although the man shut it much quicker this time. Zarrin turned to Marie. "There are so few of us these days. But often dragons are drawn to the special quality in another, regardless of gender or magical abilities. Then things would be different. I don't know how they arrange those meetings. Some dragons mingle among the humans, or so I hear. My family… does not." He glanced at the human, who was unmoving despite how the line had all but disappeared in front of him. "But when dragons choose another who is not dragon, there are no strict ways of doing anything. In fact there was… well. I shouldn't say."

"What?" Marie poked him. The human, who was a teenager, now that Zarrin was paying attention enough to notice, leaned in as if fascinated.

"A rumor of an amateur video of a dragon and a fairy." Zarrin lowered his voice. "A pornographic video," he elaborated and frowned when Marie grinned lasciviously. "But I've never seen it, and I doubt it's real. No dragon would share that, or a fairy lover for that matter. Anyway—" He couldn't help glancing to Joe as he imagined the things that might go on in a video like that one. "That isn't dating."

"Dude," the teenager exhaled. "You watch porn? Wait, there's *dragon porn*? Are you like… *you know*… in it?"

"The line moved," Marie informed him bluntly. "It's your turn."

The teenager hopped around to face the counter, then turned back in one agitated motion. "You know what? I have to get home and get my laptop to look something up. I'll, um…." He started walking toward the door before he'd finished whatever he was going to say.

Zarrin had forgotten him already. He stepped forward until he was close enough to breathe the same air as Joe. Then he placed his hands on the counter and closed his eyes to inhale the mix of feelings he never understood but which he knew meant *Joe*.

The latte had barely smelled of him. This was much better.

He opened his eyes. Joe was still and quiet, almost frozen. He had rolled up his sleeves sometime when Zarrin had been talking about porn, and the sight would have been distracting if Zarrin hadn't been basking in his presence.

"I missed you," Zarrin said, and Joe's eyes widened. "When you came to the house," Zarrin added quickly, before nodding his head with practiced courtesy. "Thank you for the latte."

Martin made a noise as if he was choking on his own spit. "You did what?"

Joe darted a glance to Martin, then another to Zarrin. Zarrin's heart pounded madly, and then Joe's gaze slid to Marie. His unhappy expression made Zarrin clench his hands in anxious anger.

Joe hadn't been frowning when he'd seen him. Whatever had brought about this change, Zarrin didn't like it, and he intended to deal with it.

"Thoughtful," Marie commented. Zarrin could *hear* her grin. "To bring a gift like that. Proper."

"It's nothing," Joe said, to *her*. But before Zarrin could offer a comment, Joe directed his frown at Zarrin. "You didn't have to drink it."

"I don't have to do anything," Zarrin started to snap at him, before it registered that Joe didn't have to do anything either. He certainly hadn't been forced to bring Zarrin his regular drink, which he'd remembered. Joe had known his drink order. "You didn't give me sugar—this time," Zarrin tacked on, in a much lower voice, and pulled his lower lip between his teeth when Joe shivered.

Joe shot a wide-eyed look to Marie, but then his gaze went to Zarrin and stayed there. "I forgot."

Marie puffed out a small laugh that made Joe scowl and finally tear his eyes away.

"I… everyone wanted you to know you're welcome here," he explained stiffly. "The fire… your fire… startled them, but only a little."

Zarrin drew himself up. "But everyone didn't bring me a latte."

Martin made a strangled sound.

Joe seemed to freeze even more. Once again, his eyes went to Marie. Zarrin couldn't see why; Marie was smiling. It was her friendly smile—much less wolfish.

"It was a holiday," Joe remarked. "No one else was around." He focused back on Zarrin, and for a moment, Zarrin would swear Joe wasn't breathing. Then Martin nudged him, and Joe cleared his throat. "You want the same today?"

Zarrin nodded absently, despite not wanting a latte.

"I see what you mean, Zarrin," Marie commented suddenly. She waved to indicate the other room, and when Zarrin glanced in that direction, several humans gave him guilty looks before ducking over their phones or books. "Have they never seen a werewolf before?"

"Only weres passing through on their way up the highway, or heading to the state park. Beings don't come to Everlasting, probably because of… the town's reputation." Martin spoke up, after communicating something silently with Joe. Joe made a face at him, then seemed to realize Zarrin was watching him.

Joe drew his eyebrows together. "It's not that. It's that you and Zarrin… that you're with Zarrin." The sound he made after he said that was nearly one of Marie's growls. Zarrin was distracted by Joe's unhappiness, but didn't miss the startled anger on Martin's face aimed at *Zarrin*. Zarrin stared at him in amazement, and then Martin's expression went blank.

"I'll make your drink," Joe offered, although Martin was already in front of the espresso machine. But Martin stepped out of the way and approached the register to take Joe's place. He wasn't smiling. Zarrin looked from him to Joe and made a quiet noise of frustration.

The line of Joe's back, while lovely, was too far away, and too tense.

"I don't understand," Zarrin whined again, to no one in particular.

"Oh, if you could smell what I smell," Marie leaned in to whisper in his ear.

"What?" Zarrin didn't whisper or take his eyes from Joe. Marie pointed her fingers at Joe in a gesture Zarrin thought was called "finger guns" and made a clicking sound with her tongue. Zarrin didn't think that was a werewolf thing, since it made Martin gape at her, but he nodded along nonetheless. "And?"

Marie clucked her tongue again and withdrew her finger guns. She leaned against the counter. "So, Joe. Do you prefer Joe or Joseph?"

"I—" Joe cut himself off and stopped, with both hands on a pitcher of milk. "It doesn't matter. I'm used to Joe."

"Joseph to some people, I bet," Marie remarked, filling Zarrin's head with all sorts of ideas.

It got worse when Martin nodded. "When he's being a teddy bear."

Joe turned enough to glare at his coworker. "You said no more getting high at work."

"I'm not." Martin raised his hands innocently. "I'm stating a fact. You're Joseph when you're scheduling Gina with extra hours so she can pay her bills, and when you don't charge the old folks on limited incomes for extra milk or anything, and when you—"

"Not a teddy bear." Joe sounded as if he was speaking through gritted teeth.

Zarrin continued to stare at him in wonder. “Joseph,” he repeated aloud. *Treasure.*

“So, then, Joseph, who brings upset dragons their favorite drink—” Marie began, only to be interrupted by Zarrin snarling in embarrassment at having his emotional state bared to the world, and Joe, who simultaneously informed her that lattes weren’t Zarrin’s favorite drink.

Then everyone went silent, and Martin suddenly regained his smile. “*Ah.*”

“So, Joseph,” Marie started again. “We didn’t get to talk much yesterday.” Joe turned around to place Zarrin’s latte on the counter. He put a lid on it before he raised his head, but this time he looked right at her. His Joseph, so brave that not even a werewolf could hold him back for long. “I understand that,” Marie continued, not really gentling or lowering her voice. “After all, you weren’t there to see *me*.”

Joe’s stare moved to Zarrin and became somewhat less defiant and more stubborn.

Zarrin felt as foolish as he had when he’d returned home and found a latte waiting for him, in a cup that smelled of Joe. He exhaled. “I’m sorry I was out,” he said softly and truthfully. “I would have welcomed you into my home.”

Martin let out a long, low whistle.

Joe’s lips parted. He stared at Zarrin for another moment, and then behind him, where a line was most certainly gathering, not that Zarrin could make himself care with Joe bothered and tense. Then Joe stepped back and glanced to Marie again. “And what did you want? I don’t know your order.”

“Something sweet,” Marie immediately responded. “And hot. I like them hot. Do you know how hot I mean, Joe?”

Joe clenched his jaw. He appeared so desperately unhappy Zarrin bumped into the counter in a silly attempt to step closer to him, but then Joe turned to the espresso machine and the moment was lost.

“Caramel okay?” Joe’s blank voice had returned. Zarrin turned to Marie with a glare. She had done this somehow.

“So….” Martin punched the register keys rapidly. “So…,” he said again and then cleared his throat. He finally focused on Marie. “Have you ever been to Everlasting before?”

"Nope." Marie popped the *p* sound. "But you might say it was love at first sight."

Joe drew in a deep breath. But it was the hissing sound from Martin that made Zarrin straighten up. He let out a puff of black smoke that at least got Marie to face him. He raised his eyebrows in silent demand, then lowered them in a frown. She smiled benignly at him, or might have, if her smiles weren't so fangy.

"It's a pretty town," she explained, all while giving Zarrin a significant look. "I can't wait to see more of it. Zarrin is taking me on a tour today."

Joe pushed a latte onto the counter between them. "Be sure to check out the lower income housing down by the harbor. It will be out of sight of the big vacation homes with the view of the water, but it's there." He put a lid on the cup without raising his attention from it. "There's also the factories. And, if you get bored, the memorial to the original Chinatown built by the Chinese workers who weren't allowed to live in the white part of town. Go a little farther north and you can see the signs telling you about the tribes who used to live here. They had to fight the city council to put them up at all." For that, he did glance up, but to Marie. "I guess it was too depressing for the tourists." Then he tossed a sugar packet onto the counter next to Zarrin's latte.

"That will be eight bucks," Martin jumped in, almost desperately.

Marie took her drink. "Those are good ideas. I'd like to see those."

Zarrin curled his hand over his packet of sugar before sliding it into his pocket. Then he peered up at Joe. Joe wanted him to see these places. They must be important. "I knew about the old Chinatown," he told Joe, just Joe, because this mattered to him, and because it was Zarrin's history too. "There are drawings of it from that era at the house." Joe gave a start. Zarrin stared into his eyes, which were warm like black tea. "Dìzhèn either commissioned them or chose to keep them."

Joe put his hand on the counter. "She wanted it remembered?" he guessed, and his hopeful tone made Zarrin want to bare his family's entire collection to him.

"She is true dragon," Zarrin confessed, in nearly a whisper, and felt his middle burn with a new heat when the corners of Joe's mouth softened. "Thank you again for the latte. I was very pleased to see it."

Joe dropped his gaze to the counter. "Well, it got you here, which is what everyone wanted."

"Please, just, I'm sorry, but eight dollars." Martin's voice had gotten high and nervous. "Sorry. There's a line and everything."

Zarrin stepped to the side and reached into his pocket at the same time. He regretted his gloves once again when Joe took the card and their fingers didn't touch. But that was nothing compared to his regret at how Joe raised his head to stare at the people in line, and how all the expression on his face disappeared again.

He went back to the espresso machine and began to prepare drink orders he must have known by heart. Martin handed Zarrin his card, which Zarrin took before reaching into his pocket again for his tip.

He was about to drop it into the jar when Marie's voice stopped him. "Is that *gold*? What are they supposed to do with that, Zarrin? They can't exactly spend it." She was loud enough to draw everyone's attention, even if they hadn't already had it.

Zarrin clutched the coin to his chest. "It's *treasure*," he explained, and tilted his head toward Joe so Marie would get his meaning.

Marie clearly didn't understand the importance of giving treasure to treasure. "Yeah, well, it's also not spendable." She angled her head toward Joe as well, but this time Joe had turned around to listen. "Dragons, right? You can't buy groceries with doubloons, Zarrin."

"It's not a doub—" Zarrin turned to Joe in horror and embarrassment. "You can't spend these? Why didn't you say anything? These aren't suitable. These aren't suitable *at all*. Instead of something you would have actually treasured, I gave you something useless because I thought humans liked—oh! There was no practical value, only gold and history. Are they… are these quite expensive? Did you think I *expected* something for them?" He clutched the coin even tighter.

He wondered if it was his imagination that the people behind them seemed to be holding their breaths.

Joe looked at him. "I figured they were like pennies to you. I know you didn't expect anything." He glared at everyone else in the room, then turned back to Zarrin. "I still have them if you want them."

"Never," Zarrin nearly hissed. He lifted his head and spoke amid spiraling wisps of smoke. "Pennies?" He was outraged. "They were a gift. I *gave* them to you."

Someone in the crowd croaked, much like a frog, and Zarrin turned in distraction to the unpleasant woman he had seen in here before. Joe didn't smile for her. Neither did Martin. She was red in the face. Perhaps she was outraged that he had so insulted Joe.

Zarrin faced him again and held his hands out in apology. "I should have realized they weren't proper legal tender. How inconvenient for you. I'm so…." He would not hang his head, not here. But tonight, at home, in bed, he was going to think of this with shame. He could not even give gifts his treasure wanted. He stuck the coin in his pocket. "Of course you wished to spend them, and instead I gave you something useless."

"I could have traded them in somewhere for money if I wanted," Joe argued, his tone fierce and his voice rough.

"Yes, he could have," Marie agreed and then waved to indicate the people in line should order even if they were watching all this.

The little girl held on to her father's hand as he moved to the register, but she was staring openly at Marie. "He's a dragon, but what are you?"

"I'm wolf." Marie was all toothy grins again. "Or a were, as you people might say."

"You're not a wolf," the girl argued. She seemed very certain.

"Oh, but I am," Marie answered, and Zarrin had a feeling her eyes had changed color. The little girl gasped and then a second later started to giggle. "I am a wolf even when I look like this. Just like Zarrin is a dragon even when he looks like that. That's how we met, in fact."

"Marie!" Zarrin interrupted her in embarrassment. "They don't need to know that."

"Yes, they do." She gave him a brief, chiding glance, and her eyes *were* golden yellow. "How else will they learn?" She looked back down at the tiny human child. "You see, I was in the Preserve in my other form, and Zarrin saved me."

"Oh, I…. Marie…." Zarrin tried to make his voice ring out, but he stammered uncertainly instead.

"I wasn't paying attention, and I got caught in a trap," Marie went on, ignoring him. "I shifted to human, but then the pain was worse, and I was cold and scared, and then a dragon came and protected me while I was at my weakest."

People were looking at Zarrin. *Joe* was looking at Zarrin. They would see how weak and soft he was. Zarrin fluttered his hands. "I simply got rid of the trap."

"He melted it!" Marie announced, with relish. "He melted it right there and left it as a warning to them. Then he took me to his house while I healed." The fire in Zarrin's belly was raging. His skin seemed to tingle. He couldn't look at Joe. Marie was making sure everyone heard her. "He gave me a place to stay and clothes to wear—I, um, naturally didn't have any with me. Still don't, in fact. I forgot all my stuff—and my car—in the last town I was in, which was… miles and miles from here." She paused and dropped her voice. "As I said, I was distracted. Weres only get lost like that when we're avoiding something, and I was being very careless with my stupid heartbreak."

"Heartbreak?" Zarrin asked quietly. "I didn't know. You should have said when I was telling you about—everything."

"This guy." Marie leaned over him and startled him completely by nuzzling his ear with her nose. If the crowd reacted—if Joe reacted—Zarrin had no idea. He was too surprised. "I didn't lose a mate or anything, Zarrin. Too much soap opera for you. Don't worry about me. It's enough that you rescued me, and cared for me, and shared your home with me."

"It's a big house," Zarrin insisted as regally as he could while being nosed and nuzzled by a werewolf. "There's plenty of room." He darted a look to Joe, hoping Joe wouldn't think he was too soft. "It's my preserve to oversee, and she was wounded there. I'll have to find the trappers. She healed on her own," he continued, unable to stop with Joe's attention on him. "I wouldn't say I cared for her."

"You fed me and checked my paw." Marie pulled away to study him. "Why are you acting weird about it? Are you *embarrassed* that you helped me?" Her eyes flashed as she said the word, and her voice slid into a growl. But then she followed Zarrin's stare to Joe, and the wild animal disappeared from her expression. "*Oh*," she said, in a knowing tone very similar to Martin's. "Oh. You want to impress him," she whispered. She nodded to Joe. "He was very fierce when he melted the traps, Joseph. Dragonfire is… very impressive."

"I know." Joe's answer, although a grunt and barely audible, was enough to keep Zarrin from wanting to slink out of the coffee shop and never return. He could have set fire to the whole place with all the emotions storming in his gut, but then Joe focused on him with a gentle frown and shook his head. "Alice Reyes told me you melt the traps," he told Zarrin, in a voice Zarrin had never heard from him before.

Zarrin spent a moment imagining Joe talking about him with someone else. Then he thought about what Joe had said. "Who is that?" he demanded, hot and furious enough to make humans inch away from him. "Where was she to see me do that?"

Joe narrowed his eyes. "In a cabin in the state park. She wasn't on your preserve."

He had no idea why Joe would say it like that—*your preserve*—as if he was angry about what was undeniable truth. "The Preserve is mine," Zarrin hissed at him. "Everything on it is mine. Everything I find on it is mine."

"Hey," Marie cut in. "You found me on the Preserve. I'm not yours."

"Mine," Zarrin snapped at her, with his head high, and then grew inexplicably angrier when, out of the corner of his eye, he saw Joe stand up straight. Zarrin puffed out a plume of dark gray. "You are mine."

"Not yours." Marie appeared taken aback by the rising smoke, but shook her head. "Your friend, yes. But not *yours*. That means something different to us, so respect that." She faced Joe while Zarrin was considering her words. "*Just* his friend, Joseph. Sorry about earlier. I have relentless curiosity and a terrible sense of humor."

Zarrin slowly lowered his head. He took a deep breath and released it. "My friend?" he echoed cautiously. He didn't know what was on his face or in his scent, but Marie's expression softened. "My friend!" Zarrin repeated happily. "Mine."

This time she didn't seem to mind hearing that. "Zarrin, baby, you need more friends." She sighed at him, and patted his shoulder.

He lifted his chin again and narrowed his eyes. There were humans watching them, after all.

"Bernard used to say that, how I need more friends." Zarrin picked up the latte waiting for him on the counter. "He said I could travel with him, but then no one would have been left to protect the town."

"Oh, Zarrin." Marie patted him again.

"Protect the town?" Joe echoed. He didn't appear to notice, or care, about the people who had ordered and paid Martin for their drinks. "The town would get along fine. The dragons have barely been here for years anyway."

"I have to watch over what is mine." Zarrin spoke slowly, to make sure Joe grasped this point.

But Joe put his shoulders back. "I suppose we're the same as a tin of—"

"I need a macchiato and two double in-house cappuccinos. Thanks!" Martin called out. "And when those are done, a small hot chocolate with extra whip for Hazel here."

"I bet this latte is amazing." Marie looped her arm through Zarrin's and then picked up her drink. Joe's eyes dropped to their arms, and then he snapped around to the espresso machine. "Come on, Zarrin." Marie could have been oblivious to how intently Zarrin stared at Joe's back, but he didn't think so. She tugged, and her strength was considerable. "We're in the way."

Zarrin held tight to the latte he didn't want while Joe helped other people and ignored him.

Marie pulled on his arm again, and this time Zarrin let her lead him from the coffee shop. What was the point of pretending he wasn't soft? They all knew now. And Joe detested him for it.

"I don't understand," he declared mournfully the moment they were out in the cold. He realized, belatedly, that he was still wearing his hat. Marie was wearing the scarf that matched it. That hadn't seemed important earlier, but it did now for some unknown reason. "He brought me my drink. He came to my home. And then… and then he was listening to me, and I could feel the warmth from him." He stared, wide-eyed, at Marie, in a way he would never have dared with his parents. "He was Joseph. Treasure. I don't understand. The land is mine. He's wrong to deny that."

Marie yanked him against her side and began to walk. She didn't seem to have a specific destination in mind. "Zarrin," she wondered, in a careful tone, "how can you be so powerful and so…?"

"Weak?" Zarrin asked, with a hint of bitterness.

"What?" she asked in return. "No. Not weak, *oblivious*. Yesterday, I thought the situation was very different. How you talked about him, and then there he was with a wooing gift! But today…."

"He's angry with me," Zarrin summed up with a sigh.

Marie stopped walking, forcing him to do the same. "That's the thing. He wasn't."

Zarrin looked up at her as he considered what she was saying. "You mean how his anger doesn't smell like anger?" He'd thought that before. "He *sounds* furious. And he frowns. But his scent is… different from rage or even irritation. I'm not sure what it means."

"It means hurt, Zarrin." Marie had a kind smile too, one without any teeth. "I told you he was sensitive. Someone hurt him."

"Hurt?" Zarrin blinked at her and then rose to his full height. "Who hurt him? I will—"

"Shh!" She put a hand over his mouth. "I thought you *didn't* want them afraid of you," she reminded him, while jerking her head toward the humans around them. Zarrin calmed himself with effort, settling down to lean toward her. She surprised him by nuzzling the top of his head, and spoke for only him to hear. "Humans, some humans anyway, the ones without much exposure to the world and its variety, always expect us to be monsters. What's natural for us isn't natural for them—or they don't want to think it is. I get it. You want to find and punish whoever hurt your boy. I'm not even saying you shouldn't. I'm saying not now, not publicly, and not until you're sure it's what your boy wants."

"But *I* want it," Zarrin protested quietly. That was hurt that made Joe scowl and distance himself. Someone would pay for it. But then he let out another long breath. "But you're right. He's Joseph, who is kind to people. I should… I should treat him with care first. Protect him."

Marie coughed. "Yeah, that, or claim that fine ass under a full moon as soon as possible." She hummed when Zarrin pulled back from her, and smiled innocently when he sniffed the air to see if she was serious. "But, you know, dragons probably do things differently. And that one is going to take some wooing anyway."

"Claim Joe…." Zarrin flushed all over. Joe beneath him, naked except for the ink in his skin, his hair spread out on the snow like—

Snow would probably be too cold for him. Zarrin corrected his thought and changed it to Joe in his bed, held in his bed while Zarrin took his cock deep into his throat. Yes, that was good too. If the full moon was necessary, they could open a window to let the silver light stream in. And Joe would beg to come, and Zarrin would give him everything he asked for.

A light slap on his cheek snapped him from his thoughts. Marie shook her head at him. "Honestly. We're in the street."

"*Joe*," Zarrin told her softly, and nearly dropped his latte as she pulled him in for a hug.

"You ridiculous thing. I'm going to help you because you helped me. But first, we need to eat. I'm starving, and winning a mate is tricky business. We'll eat and talk, and then we'll explore, okay?"

"Okay," Zarrin agreed, although he had no appetite at the moment. "To all the places he said?"

"Of course." The amusement was back in her voice. "Isn't it best to do whatever your treasure says?"

Zarrin huffed at her, because *obviously*.

Marie's expression of wicked pleasure got worse. "Then let the wooing begin."

# CHAPTER 7

"A DRAGON and a werewolf," Mr. Marcus commented in amazement as he stirred his cup of coffee. "Never thought I'd see that." Apparently he was more forgiving toward Zarrin when he thought Zarrin was dating a werewolf. Joe didn't know if that was because the werewolf was a woman, or because she was another being, or if he was simply happy that Zarrin was settling down and might stay for good. Whichever it was, Joe wished he would stop talking about it and go away.

But Joe was never that fortunate. Everyone ordered their drinks, and then instead of leaving, they stood around talking about seeing Zarrin and Marie out and about in town all weekend, and so Mr. Marcus had been over by the sugar and creamers for twenty minutes, expressing delight over Zarrin's interest in exploring Everlasting.

Joe scrubbed at the countertop without looking up. If he did, he'd see the clock on the register, informing him it was close to noon and long past the time Zarrin usually came in.

He was probably busy. He and Marie had been to the coast and farther inland along the river that snaked in and out of both the state park and the Preserve. They had visited several restaurants in town to dine together, as well as the food trucks in Stapleton, the next town over.

Intimate meals, some people had been quick to inform him. People his age, usually, who enjoyed giving him details he hadn't asked for until Martin had stepped in to take over the register. Other people seemed curious about the whole thing. And a few had wished Joe a good morning in a tone that felt a lot like pity.

Joe continued to wipe down every surface. He was very focused on the shop being clean.

If anyone had asked him, he would have told them he hadn't really expected anything else, and they were stupid if they had. Martin might have suspected it was a lie, but Martin knew better than to say anything. Joe was not in the mood to be reminded, yet again, that he'd never been a real option for anyone. It was bad enough with all the locals knowing. Sooner or later, the talk was going to reach his mother, if it hadn't already. Then he didn't know what he'd do.

Sell the coins, maybe, try living in the city again, or another town along the coast.

"Everlasting is really going places." Mr. Marcus was so pleased it was as if he'd personally set Zarrin and Marie up. The fact that Marie, at least, had made a point of saying they were only friends didn't seem to bother him or anyone else. A week ago they'd all been willing to offer up Joe to Zarrin, and now they were rubbing it in his face that Zarrin was with someone else.

If Joe had been jilted, which he hadn't been, then he deserved it, that's what some of them probably thought—Addison, the kids from high school. Joe was, after all, the one who'd seduced a star football player as surely as any filthy fairy might have done.

He turned to start cleaning around the espresso machine and let Martin handle the small talk. Martin's quiet, neutral tone was very different from how he'd started to tease Joe on Friday after Zarrin and Marie had walked out the door, arm in arm. Marie was tall and beautiful and knowledgeable about everything Joe wasn't. She was openly wolfish, or affectionate, touching Zarrin without concern or care what anyone thought. Zarrin had stared at her adoringly, deceptively wide-eyed and innocent until he'd called her *his*.

Joe shoved a pitcher out of his way and then had to mop up the mess of splashed milk he'd made.

That moment was still as vivid as the moments after Zarrin and Marie had left.

"What's the matter?" Martin had joked. "Mad you're not the center of his attention anymore?"

Joe had walked off and left Martin to man the counter by himself. He'd come back in minutes, when he could breathe again, and when all the people who had been direct witnesses to that scene were gone.

But everyone who had been out of town over the weekend was hearing all about it now. Randi, who owned a nail salon, was of the opinion that maybe more beings hadn't come to Everlasting before because the dragons hadn't been welcoming to other magical creatures. She was hoping more beings would lead to more tourism, and more money.

"None of them made friends like that before. Not for us to see," Mr. Marcus remarked, in a wise tone that made Joe grit his teeth. "Must be something special about this one."

"Why wouldn't he make friends with her?" Joe spoke up, with his hair falling into his eyes as he swiped up spilled coffee grounds. "She's strong, and smart, and powerful. She's got magic too, and she can shift, just like he can. She's acceptable, isn't she? Special? Anything else you might not like about her can easily be overlooked, right?"

His chest felt tight.

"I'm going to take a break," he added, although he usually waited until one of the closing crew had arrived.

Martin turned to look at him, but Joe took his dirty dish towel and went to the back.

"She said they were just friends." Martin followed him as far as the doorway. Joe put the towel in the laundry bin without replying. Martin was younger, and possibly didn't know the whole story that everyone in Joe's class had loved to tell. But Joe had been in this situation before, and he wasn't dumb enough to believe it a second time.

Someone called Martin to the register, so Joe went to the sink to wash his hands and grab a clean towel to stick in his apron. Then he stood in front of the milk fridge, not doing anything but listening to the chatter outside as it quieted enough for him to notice exactly who Martin was helping.

"Is it always this crowded at this time of day?" Zarrin wondered, a curious kitten about everything when he wasn't arrogantly insisting he owned it all.

"You are later than usual, aren't you?" Martin asked, answering a question with a question. Zarrin might have noticed. He was innocent about a lot, but he wasn't stupid. He probably narrowed his eyes at Martin, because Martin spoke again, in a high, nervous voice. "It *is* a little busy today."

"I was busy as well." Zarrin had a formal manner of speaking sometimes.

"Yeah, I bet you were," Martin said. His tone was so short that Joe straightened up. He could only imagine the expression on Zarrin's face.

"I had to write and send another letter to Bernard. I had a lot to tell him." Zarrin was quiet. "Is… is Joe not here today?"

Joe's heart thumped against his ribs, and he glared at the safety posters on the walls since he couldn't glare at himself for being so stupid.

Martin was suspiciously silent. "He might be," he finally answered, the most unhelpful he'd ever been to anyone who wasn't Addison Bernes.

Joe took a step to go out there and stop Martin from doing anything else he didn't have to, but then Zarrin asked, "Is he still upset with me?" And Joe couldn't move.

"I… what?" Martin was clearly as thrown as Joe was.

"The Preserve *is* mine," Zarrin explained earnestly. "Perhaps if I spoke with him more, he'd understand."

"That's not… um…." Martin must have suddenly realized Joe could probably hear them. He changed the subject. "So you're all alone today?"

He was too pointed for Zarrin not to understand at least some of what he meant. Joe went cold as the silence from Zarrin stretched on. This was Martin's fault. Joe was going to take him off the schedule and work with Gina. The last thing Joe needed was Zarrin feeling sorry for him.

"He doesn't like her?" Zarrin said softly, confused, and then his voice rose. "Oh." After another pause, he said it again, louder and with feeling. "*Oh.*"

Joe clenched his hands while his heart raced and his blood went cold, and he flushed all over with how stupid he was. He couldn't let it go on with Zarrin thinking what he was thinking.

He stepped into the doorway and barely held still when Zarrin's attention swung to him.

"There you are," Zarrin murmured, his gaze and tone like molten gold. He took his hands out of his pockets and let them fall to the counter. They were bare. He—or someone else—had buttoned his black coat all the way up and wrapped a green scarf around his throat. His hair was tousled. He looked happy and healthy and in a holiday spirit, and it took effort for Joe to take his eyes off him and go to the espresso machine.

"I wouldn't leave Martin by himself," he answered Zarrin's unspoken question once he remembered to, and ignored the fact that he had left Martin alone last Friday.

"Of course not, Joseph." Zarrin pronounced the name with far too much pleasure for someone having intimate meals with someone else. Joe crossed his arms and felt foolish. But there wasn't anything else to do without everyone thinking he was hiding. He could have asked why he was "Joseph" now, but he was distracted to notice Zarrin had been biting his nails again, and that his knitted hat was peeking out of one of his pockets.

"I would like to order a latte, please." Zarrin ordered without a glance to the board, or showing any interest in what he was saying. His attention was on Joe again, in a way it hadn't been on Friday. People were going to see and comment. Joe already felt heat prickling beneath his shirt.

At least Zarrin's presence had shut up Mr. Marcus, although naturally he was still there.

Joe nodded, since that was easier than speech, and reached down to grab cold milk.

"A medium," Zarrin reminded him, as if Joe didn't know, and shuffled in place before going still as a statue in one graceful transition. It was as if he had to remind himself to be patient.

Joe steamed the milk and readied the shots of espresso, only to turn around again when Zarrin prompted him with a question. "Did you have a good weekend?" Zarrin leaned onto the counter, but Martin wasn't stopping him. He merely picked up Zarrin's debit card from where Zarrin must have dropped it and then ran it through. "You must have a lot to do in your free time. I… never see you around town. Perhaps, you're painting?" Zarrin raised his eyebrows hopefully. "Jessie said you painted. Not sculpting or carving?"

If he'd been able, Joe would have exchanged a look with Martin. But Martin didn't seem anywhere near as confused as Joe was. Joe frowned a little. "I draw and paint sometimes. Not sculpting. I've never felt the need to."

"Perhaps… if you would like—" Zarrin stopped himself to take a deep breath. "What do you draw, then?" He tossed his head the second after he asked. "I like to look at art, as you know."

"There's a lot of it at the house, you said," Joe agreed, to cut him off. He didn't need polite, pitying small talk from Zarrin, although he wondered if his painting was on display in that big house, or if Zarrin had stashed it wherever he put all the packets of sugar he never used. "Here." He set the latte in front of Zarrin and then stuck a lid on it. He put a napkin, a stirring stick, and another sugar packet next to it. Then he tucked his hair behind his ear. "You don't have to keep doing this. If the espresso is too strong for you, you can ask for one shot instead of two. Or you can add sweetener. Raw sugar won't stick to your teeth the way refined sugar does. Some people like it in the bottom of the cup, but others add it after. Try a little at first. See if you like your lattes better that way."

"I know what sugar is." Zarrin stuck out his lower lip in a pout, then licked it. "You want me to use this now?" he asked, with a peeking glance at Joe's face.

Zarrin was beautiful, especially when he looked at Joe like that, curious and playful and a bit demanding.

Joe turned away to take Zarrin's card from Martin's outstretched hand and place it in front of Zarrin along with his drink. He answered stiffly. "Rather than watch you keep ordering something you don't like."

Zarrin picked up the packet and tore it open with his teeth. He tapped sugar granules into his drink and stirred the milk three times with the most careful, almost dainty, gestures Joe had ever seen before he replaced the lid. Joe grabbed his garbage to throw away for him, mostly so it wouldn't look like he was staring.

But Zarrin picked up the cup without actually taking a drink. "Thank you." He stuck his debit card in his pocket. "Perhaps lattes could be sweeter," he conceded, and then took his hand from his coat.

He was holding a twenty-dollar bill, which he then placed in the tip jar with the utmost care. Afterward, he cleared his throat and gave Joe another careful, peeking glance. "I'm sorry I gave you coins you couldn't use."

Twenty dollars was still too much, but Joe couldn't say no when Martin was entitled to half of it.

“It’s fine.” Joe was weirdly attached to the heat and history in those coins, but Zarrin didn’t need to know that. “I was rude. I knew your order.”

Zarrin perked up at the confession. “I knew it!” He pointed at Joe accusingly, but his tone was delighted. “You know everyone’s order!” he announced, but then his smile slipped. “Oh. You pretended not to know mine? Only mine?”

Since Zarrin already knew how stupid Joe could be, Joe met his gaze. “Only yours.”

Instead of fury or outrage, Zarrin flicked his gaze down to the cup in his hand. He lifted his chin, but it could have been habit, because he was barely audible. “I am not a very imposing dragon. Perhaps if I were more fierce—”

“What?” Joe demanded as he moved to the side to let Martin get someone’s coffee unimpeded. Zarrin matched his movement and glanced up. Joe shook his head. “I think you’re fierce enough. You still don’t have to wait in line if you don’t want to. You didn’t when you first came in, and it… annoyed me. This town has enough wannabe queens and princes, and then you….” He paused for the unaware expression on Zarrin’s face. “You don’t see it in your house on the hill, surrounded by woods, but there are politics in this town you haven’t let yourself be a part of.” Joe fixed his attention on Zarrin’s short, bitten fingernails. “I’m going to *try* not to hold the sins of your fathers against you—well, your father and your mother and your grandparents. But you destroyed the way things were the second you walked through that door, and I thought that meant—” Zarrin continued to regard Joe with innocent eyes. Joe’s voice became harsh. “—that you would be different. That was my fault.”

“Different?” Zarrin questioned, in a puff of white smoke. “Have we not made you happy?” It took Joe too long to realize Zarrin was talking about the town’s history with the dragons. “Was Dìzhèn not much more generous than the landowners who came before her? We have done as she did. We kept the land safe for those who depend upon it. We’ve worried for them, and fought for them, and provided shelter.” His cloud around him began to shift toward gray and then paled again. “Don’t we ensure the town prospers? Isn’t the land healthy?”

Joe wanted to ask how he would know if anything prospered in his years away from Everlasting, but Zarrin had spent days exploring now, as if he intended to stay and find out. Joe glared at him instead. "The land doesn't actually belong to you."

"Ours." The volcano that was Zarrin emitted a warning curl of dark smoke.

Dimly, Joe was aware of Martin muttering, "I thought we were past this," but he didn't turn away. If the werewolf wasn't afraid, then he wasn't afraid.

He worked his jaw before answering. "It's land. It belongs to itself."

Zarrin stared at him as if he was speaking a foreign language. "When Dìzhèn came here, the hills were bald from overlogging. Lives had been lost in the resulting mudslides. The wildlife was decimated. The bears and wolves were gone."

"They weren't the only ones," Joe shot back.

Zarrin's lips parted. He stared at Joe for a long time. So did Martin. Some of the others might have too, but Joe was focused on Zarrin and didn't bother to look.

Zarrin startled him by flinching. "She didn't do that," he said, quietly.

"But it's easier to buy land when there's no one living on it to protest." Joe stopped there, although he could have gone on. He didn't even know why he was bringing it up now.

"Yes," Zarrin agreed, still quiet. The remaining traces of his agitation floated up and disappeared into the air. "You're right," he added, when the final wisps of smoke had dissipated. "And you thought—you hoped—I would be different?"

"I was rude for a lot of reasons." It wasn't Joe's job to explain these things to Zarrin or to anybody else. Nor was it his responsibility to be gentle. But he was. He always was. It was why Martin teased him and how people got away with treating him like shit. "I've never been able to be oblivious to these things—I've never been allowed to be, and it bothered me that you couldn't see them." The way some people were staring reminded him that he was at work, in full view of people who were going to share this with everyone else.

*And then what?* he asked himself. Some of them would agree, and some would think Joe was getting above himself in arguing with the dragon landowner. The rest would blame it on jealousy or something similar.

"Anyway"—Joe forced himself to move away from the topic—"you probably have to go."

"Is there more?" Zarrin stayed put. His fingers slid nervously around his latte, but he kept his head up. "Is there more you would like me to know?" he went on, when Joe stared in confusion.

It was the last thing Joe expected. "Yes," he answered without thinking.

Zarrin drew himself up. "Then approach me." For a second, his voice echoed through the air to the other room, and then he lowered it. "I'm not my mother or my father, but you can speak to me. Anyone can. We… we shouldn't have allowed that to happen." He was so serious. "I shouldn't be the only one here for you, but I'll do my best. Please believe me. I will listen, treasure."

Martin made the sound Joe wanted to, a puzzled, strangled version of that word. "Treasure?"

Zarrin picked at the lid on his cup, then swallowed. "You're right about this too. I don't understand lattes. I don't think I'll ever love them. But I'll try the sugar—if I must."

"Do dragons not like being wrong?" Joe wondered, half in amazement at how much Zarrin had visibly struggled to say that.

"Does anyone?" The way Zarrin wrinkled his nose made Joe lower his arms to his sides, where they stayed, awkwardly, as he thought about what had just happened and tried to make sense of it. He was only slightly mollified by how Zarrin appeared to be equally uncertain. He licked his lips twice and made a move as if he was going to walk away, but then didn't. "You're working tomorrow?" He was breathless and his mouth was wet.

Joe had never been so confused or distracted by one simple question. "Yeah."

Zarrin's whisper was too shy to be imperious. "Then I will see you tomorrow."

He swept past the people who'd lingered to eavesdrop on his conversation, without giving even a nod to indicate he knew they were there, although he had to. A whole crowd of locals had been staring directly at him. Not even Zarrin could miss that, although he might need someone to explain to him what it meant.

He had Marie for that now, Joe reminded himself, very sternly. But when the little volcano swept out of sight and Joe turned, Martin appeared thoughtful.

"Now, *that* was far more interesting than a werewolf," Martin remarked, with so much glee Joe bristled even before Martin's next words. "Wouldn't you agree, treasure?"

ZARRIN ENTERED the coffee shop the following morning and walked directly to the counter. Joe looked up from stacking cups and then froze. Joe's arms were bare again, and he'd secured his hair, but a few strands were in his eyes.

He looked Zarrin up and down and then glanced behind him. Zarrin glanced too, but there was no one there, so he turned back to Joe.

"Joseph." Zarrin reveled in the name and the breath Joe took before he came closer.

Someday, Zarrin was going to do one of the bold, wolfish things Marie suggested, many of which involved Joe naked against this counter. But for the moment, having Joe's attention solely on him would do.

"Tea," Joe offered abruptly, making Zarrin pause, confused, until Joe explained. "You prefer tea, don't you?"

He didn't think Joe was magic, but Marie said he'd smelled "itchy," so perhaps he was. Zarrin nodded. "But not serious tea," he confessed, while his fire sparked and his blood pounded to imagine Joe thinking of him and what he might like. "My sister is particularly fond of green tea, at the correct temperature, and never served in a paper cup."

Joe's frown, like all his other frowns, wasn't really angry or intimidating after knowing him. He was more upset than furious, and Zarrin found out why when Joe stepped over to the tea display.

"I don't know what 'serious tea' is, but you drink what you like." Joe shook his head. "I like coffee with milk, personally, although too much milk upsets my stomach. Jessie hates coffee. Martin will drink anything caffeinated. Gina likes herbal tea or espresso con panna."

Zarrin noted that information and then followed Joe over to the teas. "Joe," he said again, in thrilled disbelief. This time last week he had despaired of Joe ever talking to him, and today he had Joe's attention and he didn't understand how or why. Although Marie said promising to listen was the best thing he could have done, and so Zarrin intended to do just that.

"Coffee with milk," he repeated, so he would remember Joe's drink the way Joe knew his.

Joe stopped at that, for a single moment, before giving a minute shake of his head. He waved at the teas. "Pick one."

Zarrin darted out his tongue and then took a deep breath before narrowing his focus to the black teas.

"One of those?" Joe was very observant. Zarrin wondered again what kind of things he drew, but didn't risk ruining this lovely moment by making Joe go tense again.

"Can you…?" Zarrin peered behind him again, but obviously his parents weren't there. "There are shops I visited when my family visited Hong Kong…. Could you… make iced tea with milk and honey?"

"Milk and honey?" Joe nodded, but then his frown deepened. "We only make iced tea in the spring and summer. Iced tea would need a few hours to cool if I made it now. We don't have any cold brew."

"Then hot is fine." Zarrin very nearly hopped in place. "I haven't had it in years. You know," he confided in a whisper, "I think they use a special sweetened milk anyway. Maybe it's only *called* tea with milk and honey."

"I…." Joe paused again, his gaze lingering on Zarrin's face. Then he faced the tea display and frowned even harder. "Is it like a bubble tea? They have those in the city." He grabbed a canister of one of the black teas and turned to the coffee brewers and the hot water.

"Just one tea?" Joe asked once the tea was steeping. He went over to the register, so Zarrin did the same.

"Oh yes. And one latte please, for Marie, with the caramel you gave her last time." Marie would have teased him mercilessly for forgetting her in the presence of his *nichimoose*. "Thank you for remembering."

"It's fine," Joe said to the counter, and yanked a cup from the stack.

Martin walked out from the back, saw Zarrin, and grinned widely. His attitude was very different from the day before. But then he announced, "Going to go straighten the outer room," with a significant look at Joe, before heading in that direction.

Joe steamed Marie's milk and checked on Zarrin's tea, effortlessly efficient as Zarrin could never be. He bent down to the small fridge and pulled out a package marked Sweetened Condensed Milk. "Vietnamese style coffee needs this, so we always have some on hand," Joe said, his words stilted. He finished the latte and then grabbed a paper cup for the tea. It must have looked strong enough, because he poured it into the cup and then added the milk.

He put on lids and then brought both cups to Zarrin. "I can add more milk if you want, but the honey is over there. You might want that first."

"How thoughtful." Zarrin inhaled over both drinks before picking up his own. "You're very good at this. You do know that, don't you? How good you are?"

Joe made a strange, weak sound, and when Zarrin looked up, Joe's eyes were wide. "It's just tea."

"Joseph," Zarrin sighed fondly at him, which only made Joe stare with more flustered confusion. How had he ever thought Joe was angry? All the frowning, all that distance, and still Joe couldn't help but notice things about others and want to help them. "May I please compliment you without interruption?" Zarrin chided him, but softly, so Joe would know this wouldn't hurt. That was how one approached wounded animals, especially the fuzzy ones. Even rabbits kicked when in pain. "You noticed what I really wanted, and you're trying to help me get it." And he was being more forgiving of Zarrin's obliviousness than others would have been.

"That will… it's my job, Zarrin," Joe protested all the same. He was stubborn, but Zarrin forgave him because Joe had said his name.

But as if Joe had just reminded himself that he still had work to do, he typed in Zarrin's order at the register. Zarrin handed over his card without care for the total, which should have earned a frown from Joe, but Joe rang him up and then walked over to pour himself a cup of coffee. He splashed the leftover steamed milk in it and then took a bracing gulp.

When he spoke, his voice was husky. "You don't need to be nice to me, not even for your ideas about caring for the town. If you protect what is yours, and Everlasting is yours, to your way of thinking anyway, then you have a duty to us. All of your family does. But you don't need to do that with me. I don't need compliments."

Zarrin curled against the counter in happiness. Joe *had* been thinking about him, or at least about their conversation yesterday.

"Duty," he agreed, with a beaming smile. "I knew you'd understand." Of course, Joe was wrong about the compliments, but Marie had counseled him not to push too far, so this was him not pushing.

Joe's gaze stayed on him, but he didn't move from the coffee machines. "So you're supposed to serve us. And in return?"

Zarrin's smile faded. "I don't understand what you mean. I already told you I expect nothing."

"Nothing for nothing, Zarrin." Joe was being stubborn, but he kept using Zarrin's name. He also kept glancing from his cup to Zarrin. "You have to get something out of it. What do you—what do the dragons want in exchange for your protection?" The jut of his chin was obstinate, but this time his gaze stayed on his coffee. "I know what you don't want. But everyone in town would be happier if you just told them directly what they need to give you. They'll offer it up, no matter what it is, trust me."

The bitterness in his tone took Zarrin aback more than his words, although they were certainly a puzzle. "Offer it up?" he echoed and then realized what it meant. "Ah. This is why people gave the dragons their princesses in the old stories, isn't it? Humans thought something was owed? Or perhaps that the dragons desired these gifts?" Zarrin naturally couldn't speak for the dragons of the past, but some of them might have wanted a princess or two. Some of them might have wanted princes instead. Humans could be very unobservant about that kind of distinction.

He studied Joe, who despite his current unhappy frown was one of the sharpest humans Zarrin had ever met. Joe was *sensitive*, as Marie would say.

"What is it they think I want?" he asked curiously. "Have they been considering leaving a princess at my door?"

"More like a queen." The unpleasant woman had returned. Zarrin gave her a glare for interrupting, and then, when she went pale, he turned back to Joe.

Joe raised his gaze from his study of his coffee. "No, not a princess. But it doesn't matter, does it?"

Zarrin shook his head. "We'll take care of you regardless, because you are treasure. The only thing a dragon might want for that is for others to respect what is theirs, and also treat it well, and to never, ever touch it."

That last part was said as more of a growl than a series of words, but it couldn't be helped while Joe had that furrow in his brow. He was ignoring the unpleasant woman too.

"All people need help, Zarrin, but we don't need to be taken care of." Joe set down his cup with a bit of force. "It's nice that you've protected land that might have otherwise been destroyed, but no one asked the dragons to do that, or to look out for us."

"Be quiet," the unpleasant woman told Joe in a low voice, as if Zarrin wouldn't hear.

Zarrin raised a hand in her direction to silence her. He stayed focused on Joe. "But it's our pleasure. To take care of them. To fulfill their needs."

"It's…." Joe trailed off as a small shiver traveled through him. "It's your pleasure."

"Yes." Zarrin smiled. "Yes, it is."

"To protect them. To fulfill…." Joe's voice was growing fainter. "But you have a problem giving them up."

"Give them up?" Zarrin hissed, astonished. "Give them up!"

"What if someone here didn't want to be yours?" Joe gestured at the woman standing uncertainly at Zarrin's side, but his words still hit Zarrin hard in the chest.

Zarrin went quiet and held his hot cup with both hands. "You can't force treasure to stay. Even the old dragons, the powerful ones, the real ones, knew that. They roared their pain until the world shook, but they knew that much." Zarrin made himself take a long, deep breath to calm the inferno inside of him. "That said," he added, in a *slightly* more reasonable tone, "it's not easy to let go. It's not easy at all."

"*Some* dragons found it easy, though, didn't they?" the woman remarked, but this time Joe turned to her before Zarrin could.

"Did you dig up some nerve from somewhere this morning, Addison, or are you cranky without your coffee?" Joe snapped at her, while simultaneously starting to prepare what it was she must normally get. "Was there anything else you wanted, Zarrin?" Joe asked, then twisted around to the woman—Addison—again. "Not a word from you."

She shut her mouth, although she continued to watch them.

"No. No, thank you, Joe." Zarrin glanced between the two of them, and so barely caught the way Joe frowned harder.

"Then you'd better take Marie her coffee," Joe told him without looking at him.

He was correct of course; she was waiting impatiently outside to hear how it went, but Zarrin spent another few seconds staring at Joe before he finally moved to pick up her drink too. Martin had implied reasons for Joe's frowns that had a lot to do with Marie. Zarrin simply wasn't sure how to ask.

But if Joe was jealous, oh the ways Zarrin could comfort him.

"Thank you," Zarrin said again, politely, but with a touch of heat. It brought Joe's eyes to his one more time, and then Joe nodded and focused on his work, and Zarrin had to leave so he wouldn't seem weird.

But he paused on his way out to sweep a look over the scowling human by the register. "I'll remember you," he promised her, and inclined his head graciously before carrying on to the door.

MARIE'S BOAST that Zarrin would be able to claim Joe before the week was out had obviously been an attempt to bolster Zarrin's confidence. Zarrin found he didn't mind too much. He had never assumed keeping a treasure was easy, so gaining one probably wasn't either.

She had helped him a lot already. She advised him to win Joe's trust the way he'd won Peter Rabbit's and Captain Nemo's, and to worry about the rest later. For now, Zarrin was to listen, and encourage, and help, as well as work on discovering who had hurt Joe, and how, and ensuring they regretted it.

But she wasn't dragon, so she didn't understand everything, like why Zarrin was smiling smugly to himself on the sidewalk outside the coffee shop. Zarrin had been imagining Joe's surprise all morning and was practically beside himself. Today or tomorrow, Joe would receive more treasure.

Marie rolled her eyes at Zarrin's expression but tucked his scarf beneath his chin and then ran her hand through his hair. She made a face at the two men who stopped at the entrance to stare at them, and then resumed fluffing up and flattening Zarrin's hair.

"You're lucky he already thinks you're pretty," she remarked, before pinching his cheeks. "You are supposed to make an effort to look your best when wooing a human mate."

Zarrin gave her an offended look. "I *am* pretty," he snapped back, before going still. "Does he really? Can you sniff that?"

"You are such a pup." Marie rolled her eyes again. "This is too much. No more romance for me. I'm going to go to the drug store for some stuff for my trip home. You say hello to your boy, and I'll meet you in a few minutes."

"I don't want you to go." Zarrin adjusted her coat for a moment—his coat, really, but drenched in Marie's scent now, and he would rather she wear it than see her shiver.

She patted his hand until he let go. "You're going to do fine. You weren't doing that badly before I got here. I'm only helping the process along."

"That isn't what I meant," Zarrin protested, and got another pat for his trouble.

"I know." She urged him gently but forcefully toward the door. "Now go."

"I'm going," he insisted haughtily, but then had to wait for the two men to stumble out of his way first. He decided they were either intoxicated, or had never seen a dragon before, and so he didn't say anything when they both followed him inside, still gaping at him.

He scanned the shop. It wasn't overly busy. The fire was lit, with the little human girl with the braids in front of it staring at a tablet. He didn't see Unpleasant Addison; however, there were other familiar faces around. He'd noticed that many humans didn't leave right away after getting their drinks or go to the outer room to enjoy their coffee. Some stayed to converse with each other by the table full of milks and sugars, or chatted with whoever was behind the counter.

He nodded to them in distracted acknowledgment, although none of them had approached him yet. One nodded back, the older woman he'd noticed before, who carried her two containers of coffee out with her.

Jessie and Martin were at the counter. Zarrin stopped in dismay, then straightened when Joe came out of the rear area with several gallons of milk in his arms. The action made Joe's biceps do wonderful things.

The two men bumped into Zarrin's back, but Zarrin waved them on. "Don't mind me." Despite this breathless instruction, neither of them seemed willing to pass him, so Zarrin hurried forward to the side of the counter by the tea display. He caught Joe as he finished restocking the milk.

"Good morning!" Zarrin wished him, a little too loud but unable to care. "Three of you?"

"Holidays!" Jessie chirped at him while helping someone else. "I'm the midshift."

"Ralphie—that's the owner—will come in to help in the afternoons until after Christmas," Martin explained shortly as he finished up a drink.

Joe stood up. "You're alone again today."

It wasn't exactly a question, but Zarrin chose to think it was. "For now." But then the honest answer made him sigh longingly. Soon he really would be alone again.

Joe's expression clouded over. Zarrin couldn't have that, even if Joe's dislike of her was "A very good sign," according to Marie.

"She's a good friend," he confided to Joe, and watched Joe's hands trail, lost, along the countertop. "My good friend."

"Yours," Joe agreed, without any lessening of his frown. But he glanced over at Zarrin and crossed his arms. "I made a small batch of iced tea earlier."

The scowl on his face increased as Zarrin's smile grew. Zarrin turned to share his excitement with everyone. Martin blinked at him in bewilderment.

"Did you?" Zarrin leaned over the counter and drummed his fingers along the surface. "You're wonderful. Thank you, treasure."

Joe opened and then closed his mouth. He drew his eyebrows together and stared at Zarrin almost reproachfully, although Zarrin couldn't see why.

"I told you." Martin leaned over toward Jessie, but his words were clearly audible across the counter. Joe twisted to look at him and then stalked off to the back of the shop.

"A tea, and Marie's coffee, please," Zarrin told Jessie, and gave her his card. "Whenever you have a moment. And something from the pastry selection for her." He had to make sure Marie had plenty to eat on her journey, if she insisted upon leaving him and the safety of his house. "Is something wrong with Joe?"

"No," Joe answered gruffly as he returned. He had a clear plastic cup filled with ice and tea. Martin appeared to swallow whatever he'd been going to say. Zarrin forgot about him anyway, and leaned so far over the counter toward Joe that he was practically draped over it.

Zarrin watched Joe's every move as he filled the remainder of the cup with the sweetened milk, and hissed in pleasure when Joe spilled a drop onto the back of his hand and licked it off. He refused to be embarrassed for the smoke rising from him. He couldn't help it when he'd waited so long already.

The two humans who had followed him in, who seemed to take forever to order, murmured, “Dragon!” to each other when they saw his smoke.

“You must have a lot to do today,” Joe remarked, giving Zarrin his tea as well as a straw. “Alice says you patrol the Preserve every afternoon. That must cut into your sightseeing.”

“Who is this Alice?” Zarrin wondered, but with less heat than he could have. He absently dug cash from his coat pocket and painstakingly dropped the smaller bills that humans tipped with into the tip jar. Jessie gave him his card.

“A friend.” Joe glanced at the register, and if Zarrin didn’t know him, he would have said Joe was afraid to look at him, but Joseph wasn’t afraid of anything. “She works in the park. I might see her this weekend since I was thinking of camping for a night.”

“But you’ll be cold!” Zarrin worried, and moved around people to follow Joe to the other side of the register.

Joe reached for a milk pitcher. “I haven’t been out there in a while, and I want a good, long hike.” The sound of him steaming milk drowned out Zarrin’s furious reply that it was still too cold out, and snowfall was expected again over the weekend, and what if something happened? Who would be there to protect him?

“I don’t need protecting from snow,” Joe responded when he was done, as if he’d heard it all anyway. He squeezed caramel into the cup before he looked at Zarrin directly. “It’s camping or a drive into the city so I can get—I feel like hiking. I know the park well. I won’t accidentally step foot on your preserve. People can think whatever they want, but I’m not going to interfere.”

Zarrin stuck out his lip in a pout and then crossed his arms. “Interfere in what? I don’t understand. Do you think I’d punish you for entering the Preserve? Do you really?”

He didn’t know who was more taken aback by that, Joe or himself. But it was right the moment he said it, despite the wrenching discomfort at the idea of losing some control over the land and the trees. Joe would respect them. He would help keep them safe. He should get to see them.

“But… you guard it.” Martin stopped what he was doing. “Don’t you? I mean, no one goes there because they’ll get roast—in trouble.”

“No one is allowed on the Preserve,” Joe said flatly. “You might have seen the warning signs.”

The storm in his expression made Zarrin take a step back. But then he recovered. "How else are we to keep it safe?" He gestured eloquently at Joe.

"What 'we'? It's just you." Joe put a lid on the drink he'd made and came over to put it in Zarrin's hands. His fingers brushed Zarrin's, and he made a small sound, perhaps startled by the heat. Then his scowl deepened as he stepped back. "Your family doesn't even visit."

Zarrin dropped his gaze. "No, they don't."

"Zarrin." Joe frowned a lot, but Joseph was the gentle creature who leaned down to apologize. "I didn't mean it like that. I'm sorry."

Zarrin studied him, and brought a hand to his mouth to bite his thumbnail before he realized what he was doing. "You're right," he admitted, and lowered his hand. "There is only me out there. But it's beautiful, so I will do what I can. Even in the rain, and the snow it's beautiful. Would you… would you like to see it?"

"The entire town would like to see it," Joe answered quietly, without saying yes or no. "It's good that you're protecting it, but it's ours too."

Zarrin narrowed his eyes and lifted his chin mutinously at the idea of thousands of people trampling through his exquisite wilderness.

"He's not alone, though." Jessie broke the silence. "He's got his girlfriend now."

"Girlfriend?" Zarrin nearly tripped over his own feet in his surprise, and he hadn't been moving. "Marie? I thought everyone understood. She isn't." He turned earnestly to Joe, who must have believed that the way Marie had said he did. "She isn't, Joe."

"Well, that hurts my feelings," Marie commented as she came up behind him and then nuzzled his ear until he swatted at her. She dodged his hand easily. "Kidding. Kidding." She ducked around to whisper into his other ear. "How did it go? Did you claim him right there on the counter, or is he still holding back?"

"As you see," Zarrin sighed at her, but then perked up. "But he made iced tea for me." He handed over her latte and then went over to collect his tea and straw.

"Okay." Marie seemed puzzled but followed him. "He presents you with gifts a lot, doesn't he? And then frowns defiantly at you before you even get a chance to thank him. I don't know how you're going to get him into that menagerie of yours."

"I got *you* there," Zarrin argued smugly, and bit off the top of the paper for the straw. "My friend. Mine mine mine."

Marie snapped her teeth at him. "Don't worry about me. Focus on your darling boy over there. He's so confused and miserable I want to hug him."

"You won't touch him," Zarrin threatened, and didn't appreciate her grin. He decided to ignore it and focus on Joe, who was keeping to the espresso machine instead of resuming their conversation. "Miserable?"

"You would do yourself, and him, a favor if you claimed him." Marie always suggested that, as if Joe was a werewolf and would understand the gesture, while, to be honest, Zarrin wasn't completely sure what she meant by *claim*. Sex, from her tone, but also something else.

"I would do anything for him," Zarrin said with a sigh, while gazing in Joe's direction. The startled jump from the two men lingering near him wasn't worth the effort of taking his eyes from Joe. "I want to make him happy, but I can't do that."

"Why not?" Marie sniffed her latte, then took a sip.

Zarrin sighed again. "The people in here watch him a lot. And they watch me. I don't think he would like it if I did anything to draw more attention to him. Look how tense he is already." Zarrin chewed on the end of his straw. "And he doesn't believe the dragons have taken good care of this town. He doesn't believe that I would care for him."

"So you aren't going to get ahead of yourself while I'm gone?" Marie didn't seem surprised by Zarrin's revelation. "You'll be slow, and properly woo your boy the way he ought to be wooed? Reassure him that I'm a friend, and only make him promises you will keep?"

"Yes." For that, Zarrin turned away from Joe to look at her. He lowered his head from the intensity of her stare, then darted a glance back up. "Yes, I will."

"Ah!" Marie's exclamation drew everyone's attention to them, but she squeezed him in a close hug without appearing to care. "How do you say things like that and smell so *shy*? Honestly, shy wasn't even a scent to me before you. You're precious!"

Zarrin held himself stiffly in her arms for a moment before he curled against her and rubbed his cheek against her shoulder.

"Who is going to feed you when you go?" he complained. "You're always so hungry. Oh!" He jerked his head up. "Did you choose a pastry?"

"I fed myself before I met you, Zarrin. I'll be—pastry?" Exactly as distracted by food as he'd predicted, Marie slid past him to check out the selection.

"You showed up with no clothes and no money," Zarrin pointed out, with dignity, he thought.

"I was a wolf. What was I supposed to do? Wear a fanny pack?" Marie directed this across the counter. "He worries," she said, *to Joe*.

Zarrin felt himself heating up. "I need to make sure you're cared for."

"Sugar daddy dragon," Marie named him, with a snort of amusement. "He's paid for my bus ticket, and gave me clothes, and insisted I take money to buy food along the way." She pointed at one of the pastries, something dripping with icing, and grinned as Joe slowly, almost reluctantly, came over to get it for her. "But really," she added, after Joe handed her the pastry in a paper bag, "he's a sugar baby. Let him mature a little. *Then* he'll be a sugar daddy."

"You're leaving?" Joe just seemed to be catching on to this unfortunate fact.

Marie's smile was almost sweet for a second. "I wandered a little farther from home than I'd intended to. This visit has been nice, but I need to get back before my pack—my friends—start to worry. Just a small broken heart," she explained, with a laugh Zarrin didn't understand. "You know, the kind where you think you need to get away, go anyplace but where you are, until you realize you miss your home so much it pulls at you?"

Joe's startled stare said he knew precisely what she meant.

Zarrin pushed out a black, furious protest that plumed up toward the ceiling. "But you don't have to go. You could stay. You should stay. It's safer here. I won't break your heart."

Marie didn't even glance at him. "That bossy tone of his is to hide the fact that he'll miss me. He just can't admit it. You have to filter out the arrogant dragon to get what he's really saying."

"I'll miss you." Zarrin stamped his foot to emphasize the fact that he *could* say it. "You're difficult and prone to hugging, which took some getting used to, but I will miss you!"

In less than a second, he had Marie wrapped around him, despite both of her hands being full.

"My lonely one," she whispered to him before raising her voice as if continuing to talk only to Joe. "This one here," she said fondly, and then rubbed her cheek—and her scent—all over him.

"You're embarrassing," Zarrin hissed at her, while glancing desperately to Joe.

"You love it." She snuffled into his ear.

Zarrin didn't deny it. "You shouldn't go. Let me watch over you."

"Zarrin, I'm not yours." She pulled away to study him critically, then smiled and tousled his hair. "You're mine, so there."

"Really?" The thought was momentarily distracting. "I've never been anyone's before."

Joe choked on something and frowned hard when Martin smacked him on the back.

Zarrin clutched at Marie's coat and regretted ever giving her clothes and money. "You're leaving," he admitted sadly. "You're really leaving." He felt his eyes start to sting and blinked a few times, hoping to banish the tears. "Of course you are." No one ever stayed. He tried to smile. "You'll write? Bernard writes me. He was very fond of me and asked me to go with him, but I couldn't leave. I still worry about him, though. It's harder to protect him when he's far away."

"How is he possible?" Marie demanded of Joe. "How is he real?"

"I'm not lying," Zarrin insisted, his face flaming. "Bernard *does* like me. He made me grilled cheese!"

"Grilled. Cheese." Marie groaned at Joe. "He's killing me. Are all dragons this charming and ridiculous?"

"No, just this one," Joe answered, then went very still.

Zarrin froze too. Then he turned very slowly to stare at Joe's forbidding frown. Next to Joe, Martin had his hand over his mouth, although his hooting laugh was audible. Jessie appeared very confused. Zarrin didn't care about anything but Joe's warmly furious expression. He didn't see why Martin would laugh. The sweetest words in the world, and Joe was *worried* that he'd said them.

"My parents didn't want me eating anything unhealthy." Zarrin left Marie to carefully approach the counter. "They didn't approve of the orange-colored cheese slices. I don't suppose you've had them."

Joe shrugged as if indifferent, as if he hadn't agreed that Zarrin was *charming*. "I lived off them. Made my own sandwiches with them while my mom was at work, or she'd make grilled cheese when she got home."

"Did you like them?" Zarrin asked, fascinated with the image of Joe as a child, already self-sufficient.

"If we were feeling really fancy and extravagant, we'd use two slices each." Joe said it like a challenge, but then went on. "Sliced cheese and bologna sandwich was the first thing I learned to make on my own, besides cereal." His shoulders went back as his defensive tone returned. "I've never eaten brand-name cereal in my life."

"Neither have I." Zarrin crept closer. "I longed to try Fairy Charms, but I always got oatmeal. It was supposed to be good for me." He wrinkled his nose and some of the fury left Joe's expression. "I shouldn't be having sweetened tea either," he confessed, and shuddered in delight at Joe's quick smile of disbelief. "Although, despite myself, I've discovered I miss your lattes. They warmed me when I was out in the snow."

"Goddamn," someone behind him whispered. Zarrin thought it was one of the people over by the sugar and milk, but didn't bother to check. Joe's eyes were wide and dark enough to drown in. All that hurt and fear—Zarrin didn't know how he'd missed it before. He hadn't expected it. Joe looked so strong and fierce, but he was as delicate as a wren landing on Zarrin's hand.

Zarrin was going to take such good care of him. Even if Joe couldn't want him, Zarrin was going to keep him safe.

"My baby dragon is all grown up," Marie remarked. Even Zarrin's sister wouldn't have been that sarcastic.

Zarrin turned from Joe at last, but only to huff fondly about Marie. "I have to take my friend to Stapleton now, since she insists on leaving me."

"Don't take it personally, Zarrin." Marie came up behind him. "Your hoard seems like a nice place to be. It's just not my home."

Zarrin studied her, the plait of her hair and the glint in her eyes. He already missed her. "If you ever want to return, even to visit, you're welcome," he invited her, quite graciously considering he was mad at her for going. "You may bring more wolves, perhaps, if they are… if they're nice like you."

"You're letting her go?" Joe tipped his head to one side and studied them both intently.

"You can't force treasure to stay," Zarrin reminded him, and released a long breath. "No one can. Maybe not even Dìzhèn could, and she managed to tie her magic to so much land it should have been impossible."

"Come on, before I miss my bus." Marie shoved the bag with the pastry in a pocket and looped her arm through Zarrin's. "Don't think I won't visit. Of course I will. I need to see how things turn out. You might get more than a few wolf visitors too, once the tale of my dragon savior gets out."

"Marie!" Zarrin was going to have to remind her yet again that Joe would not want a softhearted dragon. He was supposed to be ferocious.

Marie twisted around to wave at everyone. "Nice to meet you all. Especially you, Joseph. You'll like me in time."

"Yes!" Zarrin agreed excitedly and then leaned toward Joe. "We have to go, but I'll be back tomorrow. You'll be here?" Zarrin held Joe's stare until Joe gave one small, startled nod. "Then I'll be here."

Zarrin beamed at him before he recalled himself and his dignity. Then Marie tugged at him again. She was anxious to start her journey home, but let him pause for one more look at his stunned, startled Joseph before she led him out the door.

# CHAPTER 8

THE PACKAGE arrived that afternoon, shortly before Joe and Martin's shifts ended. The shop got shipments with Joe's name on them when he did the ordering, so Joe passed the parcel off to Martin and didn't think anything of it until Martin called him to the back in a strained voice.

The set of colored pencils in his hands were the kind anyone would drool over, the kind artists would kill for. They were obviously not for the shop, and there was no return address on the label.

"In case you still had any doubts after this morning," Martin commented, not even smirking, and then left Joe alone with his wooden case of one hundred and sixty gorgeous colored pencils.

Joe held his hand above the rows of carefully arranged possibilities until his arm shook, but he didn't touch them. The case smelled of lacquer and wood shavings. Each pencil was sharpened to an exquisitely sharp point. They were all so *fine*. He'd never be able to replace them, but the things he could create while he had them….

He shouldn't keep them, but they *sang* beneath his fingertips. There were shades for every face. He could do portraits like he'd never done before, like he'd never *wanted* to do before.

"I don't understand," Joe said out loud, although no one else was around. He wasn't friendly, or nice. No one had ever made a fuss like this for him. A fairy had sat in his lap and waxed rhapsodic about his shine, but he'd also been gone in a few hours.

Zarrin didn't even know what Joe drew. He didn't know if it was good. But he knew—or had guessed—Joe needed these. Joe had only given him coffee and then tea, nothing to earn this. These were beautiful.

They were probably crazy expensive, but Zarrin wouldn't have noticed the price. He had gone through gold coins, and antique books, and a painting, and finally chosen this.

Joe flushed hot as he closed up the case and held it to his chest. He shouldn't keep them, but he couldn't let them go. He was going to have to speak to Zarrin about them—tomorrow, because Zarrin had promised to come in. Marie wouldn't be with him, and Zarrin was going to come in, and Joe would refuse the set like he ought to—or thank Zarrin for it.

In the meantime, Joe grabbed his coat and stuffed his share of the day's tips into a pocket. He wandered past a grinning Martin while wondering what Zarrin would do if Joe thanked him. If he'd duck his head in strange, shy pleasure or rudely insist Joe didn't need to. He might glance around in embarrassment the way he did when Marie said he'd saved her.

Joe nodded pleasantly at Forrester on his way out, and barely noticed the startled look Forrester gave him. If Joe didn't need to buy paints for now, then he could use his money to buy another present for his mother for Christmas. He held open the door for someone walking in, and stepped onto the sidewalk just as a loud crack split through the air and the ground rolled beneath his feet.

He slammed into the wall of Cuppa, and hugged the pencil set tight as he tried to stay steady. He had half a second to think, *This is an earthquake*, and then the rolling stopped. The cars down the street swerved back into their respective lanes, then slowed to a crawl as their drivers peered anxiously out their windows.

Joe sucked in a breath and looked up too. There wasn't any sign in the sky that anything had happened, if he didn't count the seagulls, pigeons, and crows that had all abruptly taken flight.

That had been a strong one. He turned to head back into the shop to see if they'd need help with anything that might have fallen over, and then the ground *surged*, pushed along with so much force he actually saw thin cracks form in the street.

One of the streetlights flickered to life and groaned as it listed to one side, the cement that had anchored it in place weakened. Then everything went quiet. Joe was near the center of town, but he could hear the ocean over his own heavy, frightened breathing.

He faced west for one second, trying to remember what he knew about the effect of earthquakes on the ocean. Everyone on the street had gone as still as he was. Some of them were staring at the broken, leaning streetlight as it slowly fell to the ground.

The wind was gone. Or at least, Joe couldn't feel the cold breeze on his face. He couldn't recall if two shockwaves meant one quake or two, and pulled out his phone to check for news reports on what the scale had been as he stumbled back into Cuppa. Forrester exited as he came in, his radio crackling with requests for information.

Jessie and the owner were crouched down, cleaning up the collapsed tea display. Gina was in the back doorway, already on the landline, probably trying to call home and make sure her kid was okay.

There was a fault line not far away. Everyone knew that. But it hadn't been active in so long it was like no one could remember the lessons drilled into them in grade school. Customers began to chatter excitedly about it all at once or consult their phones like Joe was doing.

The US Geological Survey hadn't rated the tremors on the Richter scale yet, or determined the origin. But it had to be close. Joe had nearly been knocked off his feet.

He slipped back behind the counter to put down his pencil set and grabbed a few towels to go help clean up the spills.

"Try hitting refresh again." Two customers at a table both peered at the same tablet. Their alarmed expressions made Joe stop to stare down at the device as well. The map of the state was clear, with all the reports of earthquakes in the past twenty-four hours, no matter how small, but there was nothing near Everlasting.

The street was cracked. Something had happened, and yet—

"Hit refresh again," Joe ordered, not really caring about the look they gave him. The colors on the screen changed. A large red blob appeared with the state park in the center of it, and then one refresh later, the red blob was smaller and blue. When they reloaded the page one more time, the blob was *purple*. Joe had no idea what purple meant. He didn't think anyone did.

"Those are different sizes," one of the customers complained, with obvious confusion. "They aren't even close to the same size on the scale. Are the machines all broken?"

The odds of every scale the USGS possessed malfunctioning had to be incredibly small. It was far more likely that the earthquake hadn't originated at the fault line.

Joe watched the blob change in size and color with every page reload and then finally realized what should have been obvious from the start: the epicenter of that quake hadn't been in the state park. It had been the edge of the Xu Family Preserve.

"Zarrin," he whispered.

One of the customers—who he belatedly recognized as Holly, Helene's partner, twisted around to gape at him. "Oh no! Is he angry?"

"How would I know?" Joe stepped away from their table and drifted toward the counter as he tried to think. Town history was full of stories of the ground shaking with Dìzhèn's wrath, but the last time anyone remembered the dragons causing an earthquake had been back when Zarrin's great aunt had died. She'd married into the Xu family, and had never lived in Everlasting, but she must have been beloved by the family. Dragons from all over the country, and beyond, had gathered at the mansion in the days leading up to her death, and when she'd passed, the newspapers had reported redwoods knocked over with the force of their grief. Some of the old houses in town had suffered significant damage, which the family had later paid to repair.

Maybe Zarrin was furious about Marie's leaving, or more torn up than he'd wanted to admit.

Although, it took half an hour to drive to Stapleton, which meant Zarrin would have said good-bye to Marie hours ago. And there was another reason dragons made the ground tremble—excitement. But it would have to be something extreme to create a quake that strong. Or so Joe assumed.

He looked around and had no one to ask. He could ask Zarrin. Zarrin might even want him to. But that was something that could wait until tomorrow. This was probably nothing to Zarrin—like a tantrum, or a crying jag.

Except the Preserve was miles away, and the street was *cracked*, and the more Joe thought about that, the colder he felt. Zarrin wouldn't do something like that. He worried about the town, and not once in the months he'd been back had the ground so much as vibrated.

And… and he hadn't been furious or overwhelmed with grief when he'd left the coffee shop. He'd been smiling in anticipation of seeing Joe again. He might even have been happy because he'd known his gift to Joe was on its way.

Joe stalked to the back to throw the wet towels in the laundry bin and to wash his hands. Then he took hold of his pencil set and went out the back door to get to his car. He had to talk to Zarrin about the set anyway.

He drove slowly, in case of another tremor or an aftershock. The roads were nearly empty, as if the earthquake had scared people into pulling over or going home. The abandoned streets didn't calm him.

He was being ridiculous. Zarrin was a dragon. If he'd caused an earthquake, he probably had a reason that would make sense to him. Joe was going to drive up and take a look at the house, and Zarrin was not going to be happy about his human presumption.

Joe wouldn't go far. He'd stop at the second sign.

But Dìzhèn's mansion had no smoke coming from any of its chimneys. Joe stopped the car outside the gate and told himself that didn't mean anything either. According to Alice, Zarrin went out into the Preserve in the afternoons.

He reminded himself of that, then eased his car forward anyway, only to stop at the start of the driveway when a wave of dread hit him. He shut off the car and breathed hard as his every instinct screamed for him to run away.

That hadn't happened last time. Stray hunters had reported that feeling when entering the Preserve, but Joe hadn't experienced it until today. Something was definitely wrong. The feeling wasn't stopping him, but he doubted he'd be able to make it to the steps of the house.

He opened the car door to let the cold air brace his nerves, and was immediately surprised by the smell of smoke. He looked up to the chimneys again, then swung around to scan the trees.

He started walking the moment he saw the lingering clouds of black.

Joe pulled out his phone, shaking with fear that hadn't gone away and the cold that he wasn't dressed for. He had no idea where he was going, and though he enjoyed hiking, he wasn't any kind of tracker, or firefighter for that matter.

He tilted his face to the sky and shouted, "Zarrin!" If Zarrin was fine, well, then, it was better to announce his presence rather than surprise a protective dragon. "Zarrin!"

A rolling aftershock almost sent him to his knees. He didn't want to think that was an answer to his shouting, but fear was settling in the pit of his stomach and wouldn't go away. Everything around him was chilled and damp, and when he entered a grove of trees, condensation from the leaves above trickled down like light rain. It had melted the faint dusting of snow. If there *had* been tracks or prints anywhere, Joe wouldn't have been able to find them anyway.

The border of the state park was to the southeast, and very close, but the smoke hadn't been that far ahead. This high up, it was cold enough that Joe could see his breath. He pulled his jacket closer and tried another yell. "Zarrin!"

If there'd been a fire, one of the smoke spotters would have seen it by now and reported it. Yet Joe pressed on, too distracted to take a look at the giants watching him progress through their sacred space.

Another, smaller shockwave carried through the earth, and when Joe leaned against a tree to wait it out, he noticed a new scent amid all the smoke. Burned meat was distinctive enough to put him off barbecues forever. Charred wood made him hurry forward when he should have run, and then it took him way too long to really take in what he was seeing.

Zarrin—a version of Zarrin—was curled up beneath the vast trunk of a giant redwood, an impossibly small, raggedly breathing figure. A metallic sheen rippled beneath his bare skin, and seemed to reshape his spine, which was splashed with crimson. Zarrin's scales turned darker and brighter with his every inhale. His face was turned away, but Joe had dreamed about that bronze too often not to recognize it.

But this wasn't the Zarrin he knew. This Zarrin was naked and not entirely human. Dark claws dug into the earth in shaky, pained spasms, and then another tremor swept outward when Zarrin shivered. His body was the epicenter, Joe realized dumbly, then finally noticed the cause. The crimson dripping down Zarrin's back was *blood*. It was redder than dragonfire.

Joe's mind worked without him, noting the pieces of equipment scattered around the small clearing, the scorch marks in the trees, the kind of paper cup the coffee shop used, the bloodied plastic bags and the abandoned hunting rifle by a backpack.

"Zarrin?" He had enough clear thinking left to let Zarrin know he was there before he came forward. The scorching, the smell of burnt flesh—Zarrin had definitely hurt, if not killed, whoever had done this.

A shudder went down Zarrin's back, and then he changed before Joe's eyes. He went paler, became smaller, and then moaned into the dirt. "Joe?" he asked weakly, and Joe thudded down next to him, although he didn't touch him.

There were darts in Zarrin's skin. *Darts*, as if he were an animal. Joe glimpsed them in the soft skin of Zarrin's stomach when Zarrin moved. He pushed past the rush of vicious pleasure to imagine Zarrin hurting whoever had done this to him so he could finally call for help.

Zarrin moaned again as Joe relayed everything he knew to the dispatcher, including the sense of impending doom that was going to greet any emergency responders.

They might not make it this far. Joe was going to have to get Zarrin closer to them.

He hung up on the operator, since he was going to need both hands for this, then inched closer. "Zarrin, I have to touch you. Okay? We have to get off the Preserve so people can help you."

"A dragon does not require human aid," Zarrin answered, and turned his face toward Joe. His scales extended farther across his cheekbones, which were smeared with mud. His pupils were reptilian one second, then round and dilated the next. His eyes were impossibly bright before he closed them. "I thought it was you, treasure."

"I'm—shit—I'm going to leave the darts in, all right?" Joe didn't even want to touch them. "In case taking them out makes it worse, or… or something. Okay? It's just me. No more earthquakes?"

"I'm sorry." Zarrin panted, then put a hand to the ground and forced himself up. His claws were gone. He was even smaller than before. Joe crept forward to slide an arm under his, and made a sound at the wet cold of Zarrin's skin.

The wrongness of it had him moving faster, while still trying to be gentle. He got Zarrin on his feet and began to lead them to his car so he wouldn't have to think about how little Zarrin weighed or the sound of his labored breathing.

"I'm sorry," Zarrin said again, after stumbling for the third or fourth time. "I'm fine. I'll be fine. It hurt, but I didn't mean to. I've never done that before. Did I frighten you?" He exhaled into Joe's shoulder and even that was cold. Joe wrapped Zarrin in his arms, practically lifting him off the ground wherever the mud was too thick.

Distantly, he didn't think lifting Zarrin like that should have been possible, but then he thought, *dragon*, and let it go for now. Zarrin was something from a story anyway, changing from gleaming scales to soft skin in the space of a heartbeat. He shivered into Joe and repeated himself. "I'm sorry."

"For what?" Joe finally demanded, strained and exhausted by the time they cleared the trees. The house was in sight, but the overwhelming terror didn't return. That could have been Zarrin's presence, or the rising fury overtaking Joe's fear. "Why the hell are you apologizing?"

Zarrin pushed his face into Joe's throat and spoke against his collarbone. "A dragon shouldn't require human aid," he said, clearly, before the rest of his words slurred together. "I thought it was you. I'm sorry I scared you, treasure."

"Treasure?" Joe asked, and sighed in relief at the far-off sound of a siren. "You keep saying that."

"I shouldn't." Zarrin shook his head and then pushed himself away from Joe. He took two steps before he tripped and collapsed to his knees. He slid to the ground from there. The way he shut his eyes was so final, Joe fell down next to him. He decided to yank the darts from him anyway and wished for the power to melt them like Zarrin might have done.

Zarrin was still so cold. Joe stripped off his coat to hold over Zarrin's stomach and chest to stem any bleeding. Maybe it would keep him warm too. He hoped that had been the right thing to do. He didn't know what he was thinking, coming up here, worrying about keeping a dragon warm.

But Zarrin shivered and let Joe tuck the coat around him. He should have been delighted about that, alive and interested in Joe leaning over him. But whatever had been in those darts was taking him under.

"Zarrin!" Shudders that seemed to rise from the earth itself made Joe lean down to shout the name until Zarrin opened his eyes again. "You think you get to scare the entire town and then just go to sleep?" Joe scowled at him and wished his hands weren't trembling. "I don't think so. Stop it or they'll… they'll send me back here to kiss you awake, and that's ridiculous. Zarrin, tell me that's ridiculous. I'm not your… I'm no one's true love."

"Treasure." Zarrin didn't give Joe a look filled with yearning at the mention of a kiss. He didn't do anything but sigh. "But not mine. I'm sorry."

"What does that mean?" Joe demanded, and leaned over him. *Not mine.* The words were somehow more terrifying than the dread the house had given him. Joe put his hands to Zarrin's face. "What happened? Zarrin?"

"I failed," Zarrin confessed in a slow, sad whisper. Then his head lolled back and his eyes closed.

A moment after that, the air shimmered, and a gleaming dragon was in his place.

ZARRIN CAME to in a small, unfamiliar room, sparsely appointed. It appeared to be a bedroom, with a chest of drawers and an end table with a lamp and a clock on it not far from him. He was in a bed with a gently used mattress, covered in what felt like layers upon layers of blankets. But if he was in a bedroom, it was a strange one. There was a door in his line of sight, but it had two locks and a peephole, which made it a front door. Across from him, another doorway led to what he thought was a kitchen. That was all he could see unless he moved, and he didn't want to move.

He… hurt. A lancing pain stabbed at him when he breathed in, his stomach felt scratched raw, and his arms and legs ached with strain. He closed his eyes and then reopened them, but the room remained the same, as did the state of his body. He put his nose to the pillow beneath him and then exhaled in surprise to realize the pillow smelled of treasure. So did the blankets.

He was in Joe's bed.

Zarrin raised his head to better take in what must be Joe's home. The movement took effort, and one of his feet slid off the side of the bed until a claw got stuck in the sheets.

Zarrin hissed in embarrassment as he became aware that he could feel the sheets all along his body, which meant he was naked. Claws meant he was himself, at the moment. He was in his dragon body, and Joe must have seen him.

He instantly tried to curl up in a ball, but the movement sent a shock of pain through him. He shuddered, then buried his head under the Joe-scented pillow. He was in Joe's bed. Surely Joe hadn't been frightened, or disgusted, or upset. Nonetheless, Zarrin flushed hot with awareness of his nudity. A human wouldn't want a dragon body, but he was naked in Joe's bed. Joe had brought him home.

Zarrin focused through his spinning, somewhat foggy thoughts, until he could return to his human form. Which may have been a mistake. His sense of smell was duller, but now Joe's sheets were wrapped around his bare skin and Joe's blankets enveloped him in a warmth not of Zarrin's making. This was what it must be like to be Joe's lover. If Zarrin hadn't been in pain, he would have spread out over the mattress and closed his eyes.

But movement hurt him, so he kept his head under the pillow until he heard voices and then the creak of a door. He peeked out and saw a sheriff's deputy enter the room.

His stomach trembled. Zarrin remembered the trees, the sound of voices, two human men whispering to each other before the pain began. Then fire.

"Are you here to arrest me?" he asked, breathing hard into the pillow.

"Zarrin?" Joe's voice surprised him. He appeared behind the deputy, and shut the door. Joe did not look as neat as he usually did. Strands of hair were in his face, and his long-sleeved shirt didn't seem warm enough for him to wear while outside without a coat.

Zarrin poked more of his head out from under the pillow. "Treasure?" he replied, then gasped. He had no right to say that, not after this. "I'm sorry."

"Sorry?" the deputy prodded. He had his hands in his belt and a wary expression on his face. He was Joe's age, but with skin flushed with the cold, and he had on a properly thick coat. His eyes were very blue, and he had marks on his nose from glasses. He must have also seen what a poor excuse for a dragon Zarrin was.

Joe came forward to frown seriously down at Zarrin. Zarrin belatedly pulled the pillow from his head. From this angle, Joe was very tall.

"Zarrin, this is Deputy Forrester." Joe paused. "Technically, his name is Ian, but no one calls him that. He's going to ask you about… what happened. If you're ready." The look Joe gave the deputy was not kind. "If."

"Forrester is fine." Deputy Forrester held Joe's stare for a moment longer, then turned to Zarrin. "How are you feeling?"

"I'm in Joe's bed," Zarrin informed him, since that answered that question, and then sat up. The blankets fell to his waist. Both of the humans immediately dropped their gazes to Zarrin's body, then away. Zarrin looked at his body as well, then briefly shut his eyes.

Four little puncture wounds with bruising across his stomach, from darts, he recalled. They had hurt.

The deputy cleared his throat before speaking. "We took you to the hospital, but you seemed to get… *bigger* in unfamiliar surroundings. And your house didn't appear to want people there, for lack of a better way of putting it. Then the doctor suggested that maybe dragons are like werewolves, and require, um, specific things for healing in times of stress, so we brought you here. Which did work."

The sheer embarrassment in the room was so strong Zarrin could identify it with no trouble, and opened his eyes. Joe glared at the deputy until he saw Zarrin watching.

"So the doctor," Forrester quickly continued, "didn't know much about how dragons heal. He said you had physical responses he could monitor and then magical ones he couldn't. Anyway, we brought you here." He cleared his throat again, then pulled a notebook and a pencil from an interior pocket of his brown coat. "For now, I just need your version of events."

"Events?" Zarrin echoed, his voice much too shaky. "*Events*." They were before his eyes, despite how he didn't want them to be. He took handfuls of the blankets—quilts, he noticed, and hauled them up to his chest. He imagined dignity and pride and lifted his chin. "I was returning from a quick trip along the southeasterly edge of the Preserve when I smelled—"

He glanced at Joe, who stood with his arms crossed and a furrow of unhappiness across his brow. He turned to Forrester. "I smelled the warm milk of a latte, and human sweat. I thought it was—" Zarrin was so very foolish, and Joe was so very still. "And I hurried forward. The sound stopped me then, like the crack of rifles in the park, but closer, and then I felt pain." His stomach hurt. He clutched at Joe's quilts. "I woke on the ground. I—we—aren't human when we sleep. I woke as they were speaking, and I smelled blood, and I… panicked. My parents warned me humans don't like us. But I never thought they would… they would… do this."

"They were already trespassing, Zarrin." The anger in Joe's voice was oddly calming. "Nobody blames you for anything."

"You caught them?" Zarrin dared another look at Joe.

"Weren't hard to find," Forrester interrupted. "Two men with serious burns made it to the ER in Stapleton, and yet refused to identify the source of the fire. It was a bit suspicious."

"Are they very hurt?" Zarrin wondered, and Joe made a noise like a suppressed growl. Forrester gave a start, then focused sharply on Zarrin.

"Second degree in most places. Third in a few others. They'll be scarred, but they'll live." He studied Zarrin, but then tilted his head toward Joe. "Joe, why don't you step out for a second?"

"No." Joe was unmoving.

"Then you need to calm down," Forrester told him flatly.

Zarrin took in the picture Joe made, nearly trembling in his stillness. He would have seemed calm to Zarrin only a few weeks ago, but now Zarrin knew his frowns as the disguises they were. Evidently, so did Forrester.

"Go on," Zarrin ordered softly, although if Joe was that upset, then the news would not be good.

Forrester tapped his notebook against his thigh. "The truck belonging to the two men had blood on the doors, which led to a search. They had furs with them, and some antlers. And…."

"Two of your scales," Joe finished when Forrester hesitated.

"We don't think they planned to kill you," Forrester rushed on, as Zarrin blinked and stopped breathing. "We think they were going to keep you unconscious to take those…. And now we know how they lured you, which implies intent, which is useful."

"I see." Zarrin stared at his hands.

"You will have to come in and talk about this in more detail later." Forrester put away his notebook. "As soon as your house lets me, I'll head back up to the Pres—to the scene and get a better look. It wouldn't let anyone near, after Joe anyway. But, you should know, once Fish and Game heard about what happened, they sent some game wardens out to watch the edge of the property for you. Said they'd lost wardens before, and it was their pleasure to keep an eye out on your behalf."

"Oh." Zarrin couldn't seem to raise his head.

"As for the rest…." Forrester got awkward again. "We got most of what we need at the hospital. Pictures and things." He stopped when Zarrin curled down into the pile of blankets. Then he coughed. "I hesitate to mention it, but there were old scars, on your back. We weren't sure about them."

"Those aren't from this." Zarrin glanced to Joe. "You're being very calm for me, thank you, Joseph."

"Yeah, well." Joe scrubbed one cheek for a moment, as if it was warm. "Forrester is capable of tact, who knew?"

"Up yours, Joe," Forrester responded. It didn't sound insulting, more tired.

Joe was tired too, or distracted. "Where was this Forrester in high school?"

"Keeping his head down and trying to survive like everyone else." Forrester sighed, then briefly turned away so Zarrin couldn't see his expression. "For what it's worth, though, I never thought you did what they said."

Joe's eyes went very wide. He wiped at his cheek again, absently, and his voice was rough when he spoke. "Did you need anything else from Zarrin?"

Forrester shook his head and turned back to Zarrin. "Doctor says you can take stuff for the pain, but he wasn't sure what would work on you."

"The pain will be gone by morning," Zarrin assured him, although he knew no such thing for sure. He'd never had a scale forcibly removed before. He tried to keep the hiccupping fear from his voice. "Thank you for your concern. The house shouldn't bother you if your intentions are peaceful. If it did earlier, it must have been because I was… threatened."

"Good to know." Forrester nodded, then stepped toward the door. "We weren't sure who to call, about this. So no one has notified your family—"

"That's fine." Zarrin cut him off there. "Thank you. I'll do it."

"You're welcome?" Forrester seemed confused at being thanked, but then continued to the door. "Joe has my card, if you need anything else tonight. Try to rest, and don't worry about the town for now, okay?"

He didn't wait for a reply, from either of them. A blast of cold air came in as he left, and Joe shivered. He rushed forward to close the door and then kicked at a heating grate. "Sorry."

"They took pieces of me, for money," Zarrin answered, and wanted to pull the blankets over his head.

Joe froze.

"You must think I'm very weak." Zarrin let out a breath. "And very stupid. But I never imagined this." He shuddered and the room shook with him.

"Here." Joe swept forward to grab another quilt about to fall off the bed, and draped it over Zarrin's lap. "Sorry about the cold. My heater is broken." He wouldn't look Zarrin in the eye.

"I know how to keep warm," Zarrin insisted, but quivered a little to have a human so close to him after that. But it was Joe, who showed his concern with scowls and kind gestures. He tucked Zarrin in and stepped back with his hands out for Zarrin to see.

"I'll make you some tea." Joe moved from place to place, like someone who didn't know exactly what to do yet, then finally disappeared into the kitchen. Zarrin heard running water, and the whirr of a microwave, and then the clink of ceramics.

Zarrin continued to shiver despite the multitude of quilts, and lowered his stare to his hands. "I don't understand," he said to the silhouette of Joe at the edge of his vision. "I don't understand how humans can say and do such cruel things, but then also do this." He pulled in a long breath. "Ian Forrester said something to you that overwhelmed you. And you have taken me into your home when you didn't have to. Yet those men…."

"Here." Joe pressed a white mug into his hands. The paper square from a tea bag hung from one side. The mug was burning hot. It shouldn't have been, but Zarrin was very cold. "Not sure about you and caffeine right now, and I made it in the microwave, which I guess makes it not 'serious tea.' But here. It's berry zinger, the cheap stuff. My mom always drinks it when she isn't well."

Zarrin stared at it and the strange color of it. It smelled like candy.

Joe sighed heavily. "Or don't drink it. I just thought it might help."

Zarrin took a sip. The water wasn't nearly as hot as the mug. The taste was very fruity. He swished it around in his mouth to taste more of it, then had another sip.

"You're such a kid sometimes, right up until you aren't." Joe stepped back again, as if trying not to stay in Zarrin's space for too long. His frown was firmly in place.

"You're trying to distract me," Zarrin realized out loud. "Or yourself. You're trying to get yourself worked up." He looked up and met Joe's startled eyes. "What's a zinger?"

"I have no idea." Joe moved his hands, restlessly, then crossed his arms. "I'm not trying to—are you okay? Do you need anything?"

There, beneath Zarrin's heart, a flare of warmth returned. Zarrin had no right to this treasure anymore, but the desire to soothe this one, to protect him, gave Zarrin something better than dignity to keep him going.

"The tea is good." Zarrin spoke softly to calm the worry Joe was no longer hiding well. "You brought me to your house."

"Apartment." Joe took a step, then held himself still. "It's not a house, trust me."

"You always do that." Zarrin was growing fond of this berry tea, though his sister would hate it. "You don't need to teach me everything, Joseph. I *have* seen the world."

"I'm sure you've *seen* a lot of things," Joe muttered, but then moved forward anxiously when Zarrin lowered the cup. Zarrin raised the mug to his mouth once again, and Joe settled.

The fire in his middle sparked hotter. It wasn't fair that Zarrin had proven himself too weak to keep a treasure like Joe, but this might be the only chance he got to care for him, and his body seemed to need it.

Zarrin ignored the begrudging tone and peered around the room, taking more care now. There were two other rooms he could see. One had the tiled floor of a bathroom, which meant the bedroom, or what should have been the bedroom, was beyond the closed door.

"Where do you keep your treasure?" he wondered, but studied Joe while Joe looked around the apartment in bafflement.

"Treasure?" Joe was so beautiful, even when anxious and confused. "Your coins are by the door." He turned in time to catch Zarrin studying him. "But you don't mean those," he added, and licked his lips. In other circumstances, Zarrin might have felt bad for looking at Joe as he did. But he was in pain and naked in Joe's bed, and in any case, Joe was no longer frowning.

"My artwork is in the bedroom," Joe confessed, after a lengthy pause. "Which is my studio. Hardly a treasure."

Zarrin scoffed politely and took another sip of tea to hide his burning desire to go into that room. "I have no doubt that it is."

Joe made a choked sound, then went silent. Zarrin watched him scrub at his cheeks, and felt warm enough to emerge from a few of the quilts. If only he'd known earlier that the way to woo his treasure was with honest compliments, he would have showered Joe with them instead of paltry coins.

"Your bed is very comfortable," he offered after a while.

Joe's frown returned. "You're doing it on purpose now."

"Whatever you need, treasure." Zarrin tossed his head, because that hurt to say. "Not treasure. I'm sorry."

"I… what?" Joe stared at him in confusion. "You said that before."

"I shouldn't have." Zarrin dropped his gaze to his nearly empty mug. "As you can see—as you saw, I'm no dragon to say such a thing."

"Because someone attacked you?" Joe grunted, as if either puzzled or furious. "No one blames you for that. You heard Forrester, Fish and Game is out there right now helping you."

"A dragon should not require human aid!" Zarrin insisted shrilly, then flushed with shame. "We are supposed to be powerful," he added, hushed.

"You are." Joe came a bit closer.

Zarrin couldn't help raising his head to look at him. "They drugged me. They lured me. They wanted the magic in my scales, and I couldn't stop them."

"They wanted the money from your beautiful scales," Joe corrected quietly. "They looked at you and only saw dollar signs. It's a sickness that drives some people."

Zarrin shook his head. "I was foolish. I should have listened to my parents. Humans don't—beautiful?" The quilts slipped from Zarrin's shoulders when he straightened. The dark wonder of Joe's eyes was the purest, truest color he'd ever seen. "Don't frown, please," he said quickly, before Joe could feel uncertain or embarrassed. "Thank you. Thank you for that, and the tea, and the use of your quilts. I… I must be bothering you, taking this much from you. I should go."

"So, you can give me things, but I can't do anything for you?" Joe tossed his head. "Humans are, what? Pets? You're embarrassed to have our help?"

"What?" Zarrin gaped at him. "No! No, my fires burn again with what you've done for me. But I'm not supposed to need your help."

Joe's lips parted. "Your fires burn again?" he repeated, a sweet little echo, and then shook his head. "Anyway, you can't go yet. You don't have clothes. There weren't any with you when you… I can drive you home, or I can call Jamie for you. Everlasting only has two regular cabs, and Jamie's is the most reliable."

The subject Joe was avoiding reminded Zarrin of something Forrester had said. He stared at Joe without moving. "Did *you* find me?"

Joe also stopped moving. "Yes," he answered, in his gruff, uncomfortable voice, and didn't explain why he'd been out there or how he'd known where to find Zarrin. "You don't remember?"

Zarrin slowly shook his head. "But I apologize if Dìzhèn's house made it difficult."

"You kept apologizing then too." Joe cleared his throat. "I'll get you some clothes."

"Thank you." Zarrin watched him dig through the chest of drawers, how he pulled up his sleeves when the changing temperature of the room seemed to hit him. Zarrin had given him warmth, but Joe had cared for him. He wondered what Bernard would have to say about that. He would be furious about what had happened today, but he might have something nice to say about this. Marie might as well. She would say something about mates.

Zarrin wasn't worthy of this one. But when Joe handed him a long-sleeved shirt and a pair of sweatpants, he held them to his cheek. "Joseph, you're very kind."

"It's sweats, cheap tea, and my crappy apartment." Joe moved away as he spoke, and scrubbed his cheeks again. "But you're welcome."

Zarrin studied the line of his back as Joe went into the kitchen and then realized Joe was giving him space to dress in private. How human of him. Zarrin placed the mug on the end table and then took a breath as he got to his feet.

Someone at the hospital must have cleaned him, although he still wanted a long shower. When he twisted around, he glimpsed the bandage above his hip, but he didn't touch it. He would grow new scales. But in the meantime, there were wounds to remind himself of his failure.

He had to call his family. He would have to tell them that he'd walked into a trap.

As he dressed, he bit his lip to keep his quiet whimpers to himself. The chill was returning, and bending down pulled at the sore muscles of his stomach, as well as the torn skin at his back.

"Your apartment is nice," he told Joe, although Joe wasn't in the room with him. He didn't want to dwell on his pain. "You disparage the things you have a lot. But it's clean and your bed is cozy, and I liked the tea, even if it was cheap. The cost doesn't matter that much."

"Cost matters when you don't have a lot of money," Joe answered from the kitchen.

Zarrin pulled up the collar of Joe's shirt so he could breathe in the scent of Joe's laundry soap. "Yes, but I didn't insult your home. You did. Are you worried what I think of it? And of you?" He paused and let the shirt fall. "I don't think I'm making sense. I should… I should go home soon. To the house. I *know* it's fine, but I *need* to see it, to be there."

Joe came out of the kitchen. He paused to take in the sight Zarrin must make in his too-big, but very soft, clothes, frowning all the while. "You don't have to go if you aren't ready. Just because they thought… what they thought, doesn't mean you have to rush out of here. Are your feet cold? You shouldn't bend down. You might tear something." He frowned harder as he crossed the room. He pulled a pair of socks from a drawer and then knelt in front of Zarrin.

"Oh." Zarrin stared down at the shining black of Joe's hair and then placed one hand carefully on Joe's shoulder. He *was* unsteady on his feet, but he hadn't expected this. His fingers grazed bare skin and warm cotton. His hand covered part of the tattooing that had driven him crazy for weeks, and without any further thought he traced part of the design with his fingers. He stopped when Joe audibly caught his breath. Neither of them moved or spoke, and then Joe's hands cupped his ankle as he rolled a sock gently over Zarrin's foot, first one, then the other.

Zarrin had never felt such fires. He was breathless. "You really don't mind that I am too weak to do this?"

Joe looked up. He seemed to realize he had placed himself at Zarrin's feet, and his scowl intensified. "You shouldn't go if you aren't ready."

How had he ever thought Joe was angry at anything? His Joseph was sweet and kind. More people should have let him show it.

"I would worry about you too, if I were in your place," Zarrin told him softly.

A tremor went through Joe. He stared at Zarrin in surprise, with a terrible hope in his eyes before he remembered to hide it. Then he got to his feet and moved away. "I'll call Jamie for you, if you don't want me to drive you. It might be better. You were… bleeding and I held you, so my car is… I'll call for you."

Zarrin watched him vanish into his kitchen once again, listened to the quiet murmurs of his conversation.

"Joseph," Zarrin called to him when Joe had hung up. He had been bleeding, and Joe had found him and brought him to safety, through powerful wards around the Preserve that must have made it difficult. If Zarrin had been a werewolf, he would have been proud to have Joe for a mate. Joe should know that, and not be so upset. "Joe. You are so *good*."

"You've had a very traumatic day." Joe stayed at the door to the kitchen. "You're still in pain."

That was true, so Zarrin nodded. "I'm not much of a dragon."

For a moment, he thought Joe might breathe fire too. "You shouldn't be ashamed that someone attacked you, stole from you. It wasn't your fault, okay? It wasn't your fault." He paused to wipe at his mouth. "Someone taking advantage of you is never your fault. It's hard to remember, but it's true."

"I come from a line of powerful dragons." Zarrin had to make him see.

But Joe was stubborn. "If dragons were so powerful, they'd be running things and not avoiding humans. You're more powerful than some, but that's all. You fought them off. You did what you could, which is a lot. To… to make people target you like that means you must have scared them. They didn't challenge you directly, did they? No. They found your weak spot and snuck up on you."

Joe was too smart not to grasp this. Zarrin put a hand to his sore stomach and shook his head. "The people in town are afraid of me too. I'd rather they liked me, or respected me. But I'm no Dìzhèn."

"Good," Joe snapped back. He narrowed his eyes at Zarrin's soft gasp of shock. "I don't much like the powerful."

Dìzhèn was a dragon of legend, but Zarrin was too distracted now to argue over her great name. "But you like me?" he realized aloud. Weak, soft Zarrin should not claim a treasure this wonderful, and yet it seemed the treasure wanted him. He couldn't say no. "Joseph," he began quietly, but stopped at the close sound of a car outside. A moment later, someone honked.

"Your ride." Joe scraped his hair from his eyes and then stuck his hands in his pockets. "My hiking boots are by the door if you want to borrow them." He cleared his throat.

He was precious. Marie had warned him, but she had not prepared Zarrin for this stage, for this awareness of Joe's desires, and his fears.

"The house will keep me safe, Joseph," Zarrin assured him, although the house would not keep him as warm as the quilts on Joe's bed, or put socks on his feet.

"It let me get close," Joe argued, before clamping his mouth shut.

Zarrin clucked his tongue. "Of course it did. You've never meant me harm." It was so much easier to offer his boy comfort than to think of the night he would spend in that house, unable to sleep for the noises outside. He would leave the TV on, perhaps, and curl up with the cats under the covers. He would think of Joe and his fire would return.

The car outside honked again.

"Well, get some rest. Don't worry about coming in tomorrow, if you were." Joe went to the door, hesitated, and then opened it. The cold air seemed to take his breath away.

Zarrin had told Joe he would see him tomorrow, and Joe had remembered. But he was right. Zarrin was in no state for the public eye. He tipped his head back to study the worried line between Joe's eyes, and the fierce glare he gave the taxi driver that the man didn't deserve, although he might not see it. It had become night, sometime while Zarrin had been unconscious, and the area outside Joe's apartment was not well lit.

Joe turned back to him, and for a fleeting moment, they stood close together. Then Joe knelt down again. "Boots," he reminded Zarrin, rough but not angry.

Zarrin allowed Joe the gesture, and resisted the urge to pet his hair while Joe helped him step into his shoes, and to lean against Joe when Joe stood up again. He simply swallowed, and nodded. "Thank you." Zarrin paused, for one more moment, and then corrected himself. "Thank you, treasure."

He wanted nothing more than to stay with Joe and call him treasure until the uncertainty was gone from his eyes. But he was dragon, and he had shown enough weakness in front of his boy for one day. So he lifted his chin and walked down the steps to the alley below in his big, clumsy boots, and pretended he felt no pain.

# CHAPTER 9

JOE DIDN'T know whether to blame being too wound up from the previous day's events to sleep well, or if he was still thrown from how Zarrin kept calling him that word he couldn't think about while at work. It didn't help that the town was in a barely controlled state of panic.

The crack in the street didn't look serious now that he was calmer. It was more like a bad paving job had been exposed by the two quakes, and none of the older buildings in town had suffered any damage more serious than things falling off shelves. Nonetheless, people were rattled.

Then word had gotten out about Zarrin.

Joe wasn't sure how or where that had happened. At the hospital, probably, or a sheriff's deputy with a big mouth, but he supposed it was news, and it did affect the town. He just didn't know how to feel about seeing "Local Dragon Attacked!" on the cover of the regional newspaper.

It was a Friday a few weeks before Christmas, which should have meant people taking off early to drive into the city to go shopping over the weekend, but people coming into the shop were staying. They wanted to talk about Zarrin, and anyone who had been paying attention knew the coffee shop was Zarrin's favorite place to be in town, and why.

Joe couldn't deny it anymore either. He still didn't understand, but even pale and shaky on his feet, Zarrin had wanted him to know it. He had kept using that word, which Joe could barely think about without dropping the cup in his hands or knocking over a milk pitcher.

Martin had finally made him work the register, where he could do less damage. Of course, that had put Joe right in the front lines of all the panicky gossip about Zarrin and the Preserve, and what the family might do in response to this.

People were crazy if they thought the family was going to punish anyone in town for something they'd had no control over. But people were as nervous as Zarrin whenever the Xu family was mentioned, and Joe… didn't want to think about that either.

Or Zarrin alone in that big empty house, or Zarrin pretending he hadn't been in pain as he'd hobbled down the steps to Jamie's waiting taxi.

It was good Zarrin hadn't come into the shop today. Swarms of concerned or fearful people might have overwhelmed him. He would have needed help he wouldn't have asked for, because dragons weren't supposed to need help from humans for some stupid reason, and then if Joe had interfered, Zarrin would have gotten that look on his face.

Joe didn't know how to describe it, except that when he'd lifted his head and seen Zarrin staring down at him, he'd gotten so warm he'd forgotten about his broken heater. Whenever he remembered it, he'd stumble over his own feet, or get someone's order wrong. After a few hours, even Jessie had noticed his distraction.

At the end of his shift, he gratefully left the shop and made a beeline for his car. The colored pencil set was still there, and he brought it inside before he started to clean up the traces of Zarrin's blood that had transferred from his hands to the steering wheel. His coat hadn't been so easy to clean. He'd thrown it out at the hospital, which left him with sweaters and sweatshirts and the thinner coat he wore in the fall. He couldn't make himself care, though, despite the expense of buying a new one.

Cleaning his car distracted him for another hour, but seeing Zarrin's blood reminded him of the bruises across Zarrin's stomach, and the gold along his back marred by bandages, and the little sounds of pain Zarrin had made while getting dressed.

Then Joe was on his knees again in his mind, on his fucking knees in front of Zarrin, who had been wearing his clothes, and honestly, Joe didn't know what he'd been thinking. Forrester had caught him off guard, he'd never liked hospitals, and Zarrin had been naked in his bed. Naturally Joe hadn't been thinking clearly.

But that look sent fire into his veins, and that word made his heart pound and his palms itch. Everyone in town had known, and yet somehow

Joe was still in shock about it. It wasn't an accident and he couldn't deny it. Zarrin had looked him in the eye and called him *treasure*.

Joe washed his hands and kicked his next-to-useless heater and pulled a sweater over his henley so the cold wouldn't bother him while he drew. He only got one step toward his studio before a tentative knock at the door stopped him.

It wasn't his mother. Her knocks were not quiet, because she was a wise woman who had raised him through his teen years, and knew how to announce her presence before entering a room. Anyway, he'd texted her during a break today, a quick line to tell her not to worry, in case she saw the paper or heard a rumor. She probably already had, but was waiting for him to talk to her first. He would have if he'd known what to tell her.

He went to the door and then stood there staring at Zarrin without managing a word.

Zarrin was dressed in another cashmere sweater and his thick black coat, with his silly knitted hat pulled over his ears and a scarf wrapped high around his throat. His scooter was parked down in the alley behind him, and in his hands he had Joe's folded up clothes. He'd set Joe's boots on the ground by his feet.

Zarrin was startled, as if he hadn't expected Joe to be home. He was so close he had to tilt his head back a bit to meet Joe's gaze. He was so close, Joe could smell the clean smoke of him and see shadows of sleeplessness beneath Zarrin's eyes.

Joe's heart began to race. They had never stood together without a counter between them. The day before, Joe hadn't realized that because Zarrin had been in pain, but today Zarrin was standing straight and his skin was rich with color again, and he was staring at Joe as if equally amazed at this development. He was at Joe's doorstep, and there was no one around but the two of them.

"I didn't expect to see you today" was what Joe finally said and then, "You look better." That it wasn't the best thing to have said occurred to him when Zarrin's expression turned stricken. Joe tripped over his tongue when he tried to keep going. "You were fine up in the house?"

"Perfectly fine," Zarrin responded, but then ducked his head. "I've been to the sheriff's station this morning already." His voice got even quieter. "And spoken with my parents. I… I wasn't in the mood for coffee today. I'm sorry I wasn't there."

Joe's stomach tied itself into a knot. He hadn't expected Zarrin, and was glad he hadn't gone into the shop if he was feeling tired or vulnerable, but saying that felt obvious and stupid. "How about tea?" he asked instead, with his mouth dry. "I could make you a cup."

"The tea yesterday was very calming." Zarrin was giving Joe that look again, as if Joe offering him tea was somehow life's greatest and best surprise. "But I already took so much from you."

"It was my pleasure." Joe's mouth was running away from him, as if the knowledge that they were totally alone was enough to make him forget himself. "I mean, we dealt with that already yesterday." Finally, *finally*, Joe came to his senses enough to cross his arms and step back. He kept his voice down. "Did you want to come in?"

Zarrin's stunned blink made him resemble the deer he protected. But he stepped into the apartment and looked around before giving a small sigh. Joe bent down to pick up his boots and place them inside before he closed the door. When he turned around, Zarrin was in front of his bed.

The bed was not made. Joe had slept in it as it was, which Zarrin might notice if he paid attention. That knowledge seemed like way too much to have between them when Joe could barely form a decent sentence.

"Here." Joe came forward to take the clothes from him and set them on the dresser, then went to the kitchen to give himself a moment to calm down. "Make yourself comfortable, if you want. I'll get the tea."

He was being ridiculous. Zarrin had already seen his tiny apartment, and was only returning his clothes. Joe knew better than to get excited over ultimately meaningless gestures. But he put water on to boil and then came back out to find Zarrin exactly where he'd left him, but staring at the door to his studio.

Joe cleared his throat. "How did it go with the sheriff?"

Zarrin focused back on him. "The sheriff seemed afraid of me, so I spoke with your friend Forrester again." He continued before Joe could protest that Forrester was not his friend. "He recorded what I said, and explained what might happen if those men do not plead guilty. Although they are both still in the hospital, and that apparently delays things. He also said if there is no trial, my scales will be returned to me. Otherwise, I will have to wait. There is a service they use to guard magical items that become evidence in a crime. Everlasting is too small for a magical practitioner of that skill level, it seems. Or, at least, the sheriff's department doesn't have the budget to pay one."

Joe gave a start. "I… kept the ashes from the fire you started at the shop, if you want them. I didn't keep them for myself, but people wanted them, and it didn't seem right to give them away."

"You didn't want them?" Zarrin tipped his head to study him. Joe shined to fairies, and apparently smelled okay to werewolves, but he had no idea what Zarrin saw when he stared at him like that. "I could give them to you. I don't mind, you see, if you ask. If they had asked, perhaps I…." He trailed off.

"I thought I'd give them to Hazel—that's the little girl who asked for your fire." Joe had never fought so hard to have a normal conversation. But if *Forrester* told him he needed to calm down, then he probably did, if only for Zarrin's sake.

Zarrin nodded. "I'll trust your choice." As though that was the least of the things Zarrin was worried about, he glanced to the bed. "If you don't mind, I—" He cut himself off and dropped down to sit on the edge of the mattress. "I'm no longer in pain, but I'm very tired today."

"Of course you are." Joe scowled at him and then shook his head. "You should never have gone back to the house in your condition. You should have rested more. My mother works as a caregiver, and that is one of the worst things people do to themselves. Instead of recovering properly somewhere comfortable and safe, they try to go home, or take care of themselves. Did you even sleep?"

"I am dragon, Joseph," Zarrin argued quietly, watching Joe with fascination all over his face.

"I know you're dragon, Zarrin." Joe crossed his arms. "Did you even sleep?" he repeated, pointedly.

"The house protected me." Zarrin exhaled, a bit shakily. "Forrester said the men must have stayed in the state park after they set their trap. If I hadn't woken, the wards most likely would have sent them running soon anyway." He avoided a direct answer, but Joe took it as confirmation that Zarrin had been too frightened to sleep. Zarrin clasped his hands together. His nails were bitten to the quick. "I spoke to my parents. They… know. Not all of it. I couldn't tell them everything."

"Okay." Joe didn't know what else to say to that. He didn't lie to his mother, but he also was deliberately avoiding speaking to her at the moment. She'd want to know if the rumors about Zarrin hanging around the coffee shop were true, and then she'd want to know why, and Joe couldn't talk about that when *he* wasn't even sure. "Hold on."

He went to the kitchen to fix Zarrin's tea, and brought out his mug with the tea still steeping.

Zarrin took it with both hands. "A more powerful dragon wouldn't feel the need to lie. They're probably right not to trust me with this treasure by myself."

"Those men weren't after the Preserve. They were after you." Yeah. Joe was not calm, at all, and he still wasn't over the fact that Forrester of all people had picked up on it and tried to help him. An ally, even a silent one, might have meant the world back in high school when Joe had been accused of stealing boyfriends, or turning them gay, or seducing them, or using magic, or whatever rumor Mads had started every day until Joe had left town at the end of that summer. But he hardly needed one now. "Fish and Game went out there for *you*. There's nothing wrong with accepting help," he added, and heard himself. But he wasn't in the mood for any dramatic personal revelations.

Zarrin stared at him through berry-scented steam. "You really don't mind? You don't think I'd fail to protect you?"

Joe shied away from even the idea of that. "I didn't ask to be protected."

"But you should be." Zarrin had the softest kitten voice sometimes, young and innocent and as dangerous as little baby claws. "As the rarest of treasures should be watched over and kept safe."

Joe stood stock-still while sparks traveled up and down his spine, and his heart rate tripled, and his every nerve ending came to life. He took a breath and realized he was staring at the ground. Nobody said things like that. Nobody *believed* things like that. And if they did, they forgot about it the second someone else found out about it.

Zarrin didn't even know him, and they weren't mated werewolves, despite the fact that Zarrin had only slept peacefully once they'd brought him to Joe's home. That was probably because the hospital had been unfamiliar, and he at least knew Joe.

"I didn't come here to upset you," Zarrin added, when Joe didn't answer, and Joe finally looked back up.

"I know." He *did* know that. He also knew Zarrin didn't know enough about humans to realize they didn't say things like that. "You've been trying to be friends with me this entire time," Joe went on, although Zarrin didn't look at him like any friend. Zarrin, as everyone in town knew, wanted to fuck him.

Joe could let him, and take care of his attentive-dragon problem in one night, maybe two. He'd refused in the first place out of spite and stubbornness. Zarrin was already in his bed. Joe could cross the room and kiss him and ask for a fuck. He could pretend it didn't mean anything, and let the town think whatever it wanted when Zarrin forgot all about Joe and the coffee shop, or someday came home to Everlasting with a proper dragon spouse.

"Friends?" Zarrin gave Joe a weak smile. "Yes, of course. I should go before I take up any more of your time. You've already been too kind, and you must have plans, and I should—"

"If you haven't eaten, I was going to make something." The gruffness in Joe's voice only made the invitation more ludicrous. "I was up early and missed lunch."

"You were very busy at work?" Zarrin sipped at his tea despite the steam still rising. "Because of the holidays, or… oh, the earthquakes. Forrester mentioned them. I was… I've never done that before, and I wasn't sure if I should be in public. Were people expecting to see me?"

"Actually, they were mostly worried about you." Joe was just relieved Zarrin hadn't noticed his stupid invitation to stay for dinner, and didn't feel like mentioning that some of the people in town were also afraid that Zarrin or his family would punish them. Or that everyone seemed to expect Joe to know Zarrin's condition and to be able to smooth things over for them.

"My scales will take a while to grow back, but I'm fine. Even a small, weak dragon like me is harder to kill than that." Zarrin wrinkled his nose and sent a puff of smoke up to the ceiling. Then he slowly lowered his head to consider Joe. "I spoke to Bernard this morning as well."

"Your housekeeper?" Joe tried to follow the conversation, but Zarrin had him flushed and confused even without non sequiturs.

"Bernard says advice from weres is only good for other weres." Zarrin leaned over to set his cup of tea on the table next to the bed. "But that Marie may have had a point. He says the way humans do things is to get to know one another and *then* express a more obvious interest. Unless of course my objective was simply a fuck, in which case only the first step would apply."

His gaze was very, very serious.

"Your housekeeper said that?" Joe wondered hoarsely.

Zarrin nodded. "Elves tend to be practical. Marie's advice, however, was responding to instinct and emotion." Here, Zarrin paused to wet his bottom lip and take a deep breath. Almost immediately, his pupils dilated. He licked his lip again before continuing. "Yesterday, you thought I was being foolish because I was upset. Today I am less upset, so I will say it again. *Joseph*, you are so, so good."

"Zarrin?" Joe's voice cracked like he was thirteen again.

Zarrin stood up and walked the few feet over to him. He was larger with every step, taller and grander and more gold, despite the knitted cap and the heavy coat. Heat and smoke snaked out around him and climbed through the air like vines.

"You worry so much, and I don't want you to," he began, and then slowly, cautiously, put his hands to Joe's chest. "You thought I was with Marie, and you were hurt, but you came to me anyway and you made me tea. I didn't mean to make you think that. I wouldn't ever want you to think you weren't special to me."

"Special?" Joe could barely hear himself.

Zarrin nodded solemnly. "It is too early to claim you, which even Marie admitted, but Bernard is also right. Dragons can sometimes demand instead of ask, or assume others understand our history and why we behave the way we do. He says I should make my interest in you clear, for your sake." He stopped there and swallowed before going on. "May I kiss you?"

His bottom lip was shining. His gaze was bright and interested and not shy. He curled one hand into the fabric of Joe's sweater, and Joe realized why when he tilted his head down without stopping to say yes. He'd lost his mind, but the smoke had him dizzy, and Zarrin's mouth was soft.

Zarrin licked at him, a tiny, curious taste at the bow of Joe's lip, and then gave him another slow kiss of light pressure and lingering heat, and when he finally pulled away, Joe's lips were parted. Joe leaned down without thinking, following the tug of Zarrin's hand at his sweater, and then Zarrin was small again and stretched up to meet him.

This kiss made Joe shiver, or maybe that was the heat of Zarrin's body. Joe felt the barest of pressures, and then Zarrin leaned away.

Zarrin was out of breath. "It was very difficult to stop."

"Then why did you?" Joe hated that his voice rose on the question and that Zarrin would hear it. He thought of being Zarrin's, in that bed not ten feet away, and bit down hard to keep from saying anything else needy.

Zarrin gave him that look again, but this time Joe had a lot of words for it, like *tender* and *proud* and *possessive*, and each one sent a tremor through him. "Because when I call you treasure, you don't believe me." His hand was still in Joe's sweater. "And that's what Marie tried to tell me. But I wanted you to know. I thought of this all last night when I couldn't sleep. If men like that ever come again, I wanted you to at least know I'm not like the one who hurt you. That I value your kindness, and I want you, and I… I don't know how to feel when you say you don't mind how soft I am."

Joe caught his breath, and Zarrin clutched tighter at him. "But it's harder to let you go than I thought it would be," he added, in a confiding tone, and stared at his hand as if willing himself to release Joe's sweater. "I would like to keep kissing you, and give you everything you have ever wanted, and call you treasure in front of everyone. But that is not what you need." He peeked up, as if he weren't the mysterious, potent dragon who had stolen Joe's reason with a few kisses. "I think I am a 'sugar daddy,' as Marie claimed. Do you mind?"

"Mind?" Joe repeated blankly, then took a few deep breaths that didn't do anything to calm him. "Half the town already thinks you fuck me on the regular."

Zarrin mouthed, "On the regular," as if he'd never heard the phrase before, then stared fiercely up at Joe. "Tell me who insults you, and I will take care of them."

That, at least, brought Joe back to his senses. "I told you I don't need protecting."

Zarrin settled back on his heels and splayed the hand at Joe's chest. The pressure of his palm against Joe's heart seemed to steady him. "You did say that," Zarrin answered, without actually agreeing with him. "But I can't help wanting to."

Joe stood there like Zarrin's small hand was holding him in place. Zarrin had been the one in danger, which Zarrin obviously knew, so Joe held back his argument. But it must have been in his expression anyway.

"Don't frown," Zarrin chided him.

"You were unconscious and you were bleeding." Joe grunted. "Don't tell me not to frown." He thought he was shaking again. "You don't know what that was like." He hated that he couldn't stop thinking about it. It shouldn't have mattered. He barely knew Zarrin. They hadn't really met as kids. They'd known each other a few months at best, and Zarrin wasn't going to stay in Everlasting forever. Joe glared at him despite all of those very good reasons. "Then you left."

Zarrin's mouth fell open. He stared at Joe without blinking, then sniffed the air like Marie did.

"Oh." Zarrin took his hand from Joe's chest, only to put it back. He curled his fingers into Joe's shirt and this time his grip was tight. "You would have preferred me to stay?" he wondered quietly and left Joe to burn with embarrassment, because yes, he'd wanted Zarrin to stay and he'd just admitted it.

"I thought I would seem stronger if I returned home, and I had things to see to. But—" Zarrin straightened and yet didn't grow an inch. "I should have seen to you too."

Joe shook his head, a bit late to deny anything, but he tried anyway. "You were hurt, scared, and—"

"Joseph." Zarrin cut him off. "I'm here now. Would you still like me to stay for dinner?"

So Zarrin had understood Joe's stupid, hopeful invitation. Joe regarded him silently, the wide, earnest eyes, the knitted hat Zarrin must have forgotten he had on. This was a mistake, but he said it anyway, "Yes," and then stood there in startled panic as he realized what he'd done.

ZARRIN PEERED around Joe's shoulder to watch in fascination as Joe slowly stirred a beaten egg into boiling broth and noodles.

"You're really interested in this?" Joe seemed confused at Zarrin's presence in his kitchen, which was exactly as small as Joe had said it was.

Zarrin absently waved the question away as the egg cooked and formed ribbons around the soft noodles. “Is it time? Can I add the peas now?”

Joe had pulled a bag of peas from his freezer and run a bowlful under the tap to thaw them out. He said vegetables were important, even on a budget, and since Bernard would have agreed, Zarrin had to as well.

Joe gave him a funny look for his excitement, but nodded, so Zarrin grabbed the bowl and dumped it in.

“It’s just ramen,” Joe said, for the fourth time. “Six for a dollar ramen with stuff added in.”

Zarrin leaned into the steam to inhale the scent of dinner. He was suddenly ravenous. He hadn’t felt like eating last night, and he’d been too nervous before going to see the sheriff this morning to attempt food today. But this smelled salty and interesting, and Joe prepared it with such sure motions.

“Bernard never let me help cook,” Zarrin confessed, so some of his excitement would make sense to Joe, and let Joe scoot him back so he could turn off the stove and grab another bowl. Joe stirred the noodles for another minute, then used a big slotted spoon to drain the pot over the sink.

He gave Zarrin the larger portion of the noodles, Zarrin noticed, and then put the rest in the bowl that had held the peas. He nudged a bottle of hot sauce at Zarrin after giving him a fork.

Joe continued to frown, but that was understandable. Zarrin could have kept kissing Joe—he *wanted* to keep kissing Joe—but Joe was also upset, and he’d started trembling the moment he’d said yes, so Zarrin was giving him space, as Marie might say.

But not too much space. Joe had invited him, after all, and Zarrin was hungry.

He gave himself as generous a splash of hot sauce as Joe had done, then followed Joe out to the living room—or bedroom, or dining room.

After a moment of hesitation, Joe went into his studio and came out pushing a rolling chair in front of him. He sat in it and waved for Zarrin to use the bed. Zarrin was more than happy to.

Perhaps Joe was right and Zarrin shouldn’t have left this bed yesterday. He perched on the edge of the mattress and dug into his noodle bowl. The hot sauce felt like it was burning his lips and teasing his tongue at the same time and he loved it. He hopped up to go to the kitchen to add more and then came back to finish the bowl.

Joe stopped for a moment but then slowly resumed eating once Zarrin did. "Don't like it?"

Zarrin slurped up a stray noodle, then licked the red sauce from his lips. "It's very good. I approve of the hot sauce." His mouth tasted like chiles and salt. The steam was warming and fragrant. Joe must enjoy this a lot in his cold apartment.

Although the temperature had been rising for some time. Zarrin couldn't help it, and anyway, Joe didn't seem to mind. He didn't even appear to really notice, although he'd removed his sweater and pushed up the sleeves of his work henley a while ago.

"You genuinely like it?" Joe was quiet as Zarrin cleaned his bowl. "It's basic, cheap food, with a lot of sodium."

"It's hot and filling." Zarrin shrugged. "That's really all I require, although I did enjoy the sriracha. I'll have to get some. Can you put it on pizza?"

Joe opened and then closed his mouth before simply nodding. He ducked back over his bowl in the next second. Zarrin carried his empty dish to the kitchen with a sad sigh, then returned to the bed. Joe's bed was arranged with the long side against the wall. Zarrin had a mighty desire to lie down in it, and bent down to unlace his boots and remove them. "Eat," he encouraged Joe, who was now staring at him again, and hopped up onto the bed. Since he'd just eaten, he pulled the pillows over to prop him up against the headboard. Then he sighed and put his head on his hand to watch Joe. "You should eat more, treasure. Don't skip meals."

Joe's eyes met his before slowly traveling over the rest of him. He opened his mouth again, then shoveled in the last of his noodles and got up. Zarrin listened to the sounds of running water while digging his nose into one of Joe's pillows. The salty clean human scent on them was making him light-headed. Joe had slept in this bed without changing the sheets first. Zarrin was going to think of that so much when he got home.

He wriggled into the quilts in approval and slid a curious look Joe's way when Joe finally returned from the kitchen. He was holding a glass of water, which he brought over to Zarrin the same way he brought him tea—which was to say, he clearly liked doing it, but was anxious about Zarrin's reaction, and his private worries made him keep his distance.

Zarrin took the glass with eager hands. "Mine," he told Joe, because Joe should see how pleased he was, and had a drink. "Thank you, treasure, but you don't need to wait on me."

"You keep—" Joe cleared his throat. "All that wonder for some noodles and hot sauce?" His expression was softer than a frown, and one Zarrin had never seen on his face before. His hands twitched. "What happens when you get used to them? You're like a god in an old story, the kind who walked among humans and got in trouble."

Zarrin turned his head to the side and pushed out his lower lip in a pout. "Not fair. I can't tell if you're complimenting me or insulting me."

"I don't know either," Joe answered, which brought Zarrin's head back around. Joe tapped the arm of his rolling chair, then inhaled sharply. "Can I…. I don't usually do this. Not ever, in fact, but you look like…. Can I draw you? You don't have to say yes." Joe tried to scowl and rescind the question, but Zarrin had heard it and would never forget it.

"I didn't used to draw portraits all that much," Joe went on, head down so he didn't see Zarrin curling into his pile of quilts and rolling his face against Joe's pillow in delight. "Natural scenes are easier. I don't like a lot of people."

"You like many people, but you hesitate to show it," Zarrin corrected him, because Joe was being very silly. The wounds on Zarrin's back pulled when he moved, but Zarrin didn't care as he took another drink of water to empty the glass. He abandoned it at the corner of the mattress and then angled his head up. "Should I pose?"

Joe appeared frozen. His eyes were so beautiful it was a crime that no one had ever drawn him. "You want to?" he asked Zarrin, strangely slow to pick up this obvious fact, but then he tossed his head. "No, don't pose. Just be you. I—" He moved his hands again, then rose to his feet and went into his studio.

Zarrin couldn't see far inside that room from where he was, although he noted papers and paint all along one wall. Joe emerged with a pencil behind his ear, and a pad of paper and a wooden case in his hands. Blood rushed in Zarrin's ears as he noticed the case. He swallowed dryly as Joe placed it on the bed, but Joe didn't say a word about it, or even glance Zarrin's way. And yet somehow Zarrin felt Joe knew Zarrin was holding his breath in excitement to see him using it. Joe didn't miss much about people, despite how he claimed he didn't like them.

Now Zarrin was going to help him create. This was the best thing he could have done today. Humans were not all terrible. Some of them were worth every scale a dragon possessed.

Joe ran his hands along the outside of the case so lovingly Zarrin was almost jealous. Then he leaned back to drag his chair closer so he could sit down. He flipped open the pad of paper and then looked at Zarrin again. The stare was searching and yet absent as he opened the pencil set. Rows and rows of colors displayed themselves for him, and Zarrin did not think it was his imagination that the air in the room went still. Joe passed a hand over the pencils and gave a start.

He pulled out one pencil at what looked like random, but Zarrin now knew it wasn't, before he sat down. He put the colored pencil—a dull sort of gold—on the edge of the mattress next to Zarrin's abandoned glass, then reached for the pencil behind his ear.

He focused on Zarrin, and Zarrin had to fight not to lean forward to pet him. The strong lines of Joe's face had softened with his mind focused on his art. Maybe he wasn't aware of it, and Zarrin had no intention of telling him and ruining the moment. Joe studied him with all the intensity that dragons were supposed to have and then blinked like someone just waking up.

"You don't have to," Joe said again, his voice muzzy.

Zarrin slowly shook his head. "I'm not going anywhere," he whispered, so as not to break the spell, and stayed motionless until Joe's fingers tightened around his pencil.

After a while, Zarrin settled down to get more comfortable. Joe's desire to sketch him amazed him, but he was also tired, and Joe's bed was warm and smelled of them together. Anyway, Joe was too busy to notice Zarrin staring at him.

Zarrin licked his lips as the hot sauce flavor slowly disappeared, and slipped out of his coat and scarf. He discovered, to his horror, that he'd forgotten to take off his hat when he'd come inside the house. But once he covertly stuffed it out of sight, he had no way to deal with his messy hair.

Joe noticed. He smiled a little when Zarrin ripped the hat off, but didn't stop whatever he was sketching. Zarrin glowered at him for a few minutes, then gave up and continued his slow push to end up back under the mountain of quilts Joe kept on his bed. When his sweater became too much, he removed that too.

Joe paused, gradually pulling his attention from his pad of paper to scowl at Zarrin's long-sleeved thermal shirt. He flicked his pencil against his sketchbook, then turned to a new page and started again.

He was so very handsome; it wasn't fair. The furrow in his brow was due to concentration this time, but Zarrin thought about running his fingertips over it to smooth it away. He might then drag them to Joe's mouth and push at his lower lip with his thumb while leaning closer to share Joe's breath. And Joe would part his lips and look up at him as he had yesterday.

The memory of that look made Zarrin breathe harder. It was too easy to imagine Joe on his knees again, and how his hair would slide through Zarrin's fingers as Zarrin drew him closer. He would be so good to him. He would lavish Joe's mouth with praise, and fuck him gently when he wanted, and roughly if he did not want gentle.

Zarrin opened his eyes at the realization that he was thinking about fucking Joe's mouth in the very bed he was lying in.

Joe stared back at him. For one tense moment, he didn't move, and then he swallowed and bent down over his work.

Zarrin sat up to keep himself from getting carried away again. But it was so difficult with Joe right there.

"I never thought I'd be here." Zarrin kept his voice low, so it wouldn't bother Joe too much. "I hoped. But I thought you hated me."

Joe was just as quiet. "I never hated you. I was… confused. You're very confusing."

"I don't mean to be," Zarrin grumbled and hugged a pillow. "You're one to talk. You make it so difficult to really see you."

Joe paused again before glancing over. "Can I ask you something?" He traded his regular pencil for the gold one, Zarrin noted with interest, before nodding for Joe to go ahead. Joe's touch with this pencil seemed lighter, as if he was adding details. "That painting you showed me. Did you really think it was lonely?"

Zarrin didn't have to think about it. "Yes. That's why I liked it."

Joe made a few more strokes with his pencil. "Most people would say it was a pretty painting of some trees."

Zarrin slumped into the pillows again. "I suppose I was very lonely to imagine that, then."

Joe continued to draw with his gaze fixed on the sketch pad in his lap. "I was lonely when I made it."

The softly spoken words almost sent Zarrin bolting from the bed. "That was your painting?" he demanded. Joe startled and looked up. Zarrin crawled closer to him. "That lovely, aching moment was yours? Why didn't you tell me?" A horrible thought occurred to him, and he froze. "You must have hated me. I tried to give it away! But I didn't want to."

"I know." Joe didn't blink. "You wouldn't let go of it."

"It's hanging in my bedroom," Zarrin confessed eagerly. "My painting of Joe's. *Mine*." The glazed brightness of Joe's eyes was fascinating. "You told me you were happy I had it, and I didn't fully believe you, but look at you." He leaned forward and clutched the bedding. "If you tell me where to find it, I will buy all of your work and decorate my lair with it."

"Zarrin!" Joe protested, wary again, or hurt and hiding it with caution. "It's enough. The one picture is enough. More than enough. You—" He made a face at his sketch pad, then blinked as if noticing for the first time what he'd drawn. He immediately flipped the page to the previous one. "I'm not that good yet anyway. I still haven't gotten you right."

"You've drawn me before?" Zarrin asked in surprise, and saw the answer in Joe's stiff shoulders.

Joe went on doggedly, as if he didn't see Zarrin inching toward him. "It wasn't wrong, how I drew you, but it wasn't you either. It's still not. Although this is better."

"Let me see!" Zarrin all but howled at him and stared at Joe imploringly. "Please?"

Joe locked eyes with him, then looked away as he held out his sketch pad.

Zarrin took it with a barely contained tremor and a puff of white smoke that rose to the ceiling. He grasped at the paper and turned the page to the one Joe was worried about, and reminded himself to be gentle, to take care, as he pulled it to his lap to see himself as Joe saw him.

He was not expecting a restless, troubled boy to stare back at him, with shadows beneath his eyes and his arms tight around a pillow. His shirt pulled up at his waist to bare a hint of thin skin, shaded gold. Zarrin put a finger there, to touch or soothe or to gently pull his shirt down; he wasn't sure what impulse he felt, or what Joe had.

Joe cleared his throat. Zarrin ignored this and went to the next page.

A dragon looked up at him, a real one to rival Dìzhèn, spread across pillows and mounds of blankets. His shirt had ridden up to expose naked skin, the lines of his hips, the low tug of his waistband. The things around him were indistinct and hazy, but his eyes were sharp and hot. His hands were caught in a moment of pleasure, pushing and pulling at the bedding. His head was raised in expectation, or command.

"You have a way of looking at me. Everyone's noticed." Joe crossed his arms, a hint of nervous motion at the edge of Zarrin's vision. "You never did anything about it, though."

"I see," Zarrin said, faintly, and raised his head. Joe was frowning at the sketch pad. Zarrin closed it and put it to the side without taking his eyes off him. He couldn't tell if Joe was furious or relieved. He was definitely embarrassed.

Strangely, so was Zarrin. He was small and weak, and he was golden and on fire for Joe. He licked his mouth, but the air gave him no answers.

"I could do something about it now?" he said, but it came out as more of a question. "If you want. *I* want."

"I know." Joe shivered. "*Everyone* knows. You look like…." He raised his head, but didn't explain what Zarrin looked like. "I want too," he added, as if the admission had been dragged from him.

But he didn't move. Zarrin waited and then scooted forward to put his feet on the floor. Joe seemed alarmed for a moment, as wary as any deer when they first crossed paths with Zarrin, and inhaled sharply when Zarrin stood in front of him.

Zarrin hesitated, more because he was struck by Joe's expression than for any fear. Hunters and their greed were frightening. Joe was not. He shivered when Zarrin put a palm against his cheek, and he let Zarrin's thumb rest at his mouth. His hair was silk in Zarrin's other hand, sliding easily free of its hairband to fall over his fingers.

Zarrin wanted to do so many things with, and to, Joseph. But he would be no kind of dragon to think of them now while Joe was anxious.

He petted along Joe's cheekbone and traced the shell of his pretty ear, and felt like Dìzhèn the Great when Joe closed his eyes.

"Don't tremble," Zarrin told Joe, in someone else's voice, someone calm and firm and there to think only of his treasure. "I'll give you anything. Tell me, and it's yours."

"People don't say things like that, Zarrin," Joe protested quietly, with his face partially turned toward Zarrin's palm.

"Dragons do," Zarrin corrected him, eyes intent on Joe's mouth as Joe's lips grazed his skin. "*I* do. Tell me." He ran his thumb along the edge of Joe's mouth, and Joe parted his lips.

A spike of electricity in the air made it difficult to stand still.

"I want that too," Zarrin admitted, his voice a little rough with surprise and arousal. How lucky he was. How good Joe was, to be so brave. He stroked Joe's cheek and pushed against the softness of Joe's lip. "Like yesterday?" he wondered, smoothing the line of worry from between Joe's eyes, then letting his thumb slip into Joe's mouth. Zarrin whimpered, but he thought anyone would have, in his situation.

Joe opened his eyes. His skin was very hot to the touch, even to a dragon. His need was making Zarrin dizzy, but he felt strong and daring.

"I thought of it," Zarrin admitted in a whisper. His throat was too tight to allow anything louder. "All through the night when I couldn't sleep, I remembered you on your knees for me. You're so pretty, treasure, I couldn't help it."

Joe closed his eyes again and leaned forward to breathe heavily against Zarrin's waist. Zarrin gave a small start at the unexpectedness of it, the needy sound of Joe's panting, then tentatively put his hand to the back of Joe's head. Joe reached up, and Zarrin shuddered at the feel of Joe's hands at his fly.

He licked the scent of desire from the air, and wondered if he should speak again, if he *could* with Joe's mouth on him. Then Joe exhaled against the bared skin at his hip, and shoved Zarrin's pants down with blind impatience.

Zarrin heard himself rumbling with pleasure. "Very good," he praised, smoky-voiced, and moaned for Joe's mouth wetting his cock. His hand fell to the nape of Joe's neck, and he focused on that, on holding steady and not immediately thrusting forward to come down Joe's throat.

He had waited so long already; he could wait a bit longer despite his tremors and fierce roar he barely kept back.

Joe took a little more of Zarrin's cock each time he moved in, and his hands splayed out on Zarrin's hip and stomach. He shivered and swallowed around more, and shivered again when Zarrin stroked the knob at the top of his spine. He was breathing hard, and when he finally buried his face against Zarrin's skin and Zarrin tightened his grip to keep him there, he moaned.

"*Oh*," Zarrin exhaled in shocked pleasure. He shut his eyes to keep from looking, to keep from coming, and held Joe there one more moment before he let Joe pull back, to breathe, to shake and swallow and then take Zarrin down his throat again.

The air itself was filled with Joe's lust, and Zarrin's fires. He grasped the fine strands of Joe's hair and held him again, easing him off, watching Joe lick spit from his lips before sucking him back down.

Letting Joe go was going to be next to impossible now.

"What else?" Speaking hurt when Zarrin wanted to roar and split the earth so everyone would know. He'd never felt like this, not with anyone else, and petted Joe with short, clumsy motions as he pulled him forward. Joe allowed it, brave one, treasure, thirsty for Zarrin to have him like this. "C… come in your mouth?" Zarrin stuttered and didn't care, although he would later. "I want to. I want to, but I won't if you—"

Joe clutched at him, and made a small sound that echoed through Zarrin's every nerve and dragged the orgasm from him.

He half bent over Joe when his legs went weak, and released Joe to grab the back of the chair to keep himself on his feet. The muffled, slick sounds of Joe's swallows and gasps for breath thrilled him. "Treasure. I'll give you everything." He couldn't say enough to answer what Joe had given him. "So pretty, aren't you? So good."

He crooked his fingers beneath Joe's chin and urged his face up, only to burn at the sight of his mouth. Joe's eyes were starry and his eyelashes were damp. He kept swallowing, and didn't move, although he must want to. He was obviously hard. Zarrin wanted to keep him, exactly as a fairy would have, exactly as Marie had said.

He wobbled slightly on his shaky legs and then shrugged and let himself fall to his knees.

Joe was wide, wet eyes and a darkly used mouth with some of Zarrin's come at the corner. He was still struggling to breathe normally, and let out a surprised, almost broken sound when Zarrin sat up to get closer between his legs.

Zarrin darted out his tongue to lick the musk from the air, then panted at him and slid his hands up Joe's parted thighs to the stiff cock pushing against his jeans. He was nearly shaking as he pushed Joe's clothing out of his way.

*Mine*, Zarrin longed to tell him, and filled his mouth with Joe's cock instead.

Joe expelled a hushed, startled breath before spreading his legs wider. He was so good. *Treasure* was so good. Zarrin wished he had more experience at this to make it perfect, but supposed it didn't matter. Joe was already twitching his hips up into Zarrin's mouth. His desire scent was on Zarrin's tongue now, the brightest he'd ever tasted, as if sucking Zarrin's cock had already brought Joe to the edge.

Zarrin used his hand with nothing more than the intent to get Joe off as quickly as possible, and kept his cock wet, and reveled in the punched-out noises coming from above him. Joe's hands tangled in his hair, then released it, then came back again and held on tight.

"—Rin." He choked on Zarrin's name and then came, gloriously hot in Zarrin's mouth.

He pulled his hands away too quickly, almost guiltily, but Zarrin continued to wring more come from him. He knew some humans didn't care for it, but to him, and he supposed to other dragons and possibly weres, it was pure desire. Proof that Joe wanted him, and had been so pleased with Zarrin's initial attempts to give him what he needed.

He had to admit he'd enjoyed using Joe's mouth like that—or letting Joe use his cock like that. He wasn't exactly sure how to define it. He would do it again, without hesitation.

He pulled off Joe's cock at last and then rested his chin on Joe's knee. Joe hadn't caught his breath yet, so Zarrin stroked the length of his thighs and gazed up at him in approval. "Good treasure, best treasure," he whispered happily, and sent puffs of smoke floating in all directions. "You were so good, better than I've ever let myself think about." His voice was a bit raspy and used, but he didn't mind.

Joe's stare was full of stars, but Zarrin could already see his worry returning. Or fear, but Zarrin didn't like to think of Joe afraid of anything.

"Joseph," he began, with his head resting on Joe's knee. "Would you think less of me if I told you I might have trouble standing up?"

"What?" Joe's frown returned, although it lessened slightly when Zarrin smiled at him.

"I didn't expect this. I'm in shock. The things you've done for me today." Zarrin placed a small kiss on Joe's knee, then peeked upward to gauge Joe's reaction. Joe appeared stunned, but not unhappy. Zarrin cleared his throat and sat up without taking his hands from him. "Would you mind if I rested here for a while?"

"Mind?" Joe reached out, then snatched his hand back in order to cross his arms over his chest. "No. Do you need help up?"

"A dragon shouldn't—"

"Require human aid, yeah, you've mentioned that," Joe interrupted in his gruff voice. "The bed would be more comfortable. I don't have a couch. I never needed one."

Joe's bed. Zarrin sighed warmly and held up a hand so Joe could pull him to his feet. The action got him another startled stare and a frown, but then Joe pushed back the chair and stood up, taking Zarrin with him.

They ended up very close. It would have been nice if Joe hadn't hesitated and then stepped back. Zarrin sighed but decided not to pursue him for the moment. Anyway, his pants were stuck at his hips and he didn't think his legs could hold him up much longer. His shuffle to the bed was awkward, but then he got to collapse face-first into the pile of comfy quilts he'd left behind. Unfortunately, his dive into the bedding sent his water glass tumbling to the floor.

It landed on the carpet, unbroken, so Zarrin sighed and wriggled farther onto the bed. He'd never bothered to straighten his pants, and part of his ass was on display, but this time Joe didn't turn away from his nudity or leave the room. He came closer.

Zarrin pushed himself all the way onto the bed and turned onto his side with his head on his hand. His cock was still wet from Joe's mouth, so naturally he touched it, idly stroking himself although at the moment he was quite satisfied.

Joe's gaze slowly traveled over him. Joe was partially undressed as well, but he didn't appear to notice as he stared at Zarrin. Zarrin stared back and licked the inside of his mouth, where the taste of Joe's pent-up need lingered.

"Want to draw me now?" Zarrin offered, leaving his clothes as they were. After a second, he let his head drop to the pillow. "I need to rest, but I liked how you drew me. Do you… do you really see me that way?" An artist with Joe's gifts was the kind to see truth. Zarrin's stomach fluttered as he imagined Joe discovering him, and putting it down on paper. He smoothed a palm over his stomach and closed his eyes.

Joe didn't answer. After a while, Zarrin cracked open an eye to look at him. Joe hadn't moved, except to straighten his clothing. His hair was still loose. Through it Zarrin could see one wide, dark eye and softly parted lips. If Zarrin was sometimes a boy with bitten nails and shadows beneath his eyes, then Joe was sometimes a young human peering out wistfully from behind a curtain.

"I'm sorry," Zarrin called up to him, in a coaxing, careful whisper. "I've never been anyone's before. Did you want to lie down with me? I should have asked."

"It's my bed," Joe answered, low and puzzled. Then, without meeting Zarrin's eye, he stepped forward to stand at the edge of the bed. "It's barely evening."

"I don't see what that has to do with it. Marie cuddled me in bed all the time. Not like that!" Zarrin added in a rush. "Just hugs while we watched TV. Werewolves touch a lot, she says."

"This isn't what I expected." Joe shook his head. "I don't know what I expected. Not this. You want me to—" His voice cracked. "—take a nap with you?"

"If you want." Zarrin found it very hard to breathe when Joe stepped out of his shoes. "Yes. Yes, I want it a lot," he went on encouragingly, and patted the bed. "Come here and let me hold you."

But Joe stopped to move the case of colored pencils carefully to the floor. Zarrin did his best not to pout over that, or to question the cautious look Joe gave him before he turned and sat on the bed. He exhaled, then leaned down onto his side in front of Zarrin. He held himself stiffly apart.

Then Zarrin scooted forward to nose at his hair and Joe trembled.

"Anyone's?" Joe wondered, as though Zarrin could remember what they'd been talking about in a moment like this. Zarrin gently pulled Joe's hair away so he could nuzzle his neck. He paused when Joe gave another shudder. But when no objections came from Joe's lovely mouth, Zarrin slipped a hand beneath Joe's shirt and stroked the warm skin of his lower back.

"I've never done anything like that before," Zarrin confessed against the shell of Joe's ear. "Was it… was I the strong sort of dragon you wanted? I hope so. It felt good to have you like that. Very good. So does this. Do you think that's strange, to want both of those things? Mmm, treasure, you have no idea how your skin feels, or your mouth." Joe was shivering. Zarrin moved his hand to Joe's stomach and urged his body closer. "Are you cold? I'll warm you. I'm good at that, if nothing else."

He dragged his lips along Joe's nape. Sweat from sex had left his skin damp. Zarrin nosed at it and swept his palm up and down Joe's stomach. He felt Joe inhale before he finally spoke.

"This is what you want?" Joe's voice was husky, different but not unpleasant.

"Among other things." Zarrin hummed at him, sleepy and sated and quite content to pet Joseph for hours. He licked curiously over some of the tattooing and then considered mouthing at the skin until a bruise formed. "This will make up for not being able to sleep last night." He thought about it, then decided to add one more warning to appease Marie. "It's a pleasure to have you here, but I'll try not to hold you if you want to move."

Joe shifted to ease one shoulder forward. The action tugged at his shirt, displaying more skin for Zarrin's mouth. "You want to hold me?" His serious words ended in a gasp when Zarrin scraped lightly at the tattoos with his teeth. The ink he could never touch would vex him until his dying day.

*Mine*, Zarrin wanted to tell him again, with his mouth and hands pressed to Joe's skin. But even Zarrin wasn't that foolish. "Yes," he said instead, and focused on warmth, on heat, on anything to stop the shivers Joe couldn't hide.

# CHAPTER 10

JOE WOKE with his body cocooned in heat and a heavy, languid sensation in his bones, as if he'd been asleep for days. His toes weren't cold despite his bare feet, and when he turned his head, the pillow under his cheek was pleasantly warm.

He opened his eyes, and Zarrin was standing at the side of his bed, fully dressed, except for his knitted hat. The shy smile on his face turned the anxious swoop of Joe's stomach into a shivery flutter.

The room was fairly light, as if it was morning, which it might have been. Joe had a sudden memory of waking up once or twice to a dark apartment, with a large body next to him. He'd felt trapped in his jeans and shirt, so he'd pulled away to remove them. He'd been so tired, and the weight across his legs—Zarrin's *tail*, he realized with distant shock—had felt so secure, he'd scooted back until he'd been against Zarrin's body with that weight—that *tail*—tucked around him.

He'd fallen asleep next to a dragon, which was alarming even before he considered that he had never, ever spent the entire night with someone he'd slept with. He was disturbingly well-rested, and frowned because that *shouldn't be*.

"Zarrin?" he asked, in a rough, early morning voice, because a large part of him had not expected to wake up to find Zarrin there.

Zarrin's eyebrows came together in a frown that signaled a possible eruption as much as the tufts of smoke curling through the air.

"Who else would it be?" Zarrin demanded with narrowed eyes, but then stopped himself. He sucked in a long breath, and unclenched his hands before nodding slowly. "You're human and sensitive. I keep forgetting. Obviously, you can have many… you can have… if you're… if you're seeing someone else, I won't hurt them, because that is your right as a human who does not understand the way things are." Zarrin forced out the words through a low growl, then gave Joe a wide-eyed, pleading stare. "You aren't, are you? You'd tell me, wouldn't you? I know I have no right to make you my boy yet, but I thought… last night…."

The Son of Krakatoa vanished and in its place was Zarrin, soft and nervous.

Joe sat up and realized how naked he was. He'd taken off his socks and underwear as well last night. *Fantastic.* "Are you jealous?" He was going to blame the question on pleasant dreams and his sleepy, foggy thinking.

"Of course," Zarrin hissed at him. "You're *Joe*. They all want you, even the ones who act like they hate you."

Joe looked at him, then rubbed his eyes and looked again. Zarrin was serious.

"They don't want me, Zarrin," Joe explained, very slowly. "Some of them think I'm a troublemaking, uppity slut, and the rest have done everything but serve me to you on a platter."

"Serve you? You mean, offer you?" Zarrin fell back a step. "You didn't want me?" he wondered sharply. "Last night wasn't real?" He began to chew at his bottom lip. "Did you *want* to sleep with me?"

"Since the first time you came into the coffee shop, Zarrin," Joe answered on a sigh, but then gave Zarrin a furious look. "It was real. Sleeping with you, and kissing you, and… everything else." *Everything else* was encouraging Zarrin to fuck his mouth, Joe's cock hard because Zarrin had told him he was pretty and good while keeping a firm hand on the back of his head. A spike of lust went through Joe at the memory. He glared down at the quilts Zarrin must have tucked around him after getting out of bed. "I've never done the things some of them think I did, and I wouldn't trick you, and I sure as hell wouldn't fuck you to make them happy. I wouldn't have anyway, but I know you now, and… you wouldn't want that."

"No," Zarrin agreed in a whisper. "I want you, not a… princess left at my door."

Joe raised his head, some of his anger fading away. "You barely know me." The stinging sensation at his neck that felt like a love bite said otherwise, but he ignored it.

Zarrin drew himself up. "I have been attempting to get to know you," he declared, as if indignant that Joe hadn't noticed. "Didn't I tell you I was making my interest clear? *Humans*."

Joe wiped at his mouth and noticed his terrible morning-after breath. But that was something to deal with later. This was far more important. "But you were leaving?"

"I was waiting for you to wake up!" Zarrin remained outraged, although he eased down into something calmer. "I have to get home. I should have last night, but I was so tired, and you and your bed were so nice, I completely forgot the things I had to do and stayed here all night. This morning I remembered them."

"You're going home?" Joe didn't know why that surprised him. Of course Zarrin had to get back to his house. He might want to shower and eat proper food and take care of whatever it was he did when he wasn't patrolling the Preserve.

If he even did that anymore. Lots of people wouldn't have, after something like that.

"I have to see to my treasure," Zarrin said, as if that was a reasonable thing to say.

"I thought *I* was—" Joe swallowed the rest of the words before he made a complete fool of himself. "What were you going to say when I woke up?"

"Oh, that." Zarrin waved a hand. "I was going to ask if, perhaps, since it's the weekend and you don't work, if I could see you again. You fed me, so it's my turn to feed you. Isn't that how humans do things?"

"Do you mean a date?" Joe was really, truly stupid after a night of sex and solid sleep.

Zarrin nodded. "But if you're worried about this 'on the regular' business, we don't have to. I just don't want to have to wait until Monday to see you again."

If Joe had heard something like that as a teenager, he would have done anything Russ had said, stayed a secret for him, lived in town to be near him, answered every furtive call to come over as if he had nothing better to do.

He threw himself back onto the bed, not unlike how he would have at sixteen, and replayed those words. Zarrin didn't want to wait to see him again. Zarrin had things to do, but had stayed so Joe wouldn't think he was sneaking out. Zarrin wanted to take him on a date.

He was breathing too loud.

Zarrin leaned over him to peer at him in concern.

"Were you really jealous?" Joe searched Zarrin's face for hints of deception, or even confusion, but Zarrin just looked disgruntled.

"Yes," he said, accompanied by a puff of smoke. "You could have anyone. Marie says you smell like sea air and strong wood. Your features are sensitive and handsome, your body is very attractive, and your mind is sharp. You're desirable—fuckable, as someone said on TV. Naturally others want to—fuck you, that is." Zarrin's eyes were very gold. "I would prefer they didn't."

"Yeah?" Joe was ridiculous, but Zarrin was about the same. "What are you doing today?"

"Today?" Zarrin blinked his beautiful eyes. "I'll see to the house, and possibly some of my chores. Normally, I would… do things that I won't be doing today." He bit at his fingernail for a second, then saw Joe watching and tore his hand away. "I should call my family again, at least my sister, but I don't think I will. Why?"

"You're going to be in that big house all day? Alone?" Joe could feel his frown returning.

"Yes." Zarrin brightened. "Did you want to come with me? I'd like having you in my home, Joseph, if only for a little while."

"You're inviting me into Dìzhèn's mansion?" Joe was on his back, staring up at Zarrin with probably way too much attention, but maybe it was okay.

Zarrin was all shy smiles again. "Of course. It was only a matter of time before I would. Didn't I tell you that before?"

Joe started to say no, then changed his mind and said nothing. He didn't know what might have happened if he'd brought that latte and Marie hadn't been there, but he was starting to think it would have been something like this. This was what happened when it was just the two of them, and no one in town was allowed to see.

A visit to Dìzhèn's house would be equally private—and Joe had always wanted to visit it. "I'd need to shower and get dressed, get some coffee."

As if that was nothing, Zarrin clucked his tongue. "I can wait."

His steady gaze said he meant it. Joe was suddenly very, very warm.

"Zarrin—" He started the question, then paused before making himself ask it anyway. "If I'm the bay and the trees to Marie, what do I smell like to you?" His heart was pounding. It was difficult to hold still.

"You smell…." Zarrin tipped his head to the side, then darted out his tongue to wet his lips and breathe in. His eyebrows went up with almost comical surprise, but he answered with burning glee. "Like you want me to kiss you."

"Yeah?" Joe asked again, in a voice he didn't know. He eased his head back onto a pillow and watched as Zarrin put a hand to the bed. Zarrin tasted the air again, as if confirming Joe's desire, before leaning over him.

Joe abruptly remembered his morning breath and put a hand over his mouth. "Morning-after breath," he explained quickly.

Zarrin's hurt little moue instantly changed to a nod of understanding. He reached into his coat pocket and pulled out a familiar tin of mints, then shook two into his palm. Joe was so distracted that he took them and then blinked at the shock of cold, sweet mint in his mouth.

"Treasure for treasure," Zarrin told him smugly, and kissed him before Joe could even begin to ask what he meant by that.

ZARRIN HAD two cats. Joe didn't know why this fact was so surprising. Alice said he protected the animals in the Preserve, but cats were something else. Joe watched the two of them circle Zarrin's ankle with a fraction less amazement than he'd felt crossing the threshold of Dìzhèn's mansion.

Treasure was the first word that came to mind the second Joe passed through that stained-glass entrance to Zarrin's home. He'd been worried at first that something would stop him from crossing the threshold, but the only thing that stole his breath and made him freeze in place was a glance around the foyer. A gleaming wooden floor led to a huge central staircase that angled to the side at the landing, cutting off his view of the second floor. Statues stood guard on columns on either side of six arched doorways. Dragons, carved from ebony and jade and possibly yellowed ivory, flanked the end of the banister, and roared silently at either side of the front door. Some of the dragons were the large, winged kind of European folklore, while others seemed to dance on air like the dragons in Lunar New Year parades on TV.

Way up high, where Joe could see when he'd finally walked farther into the house, was a sky well of sorts, a glass version of a skylight. Thin, old glass would make the house difficult to keep heated, but then, it had once been filled with dragons, and judging from the chimneys, there was a fireplace in nearly every room. And someone in the Xu family had modernized everything sometime during the past decades.

The house was comfortable enough for someone wearing a sweater and thick socks, and the kitchen, where Joe stood to watch Zarrin give his cats their treats, was getting warmer the longer Zarrin stayed there. The kitchen itself had very obviously been remodeled somewhat recently, and the technology in it was up to date, down to the microwave where Zarrin cooked frozen breakfast sandwiches for them before going back to loving up his pets.

"My little ones," Zarrin crooned at them the way he had when they had first dashed down the grand staircase to see him. "I'm sorry I wasn't here. I'll make it up to you! Two treats each!" Both cats continued to meow at him while also butting their heads against his ankles. The gray one had a bad eye and a piece missing from its ear, and skittishly glanced at Joe without approaching him. The orange one paused to study him a few times before continuing to aggressively purr against Zarrin's legs.

"My babies, mine," Zarrin whispered to them as he fed them far more than the two treats each he'd promised.

Joe finally remembered to eat the sandwich in his hand, and did so with strange hyperawareness that he was on the Xu Preserve, in Dìzhèn's very house, in its oddly modern kitchen, eating a microwaved breakfast sandwich while the dragon he'd slept with fawned over his two greedy cats.

Maybe if Everlasting had more magical beings around, things like this would be commonplace. Then again, this house, like Zarrin, was one of a kind.

"This is what you had to come home to see to?" Joe realized out loud, as Zarrin picked up the gray one, Fogg, to let it rub its scent all over his chin.

"They have a machine with a timer that dispenses their food," Zarrin answered defensively. "But that doesn't mean they don't need attention."

"And treats," Joe finished for him, although it was obvious Zarrin had missed the cats as much as they'd missed him.

Zarrin's expression went sulky as he put Fogg down in order to pick up the orange one, Nemo. Nemo squirmed in his arms and then climbed up onto his shoulder, where she rested, perfectly at ease, with her tail curled around his neck.

Joe stared at her, and she stared back. She reminded him of Marie, in a way he could never say out loud anywhere Marie might hear.

"You have cats," he said, not for the first time, but softer now as his mind adjusted to the information. "Just two?"

"Two cats." Zarrin stroked the orange tail at his neck and studied Joe carefully. "What?"

"Nothing." Joe hadn't looked away for a while. He couldn't help it. People in town thought Zarrin was going to roast them. Zarrin, who ate egg-and-cheese sandwiches for breakfast, who'd sat politely on Joe's bed while Joe took a quick shower. Zarrin, currently being used as a cat tree.

Joe had a feeling he could draw Zarrin every day and never get him exactly right.

"It's not soft to have cats. Lots of people do. Cats are worshiped in some places." Zarrin was nervous, Joe realized. He was worried about Joe's opinion of his pets.

"They love you a lot, I can tell." Joe wondered what the gray one would do if he knelt down to pet it. Probably run. Fogg hadn't had an easy life, from the look of him. Yet he openly adored Zarrin in a way people said cats didn't do. But maybe they did, and aloof cats were another myth. "I never had a pet, but they look happy to me. Do they always greet you like that?"

"Sometimes, usually when I've been out for longer than usual." Zarrin stepped closer to Joe and didn't seem to notice when the orange one leaped from his shoulder to the floor. "They've had enough treats. Would you like me to show you the house? They should be calmer by then, so I can properly introduce you to them."

"They missed you, Zarrin. Let them freak out a little." Joe shrugged, as if he weren't fascinated by the fluffy tails continually being brushed against Zarrin, and the meows that stopped when Zarrin would look down to address them.

"All right," Zarrin told Joe, in his dignified dragon voice, before speaking to his cats again. "Three more treats each, but you'll be nice to Joe. No clawing at his pants." He raised his head and then blinked in surprise. "What?" he demanded again.

Joe realized he was smiling, probably a stupid smile, but it was too late to hide it. He tried anyway. "This isn't what I thought it would be like to be inside your house."

"What did you think it would be?" Zarrin's interest made it difficult to answer, so Joe took a moment to swallow the last of his sandwich.

"I don't know. Every kid in Everlasting grows up hearing about it, and the Preserve. You don't expect to ever see it." Joe held out his hands. "It's nothing like what I imagined, but also exactly how it should be, antique and grand and rich. Then there's Zarrin and his little ones."

"Dìzhèn's house was built to impress humans," Zarrin told him seriously. "I wasn't." He bit his lip for a moment, then added, "But I love my little ones."

The surge of fluttery, rising warmth in Joe's chest was as disarming as Zarrin kissing him awake, or finding out that Zarrin thought of grilled cheese as a sign of affection.

"*Dìzhèn*'s house?" Joe had to clear his throat to speak. "Not yours?" He'd noticed that earlier as well. "You live here."

"It's my home," Zarrin agreed as he washed cat treat remnants off his hands. "But the house is her treasure, with some additions from her descendants." He kept his head down as he used a towel. "Before they left. Most of them leave. It can be difficult to live in her shadow. Even her children left and did not return."

"Tell me about it," Joe muttered without thinking, although obviously things were different for a human in Everlasting then for a dragon in her actual house. "So… everything in this house is either hers, or was abandoned here when people left? And then it becomes hers?" Joe resisted pointing out that Dìzhèn had been dead for over a century. History wasn't always in the past, and death meant a lot of things in a lot of cultures. And he had an uncomfortable memory of a dark night with her statue.

"It was always hers. Even the magic that protects is still Dìzhèn's. Although, sometimes I think it's too much for one dragon, even one such as her. Almost as if she did something else to ensure the town would survive. There were so many threats at the time, outside interests challenging her and the town she saved. She did something unusual and now that I can truly sense the magic involved, I don't think—" Zarrin seemed to have a thought, then dismiss it. "She has power that current dragons have lost." Zarrin referred to past events in the present tense sometimes. Joe didn't know if it was a cultural thing or a language thing. He didn't even know if Zarrin spoke any other languages.

"That's why all the dragons left?" Joe wanted to be gentle but couldn't. "They couldn't handle having a great ancestor, so they split? I thought they cared about the town. My dad might not have been the greatest, but he cared about me and my mom and worked hard to stay with us. Even when he couldn't get a good paying job in this town, even when he got sick, he stayed. Your relatives sound weak as hell."

Zarrin twisted to stare at him with open surprise. "Joseph!"

"Sorry to insult your family, but you keep going on about what a dragon is supposed to be." Joe shook his head when Zarrin looked ready to protest. "Maybe your relatives are all those things like she was, but you're the only one who's still here."

"I don't mind caring for what is hers. My treasure is no challenge to her," Zarrin argued softly.

"Except for how your treasure is a whole town, according to you." Joe crossed his arms. "Unless that's still hers too."

"I…." Zarrin trailed off, distinctly uncomfortable. "I would help Bernard clean the house, but it was too much even for an elf and a dragon. It needs the attention of experts in preservation, especially with the damp from the redwoods and the bay, and someone to oversee all of that. If I were properly caring for it, I would have hired someone like that already, and brought in more staff to keep it clean."

It was on the tip of Joe's tongue to ask why Zarrin hadn't done that, but Zarrin was starting to chew on his bottom lip, so Joe let the subject rest for now. "I don't mind dust, if you still wanted to show me around."

"Yes!" Zarrin moved forward energetically, as if eager to change the subject. "Where to begin? The architecture firm Dìzhèn originally hired was the same one who designed the state capitol, but they refused to incorporate her ideas, so she turned to her secretary, and several of the Chinese builders living on the outskirts of town. The people in town, and the other timber barons and factory owners, tried several times to be rid of her. I suspect her tie to the land began then, to ensure Everlasting's survival." He swept past Joe, then stopped to give Joe an impatient glance over his shoulder.

"Much of the wood paneling was replaced by her son in later years. He chose a wood more resistant to the damp, but kept his mother's designs." Zarrin continued once Joe followed him back out into the main hall. "The many dragon statues were gifts sent to him by business associates. Orientalism was a craze in décor at the time. There was also a desire to have some of the more glamorous beings appear in the homes of the very wealthy. The dragon statues were believed to be attempts to curry his favor. He had the pool built and expanded the garage to house his automobiles as well."

"But he left eventually?" Joe wasn't exactly guessing.

Zarrin took him into another room, a study or a parlor, with furnishings draped in white dustcloths. "His two younger sisters expanded the fleet of fishing ships in the harbor and founded the town library. The elder sister loved to explore and sent back the rugs in this room and the library, as well as the trinkets you'll see throughout the house. She spent her last years in India. The younger briefly traveled to France before returning here in the thirties. She had an affair with an English dragon and raised her children here for many years before they left again."

The parlor room had several thick rugs beneath heavy chairs of polished dark wood. The grand piano in one corner was probably out of tune, but had a giant harp to keep it company. The wallpapered walls were covered in framed paintings.

"This is art she brought from Europe?" Joe asked as he walked past Zarrin to make a slow circuit of the room. The dehumidifier in one corner of the room wasn't going to be enough to preserve everything, although it was a start. Joe didn't know much about art conservation, though.

He stared at large works on canvas for a long time. Some he'd only seen in books, others he'd never seen, or heard of the artists. Not all of it was modern, like he'd expected after hearing how it got there. Some of it was much older. Still others were simple sketches, artist unknown.

Joe knew by now that meant the younger daughter had liked it enough to want to own it, even if the artist wasn't a famous name.

He smiled a little, even though those artists were long dead and couldn't appreciate how loved their work had once been.

"This is incredible," he whispered after a while, in a rough voice. "But she left too?"

"Eventually." Zarrin stayed in the doorway. "She returned to England after the war, but her child came back. Dìzhèn's son, Shǎnliàng, hadn't raised any heirs, but he had contacted the family who stayed in China. Many of them came over to live here in the middle of the century before they found her magic greater than theirs, and they also went away. Would you like to see the library?"

Joe nodded, because it was that or stare at the paintings until his eyes went dry, and this might be his only chance to see the whole house. Zarrin led him farther down the same side of the hall and pushed open the doors to reveal a library of the kind old white guys had in period movies. The room could have been a ballroom in another life.

"The dining room and game room are closer to the kitchen. There's a billiards table and a bar, if you're interested." Zarrin hurried into the library despite his words, and sank down into one of the many plush benches of velvet throughout the room. The air smelled of old books, but there was no sour-faced old woman to stare Joe down as he walked in.

"And the books?" he asked, after taking a moment to let it all sink in. The fireplace at one end of the room was tempting, but so was the window along one wall. The drawn curtains revealed a view of the redwood covered hills.

"Organized by time of acquisition more than any other system." Zarrin was studying his reaction, but Joe didn't mind. "The paperbacks are closer to the fireplace. You know, some of my aunts and uncles were very fond of genre fiction, romances in particular. I don't suppose someone would want to curate those."

"I suppose someone would." Joe went over to the fireplace to study the carving work in the mantel and the antique clock on top of it. "Real librarians—not like the uptight woman at the town library front desk—live for that stuff." Every once in a while, an oddity stuck out among the books: a series of graphic novels all in a row, photo albums, cookbooks. But mostly the library appeared to be full of ordinary-seeming books and novels and not a collection of magical tomes, although they could have been there. It's not like Joe would know them by sight.

He came back to Zarrin. "Where are the old maps and drawings you mentioned?"

"*Ah*. Those are among *Alfie*'s things." Zarrin said the name the same way he spoke of Dìzhèn. When Joe only stared at him in confusion, Zarrin lowered his voice to a secretive whisper. "Alfred Van Kirk was Dìzhèn's human secretary and then her boy. His things are kept in the room adjacent to the bedroom she used."

"Her boy?" Joe had to ask. Zarrin had the most intense expression on his face.

"Her lover… her… mate, as Marie might say. Her one, who was also human, which is why we use the term boy, despite his age." Zarrin sighed happily. "He was very devoted, although he disappeared from the records after her death. Even Shǎnliàng didn't know what became of him."

Dragons mating like werewolves was news to Joe. He wondered if it was rare and that was why Zarrin spoke of it reverently. But he held in his questions, because it meant that someday Zarrin might see someone, or smell them, and choose them for his, and Joe didn't want to hear about that.

He focused on the story itself. "So the family kept his things the same way they kept hers? That's quite a way to honor a human. If he has some of the town's history among his things, you really should have someone come in to take a look at it. History is important, Zarrin. People forget it too easily."

Zarrin's lips parted. "You're right. Of course you are. But I haven't. I don't think my family would trust my decision." He snatched his hand from his mouth before he could bite his fingernails, then got to his feet. "What do you think of the house so far?"

"The new houses in town have nothing on it, although they wish they did." Joe gave the books one more glance. "Maybe I'm used to small apartments, but big houses seem to echo, don't they? Funny that this room doesn't."

"Have you been in many of the big houses in town?" Zarrin frowned, probably thinking Joe was somehow insulting his home.

"Just one," Joe said curtly. "But I never got a formal tour." He shook his head to dismiss the subject. "Are you going to share your treasure with Dìzhèn too?" According to Zarrin, that meant he'd be leaving.

"I don't want to share my treasure with her." Zarrin was petulant and then appeared surprised at himself before growing sulky again. "I take care of her house, but my treasure is mine." He narrowed his eyes—at the walls of the house, apparently—before focusing on Joe. "Would you… would you like to see mine?"

"You want me to?" Joe cringed at the hope in his voice, but Zarrin hardly seemed to notice.

"Naturally." He rolled his eyes, as though Joe was very silly, but then didn't actually move for another few moments. "Okay. *Okay*, I can do this. I can *share*. It's different with you. Marie didn't know and charged ahead. But I want you to like it. It took me a long time to figure out what you like, and even now I'm not sure. If you think it's stupid or a waste of time—"

"You don't have to show me," Joe tried to remind him, although he was frowning to think Marie had seen it.

Zarrin raised himself up. "I promised you a proper introduction to the little ones." He took Joe's hand and pulled Joe from the library.

As he was led up the staircase to the second floor, Joe thought about asking how Zarrin's cats were related to his treasure. But the paintings at the landing distracted him, and then he got his answer, so it didn't matter.

Zarrin took him to the very end of what must have been an entire wing of the house and then waved Joe through an open door with a nervous hitch in his breathing.

What waited on the other side were not piles of gold coins or chests of jewels. Zarrin's room—or rooms, really, were a suite of three rooms, not including the bathroom, each one leading into the other through an open, arched doorway.

The first room had a large rolltop desk against one wall, beneath two large bookshelves. The books were nonfiction, and seemed to be a mix of antiques and recent releases, all of them about the natural world. Zarrin kept his books separate from the ones downstairs, but maybe that was for convenience. Every book here seemed used or filled with bright strips of sticky notes for bookmarks.

The desk looked used as well, with a laptop incongruously on the writing surface, and a cup of pens next to a notepad and a pile of smooth river stones and bird feathers. Drying leaves and flowers hung from the wall and the top of the desk by bits of string, and for some reason, Joe thought of magpies or crows, nesting and hoarding pieces of useful, shiny things. But then the rest of the items along the walls caught his attention. He'd never seen so many shadow boxes, and in each of them was something different: shells, feathers, a single butterfly. Each one was labeled as well. *Tail feather, Accipiter striatus, Sharp-shinned Hawk.* Or, *Danaus plexippus. Monarch Butterfly.*

"I found the butterfly like that," Zarrin commented, in a funny, high voice. "I didn't kill it. Or the others." "The others" were in displays of the kind in natural history museums. Dozens of dead insects pinned to a board inside a glass case. "They were already in the house, in storage. One of Shănliàng's playthings must have been a naturalist. I kept them because they're useful, and I didn't want the insects to have died for nothing."

Joe looked at Zarrin, who must be a naturalist too, even if he seemed anxious and embarrassed about it. "Do you know the Latin names of everything on the Preserve?"

"If I don't, I learn it." Zarrin dismissed that. "You have to know the land to protect it. If I don't know what a healthy ladybug looks like, how would I know if one had a problem?"

"You didn't go to school?" Joe knew he hadn't, but it was something he hadn't thought about before—Zarrin as self-taught. His sister had gone to college. His parents probably had too.

Zarrin shook his head. "But this is only the Preserve. You're right. I should look through Alfie's records and learn more of the town's history. By all accounts, he was very thorough, so that might take some time. I like that about him. I also try to get as much detail as I can into my records."

The image of Zarrin at that desk, faithfully cataloguing ladybugs and ferns, made Joe's heart beat faster. He turned away when he couldn't take it any longer, and went into the next room. It had a door facing the hallway, but the doorway was blocked by shelves. The room was small, probably an antechamber or sitting room. Two cat beds and three cat trees lined one wall. Terrariums and empty cages were stacked on top of what looked like pricey cabinets, along with bags of feed and water bottles, and planters full of dirt. A metal shelving unit was half-full of notebooks as well as bottles of antiseptic and what looked like animal medications.

Zarrin cleared his throat and hurried on to the last room—his bedroom. His bed was ridiculously huge and comfortable-looking. The kind of bed with matching pillows and comforters Joe would never be able to afford. But Joe barely glanced at it despite the two familiar cats curled up on it, patiently awaiting more snuggles.

There was a rabbit in Zarrin's bedroom. A big brown bunny with alert eyes and a twitching nose sat in a large cage, complete with bedding and a warming lamp and water. Zarrin clucked his tongue at the empty food bowl and bent down to reach into a small refrigerator by the side of the bed. He pulled out lettuce and a single raspberry, which he placed into the cage before closing it again.

The rabbit, skittish and probably wild, began to eat even before Zarrin's hand was out of the cage.

"That's Peter," Zarrin explained. "His leg is much better, and his weight's up. I'll have to let him go soon. I hate that part." He grasped anxiously at the air in a way that shouldn't have stabbed Joe in the gut like it did. Zarrin must have cared for many animals and then released them, but only the cats had stayed.

Marie's story about Zarrin taking care of her hadn't been a joke.

"Fish and Game had it right. You are one of them. Forest Ranger Zarrin." Joe intended to tease, then realized he meant it.

Zarrin gave a start. Joe wanted to stare at him for a long, long time, until he made sense, or he turned into an arrogant jerk of a dragon, perched atop a pile of gold. But though everything in this house, in these rooms, cost a great deal of money, Joe had yet to see any gold in Zarrin's personal possession. Only cats and an injured rabbit, and stuff Zarrin had found on the forest floor, and books.

Joe looked away from Zarrin's hopeful gaze, and faced the bed. It was beneath a giant window, which had to make it cold in the winter, but there were thick curtains, and anyway, Zarrin was his own furnace. He could lie in that bed and look out at the Preserve if he wanted, which he probably did.

Or he could stare at the TV, which took up half the opposite wall. But Joe's attention went past the TV to the nightstand by the bed, which had unfolded handwritten letters on it, and a glass of water, and several familiar sugar packets. Above it was his painting of the trees.

It was the only painting Zarrin had chosen for his own, even with the others in the house. Positioned where it was, Zarrin could look at it while in bed too, a lonely subject for a lonely dragon.

Zarrin came up behind him, although he seemed hesitant to speak. "You don't mind?"

Joe ignored that, for the present, like the lump in his throat. "I was expecting riches, I guess."

"Riches?" Zarrin's breath was warm enough to make Joe shiver. "There's the family trust, I suppose. But this is all Dìzhèn's, really. If I wanted to gather riches I'd have to join the family business, and I don't want to. They… wouldn't have me, anyway. Every dragon is different, but most have the sense to hoard some things of value."

"Your family thinks you're soft for this?" Joe kept his eyes on the trees in his painting. Zarrin had also said they gave him hope.

"I'm dragon." Zarrin sighed.

Joe finally looked at him. "You confronted criminals, who *attacked* you. You gave Hazel fire. That's dragon."

"We aren't supposed to share our fire with just anyone," Zarrin admitted in a whisper. His peeking, careful glances were making it hard for Joe to think straight. "But she asked me, and I was cold, and those two women had been so horrible moments before, and I wanted… I wanted you to see me and notice me and never forget me again."

Joe had never forgotten him, and flushed in embarrassment for ever pretending he had. "Zarrin," he began, "why did you come down into town and start talking with people? You said your parents didn't approve, but you did it anyway. You didn't even like coffee."

Zarrin shrugged and then fluttered his hands. "It's very quiet here. Bernard was gone, and I wanted to see our humans in their natural habitat. Then Bernard recommended I go to that particular coffee shop. I didn't understand why at first." He met Joe's eyes. "The interior was warm, and the music was calming, and you and Martin were making jokes about something in the newspaper with an older human man with a weathered face and frayed clothes. You gave the elderly man a cinnamon roll from the pastry display and didn't charge him for it, and then when you rang him up, it was for a small coffee instead of a large. And after the man left, Martin teased you about it, and I saw it then, in that moment before you frowned and hid it away again. I saw you and how much you care, about everything."

He inched forward and nodded earnestly. "It wasn't as cold then, but your hands were bare, and you kept rubbing them together after you got milk from the refrigerator. I wanted to warm them. I wanted to warm *you*, to curl up on top of you and keep you safe and protected." His small sigh was pained. "But the other humans didn't like me, and you didn't like me, and I thought, if I kept going, I could figure out why."

"I like you," Joe said, then went on before the look in Zarrin's eyes would actually kill him. "So do Marie, and Hazel, and Martin. I think Alice does too, in her way. But no one hates you. Well, some people are assholes and always will be, but most of them don't. They don't understand you, and they're afraid of you, and your family, but…." He trailed off when he realized he was repeating himself. "Everyone at the shop was outraged at what happened to you." Some of them had been more worried about the Xu Family's reaction to harm done to their son, but not that many of them, surprisingly. Anyway, Zarrin didn't need to know that right now.

"My sister would never have been lured by the smell of a latte into letting her guard down." Zarrin made a face. "You don't need to pretend, or be kind about it. The best I can do is offer you comfort. We could watch TV, or eat. That wasn't much of a breakfast, and it's long past noon. Do you want something else to eat? My skills in the kitchen aren't as good as yours, but I could make something. Maybe. I need to go to the store. Werewolves eat a lot. Oh, I, if you want meat I don't have any." Zarrin gave Joe a look of pleading hope before lifting his chin. "You won't tell my parents."

As if Joe would ever talk with Zarrin's parents. He took a step back at even the idea and then blinked and reconsidered Zarrin. "You don't eat meat? You live in a fishing town and you don't eat fish?"

Zarrin's wrinkled nose was so cute it was terrifying. "They have *faces*, Joe," he confided seriously.

Joe realized he was shaking with the need to *touch*. He reached out to take Zarrin's face in his hands and pressed his mouth to Zarrin's with a desperate sound that embarrassed him, then thrilled him, because Zarrin immediately kissed back. He pushed forward and placed one hand against Joe's neck. The contact was hot and steadying. So was Zarrin's whisper as he briefly pulled away. "Shh, treasure. You can have me. Please don't be upset."

He followed the words with more kisses, and petted Joe's skin, and curled his palm at the back of Joe's neck to draw him down. Joe slid his fingers into Zarrin's messy hair and gulped air as he imagined those dark gold fingertips pressed into his skin. Then he sought out Zarrin's mouth. Zarrin fit himself into Joe's arms, and when Joe stopped to breathe, to think, Zarrin kissed along his jaw and then along his throat. Joe made that needy sound again, and Zarrin nuzzled at the hollow of Joe's throat.

Zarrin growled softly. "None of that. You don't need to hide here. Make all the noise you want." He nipped at Joe's shoulder, over the love bite he'd already left, and tugged at Joe's clothes to bare the skin. Joe tilted his head up and exhaled hard. He closed his eyes when Zarrin sucked at the bruise and it felt unexpectedly good. "Tell me, and I'll give it to you. Please." The scrape of Zarrin's teeth was like lightning, there and gone, and then Zarrin's strong, greedy hands were hauling Joe down so Zarrin could nibble at his bottom lip. This was gentle, but no less insistent.

Joe opened his eyes and Zarrin eased back to study him, all widened eyes and hunger. "You kissed me." He could have been reminding Joe, or just incredibly pleased about this fact.

Joe stared at him, with his lips buzzing and his shoulder stinging. "I had to."

Zarrin hesitated before reaching for him again. He stroked his thumb beneath Joe's jaw. "You don't have to wait. You are… if you're worried about what I think, and that's why you hold back so long, you don't have to. Whatever you were feeling—"

"Your hair," Joe grunted, and sighed the rest. "Your cats. That library. *Your* library. Feathers and rocks and a lame rabbit and my painting, Zarrin. My painting, and my sugar, and I couldn't—" He clenched his hands. "You take care of them, and I—"

"You wanted me?" Zarrin finished for him, delighted, before slinking forward to press his body to Joe's. "I can take care of you." He kissed over Joe's throbbing pulse and along his collarbone. "I would love to." He dragged his hands down Joe's chest to his stomach and then pushed them beneath Joe's sweater and T-shirt. Then he left them, hot and still, at Joe's waist. "Let me." He huffed warm and damp, against Joe's skin, leaving Joe to shiver at the rising temperature.

He wound his arms around Zarrin's slender body, and Zarrin responded with another puff of hot breath and a soft press of his teeth. Joe grabbed at him, and Zarrin finally moved to kiss him again, slow and deep. He stole Joe's breath and then did it again, taking his time with Joe's mouth while holding Joe still with the barest pressure.

His fingers curled into Joe's skin, warm and greedy, too far from his waistband for Joe to do more than whimper. Zarrin shushed him but didn't move his hands. He took heavy, drugging kisses from Joe, over and over, and urged Joe back, one step at a time, until Joe was against the wall.

Joe realized his eyes were closed and his breathing was strained. His legs were weak. He smoothed his palms over Zarrin's back and Zarrin murmured in encouragement and slid his entire body against Joe's. He swallowed Joe's groan and yanked Joe in by his hips. His cock was hard, and when he realized Joe's was too, he growled in clear satisfaction.

"Zarrin." Joe tried to speak, but he was out of breath and had no idea what he meant to say.

Zarrin clutched tighter at his hips and rolled against him. He gasped while Joe shuddered and pushed back to feel that again. Zarrin slid his fingers into Joe's jeans and lowered his head to watch.

Joe was dragging Zarrin's sweater up his back, but Zarrin didn't slow as he popped the button of Joe's fly and squeezed his dick.

"We were too fast last night," Zarrin commented, a talker during sex, like before. "Too fast for me to appreciate all of you. What a good handful you are, treasure."

Joe bit his lip, but a weak sound emerged anyway. Zarrin huffed, as if chiding him, and thumbed at the head of Joe's cock until Joe whimpered. "I want to suck you again, but I want you naked first. Naked Joe, spread out on his back in my bed." The sounds he was drawing from Joe were humiliating, but the pleasure he took in them made it impossible for Joe to stop. The things he was saying were things people didn't say—unless they were dragon, unless they were Zarrin. "I didn't get a proper look at you last night. Not naked. Only your nice cock."

"Zarrin," Joe protested faintly, and got another huff.

"It's a very nice cock," Zarrin continued, and gave it another squeeze. "I'm going to kiss it as soon as you're naked and in bed. Then I'll kiss you too. Like this." He placed a small kiss at the corner of Joe's open mouth. "Yes?"

"Yes," Joe agreed, and shuddered as Zarrin pulled his hand out of his jeans. But it was only to reach for the bottom of Joe's sweater. Zarrin tugged it up, then went for the T-shirt beneath as well.

"Yesss," Zarrin drew out the word when Joe raised his arms. "Like that." The moment the clothes were gone, Zarrin's hands were back on him, then his mouth. He licked across the tattoos he seemed obsessed with and then moved to Joe's nipples. He splayed his hands at Joe's back and held him close while he nipped experimentally at sensitive places.

Joe was going to die from one dragon's attention. Zarrin was learning him, tasting and darting away, returning to suck hickeys into his skin and bite at spots he'd already left puffy and hot. "Rin." Joe couldn't seem to get the full name out. "Za'rin." Words were difficult, his tongue thick in his mouth. He was so hard, and Zarrin seemed to have forgotten about his "pretty cock."

"Yes." Zarrin exhaled against his ribs. "Treasure."

Joe pushed away from the wall, trying to grind against him, and Zarrin straightened to give him a stern, if bright-eyed, stare. It lasted for a moment before his gaze traveled down over Joe's body. Then he swallowed. "Tell me," he commanded, bright and hot as lava. "Tell me, and I will give you everything."

Joe reached for him and kissed him, mouths open and panting, hands burning on scraps of bared skin. He left the wall because he wanted the bed, exactly as Zarrin described it. The back of his legs hit something soft. Zarrin pushed him down, displacing huffy cats, and then climbed over him. His gaze was shining, intense. "Tell me."

"What you said," Joe gasped, wriggling against velvety bedding and getting nowhere. Zarrin was suddenly heavy. He kneeled over Joe and held him down by his wrists. The air stung with heat.

"Tell me, Joseph, and I will kiss your pretty thighs too," Zarrin promised, or threatened, and Joe whined.

He would have flushed, shamed, but Zarrin spread his hands out to link his fingers with his, and trailed a long, wet kiss from Joe's throat to his chest. When his hands slid away, Joe kept his where they were. He grabbed fistfuls of the comforter and trembled while Zarrin pulled his zipper down and then pushed at his jeans.

He helped, or thought he did, kicking at his shoes, lifting his hips, but Zarrin sucked another hickey into his untattooed shoulder, and his thoughts narrowed to sharp heat and the teasing hint of teeth.

Then Zarrin sat up so abruptly Joe shivered with actual cold.

It didn't last. Zarrin's gaze made sure of it. He was seated on Joe, fully dressed, and staring covetously at his naked body. He bit his bottom lip so hard Joe half expected to see blood. Then he bent down slowly, to place a single kiss to Joe's stomach. He slid down until his feet were on the floor and he was between Joe's legs, and then he did what he'd promised, one gentle kiss to each of Joe's thighs, then a soft, pleased kiss to the head of his cock.

He played with the foreskin for a moment, his gaze on his hand, before he brought his eyes up to meet Joe's. "Joseph."

"Come back," Joe said before Zarrin could command him to speak again. He raised a hand, and Zarrin moved so that Joe's hand slid into his hair as he climbed over him.

He didn't seem to care when Joe tangled his fingers into the short strands, or that he still had all his clothes on. He reached down to undo his fly and then he curled against Joe, his cock hot and bare against Joe's stomach.

Joe hissed. Zarrin buried his face in the crook of his neck and moaned. The chafe of Zarrin's jeans was painful, but only enough to make Joe yank at Zarrin's clothes with his one free hand. Zarrin wriggled and let him. Then he moved down a few inches until their cocks brushed together.

"This. Yes. Spread your legs for me," Zarrin all but purred into Joe's chest. Joe bent his knees and suddenly Zarrin was close against him, silky and hot between his thighs. He rolled his hips, bringing their cocks together again. Zarrin was uncut too, and the contact made him reach down to squeeze himself. Then he panted and bent his head as he rose up. He stroked himself for another moment and then raised his head to watch Joe's face as he wrapped his hand around Joe's cock.

Joe threw his head back and jerked his hips up. His heart was loud, his breathing strained. "Good," Zarrin told him, his mouth so wet, his grip tight. "So good." He said it easily, if breathlessly, as if Joe weren't grasping at his hair and thrusting up into his hand like no one had ever jacked him off before.

Joe's other hand was strangely empty, so he ran his palm over Zarrin's lower back and pushed him down in search of pressure, friction. Zarrin moved in response, slinking along Joe's body again to grab his hands and hold him down.

Joe exhaled in shock. It felt good, like trickling heat through him, and a stillness in his mind, and awareness that Zarrin had him, Zarrin was going to take care of him.

"Joseph." A volcano said his name, and ground down against him, again and again. Joe turned his head and breathed harshly through his open mouth. He wrapped his legs around Zarrin and felt a rumble travel through him. He arched up from the bed, or tried to, and Zarrin rumbled again, in approving pleasure. "Treasure."

"Za… Zarrin," Joe tried to tell him. He was so hard, his balls tight. But Zarrin continued to fuck between his legs and hold him down. He was slight and little and all gold. He was going to leave bruises, and Joe didn't care. He wanted the rumble against his thighs, and the soft brush of cashmere at his chest, and Zarrin's cock lined up to slide perfectly against his. "Zarrin?" he said again, shaky and quiet.

"My boy," Zarrin whispered back at him, and rose up to grab Joe by the hips and grind down fiercely. He was talking nonsense. "My boy. Pretty and good and *mine*. Mine from the first moment. Joseph."

Joe saw white. His whole body tightened as he came. He thought he pushed up from the bed, but Zarrin stayed on top of him, hot and steady until Joe was gasping for air, and then he reached down and stroked his cock until he came, messy and fast, across Joe's stomach.

He collapsed to the side in the next moment, falling onto his back with a tired groan.

Joe stared at the ceiling. His chest was heaving, and sticky with spunk. He could still feel Zarrin's weight on top of him, the heat of Zarrin's hands at his wrists. Zarrin was—or could be—stronger than he appeared when he wanted to be. He was fierce and foreign as any dragon, despite what he thought.

But he curled up to Joe's side and put his face to Joe's arm while he caught his breath. His hair was as soft as Joe had always thought it would be. His breath tickled.

He panted for a few moments before he propped his head up with one hand.

Joe could feel him watching.

"You're very quiet," Zarrin began, hesitantly. "I don't know if that's usual for you."

"And you worry," Joe remarked. He'd been warned about that, hadn't he? He turned his head. Zarrin regarded him with bright eyes. Joe's every muscle felt so drained he had to concentrate to speak clearly. "I don't know if it's usual. I feel… quiet, right now." His body was exhausted and warm, achy where he'd been held down, or kissed, or bitten. His skin was humming too much for him to frown. He wanted to know how Zarrin knew what he wanted like that, but didn't have the energy to talk about magic, if it was magic. "Do you like doing that to me?" he asked haltingly instead. "The way I—"

"Very much," Zarrin answered, smoky-voiced. "No one's ever wanted that from me." He sat up and smiled down at him. "You were very good." He smoothed some hair from Joe's face and clucked his tongue when Joe glanced away, bemused. "So good. Thank you." Zarrin hummed happily. "Do you need anything? Water?"

Without waiting, he slid to his feet and walked over to his minifridge, yanking up his pants as he went. He returned with a bottle of water, which he placed next to Joe before disappearing into the bathroom.

When he came out with a warm, damp washcloth, Joe at least kept the surprise from his face. But Zarrin didn't seem to notice Joe's stillness as he cleaned Joe. He wiped up the mess they'd left on Joe's chest with slow, careful circles. Joe watched him for another moment, too tired and too sated to fight it. He shut his eyes and then let out a long breath. "Never asked that from anyone else. Wouldn't get it."

Zarrin stopped, then resumed gently washing Joe. When he apparently thought Joe was clean enough, he left the bed for a few minutes. Joe opened his eyes in time to see Zarrin returning from the bathroom, then shut them again and tried not to tense up when Zarrin settled at his side. He rested his head at Joe's shoulder and pressed close. "Pretty and good," Zarrin told him, with his hand creeping along Joe's waist, as if still holding Joe the way Joe had wanted during sex. Joe didn't ask him to stop. He turned his head until Zarrin's hair tickled his nose. He shivered and Zarrin burrowed in closer. "I will keep you warm, treasure."

"Not Dìzhèn's?" Joe wondered, without opening his eyes, and shivered again for the steamy growl beneath his ear.

"No," Zarrin told him firmly, and threw one leg across Joe's knees. Half pinned down and surrounded by heat, Joe risked another glance. Trickles of white smoke curled above them, like emphasis, or a declaration. "No," Zarrin murmured again, as Joe's breathing evened out and his eyes fell closed once more. "Not hers."

# CHAPTER 11

"ARE YOU sure about this?" The question from Joe made Zarrin stop dead before he remembered he was in the middle of crossing the parking lot in front of the grocery store. Joe strode ahead, only to turn around at the curb when he apparently noticed Zarrin had fallen behind.

Traffic or no traffic, Zarrin crossed his arms. He hoped his expression conveyed hopeful attention and not unimaginable hurt, but he didn't think it did. He had touched Joe, and kissed him, and nearly fucked him, and gotten to sleep with him twice. He'd woken to Joe in his arms in the safety of Dìzhèn's house, with Nemo and Fogg curled up at his back. It had been Joe's suggestion—after seeing the state of Zarrin's refrigerator—that they go into town to get something to eat. Now Joe was hesitant.

The sky was still light, but the late-afternoon time should have meant the store would be less crowded. Yet as Zarrin studied Joe, he noticed that the parking lot had plenty of humans in it, and many of them were now glancing his way.

Joe cleared his throat. "Maybe you don't need me with you when you buy groceries." He waved around him in a short, annoyed gesture. "People are going to think—" He cut himself off and worked his jaw before going on. "It's not their business what we do. But they might say things… about me." He seemed to feel this wasn't enough. "You should know."

Zarrin released a relieved breath. He'd thought Joe was tiring of him, or already regretting Zarrin's weakness.

He turned to level a look at a shopper who should have moved along instead of stopping to watch them, and then, when that shopper hurried on their way, he returned his attention to Joe. Zarrin stepped forward deliberately, and sighed again when Joe let him come closer.

Once in front of Joe, he raised his head to meet that nervous frown directly. "Do you mean"—Zarrin tread lightly—"that they will say you stole someone's boyfriend? Or that you turned someone gay?" He reached out when Joe flinched, and brushed his hand down Joe's arm. "Or that you must have magic?" Zarrin shook his head. "Of course you have magic with your *talent*. But the rest of it is obviously not true. You cannot steal someone's affection any more than you can change someone's sexuality for them—provided you aren't using an illegal potion of some kind, which you would never do. Not my Joseph."

Joe raised his eyebrows, but then his frown returned.

"I didn't." He didn't shake off Zarrin's touch, but he didn't lean into it the way he had in Zarrin's bed either. "I didn't use a potion or a spell. I didn't use some bullshit racist curse. I didn't do anything but look." He took a sharp breath. "I just looked. He's the one who said that they were only friends, that he loved me." Joe sounded furious, although his scent made Zarrin want to hold him. "And I believed it, because I was stupid and lonely. And maybe… maybe it was true, a little bit. Just not enough."

"Shh." Zarrin couldn't soothe him properly with so many layers of clothes in the way, but he kept his hand on the sleeve of Joe's coat, and inched closer to keep Joe within his circle of warmth. "Please don't be upset. We don't have to go to the store." He used the same voice he'd used for injured Peter, and petted Joe's arm until Joe's expression became less severe. "We can return to the house, or your apartment. You can even send me away if you don't want the attention again. I can't help being dragon, but I don't want it to hurt you."

"Send you away?" Joe echoed, barely audible, in a tone that said he hadn't known that had been an option. Then he surprised Zarrin with a quick, soft smile. "You're so dramatic." He didn't sound angry. More like Joe's version of teasing, which was gentler than Marie's and more subtle than Bernard's. But then he sighed. "Sorry if I spoiled your good mood."

"Joseph, not even those hunters would spoil my mood today." Zarrin meant it. He had identified them through pictures, which so far had been enough, and he was not looking forward to having to face them, but at the moment he had no terror about it. Bernard had said that might happen later. Zarrin privately thought dragons were not supposed to be afraid of a conquered enemy, but he knew better than to tell Bernard that. Bernard had already threatened to drive back here, and Zarrin was finally starting to do well on his own.

He could do this on his own too, like calling his parents or making another visit to the sheriff's station. And in the meantime, he was with Joe.

"We could go get something to eat, then hide away someplace." Zarrin paused. "I mean, not *hide*—a dragon would never hide. Obviously."

"Okay." Joe's agreement shut him up. "There are some takeout places on the next street, unless you want a burrito."

Zarrin shook his head, although he suspected burritos from a restaurant would not be like the small frozen ones he'd made for himself a few times.

Joe started off in a new direction. Zarrin walked alongside him, hoping their hands might brush and that might turn into more. Joe had let Zarrin hold his hand back at the house, but they'd been alone then, and now Joe was anxious.

"Zarrin," Joe commented after a while. He stared resolutely ahead as he walked, as if he didn't see people sneaking glances at Zarrin. "I think it'd be okay, if you wanted to hide. I would—I left town for years, and that wasn't for anything like what happened to you."

"How can I protect anything if I'm hiding?" Zarrin tutted at him, while pretending he wasn't slightly panicked at the idea of everyone knowing about his failure.

Joe stopped long enough to scowl at him. Zarrin made a face and didn't answer. Then Joe continued on. "Are there really love potions that can do that?" he asked, after a few minutes of silence. He was very quiet. "I thought that was TV exaggerating things."

"I've never known a witch that well, but I believe so." Zarrin growled a bit, because Joe shouldn't have ever been accused of something like that. "But you wouldn't. Look how horrified you are to think about it." He didn't like this. He wanted the return of Joe from this afternoon, when Zarrin had gathered up Joe's clothes for him and kissed him as he'd returned each article of clothing. Joe's wide eyes and stunned silence had said more about what Joe was used to than Joe probably ever would.

"I am going to treat you so kindly," Zarrin promised him. "Just you wait. You are going to get so many kisses from me, Joseph. One for every frown, if I have to."

He might have said that louder than he'd meant to. The lady walking past them tripped over her dog's leash and was only saved by a mailbox.

Joe stopped walking.

Zarrin glanced at him, noting Joe looked more startled than angry, and hurriedly changed the subject to something less embarrassing for Joe.

He put his hands to a shop window to peer inside. Someone had painted the window with holly sprigs. Inside the shop was filled with mostly women buying bottles of what he thought were lotion or shampoo.

"Christmas is soon, isn't it? Do you celebrate?" He would have to find something special for Joe, but nothing to make Joe worry about the cost. His treasure could be so particular about that.

Joe came up next to him. "I sign the card my mom sends to my dad's family, and get her some presents. I spend the morning with her too. Sometimes we walk around town on Christmas Eve to see all the lights and the town's tree. When I was little, I remember some of the dragons attending the lighting ceremony every year."

There was a question hidden in Joe's words. Zarrin shrugged to conceal the nervous fires building in his chest. "I don't know what I'll be doing this year," he answered, then turned away from the shop window. He stopped in front of the next one when the smell of baking bread made his stomach rumble.

He'd eaten at the French bakery before and loved it. "Here?"

"It's good, but pricey." Joe was adorable. Zarrin had chosen well.

"I can pay, treasure." Zarrin rolled his eyes playfully. "And later, if you like, you can cook for me again, if that bothers you."

Joe opened and closed his mouth a few times, then snorted. "Boiling water for ramen isn't really cooking."

"But I get to buy you food now?" Zarrin focused on the most important part of what Joe was telling him. He grabbed Joe's elbow in his excitement, but remembered to let go before he swept into the building.

Several people were seated at the tables, but no one was in line or at the counter, which was fortunate since the warm doughy smells were making Zarrin aware of how hungry he was.

The older human woman behind the counter had a wonderfully sleek haircut and two clips holding her bangs from her face. She blinked several times when she saw Zarrin, but then came over to take his order.

Zarrin turned back in question. Joe was a few steps behind, glaring around the room with a stubborn expression on his face. Somehow, Zarrin did not think his annoyance was about the cost of the food. He glanced to the people at the tables. They'd stared when he and Marie had visited different places in town, since, as she had said, a werewolf and a dragon together were quite a sight even in a big city. But they should have been used to Zarrin by now, and recognized Joe by sight if not by name.

Zarrin held back smoke with effort and turned back to the counter woman. He ordered pumpkin bisque and a brie and apple grilled cheese before turning to Joe again. Joe was staring furiously at the floor, and Zarrin huffed out some smoke meaningfully so everyone in the bakery would know he meant business where Joe was concerned.

"The same for him?" the woman at the counter asked, in a delicate, almost conspiratorial whisper. She had a French accent. Perhaps she was the owner.

Zarrin nodded. "And a selection of rolls and sweets for later. And two hot chocolates. All to go."

She wrote out a little slip, which she handed to someone in the back before ringing him up. "Don't worry about them. They all wish they had a dragon to spoil them."

"Do they really?" Zarrin asked, then realized they thought he was keeping Joe in the way humans meant. Like a toy. Like one of Shǎnliàng's playthings.

She went over to a pastry case to pack a box for him, then tied it with string.

"Joseph isn't a fling," Zarrin told her, as coldly as he knew how.

She paused. "You look as though you want to hand-feed him every pastry in this box," she said, as she handed it over. "Who would do that for a fling?"

Zarrin froze, mesmerized at the thought of feeding Joe small pieces of warm chocolate croissants and caramel-drenched cream puffs.

The woman gave a throaty laugh and then went into the kitchen.

"Joe," Zarrin called over softly to him. "You're not a fling." He told Joe that the second Joe was close enough for him to whisper and then faced the counter again when the woman returned with their order in a bag and a cardboard tray with two cups in it.

"Thank you." Zarrin wasn't certain he liked this woman yet, but she'd given him some ideas, and she smiled warmly at Joe and had good vegetarian options, so he reserved judgment.

Joe took the box of pastries and the bag of food before Zarrin could, so Zarrin followed him outside with the two hot chocolates in his hands.

"I'm sorry you were embarrassed." Zarrin didn't think Joe was walking with any particular direction in mind. "I didn't mean to imply anything. Marie says I can be high-handed, but I only wanted to get some food with you."

"You didn't do anything." Joe made a frustrated sound but then glanced at him. "It's all over town by now anyway. Your scooter has been outside my apartment all night, in case you forgot. I don't care if people know. I'm not hiding anything. They'll think what they want. But… people are back in town right now for the holidays. That's all."

"We could take this to your apartment," Zarrin suggested.

"No." Joe went stubborn again. "It's a nice afternoon, and I don't feel like hiding if you don't." By nice afternoon, he probably meant it wasn't raining and the clouds were high enough that it almost felt sunny, even if it was still cold. He looked to Zarrin again. "We could eat in the park. I do, sometimes."

Which Zarrin knew, even though he'd never been bold enough to approach Joe there.

Zarrin turned around to take them back toward the park. Joe was upset, judging from his silence, but he didn't seem to mind walking close to Zarrin either. Zarrin smiled to himself and sipped from his cup to help keep his warmth up. Joe would need it soon. It wasn't *that* nice of an afternoon.

They entered the park from the north path, which still took them to the center and the benches a few yards away from Dìzhèn's statue. Zarrin waited until they were seated and Joe was enjoying a spoonful of his soup before he looked to his ancestor.

She regarded them impassively, watching, he thought, waiting to see if he'd mess things up. Perhaps she would want Joe among her treasure after all.

Zarrin scooted over until his thigh brushed Joe's.

"I know how to eat, Zarrin," Joe told him, teasing again, hot-voiced and quiet. He was—to use a vulgar phrase—being-bait, from his head to his toes. Zarrin yanked his knitted cap down over his ears, hunched over his sandwich, and stared defiantly at Dìzhèn.

She was right to judge Zarrin's wooing skills. The air was too cold. This was no sort of date.

But then Joe leaned into him, likely seeking out his heat, and Zarrin relaxed. He finished his sandwich, then decided to have his soup later so he could enjoy his hot chocolate. "Mine," he murmured before he had another sip. Joe shot him a quick look. He was nearly flush against Zarrin's side, so he truly must not mind being seen with Zarrin.

Zarrin threw his sandwich wrapper back in the bag it came in, then reached across Joe to grab the pastry box so he could put it in his messenger bag. Then he picked up Joe's drink and handed it to him.

Joe gave him another look. Zarrin stared back innocently, but sighed in happiness when Joe took a sip. Then he stowed away Joe's garbage as well and drank his chocolate next to Joe in contentment.

He kept an eye on Dìzhèn, though.

Joe must have as well. "Sometimes that statue almost seems alive," he offered, with his fingers tight around his paper cup. His tone was strange, almost like he was asking.

Zarrin sat straight up to glare his glorious ancestor into submission. Then he realized what he was doing and barely contained his shocked gasp.

"Like right now, the clouds and the shadows make her seem amused," Joe went on, touched by magic enough to see what others couldn't, and yet blind to Zarrin's predicament.

Zarrin watched the statue carefully, searching for fury or indignation, and seeing only what Joe had said, benign amusement, or perhaps approval.

It didn't calm him. If he'd had a tail at the moment, it would have been twitching. Joe was his, and Zarrin would challenge even a true dragon for him. He had only been more frightened once in his life, but no amount of fire was going to chase this away. He would defend Joe from anyone. He would fight for him the way someone should have long before Zarrin had ever spoken to him.

Then Joe stiffened next to him, and pulled away so abruptly Zarrin whined in complaint. Joe was staring at the path to the street, near the statue's base, where two humans stood.

One of them, the woman, was familiar, although her hair was not in two braids today. Mads was her name. She met Zarrin's eyes and then wisely looked away. She pulled lightly on the sleeve of the man next to her, but he wasn't moving.

He was handsome, with short, parted hair and broad shoulders. He seemed tall and fit, and the plum scarf around his throat went well with his peach skin and brown hair. Zarrin would guess he was about Joe's age.

Zarrin turned to Joe, and found Joe steadfastly staring at his hot chocolate.

Zarrin grasped his paper cup to feel the heat against his palms. It helped him keep his voice even. "Is that him?"

Joe raised his head to blink at him. "What?"

Zarrin would not be denied. "The one those women referred to. The one who lied and hurt you. Is that him?"

The delay in Joe's response was the answer Zarrin needed, although it didn't tell him what to do. Only Joe could tell him that.

"That's Russ. It's always weird when we run into each other in town. It's as if he wants to talk to me, but never makes it over." Joe tucked a strand of hair behind his ear. "I don't think he likes to see me having a life, or he thinks…. Who cares what he thinks? I wouldn't have been someone he'd bring home, even if I didn't have a dick. I've got a Mexican last name and an Indian mother. According to assholes like his parents, I'm not good enough… but that shouldn't upset someone if he really—anyway."

Joe focused on Zarrin again, and gave a small shrug that Zarrin didn't believe for a second. He smelled not-angry. Joe smelled of hurt and a need for sweetness. "Now, I think he was scared. He did want me, maybe, but not enough. Or… he still found it easy to let others blame me."

Zarrin swung his head toward Russ, who had finally noticed that a member of the Xu family was sitting next to Joe. He stared at Zarrin in amazement and fear and then at Joe with something else entirely in his eyes.

That man dared to still think of Joe as his.

Zarrin reached over and took Joe's hand.

Joe made a noise, more confused than complaining.

"Would you like me to deal with him?" Zarrin asked, their fingers locked together and his thumb sweeping along the outside of Joe's hand.

Joe glanced down and then at Zarrin's face. "I don't need protecting," he insisted, although his voice was rough.

"Perhaps I want to, even if it's not needed." Zarrin brought Joe's hand up to his mouth to kiss the back of it, so Joe wouldn't be upset. But Joe's eyes went even wider, as if he couldn't comprehend any of this. Zarrin released his hand so he could drag his knuckles along Joe's cheekbone and brush his lips with his fingertips.

Joe exhaled a harsh breath. "What are you doing?"

Zarrin petted him again, putting his hair back for him and tracing the edge of his mouth. "Thinking about kissing you."

Joe's eyebrows twitched, as if he wanted to frown, but couldn't. "Because he's there?"

"Partly." Zarrin inclined his head to acknowledge the man who would never come near Joe again. "And because you're unhappy and I don't like it."

"Yeah?" Joe always asked that question as though he didn't believe what he was hearing. So Zarrin tipped his head up and leaned in and pressed his mouth to Joe's, as softly as he knew how. He darted out his tongue to taste chocolate and the unraveling loveliness of Joe's desire for him and then eased back to take a breath.

The dark wonder in Joe's eyes made his chest tight. "Perfect," Zarrin praised him, to watch the startled hunger sneak into Joe's face. He looked the same when Zarrin pinned him to the bed. "Again?" Zarrin asked, and moved forward when Joe parted his lips.

He cupped Joe's jaw and swayed toward him when Joe let him in with a breathless moan. "Mine," Zarrin whispered, nibbling at one full lip before sliding their lips together. Joe's quiet moan was almost lost. Zarrin ended the kiss before he pounced on Joe right there, and that was only because Joe was not to be shared. Joe opened his eyes when Zarrin leaned back, so Zarrin returned to plant a brief kiss to that beautiful mouth. "So good, treasure. It's so hard to let you go."

"Yeah?" Joe asked again, as if Zarrin wasn't lingering in his space to inhale his breath or brushing his lips across his jaw.

Zarrin placed his thumb to Joe's lower lip and felt like fire itself. "Yes." He had to kiss Joe again and then once more before the slosh of liquid in the cup in his hand reminded him he was holding something, that he was in a park, and this was very public. "I think," he said, his voice scratchy, "that if you and I had met where no one else was around, I would have kissed you immediately."

A line appeared between Joe's eyes when Zarrin didn't kiss him again, and then he stared at Zarrin in dazed confusion. "What?"

"But of course, it would have been different then," Zarrin conceded, and stroked Joe's cheekbone once more before pulling away. He needed to breathe air that wasn't rich with Joe's needs.

Joe sucked in a breath, abruptly looking much more alert, so Zarrin took his last chance to check on the liar who had broken Joe's heart. He was still there, although Mads had left.

Zarrin stared at him smugly before turning back to Joe.

"This will definitely be all over town by Monday," Joe warned him, his words slow.

"Drink your hot chocolate, or it'll get cold." Zarrin could not care less about what would be all over town, unless whatever it was bothered Joe. If people in town wanted to gossip about Zarrin buying Joe anything he wanted and feeding him treats in the park, then so be it. It was hardly a lie.

"You said…." Joe faded into silence without finishing his thought and glanced toward the statue. When Zarrin looked, Russ was gone, and Dìzhèn was placidly watching them. "Thank you."

Zarrin raised his eyebrows, but couldn't imagine what he was being thanked for, unless it was getting rid of Russ. He leaned against Joe's shoulder and remembered his own chocolate. It wasn't kissing, but it was still good. "Anything you ask, treasure."

"Zarrin." Joe's voice wasn't quite thick with arousal, but he did stumble over Zarrin's name the way he did when he was close to coming. "You say that stuff, but… do you take me seriously?"

"Yes. Of course." Zarrin huffed to demonstrate this, sending smoke to the sky.

Joe did not seem impressed, and he still didn't turn his head to look directly at him. "I'm more than just someone you want to fuck?"

Zarrin hissed a little at the word, at the *image*. "Yes."

"I want to believe that." Joe licked his lips and then took another drink. Zarrin lifted his chin to argue the point, but Joe wasn't done. "Zarrin, if you… want company when you go to the station or back out to the Preserve… you can ask me." He exhaled when Zarrin didn't move or speak. "Or don't. Never mind. It's not like we're serious."

"I…." Zarrin put his cup on the bench and clasped his hands tightly together. All his earlier heat was gone. "I can't let you see me tremble at the sheriff's station. I would be no kind of dragon to allow that." He shuddered and closed his eyes. "But I… I would love to show you my Preserve sometime, Joseph, if that will do. I haven't gone back yet."

He felt himself shaking, the beginnings of a temblor forming deep inside him, and then Joe pushed against him, warm along his side, and the panic eased.

Zarrin left his eyes closed so he wouldn't see Dìzhèn's expression, and lowered his head to Joe's shoulder.

The hand Joe carefully rested on his knee relit his every fire.

THEY AGREED to go their own ways for a few hours, which was a terrible thing to ask when Zarrin was still new to kissing Joe. But Joe had wanted to clean up, take care of some things around his apartment. Zarrin hadn't wanted to let him go, and Zarrin hadn't wanted to crowd him or scare him away.

But it didn't really matter in the end. Zarrin finally went to the grocery store before returning home, and he had barely put the groceries away when Joe knocked at the door. Joe stood there on the doorstep, with a duffel bag in one hand and his hair sleek in its little ponytail, so uncertain of his welcome that Zarrin had dragged him inside to kiss him against the door.

Joe had taken a shower, and changed his clothes, and Zarrin kissed him until his mouth was as plump as it had been that afternoon. Then he finished bringing Joe inside, and led him upstairs, and curled up with him on his bed to watch recorded episodes of his favorite soap opera.

Zarrin was a few episodes behind, but felt less interest than usual over the developments on *Diedre's Secret*. Probably because he was half in Joe's lap, with his back to Joe's chest as Joe leaned against the wall beneath the window. Zarrin was comfortable and distracted at the same time. It didn't help that Joe kept asking questions about the characters, or snorting to himself at the dialogue.

Zarrin shushed him, then spent a few moments in worried terror—he hadn't gotten Joe to finally be with him, only to tell him to be quiet.

But Joe snorted some more and at least waited until Zarrin was fast-forwarding through a commercial to speak again.

"You know, this isn't how I imagined my first sleepover would go." His tone said he thought something was very funny, but when Zarrin twisted around to look at him, he wasn't smiling.

Zarrin considered the meanings of "sleepover" before leaning back to see Joe better. The mound of cushions around them kept him from falling.

"Did you want more popcorn?" Zarrin liked caramel microwave popcorn the best, although Joe, like Bernard, preferred salt and butter. He had his own bowl, mostly empty, at his side. Nemo had stuck his face in it.

Joe shook his head and smiled. Zarrin smiled back at him and gave a small sigh of contentment before returning his attention to the TV. He stayed as he was, more lying across Joe's lap than sitting in it.

A few minutes later, Joe spoke again. "You really asked me here to sleep over, didn't you?" Luckily, it was in the middle of a plot point Zarrin didn't care about.

For about five seconds, Zarrin managed to sound lofty. "If you are trying to ask if I invited you here for reasons of a sexual nature… well, yes. I like having sex with you. But this is nice too, having you here. This house is quiet, sometimes."

"All the time." Joe's sense of humor could be very dry.

Zarrin glanced at him and found Joe watching him. That was far more interesting than TV. Zarrin hit Pause and then shoved the remote aside.

"Finally spending time with you is all I wanted. Or—" Zarrin nodded to concede the point. "—not *all* I wanted, but if you fell asleep right now, or decided to stay up all night to watch every single anime DVD Bernard left behind, that's good too. Well, not the anime. Some of it never seems to end, Joe!" He shut up when Joe's smile split his face. "What?"

"Nothing." Joe shook his head, using his unfair teasing voice, and then focused on the TV as if he cared about the struggles of Blake, Stupid Werewolf. Zarrin hit Play again, but with a suspicious glance at the human watching him.

Zarrin meant to say something, but then the fairy appeared, and he smacked his hand over Joe's mouth instead. "Look at that fairy! Look at his sparkles! He's supposed to hate the villain and yet he *sparkles*! I need to buy those soap-opera magazines and find out what is going on between those two."

"Fairy sparkles don't always mean anything," Joe said, muffled behind Zarrin's palm.

"He loves him, I tell you!" Zarrin insisted, then dropped his hand to grab at Joe's sweater when the fairy turned toward the villain with a frown, acting to the best of a fairy's ability, as if his heart weren't on his sleeve.

"Oh," Joe murmured, when the fairy's glitter blazed with color. Then he fell silent.

Zarrin watched the fairy moon over his chosen human for as long as they were onscreen, then switched his attention to Joe. "When this episode's over, we can watch something else."

"Watch whatever you want." The furrow in Joe's forehead was puzzling when he'd just been smiling. "I don't have TV and have no idea what's on anyway."

"Marie said I should be kinder to Blake. Love is hard, even for werewolves." Zarrin sighed. "I suppose she's right. Even when you know, everything can be complicated."

"Well, Valerie has made it pretty clear she's waiting for him." Joe briefly closed his eyes. "Please don't tell Martin I've watched this enough to know their names."

"Martin has enough things to worry about," Zarrin huffed, while Joe frowned as if he had no idea what Zarrin was referring to. Martin's very obvious struggle with his bisexuality was something Joe had commented on, at least once, when in Zarrin's hearing, but perhaps Joe didn't believe his own insight. Silly, when the only reason Zarrin had ignored Martin's small crush on Joe was that *everyone* seemed to have a small crush on Joe, and it was the one thing Joe was blind to.

But he was here with Zarrin now. So Zarrin sat up enough to curl against his side again. Joe caught his breath and then carefully eased an arm around Zarrin's waist.

It was much easier to ignore the feelings of awe his treasure inspired in others when his treasure was touching him shyly and sneaking popcorn from Zarrin's bowl. Zarrin didn't feel even the faintest need to try to stop him. The wonders of finding one's treasure!

Tomorrow morning, Zarrin was going to feed Joe pastries in this very bed. He would feed him, and keep him, for as long as Joe allowed. No one would get in his way.

But he yawned a moment later, not sleepy, but comfortable and warm. The cats were curled up by his feet, and Joe's hand had slipped under his shirt.

Another series of commercials came on, but the remote seemed far away. Zarrin wasn't inclined to move with Joe's heartbeat against his back and Joe's breath above his ear and then down along his neck.

Zarrin made a strangled sound when he felt Joe's lips graze his skin. Joe trailed a few kisses behind and beneath Zarrin's ear, then stopped, cruelly, when the commercials ended and the show came back on. His hand, however, stayed under Zarrin's shirt, and he slowly swept it back and forth as the characters on TV talked about… something. Zarrin honestly had no idea what.

He arched his neck invitingly, but there were no more kisses—at least until the next bunch of ads came on. Zarrin shivered when Joe's fingertips dipped into his waistband, and Joe renewed his gentle, teasing kisses at the side of Zarrin's throat.

"What are you doing?" Zarrin wasn't protesting, far from it. He gasped and slid a hand over Joe's on top of his sweater to encourage him. "Do you want more?" He sounded breathless and confused and then roughly thrilled when he felt the light scrape of Joe's teeth. "I can give you more."

"I know." Joe paused, as if he was thinking about his words. "I like when you do. But… I've always wanted to do this." Joe ended that sentence by kissing Zarrin's neck in a way that was going to leave a mark, at least for a few hours.

"What?" Zarrin panted at him, absolutely blind to what was onscreen. "What are we doing?"

"Making out?" Joe paused long enough to move to the other side of Zarrin's neck. "Necking, I think is what people used to call it. Fooling around while watching TV." He stopped again when Zarrin didn't respond right away. "You… know what that is, right?"

"Of course I do!" Zarrin made a face Joe couldn't see, then quietly admitted the rest. "I've never…. My only partners were other dragons. Our parents wanted us to get along, and we were teenagers, so the inevitable happened once we were alone. But none of them ever watched TV with me."

"Just sex?" Joe stopped kissing him and rested his forehead on the back of Zarrin's head. "I kind of wondered how you could be like this, and fuck like you do, and still have never been anyone's."

"I could be yours," Zarrin replied without thinking, then squirmed away from Joe in order to twist around to study him. "You like how I fuck? I'm good for you?" He wriggled forward so he could straddle Joe's lap and then used both hands to push Joe's hair behind his ears.

"You're good for me." Joe's voice was husky. He spread both his hands out on Zarrin's bare skin and tugged him forward by his hips. "I just want to do this right now."

The way he sucked and kissed at the hollow of Zarrin's throat was going to drive Zarrin crazy. "Then please proceed."

"But your show is on," Joe teased him. He dared to *tease*, as if he weren't pulling Zarrin's sweater up to expose his chest. Then he gave a small laugh, as if he didn't quite believe himself either. The laugh faded to heavy silence when Zarrin merely lifted his arms to let Joe strip him.

The sweater and shirt landed on top of Nemo, who flopped over onto her side, apparently not bothered enough to move.

Zarrin closed his eyes at the feel of Joe's fingertips traveling up his spine and along his back. They paused at the tiny patches of scar tissue near Zarrin's shoulder blades, but then swept down to Zarrin's hips. Zarrin leaned forward to capture his mouth, which tasted of Zarrin's caramel popcorn. He hitched his body closer, and Joe's hands fell to his ass.

Zarrin rocked against Joe a little as he grew hard and felt Joe do the same. Joe tightened his grip and made pleading, quiet gasps into Zarrin's mouth that became pleased grunts when Zarrin ended the kiss to suck marks at the juncture of Joe's neck and shoulder.

"Do we get to come eventually?" he wondered, while considering the outline of his mouth on Joe's skin.

Joe's startled shiver at the rush of Zarrin's breath over his wet skin was very satisfying. So was his soft laugh. "I wouldn't say no."

"But this first?" Zarrin raised his head to look Joe in the eye, then was distracted by Joe's well-kissed lips and hungry stare. "Yes," he answered his own question, anything to keep Joe gentle and happy. He stroked Joe's cheek until Joe closed his eyes, and then pressed his mouth to his forehead, where there was no frown. Joe's hands had him shivering in anticipation. He wondered if he could bear the wait, but from the way Joe kept squeezing him and inching his hips up, he didn't think it would be much longer. He wanted to grind down, and restrained himself, barely, by remembering this was supposed to be slow.

"Humans do this?" he panted, while Joe grasped at his skin as if trying to drag Zarrin on top of him. He kissed Joe again, but harder, and Joe shuddered before pulling away. He caught his breath beneath Zarrin's ear, as if Zarrin's pants weren't painfully tight. Joe's probably were too. "Why?" Zarrin asked, not in agony, but aware it could happen.

"Because it feels good." Joe seemed to be trying to convince himself, because in the next moment he slid his hand up Zarrin's back. "You feel good too," Joe added, the words nearly a hum.

Zarrin would have preened for him at any other moment. Now he felt like begging, weak and foolish, for Joe to say more. He stopped instead, until his blood wasn't pounding and his breathing was quieter. Then he arched back until Joe lifted his head to look at him.

Zarrin immediately placed a soft kiss on his lips and spent a moment tucking his hair safely behind his ears once more. "Then please proceed," he told Joe gravely, and lit up with pride at the smile on his treasure's face.

JOE HAD never spent all night and all day in bed with someone, never woken up with the early morning sun in his face, hugging the warm spot where someone had been moments before, never secretly watched someone come back from the bathroom and curl up next to him.

Zarrin hadn't either. Maybe that was why, when he saw Joe was awake, he gently displaced the two cats that had taken over his pillow in his absence and scooted in to kiss Joe good morning. In the bright light of sunrise, the scales in Zarrin's skin were nearly blinding. He had a strange sense of modesty, and went downstairs without any clothes on to grab the box of pastries from the day before, but then turned shy while lying on his stomach, with Joe kissing the scars at his shoulder blades.

He pushed pieces of flaky, buttery croissant between Joe's lips as if nothing had ever been more serious, then watched another episode of his soap while Joe was in the shower. He pouted when his favorite fairy didn't make an appearance.

Joe couldn't stop staring at him. He heard himself saying, "I'm sure he'll be in the next one." He ate two pastries too many because Zarrin seemed to enjoy feeding him so much. And when the simple act of Joe tying his hair back made Zarrin ask in a tremulous voice if he was leaving, instead of pointing out that he would have to leave sometime, Joe said nothing but Zarrin's name.

"I know, I know," Zarrin had grumbled at him a second later, making the grabby hands gesture Joe was starting to associate with moments of Zarrin's anxiety. "You must leave me. I *know*. But I don't have to like it."

"I don't have to go yet," Joe answered, standing there in the doorway of the laundry room while Zarrin washed the bedding they'd dirtied. Maybe it wasn't normal to spend this much time with someone this early into something, but he wouldn't know. And he wanted to. And Zarrin wanted to, and that did something to him where his heart would beat faster despite how peaceful he felt.

Sunday was a day for chores, even for dragons. Even for dragons on whatever number date this was, if this counted as a date. Joe had no idea, about any of it. He had a hickey at the base of his neck, and a pleasant ache in his muscles, and a suspicion there was a funny look on his face, because every so often Zarrin would stop and grin at him.

Then Joe would say, "Your hair," because Zarrin's hair was so soft, even though he hadn't meant to say anything about it, or, "Stop looking at me like I'm a smooth river stone, Zarrin," although he didn't mind how Zarrin looked at him when he thought Zarrin meant it. Then Zarrin would proudly insist that Joe was better than the prettiest rock from the river, only to get distracted into showing Joe more of his rock collection in order to prove it.

"Is this what you'd normally be doing today?" Joe finally asked, after Zarrin had gone on about the mineral content of the river water for a while. "Working on your research?"

"Well, no." Zarrin blinked up at him, for all the world as though he would have had glasses if he hadn't been dragon. "In the afternoons, I usually go into the Preserve."

"Don't let me stop you," Joe answered without thinking, then quickly shook his head. "I just meant—"

"Would you like to see it?" Zarrin lowered his gaze to the pyrite in one of his hands. "I could show you. Not… not there. Not that place, yet. But the rest. Or some of it. It's more exciting than my rocks, I suppose. Bernard tried, but he never thought they were interesting. Maybe if you saw them in context?"

"Rocks in context?" Joe echoed, in the embarrassingly fond tone he'd been using all day. "I want to see the Preserve, Zarrin, but you don't have to show me right now."

The peeking glance upward Zarrin did when he was scared and didn't want anyone to know might be Joe's undoing someday. "I have to go sooner or later," Zarrin told Joe seriously. "It's mine to protect, and I miss it."

Fear was normal for anyone in Zarrin's situation. But according to Zarrin, dragons should never be in his situation. That was obvious bullshit, since if dragons were so fearless, they would never have hidden away like all the other beings. However, since it did no good to say that, Joe took the pyrite from Zarrin's hand and returned it to the desk.

"Then the shoes I brought will do for a short hike," he said, as lightly as he could, not that he fooled Zarrin. Zarrin wouldn't want Joe to acknowledge his fear of returning to the Preserve. But they both knew it was there, and that was as much pretense as Joe was capable of.

Zarrin narrowed his eyes and hissed a little before releasing a puff of dark smoke. But he stood up. "You do things to me, treasure," he growled, in a voice that would have been scary if Joe hadn't known exactly what he meant.

Then he bundled up in a big coat and his knitted cap while Joe put on his shoes, and clucked his tongue when Joe didn't bother with a scarf or a hat. He seemed confused that Joe would want to take supplies like water with him even for a short hike, but apparently shrugged it off as a human thing, because he stopped peering at the water bottle and phone stuffed into Joe's coat pocket before they were even off the porch.

Joe was kind of curious about the other buildings, and the rest of the property close to the mansion. He hadn't gotten a chance to see the rest of the house, much less any of the surrounding structures. But Zarrin clenched his jaw and began to walk toward the not-so-distant tree line, so Joe followed without asking for more of a tour.

Zarrin led him away from the driveway, in the opposite direction of where Joe had found him after—during—the earthquakes. Someone must have maintained the property around the house once. Overgrown bushes could have been topiaries. There might have been a lawn, or at least flowers, and even the rich had gardens for herbs and vegetables back in Dìzhèn's day. There was no sign of one now. His mom had always wanted a little garden, but they'd never lived in a place with anything that would be considered a yard.

He thought he saw a pool, and a greenhouse, and maybe a garage, but Zarrin passed them as if he didn't notice them. He could have been used to them. Or he could have been more consumed with whatever he felt as they got closer to the cool darkness of the trees.

"Joe." Zarrin didn't look around to see if Joe was listening. "If I shame myself, could you pretend not to notice?" Joe felt his eyebrows twitch. He was probably frowning, but Zarrin couldn't see. "I know you don't like lying, or liars," Zarrin went on, in a small voice that didn't quite have a tremor in it. "But please?"

Joe studied the slight, golden shape of him, obscured by his puffy coat, and then sighed.

"What could you possibly do that would shame you?" Joe asked, and shoved his chilled hands into his pockets.

Zarrin stumbled, then righted himself so swiftly it might not have happened at all. He glanced back, reproachfully, or pleased, or both, and then sailed regally through the first stand of redwoods.

They headed northwest at first, hitting on a barely discernable trail. The trail was about four or five feet wide, wider than that in some places, as if a swishing tail had left its mark.

Zarrin moved with the same grace over fallen tree limbs and damp earth that he did down city streets. Sometimes his breath would leave him in a huge fluffy white cloud of steam, and he'd shiver despite his great big coat and all his knitted accessories.

"How is it you're cold all the time?" Joe's breath was a little steamy too.

Zarrin stopped and turned back to him with wide eyes. "It's this body!" he declared indignantly. "I'm very fond of it, but it doesn't keep the heat in."

Joe thought about asking how it was Zarrin could grow bigger sometimes, and yet still chose a little human body. "I like your body," he said instead, and felt a flush in his stinging cold cheeks.

"Joseph!" Zarrin purred in approval before his shoulders drooped. "I can't keep you warm like this, not really, not how I should. But you wanted to walk with me into the Preserve, and this is the only way to do that. I should—" He scowled in determination. "I *will* ask Bernard to knit you a scarf and hat. That will help."

He nodded while Joe knew he was staring in confused surprise, and then resumed walking.

"A peregrine falcon used to live in this tree," he remarked, with an airy gesture up toward the increasingly crowded canopy. There were more shadows than spots of dappled sunlight. "The topsoil is red because of its high iron oxide content. It's very nutrient rich because the redwood forest floor is full of decaying leaves and wood and other natural elements. You… probably know that already." Zarrin was briefly sheepish and then excited once more. He laughed as one of the occasional drips of water from the branches above them hit his cheek. "These are old-growth trees, each one its own ecosystem that takes water from the fog and shares with the plants below it, as well as with the fungi in its branches. If you cut one of them down, you'd take a water source away from everything below it. You… probably know that too. I'm being silly. But I've never gotten to show this to anyone who hasn't already seen it, and it's exciting to think that you could love it as much as I do."

Zarrin stopped dead and turned around to give Joe a look of amazement. "Is this why humans like sharing so much?"

The pang in Joe's stomach was all need and yearning for the earnestly dorky park ranger in front of him. His voice was soft. "What did you name the falcon?"

"D'Artagnan." Zarrin stared at Joe in wonder, then shook his head. "I'm not sure why he stopped here for so long, but he found his mate and nested by the ridge. Do you like birds of prey? They're fascinating, although I don't like to watch them eat their kills. They attack other birds," he added, in a whisper, before sweeping forward along the trail again. "This was the first trail my sister and I were allowed to run free on when we were children. It's my favorite, except when I want to be closer to the river, or when I haven't been up into the foothills to look down in forever and I miss it. Or the ridge at the very north edge of the Preserve, where there is a waterfall when the snows melt. Or my grotto at the heart of the forest."

"Your grotto?" Joe walked nearly silently after him, trying to imagine the dragon children playing here. Dìzhèn's children might have played here. Only dragons would have set foot here in a hundred years.

He'd known that before—everyone in town knew that. Unless a secretary or a plaything had been permitted to wander the property, no one but dragons had walked this land in more than a century. He could see that with his own eyes. The stands of trees were thicker, the trees greater and taller than anything near the trails in the state park. And it would be like this throughout the entire ninety-nine acres.

"The, um, grotto," Zarrin's explanation was background noise as Joe stepped off the trail. "Isn't really a grotto, except to me at ten, when I read adventure books and convinced myself it was. There's a stream that winds that way, and a collection of boulders that almost form a cave—if you're a boy with too much imagination."

Joe smiled to himself at the image, and the wet, rough scrape of bark against his palm as he put a hand to the base of one tree and then looked up. He could barely see to the top, but he thought the tree was gazing back at him, curious and distant. A few branches swayed in the wind, and droplets of water continued to fall, creating a soft hush of noise where he'd expected silence.

But then, the land hadn't been dead and gone this whole time. It had been alive and well; it *was* alive. Not waiting for him, because the land had been here first, and would be here long after humans were gone, but aware, somehow, that a human was present.

The tree didn't shiver with apprehension. It stood, solid and strong, until Joe twitched with the need to paint it. He had nothing on hand to let him, so he moved on to another tree, one with a trunk wider than his car. This one he didn't touch, and left it to its disinterest.

He knelt down to consider the wet, dark layer of decaying leaves and the red soil beneath it. He wondered if there were salamanders watching him, and what Zarrin thought of them, and then looked up to see Zarrin by the curious tree.

"This land hadn't been touched by the gold miners or the timber men when Dìzhèn claimed it and did whatever she did to keep it safe." Joe wasn't really asking. Some of Dìzhèn's land might have been damaged by overzealous loggers, but not this part. "And of all the people who end up walking it again, it's me?"

Zarrin opened his hands in a helpless gesture. "Who else should it be?"

Joe swallowed the lump in his throat and shook his head to indicate that he didn't know.

"We don't have to stay, if it bothers you." Zarrin came a few steps closer.

"I'm—" Joe struggled for the right word. "—overwhelmed, not bothered." For some reason he hadn't been prepared. He'd been focused on Zarrin's fear, or confused this with every other hike he'd been on. "I like it here. I—" *Love it here.* The state park was huge and beautiful, but it was the kingdom that had sprung up from this ancient civilization.

"The *awe*," Zarrin said, wisely. "It never really goes away." He sighed. "I adore them, but I think the trees only tolerate me. They probably remember that I was a very silly child, and have decided I'm not fit to protect them. But at least they accept that I mean them no harm."

"Is that what you think?" Joe looked up at the trees again, and put a hand to the ground so he wouldn't fall over when the height made him dizzy. Of course the trees were alive to Zarrin. He'd seen the same thing in Joe's painting.

"But they seem interested in you." Zarrin crossed his arms as if sulking, but his tone wasn't pouting. "That one pretending it doesn't care, this one openly curious about you." Zarrin *was* sulking. "But you were mine first."

There were too many things to say to that to say anything.

Zarrin came a little closer, then a little more. He kneeled down beside Joe and wiped droplets of water from the back of Joe's neck that Joe hadn't noticed.

"Protecting something doesn't always mean keeping other people away from it." Joe shivered at Zarrin's temperature, and the care he took for a few drops of water.

"Are you suggesting I let others out here?" Zarrin didn't quite sputter, but he did raise his voice. His words echoed faintly back to him, and he must not have liked the sound of them, because he grumbled. "Humans have done bad things to places like this," he insisted, although Joe wasn't arguing. "They have done bad things *in* places like this," he added softly, then stood up. He got one fingernail between his teeth and then tore his hand away from his mouth.

Joe got to his feet too. "But I'm different?"

"Don't be stupid. Of course you are." Zarrin cut him an irritated but questioning look.

"And beings never do bad things?" Joe pressed. "You're the last dragon here. What if the next generation of Dìzhèn's descendants doesn't like the Preserve and leaves it forever?" Zarrin's annoyance turned to shocked silence, but he still wasn't arguing. Joe went on. "How could anyone love it without knowing it?"

"You loved it before you ever set foot on it." Zarrin stuck out his jaw, mulishly, then exhaled. "But I just said you were different. Which you are, Joseph. Never forget that."

Joe squared his shoulders. "Zarrin, the first time I set foot on the Preserve, I was eighteen and I spray-painted over the sign telling people to go away. I'm not that different."

"It doesn't tell people to go away. It says—" Zarrin shut his mouth with a snap, then reopened it. "*You* did that? You wrote 'There are no dragons' on the sign? *Joseph*!" He was scandalized. "My mother was furious! Why would you do that?"

"Because there were no dragons here." Joe could cross his arms and be stubborn too. "There were supposed to be, but they were gone."

"You were waiting." Zarrin's anger seemed to vanish in the blink of an eye. "You were hurt." He swept forward to curl around Joe and rest his head at his shoulder. "I'm sorry I wasn't here. I was young, and by then I'd forgotten most of the details of you. Sometimes I'd be in the car, on my way out of Everlasting, or being driven through town to visit the house, and I'd see *something*, like a shape or an outline, but that's all. You grew up and you waited while I let them tell me to date other dragons—you can be jealous about that. I don't mind."

Joe was too bemused to be jealous. Zarrin didn't seem to notice.

"You got tall and strong and changed your hair. You put music and art beneath your skin, and they look like *scales*. They *tempt* me." Zarrin's breath was hot at his neck. "May I tell you something?" He was whispering, although nothing but the trees would hear him. "You're so right that I don't know what to do. I want to give you what a dragon should, but what if I can't? What if I fail you? It was an accident that made the house respond to my need like that. I'm not that strong."

Joe put a hand to Zarrin's shoulder, then slid it up to tangle in Zarrin's hair. His grip was probably painful, but he couldn't relax his hand, and anyway, Zarrin didn't complain.

"If you fail me?" Joe asked. He was quiet too.

Zarrin snuffled beneath his ear. "My family sent me out here because I wasn't interested in school, or business, or finding another dragon, or traveling the world in search of shiny things. They didn't know what else to do with me. I'm a failure, but a failure who has always preferred being here. Because I am weak, and no challenge to Dìzhèn, I don't mind staying here. I want to live here."

"This is your home." Joe hoped what he was saying made sense. His thoughts were whirling, and he found it hard to breathe the cold, wet air when Zarrin's heat was making him shiver. Or perhaps Zarrin was shivering, and it was radiating out to Joe. He eased his fingers from Zarrin's hair and tugged his cap over his ears. Zarrin made a pitiful sound a starving cat wouldn't have made and wrapped himself tighter around Joe.

"Do you have to do what your family says? I know I'm disconnected from what should be my family, so I don't know how larger families work, but—" Joe thought about it, then frowned. "Fuck them." Zarrin flinched, so Joe took a calming breath. "You might not be a superdragon, but you're learning. And you know what else? You know how to let things go. I bet most dragons don't, do they?"

"What?" Zarrin pulled back enough to look at him. His eyes were close to sparkling with tears he probably wouldn't want Joe to mention.

Joe wasn't about to stop, though. "If it's in the best interest of what you want to protect, you let it go. The rabbits and the deer and… Bernard and Marie. That's strength. Some people never let go. Shit, Russ still comes to town and I can tell he wants… he thinks he could…. You should…." He ran out of steam there, when the quiet reminded him that the trees were listening. "You should get to keep something."

Zarrin blinked a few times. "Like what?"

*Like me.* Joe bit back the stupid, stupid words and forced them down, next to the pains in his stomach and beneath his pounding heart. "I don't know."

Zarrin put a hand to his chest, as if he also felt something painful there. Then he leaned against Joe again and clutched at Joe's coat. "And you should believe that you belong here. I'm sorry I was gone, that I couldn't stand up to them to stay."

"Would you now?" Joe wrapped his arms around Zarrin and held him close, which was another first in a weekend full of them.

"Someone has to look over things," Zarrin said, after a pause, mumbling into Joe's coat.

"You've traveled. You've seen the world," Joe reminded him, scowling for no reason he could name. "I had to go away to realize Everlasting is home to me. So did you, I guess. But you shouldn't have had to if you didn't want to go."

"My home." Zarrin's greedy statement was muffled. "Mine."

"Not Dìzhèn's?" Joe wondered, with a knitted cap under his nose.

Zarrin growled, and the earth rumbled, a small but nerve-wracking tremor. Zarrin seemed startled, but then he pushed his hands beneath Joe's sweater to rest them against his skin, and the land was still. "*Mine*." He shuddered closer. "My rocks and my deer and my bend in the river. I am the one who shivers for the turn in the air that means spring. I'm the one to frighten away hunters and who worries over the rainfall. I'd do the same for the town, if it lets me. And if I can't do it well, then I don't deserve it. I wanted to be here, but I didn't fight to stay. So it wasn't mine then."

Joe blinked upward, then closed his eyes. "You wanted to stay?" He didn't know why that made a difference. Their paths would never have crossed, not even in a small town.

"I'll make it up to you, and to everyone in town who looked for dragons that weren't there." Zarrin ran his hands down Joe's stomach in slow, soothing motions, although somehow Joe didn't think it was meant to comfort *him*. "I'm not Dìzhèn, or even Shǎngliàng, but I'll prove I can be trusted. I'll give you so much, treasure. Whatever you want."

Joe waited until he could speak without his voice cracking, but he couldn't stop the question from coming out of his mouth. "What if I asked for it? For this?" His lips were dry and already chapped with the cold. The sound of his heartbeat was almost deafening.

Zarrin answered the way he always did. "Anything, treasure." He said things like that, and probably meant them, but he didn't realize how crazy it was, how easy it was to make promises that couldn't be kept. Even if he wanted to mean it, he couldn't.

Joe enjoyed another second of Zarrin's hands on him. Then he took a deep breath. "What if I asked for this?" The cold at his back was going to be even worse when Zarrin pulled away. "What if I asked for the Preserve?"

Zarrin could have been made of stone. The warm little dragon Joe liked so much that it scared him became an unmoving statue in his arms.

Then he slid his hands from Joe's skin, and Joe couldn't quite hold back a soft, wounded grunt, although he'd expected it. Even a well-intentioned lie was still a lie. Russ had said his girlfriend was only a friend, said he was working up the courage to do what was right, said he loved Joe, but when it came down to it, anything he'd felt for Joe hadn't been enough to overcome his fear. Zarrin liked Joe, a lot, and he wanted to believe in his own bravery, but when he said *anything*, he didn't mean it.

Something plucked at the bottom of Joe's coat. Zarrin grasped nervously at him, then stopped. He drew in a ragged breath and kept his head down so that he spoke against Joe's shoulder.

"What—" Zarrin took another long breath. "What would you…? What would you do with it?" He tugged at Joe's coat and then his sweater, and then he pressed his fingertips to Joe's skin.

He was anxious, so Joe drew him closer before he could stop and think about what he was doing. But Zarrin buried his face in the base of Joe's throat and made small worried sounds, almost to himself. He spoke in a frantic whisper. "Would you… live here, or paint it, or never let me see it again? I know you love it, but it's mine, the one place I had that was mine and not theirs and not *hers*. You won't destroy it, I know that. Not you, not Joseph, but I… this hurts so much. Only the great ones must love humans, because you ask things a dragon would never ask."

"Zarrin?" Joe's brain stalled at "love" before rushing off in a dozen different directions as he realized Zarrin hadn't said no. Zarrin was asking what Joe would do with the Preserve if he did give it to him.

"Would it make you happy? I want you to be happy, but giving this up would hurt. Are you really asking?" Zarrin seemed so distressed that Joe cupped the back of his head and shushed him.

He had no answer. Zarrin had honestly considered handing over the Preserve to a guy he'd dated for a single weekend, even if he couldn't do it. And he wasn't a spoiled rich kid who didn't know the value of this place. Zarrin was in actual pain at the idea of giving it away.

Joe shushed him again, this gentle sound he hadn't known he could make, and rubbed at Zarrin's back. "I *could* ask," he explained, finally. "I could. You shouldn't say those things, Zarrin. I… I don't need promises. Not like that."

Zarrin lifted his head to reveal bright, wet eyes. "Yes, you do," he argued sadly. "Do you think I don't know how much you hate having the town's attention on you? And you did it anyway, because of me."

"Because of you?" Joe frowned. "I did it because I wanted you. It's not a sacrifice for me to be here. They can all think whatever the fuck they want. We know the truth."

"Do we?" The tip of Zarrin's nose was red either from the cold or from his barely suppressed tears. "What's the truth?"

"You like me," Joe explained, softening for something as ridiculous as a dragon with a red nose. "I like you. You don't need to make it… more. It's good as it is. We're not, you know, how they say." *Mates.* Joe couldn't even say the word because it wasn't true for so many reasons. "We're just better at this when the others aren't around. That's all. It's funny, really," he added, because Zarrin was staring at him and sniffling. "With Russ, it killed me for it to be the two of us, two kids in his big, empty house and no one else in the world. But being alone with you is the easiest thing." He wasn't sure what he meant by telling Zarrin that, but Zarrin listened with a serious, tense expression. "This whole weekend has been great, but it's not, uh, destiny, or magic or anything. We like each other. When you promise me *anything*"—it felt good, as good as Zarrin said, pretty, and right, and just *good*—"you don't need to do that. I know how things are."

"Do you?" Zarrin wondered quietly. He took one hand from Joe's stomach in order to wipe the traces of tears from his eyes, and then he lifted his chin. "Marie is a smart woman. Now I see what she was trying to tell me."

"What does that mean?" Joe wasn't going to waste time glowering about Marie. But he wanted to, since she always seemed to know something he didn't.

Zarrin put his hand to Joe's cheek, and exhaled roughly when his thumb grazed Joe's mouth and Joe licked the taste of salt from his lip. But he didn't take it further, didn't kiss Joe or call him treasure.

He regarded Joe steadily for one more moment and then squeezed his eyes shut. Before Joe could ask what was wrong, Zarrin had straightened his shoulders and reopened his eyes. His scowl was determined.

"It's getting late, but there's more for you to see." Zarrin's voice alone could have melted the snow farther up in the mountains. "Too much for one day, but I don't want to stop yet. There's so much more to share with you."

"Oh." Joe had no idea why he was so surprised by that answer, or confused by Zarrin's tone. He looked around them, at the silently watchful trees, before giving a nod. "I can stay a little longer. I'd like to see more." Honesty pushed him on. "I'd love to see it all, someday."

Zarrin released a long, slow breath and then smiled again, for the first time in what felt like hours, though it must have been minutes. "I can do that," he said, fiercely, then took hold of Joe's hand.

Joe let him tangle their fingers together, and Zarrin seemed to take that as his cue to continue hiking. He led them back to the trail without a word, and kept Joe's hand in his as he talked softly about spiky woodpeckers and sneaky tree voles and small gray foxes as if he wanted to show Joe everything he loved about them.

# CHAPTER 12

MONDAY MORNING, Joe woke to a freezing apartment and got dressed in the near dark before heading out to open up the shop. He gave the alley cat milk to stop its howling and started the coffee before getting the register ready. But when he went to let Martin in, Martin studied him in silence for so long that Joe eventually gave up and left him to freeze until he felt like coming in. Which he did after another moment and then helped himself to some fresh coffee.

Before sunrise was too early to deal with smirking coworkers, especially when Joe was nicely sore from a long hike and a final, desperate grinding session and blowjob up against the wall of Dìzhèn's mansion, and there was a stinging love bite on his shoulder, temporarily hidden from view, and Joe had spent a long, cold night alone with his doubts and questions.

Martin's narrow-eyed stare flashed into a grin the second Joe snapped at him. "What?"

"It's true!" Martin crowed, and raised his cup in a toast. "Oh man. I wasn't sure you were going to do the coy thing for much longer, but I should've guessed this from how you reacted when he was…." Martin's tone was briefly somber. "You look like you do when you come back from one of your Saturdays in the city getting laid. But, like, cranky at the same time. Uh-oh."

"Coy thing?" Joe rubbed his eyes, then got himself some coffee too. "This is what it's going to be like all day, isn't it?" He was probably going to want to hide from everything and get as high as Martin got by the time his shift was over.

"Well, people *have* been talking." Martin patted Joe's shoulder before stepping away to gather the newspapers and turn on the string lights. "Not everyone. But, um, I heard it from my mom. She can be… weird about this kind of stuff. She doesn't, uh, like gay stuff. She says it's beings influence on good people. Probably why she was freaking out so much and called me. She likes you."

"But thinks a dragon made me gay," Joe finished for him, too tired of it all to be really offended at this point. Martin looked torn up about it for him anyway.

"Well, no. No one thinks that. Not with your history." Apparently Martin *had* heard all the old high school stories about Joe, probably also from his mother, who was not a kind woman. Joe scrutinized Martin's face, but there was no sign Martin believed any of the rumors. Joe hadn't known how much it would have bothered him until he saw that Martin didn't even seem to have doubts. If anything, Martin was apologetic for mentioning the gossip. "But she thinks Zarrin might be using you. My mom is fond of you, despite some of the shit she says. I swear she is."

"Huh." Joe paused before turning on the music. It was all Christmas carols for the season, so he turned the volume down for the sake of his sanity. "Not used to anyone else's mom being fond of me, but then, I suppose I'm not dating you."

"True," Martin said, around a cough, and then got himself a refill. His Adam's apple bobbed as he swallowed. "So, you are dating Zarrin? It's not just freaky dragon shenanigans, or you doing some weird martyr thing for the town, or a onetime thing, or—"

"We're friends," Joe interrupted to stop Martin from saying Joe's every late-night thought out loud. Everything that was natural when he was alone with Zarrin was too easy to question when Zarrin was gone. Zarrin meant well, but he was always making promises. He wanted Joe now, but it couldn't last. Sooner or later, Zarrin's parents would insist he leave, or he'd find another dragon of a powerful line to walk the Preserve with him. Or—the thought that ensured Joe hadn't slept well—Joe had been lied to again, or misread everything, or tricked because he'd wanted to believe it. What if Zarrin had looked at him with those dragon eyes and seen everything Joe secretly wanted? What if he *had* slept with Marie and the two of them had laughed about Joe? What if Zarrin thought sweet words and gifts were enough to win Joe's affection, and he'd been right?

It was all bullshit. It had to be. Joe had seen Zarrin at his most vulnerable, drugged out of his mind, and even an unconscious Zarrin had trusted Joe more than anyone else.

They weren't forever, Joe reminded himself before his heart could start racing. But if it was only one weekend, then he shouldn't have left last night. One more night of being called treasure would have been nice.

"Friends," he said to Martin again, and shook his head. "I'm not his boy toy, or his bride—a label which I'm not even going to discuss."

"Then you'd better make that clear to everyone who comes in here today, because they'll all have their own ideas." Martin unlocked the door and then came to the counter to put on his apron. "I know there are a lot of different ways for, um, men to be together that aren't exactly dating. I mean, from what I understand. Not that I…. But lunch in the park?" Martin handed an apron to Joe without looking at him. "Letting someone kiss you on the mouth in front of everyone? Sounds like dating to me."

He wasn't wrong. And as usual when he was sober, he hit the nature of the problem exactly on the head.

Joe put down his cup and stared at the counter as the bell over the door rang. "But what if it isn't?" he asked at last, then greeted their first customer before Martin could say anything.

MARTIN'S PREDICTION wasn't wrong either. While a few customers were clearly there to get their coffee and go, the regulars all seemed to have heard the gossip before they'd come in. If they hadn't, someone was probably happy to tell them whatever story was currently popular. Then they'd come to the counter, full of questions about what Joe had done over the weekend.

Joe stayed at the espresso machine and let Martin take the full brunt of the customer service. When he wanted to, Martin could be so chipper it was off-putting. Most of the regulars didn't know what to do when someone responded to their questions with a wide smile and cheery yet impersonal inquiries about their weekends.

Helene came in later than her usual time, and unlike the others, she knew enough to dodge Martin and go straight for Joe. She waited close to the espresso machine and didn't immediately leave when Joe pushed her drink forward.

"How is he?" What she finally asked surprised Joe into looking directly at her. "After everything, I mean. Is he okay? Your deputy friend is being tight-lipped, and no one else seems to know anything."

"He'll be fine," Joe explained, in close to a grunt. "He's tougher than he looks." Zarrin had gone through that and then walked into the sheriff's station by himself. No one should have demanded that from anyone.

"Good. Good." Helene nodded. "He seems like a sweet kid. Glad you were there to look after him."

Joe opened his mouth to tell her Zarrin didn't need Joe to look after him, but it would have confirmed whatever she was thinking.

Helene held Joe's stare for another moment. "The wolf girl wasn't from here. I'm sure she's great as a person, but she's not someone we'd want to trust with our dragons." Joe gave a start, and Martin turned from the register as if he'd heard that and was equally shocked. Helene picked up her drink. "This town only looks like a regular small town. Maybe we all thought we were for a while because that big house was empty. But we aren't. There's something special here, despite all the crap you get like in any other town. It's why Holly and I moved here, and why you came back, I bet, even though life in the city might have suited you better."

"And?" Joe asked gruffly, although city life hadn't suited him better. Helene's gaze traveled to his shoulder, and the bruising bite mark Zarrin had left there. Joe had tried to keep his henley on for as long as possible, but eventually the temperature and his growing irritation with everyone had made him take it off. Whether or not Zarrin came in today, they were going to stare. Joe had let Zarrin kiss him in the middle of town. If he never saw Zarrin again, he was always going to be the guy who had done that. So there was no point in pretending anything.

Helene stopped ogling Joe's hickey. "That dragon is yours, but he's also ours. I'm glad you were there for him. I bet he was too." At that, she winked before taking her coffee and heading to the other room.

"The fuck?" Martin breathed, echoing Joe's exact thought.

Hazel's dad gave Martin a stern look, and Martin gulped. He peered over the counter to wave at Hazel, who regarded him solemnly. Joe had a feeling she'd be repeating "fuck" in a few minutes, and it'd be Martin's fault.

Joe had his first urge to smile all day at the thought. It had nothing to do with Helene's weird blessing.

His smile lasted through a minirush, and then Jessie clocked in and gave them some space to breathe, which meant Joe could now pay attention to the conversations around him. He could also notice the clock, and that it was past the time Zarrin normally made an appearance.

Zarrin hadn't been in since he was attacked. Joe had no reason to think he would today. But reason and hope were different things. He looked at the time and then at the door before disappearing into the back to grab more milk. He'd brewed Zarrin's iced tea, which was so obvious it made him squirm.

He didn't have Zarrin's number and wasn't sure he could have contacted him if he had. They'd never made any plans. It had felt like it, somehow, with Zarrin pulling him down for kiss after kiss, his lips buzzing from them all, Zarrin clinging to him. Everything was so different when Zarrin was there.

But he wasn't here now, and if anyone should have learned not to trust his feelings, it was Joe.

Martin shot Joe a concerned look when he came out. Joe was an idiot, and the world knew it. That was nothing new.

He grabbed a towel and a spray bottle and went over to clean tables.

"Yeah, but I still don't know what it means," he overheard as he swept some crumbs to the floor and picked up an abandoned paper. "Everything hinges on whether or not the Indian was good in the sack?"

Joe glanced up.

"No. Don't be stupid. And gross." A boy about Martin's age didn't turn away from his laptop screen while addressing his friend. He was typing madly. Despite the Christmas break, he must have still had something to turn in. "Although he couldn't have been that good, since the dragon's not here. Sucks. I wanted to see it."

Joe straightened. Helene caught his eye. She seemed like someone about to say something.

Joe was faster. "You sure about that?" he asked the boys, with his arms crossed. "The last humans who saw him as an 'it' wound up in the hospital with third-degree burns."

The two of them raised their heads at the same time and gaped at him.

"His name is Zarrin," Joe informed them, and everyone else nearby, with the meanest scowl he had. "I have no idea if he has plans for the town, and I doubt he'd tell me if he did, no matter how good of a fuck I am."

Helene put a hand over her mouth. Hazel's dad said, "Son of a bitch!" And then looked like he bit his tongue.

"If anyone wants to know what Zarrin or any of the dragons are up to, try asking them. It's obviously got nothing to do with me." Joe exhaled roughly and pushed in a chair that was fine where it was. "So, sorry to anyone who thought they could ask me. 'The Indian' has no idea."

He slammed the chair into place again, something else that wasn't needed, and then stalked back toward the counter. He was flushed and acting stupid. He should be happy that he'd had such a good weekend, not snarling at people who were only confirming what he already knew—Zarrin liked him, but not like that, not seriously. He was just dramatic and prone to making outrageous promises.

It did not improve Joe's mood to see Addison Bernes waiting for her drink, although at least she wasn't talking. She met his gaze as he passed by but didn't say a single thing. Maybe she was riveted by whatever Mr. Marcus was on about today.

Joe already knew he wouldn't like it, because even Jessie had a strained expression.

"The crack in the street." Mr. Marcus was agitated. "Who is going to pay to fix that? Tourists won't want to see that."

In contrast, Martin was grinning smugly. "You could always tell them Zarrin did it. Tourists like stories about the dragons." Martin was really going to be something one day when he finally got his shit together.

"Oh yes. Tell them our oh-so-powerful dragon got attacked. What good would that do?" Mr. Marcus was close to getting himself kicked out. Joe might lose his job, but maybe that would be fine in the end. Maybe it would be the push to finally make him leave this town for good. He'd find someplace else with redwoods and sea air. Anywhere up the coast would do.

"I don't get it," Jessie piped up. "Those hunter guys attacked him, right? Like, I would have pissed myself. All he did was shake the ground a little. It was cool."

"The dragons always pay for the damages," Addison said, out of nowhere. She blinked when Joe slowly turned to give her a look of disbelief. "Well, they always did before."

"It's a Christmas miracle!" Martin clapped his hands together. "Addison sides with the dragons!"

"What? They do!" Addison insisted and then gave Joe a serious stare. "They take care of what's theirs—provided it's actually theirs. Even the little one should know that, no matter how confused it is about everything else. It might mean well, Joe, but you need to be care—"

"Happy holidays, Addison." Despite the pleasant greeting, Forrester stepped in front of Addison as though she weren't there. "Martin." He nodded to Martin, then stood there, effectively blocking Addison from the rest of the conversation. As if he didn't know that, Forrester nodded at Martin again. "Martin? My usual?"

Martin hopped over to the espresso machine so quickly he nearly stumbled.

"But what if he doesn't repave the road?" Mr. Marcus was not going to let it go. Joe continued going behind the counter so he wouldn't have to answer him. He clenched his jaw to keep from reminding yet another person that he wasn't Zarrin's keeper, and that Zarrin wasn't his. Zarrin didn't have some irresistible drive to be with him.

Joe bent to pull out a new carton of milk, and as he came up, he caught sight of Zarrin slipping through the door with such smooth grace that the bell didn't chime.

He was in his big coat, and had remembered his gloves. His messenger bag was bulging, as if he'd gone to the store, but he wasn't in any hurry. He tugged his hat off his head and put it in his pocket, and did the same to his gloves before running his hands through his hair.

Joe had a distinct memory of gripping that silky hair, and bit down on his lip to keep from saying something embarrassing.

Then Zarrin looked across to him, and smiled, and Joe's knees went weak with relief. The carton of milk was painfully cold at his fingertips when the rest of him was so hot. He stepped forward, because everything was so much better when Zarrin was closer, and Zarrin ducked his head in shy surprise.

Joe's heart felt like it was fluttering, which was probably bad, but he didn't care. Zarrin had been nervous about Joe's reaction today. They were both idiots, but Zarrin was here.

Joe pulled in a long breath. "Zarrin." Zarrin froze when everyone's attention swung to him. Everyone had a few seconds to see soft, glowingly happy Zarrin, and then Zarrin took his eyes off Joe to consider the others.

His chin went up. Joe leaned his head toward the group without looking at any of them. "Mr. Marcus, you had something you wanted to ask?"

Zarrin focused on Mr. Marcus with curiosity, most likely guessing who he was by process of elimination. "Yes?" He was in full volcano mode, and for some reason that put Joe in a better mood.

Mr. Marcus widened his eyes and lost what color he had.

Zarrin continued to wait.

Mr. Marcus probably thought the bright interest in his eyes was hunger or anger. He was getting twitchy. "The street outside," he managed to say and then nothing else.

Zarrin swept forward. "Are you responsible for the street? I've been meaning to find out who to talk to about the drains. There are some leaves piling up at the corner of Cannery and 2nd Street, and with this much rain and snowfall, I've been worried about flooding."

Addison closed her mouth hard. Joe let out an audible sigh of pleasure, which, thankfully, no one seemed to notice.

"I, uh, suggest the Chamber of Commerce meeting. Or the town council." Mr. Marcus was more than a little flustered. It was those gold eyes. They were innocent and knowing at the same time, and they made thinking difficult. And that was before dragonfire factored into the equation.

"Chamber of Commerce?" Zarrin pouted thoughtfully. "Don't they have a pancake breakfast once a month? I like pancakes." He was going to show up there, Joe could already tell. His family did own several businesses in town, so he sort of had a right to. But as if the mention of pancakes settled the matter, Zarrin turned back to Joe with a puff of white smoke that magically didn't set off any of the detectors. "Good morning, Joe."

It wasn't just Martin and the others looking at them now.

Joe licked his lips, which made Zarrin lick his. That helped him notice scents in the air, Joe knew now, but it didn't make him feel any less warm. If anything, it made it worse, because it made Joe think of Zarrin blowing him against the side of Dìzhèn's house, and how he hadn't let Joe return the favor, but pulled up Joe's shirt to jerk off on his stomach instead. The trees couldn't witness it, apparently, but the house could. Maybe Zarrin wanted it to. He was surprisingly—or not—vicious about delineating what belonged to Dìzhèn and what didn't.

He approached the counter, and for once, Joe couldn't be bothered to be upset about any people who might have been behind him waiting to order. "You're late," he told Zarrin in a husky voice.

"I'm sorry." Zarrin placed both hands on the counter and dragged his gaze up from Joe's shoulder to his face. No one should look that proud of one love bite. "You worried?" Zarrin clucked his tongue, and nodded toward the hickey again, as though it conveyed a message other than "Zarrin and Joe are sleeping together." "This part is important. I wouldn't miss it."

Joe's thinking got a little foggy. The longer he stood there, shivery-hot and silent, the more Zarrin seemed to shine.

Then Martin poked him in the side, and Joe remembered they weren't alone. He cleared his throat. "Sweet tea?"

Zarrin gasped. "No one's ever called me sweetie before."

Forrester choked on his first sip. A high laugh escaped Martin before he strangled it. He turned away from Zarrin's inquiring stare, only to blanch when he saw Forrester frowning at him.

Joe took a breath, as if that were going to do anything for his embarrassment. "I meant, your tea with sweet milk."

"Oh." Zarrin sighed softly. "Yes, please. If you don't mind."

"If I don't mind?" Joe recovered enough to roll his eyes at that, because it was his job, and because if he'd minded, he'd never have started making out-of-season iced tea for Zarrin in the first place. "I'll be right back."

"I'll wait," Zarrin told him, and Martin made that panicked, amused sound again. Joe left him to the laughter he was fighting, and also all the customers in line, and went to get a glass of tea.

Zarrin had politely moved to the side of the counter by the tea display, but was otherwise as Joe had left him. He shifted in place with small energetic motions while Joe prepared his tea, and then accepted his plastic cup with a quiet "Mine" that made Joe shiver.

"Did you have a good night?" Even Zarrin's coat couldn't hide the sleek lines of his body, which Joe was now familiar with, and had wanted against his back last night. Zarrin must have wanted that too. "I missed you," Zarrin added, longing and warm.

"I had to get up early for work." Joe had explained this to Zarrin yesterday, while avoiding saying anything about needing space to think.

Joe had never dated, but he was sure most couples didn't immediately spend all their time together. "I didn't want to bother you in the dark of morning and then drive into town." And he'd thought he'd get some sleep, but he'd been wrong.

"I suppose." Zarrin was huffy for one moment, and then he leaned forward. "Call me sweetie again?"

Of the many things Joe could have called Zarrin, he would never have said "sweetie." "What did you do this morning?" he asked quickly.

Zarrin grimaced and glanced toward Forrester, who was now ignoring them, or pretending to. "I went to the sheriff's station to see if there was anything else they needed that I should tell my family about." He looked down to pick at his nails, then seemed to remember he had an audience. He straightened abruptly. "One of them is going to be released from the hospital into jail. There will be a bail hearing, which means I will have to call my sister again."

"That's not so bad, right? You said she was a lawyer. She'll handle it for you. Or assign a team of attorneys or whatever." That's what rich people did in movies.

"She'll discuss it with my parents, and they will send someone, if they haven't already." Zarrin stripped the wrapper off his straw and jabbed it into his lid. "They weren't surprised. I could hear it in their voices during the last call. They were worried, but I could hear their disappointment that I let pieces of myself be taken." He chewed the end of his straw so much it didn't look usable. "Zarrin, too scared to come out of his shell. Zarrin, who can't protect anything on his own, not even himself." He dragged in a long breath and gave a start when Joe gently reached for his cup to replace the straw.

Zarrin glanced over at Martin and Jessie and Addison and Mr. Marcus, who was still there for some reason. He put his shoulders back and lifted his chin. "I would do all that a dragon should for this town, but I'm not much of one."

"You're enough for me," Joe told him quietly, and gave Zarrin his cup with its new straw.

Zarrin blinked at him, all bright-eyed and wobbly-lipped, and then took another long, steadying breath. "Treasure."

This time Martin didn't make a sound.

"The state of the street drainage is a very important thing," Mr. Marcus announced, out of nowhere, and then left after a vague nod toward Zarrin.

"Drainage?" Forrester yawned ostentatiously. "Well, that's my cue to leave. Nothing interesting in here today. Nothing that is any of our business, right, Addison?"

"*Dude*." Martin watched him go, then turned to Addison. "Did you ever actually order?"

Joe put his back to them before Addison could do more than narrow her eyes at Martin's rudeness.

"Are you okay?" He kept his voice down for the sake of dragon dignity, but he wasn't going to pretend Zarrin wasn't upset.

Zarrin gave him a stunned, owlish look, then shook his head. "There's nothing to be done about it now. I could use the legal help anyway, and… there's just nothing to be done. How was *your* morning?" he moved on firmly, and leaned against the counter again. "Busy?"

Joe nodded. "It's slow now, and then it will pick up again around lunchtime. Then I get to go home. Clean up, take a nap."

"You didn't sleep well?" Zarrin all but purred. "I could have helped with that."

"Zarrin." Joe was not smiling, even if he wanted to. Zarrin had no discretion at all sometimes, and Joe really shouldn't be as into it as he was. It was only going to come back to haunt him in the end.

He got a pout and then a small bounce. "Do you mind if I stay for a while? I have no plans at the moment."

Joe gestured at the few empty tables. "You want to stay? There's plenty of seats."

"But they're all so far away." Zarrin considered them, then sailed over in the direction of the nearest table. Joe was about to remind him of his tea when Zarrin began to drag the table closer to the counter. When he had it on the border of the two rooms, he went back for a chair. Once again, people were staring, but this time more for the sound the table legs made against the floor.

"What are you doing?" Jessie asked before Joe could.

Zarrin smiled at her, took his drink, and then sat down with a regal flounce. "I'm making sure no one talks shit to Joe."

"Talks shit?" Joe echoed in disbelief, while thinking that Hazel's dad was going to kill them. "What have you been watching?"

"People were, weren't they?" Zarrin argued, somehow both superior about it and softly earnest. "I could tell. You were not angry. Hurt." He met Joe's eyes. "They won't bother you if I'm here."

Joe stared at him, then at the counter. He swallowed a few times so he could speak. "Do you have a book or anything?" he wondered, gruff but still too soft. "If you're going to stay there, you might get bored."

"Next time." Zarrin bobbed his head. "I won't stay long. Only enough to make my point."

"Stay as long as you like," Martin interjected, while ringing someone up. "I'm enjoying this. I've never seen Joe fight a smile so hard."

"Really?" Zarrin peered at Joe with fascinated interest.

Joe had to do something that wasn't mooning over his—Zarrin. "Nothing. Ignore him. You can stay. But you don't have to do all this. I'm fine."

"*Hurt*," Zarrin repeated, with a sniff, as if that meant something, and finally took a sip of his tea. He pulled a yellow notepad from his bag, and a pen, and started to write.

Joe hoped Zarrin wasn't making a list of people who had been mean to him, but kind of thought he was.

Addison must have had the same idea, because she locked eyes with Joe and then took her drink outside.

As she left, another customer stepped in. Because Joe's life was now even more public, of course it was his mother.

He hadn't known she was off today, but he'd been avoiding talking to her so she wouldn't worry about him. He'd been stupid to think she wouldn't find out and get anxious that Joe was going to be publicly used and abandoned again. This was Zarrin Xu they were talking about—everyone knew, not just kids in one high school class. She'd probably known from the first moment Zarrin had given Joe a gold coin, and she'd been waiting to see what Joe would do.

He couldn't blame her. On paper, Russ and Zarrin were a lot alike: rich, lonely children of established town families. She'd have to know Zarrin to find out how different he was, and now she was here to do just that.

She unwound her long scarf so the ends hung down over her chest and the bottom half of her face was visible. She had her hair parted neatly down the middle and then twisted up in two buns, one behind each ear, and big, beaded earrings to make that look less severe.

She had on loose jeans despite the chill, and winter boots, and a pale pink trench coat she'd tailored to fit herself, and thick gloves.

She bestowed a smile on Martin and Jessie, a frown on Joe, and then her expression closed off entirely when she saw Zarrin.

Hard at work on his list, Zarrin had no idea what was about to hit him.

Joe was motionless for a few seconds too long. His mother went over to grab a chair, and carried it to Zarrin's table. She was all wiry muscle.

"Mom," Joe finally protested, right as she put the chair down.

Zarrin jumped as she took a seat opposite him.

"Zarrin, isn't it? How are you?" Joe's mom asked. She meant it. Whatever her other feelings about boys using her son, she'd never wish harm on anyone. She had named her gray hairs after Russ, though.

Zarrin didn't blink. He very slowly sat up and then put down his pen. "I'm fine."

"I heard about you." Joe's mom was either unfazed by the draconian stare or pretending to be. "I was worried, believe it or not. But you look strong, and quite content at your table here. Is this to be closer to Joe?"

"Oh shit." Joe left the counter to Martin and Jessie and came around to the front. "Zarrin, this is my mother. Mom, this is Zarrin. Which you know, clearly."

His mom didn't so much as glance at him. "We all know *of* the dragons. But we don't *know* the dragons." Zarrin still hadn't blinked. Neither of them had. His mom gave no indication that she was likely shaking in her boots as she observed Zarrin carefully. "What are your intentions?"

Zarrin cocked his head to one side. "Intentions?"

"Mom." Joe pushed out a sigh. "It's not like what you're thinking."

His mom sat back and crossed her arms. "I'm not talking to you right now, Joe. You had your chance. Now it's my turn. You, Zarrin, the youngest of the Xu family, it's you who needs to talk to me, because there's no one else."

Zarrin squeaked out a breathless sound, delighted or irritated or puzzled, Joe honestly couldn't tell. "What would you like to know?"

"What do you intend to do with Everlasting?" Joe's mom asked the one question everyone had been afraid to ask, and did not seem impressed when Zarrin raised his eyebrows. She tapped two fingers against the table. "We have an interest in the fate of this town too. Did you all forget that?"

"The town?" Joe looked between them. "You're asking about the town?"

Zarrin was beginning to lose his air of startled interest. In its place was a watchful, wary dragon. He leaned forward ever so slightly. "We are supposed to look out for what is ours. Our treasure."

Joe's mom snorted. "But you haven't been, not really. No dragon has laid more than a nominal claim to Everlasting in decades. If you love something, you at least check on it once in a while. They say they watch out for us, but do any of them know who we are, or ask what we want?"

Joe clamped his mouth shut and turned toward Zarrin. He'd bet anyone else listening in did the same.

If Zarrin noticed the attention, there was no sign other than the angle of his chin. "I do." A plume of gray wafted toward the ceiling, but then Zarrin looked over at Joe. "I will," he added, in a softer tone, and inclined his head in Joe's mother's direction. "What do you want?"

Joe's mom didn't hesitate. "The Preserve."

Joe thought his heart actually stopped, but there was nothing from Zarrin. No dark or light smoke, no tremor beneath their feet, no barely suppressed roar.

Zarrin kept his eyes on Joe for a long time, while everything around seemed to grow shadows, and the temperature of the shop spiked higher. Then Zarrin shivered and looked away. He settled into his chair and faced Joe's mother. "Joe is definitely a child of your blood."

"Mmm-hmm," his mom agreed. "Of course he is." She made a dismissive gesture. "You can relax. I'm a realist. I didn't expect you to hand over the Preserve. I mostly wanted to see what you'd do if I defied you. No roasting or tantrums, so that's good. And it was worth a shot, anyway."

Joe closed his eyes.

Zarrin's warm voice made him open them. "You must come from a powerful line."

"Yes, I do. But Dìzhèn's no one to sneer at either." His mom could not have known the effect that name would have on Zarrin.

Zarrin bit his lip, then seemed to force himself to speak. "She was much stronger than I am, with different threats to face."

"I'm grateful that someone was around to at least stop the overlogging and consequent environmental disasters." Joe's mom tapped the table again. "But who was it for? Not for us. Not for anyone in the town she claimed either. We aren't allowed to see it. The park is fine, but it's for everyone in the state. The Preserve was supposed to be for Everlasting."

"You… want everyone to see the Preserve?" The rising volcano straightened and put both his hands flat on the table. His voice was smoky. "My family would never allow that."

"But you would?" His mom had the sense enough at least to stop there. Or so Joe thought. But she was only waiting to strike again. "Where *are* your family, Zarrin?"

"Mom," Joe interrupted when Zarrin flinched. "That's enough."

She raised a hand to shut him up. Her voice was solid as granite. "If you were mine, and someone hurt you like that, I would have raced to your side, and nothing would have stopped me."

Zarrin flinched again, and let out three distressed little breaths that floated away in puffs of pale smoke. He clasped his hands together, but he kept his chin up enough to do his ancestor proud. "I've healed already."

Joe clenched his hands. Zarrin's scars were oddly smooth, and Zarrin made shocked, wet sounds when Joe touched them, like it hurt and felt good, but more like he'd never expected anyone to be kind about them.

"Joseph." Joe's mom abruptly acknowledged him. "Don't scowl."

"He scowls when he's upset," Zarrin informed her. "When something's hurt him."

"I'm not the one who's hurt," Joe grunted, then heard himself, what he'd said and how he'd said it, and why he'd said it. He could tell Zarrin had heard it all too.

Zarrin blinked at Joe as though he'd never seen him before. "Oh," he said, then softened his voice. "Treasure, I'll be fine. Dragons lose scales all the time, and I told you I healed already. You don't need to fret over me."

"I—" Joe stopped there. He glanced to his mom. "None of them were here for him."

His mom sighed shakily. "Joseph Andres, your heart is going to change the world." Then she uncrossed her arms and seemed to force herself to relax. "I'd like a coffee please, Martin," she called out, and waited while Martin got it for her, black with a sugar packet and a cube of ice to let her drink it right away. She poured in her sugar while watching Zarrin. "I came here to get coffee, and see my son," she explained. "Instead I find you. The dragon who sits with my son in the park, and who—countless nosy birds tell me—spends the night in his apartment."

Zarrin didn't look startled anymore. "Yes?" he agreed, but with a question. "Here I am."

"Mmm." His mom sipped her coffee before speaking. "Down among the people. Why is that? For us? Or for him?"

"Both." Zarrin drank some of his tea, with much the same attitude. Joe glanced to Martin, who shrugged helplessly.

"Joe would be worth it by himself, don't you think?" Apparently Joe's mother was feeling ruthless today. As if it weren't enough to be under discussion already, now people were going to be repeating this whole conversation.

"Mom," Joe objected, again, although normally he would never have interrupted her.

Zarrin focused on her like she was a Latin phrase he needed to learn. "Yes," he answered, utterly serious. "Yes, he's worth it. But he doesn't believe me when I say it, unless I say it in bed. I'm going to have to show him."

Joe scrubbed at his hot face and tried not to look at his mother.

He could hear her amusement, with a tinge of embarrassment, not that it would deter her from whatever her goal was. This woman had worked full time and gone to community college in another town and raised a son all by herself. She didn't do things half-assed.

She waved toward Joe. "That is a good-looking, hardworking, well-mannered boy. A catch for anyone who is brave enough to really try for him. Tell me…. What do you think of my son? Isn't he talented? I mean, outside of bed, Zarrin. He's clever, isn't he? And sensitive."

Zarrin ducked his head. Talking about sleeping with Joe didn't embarrass him, but whatever he was about to say did. "Yes. I—he didn't tell you? I… bought his art before I knew it was his."

"Joseph doesn't talk about the things he wants when he thinks he won't get them." His mother dismissed Zarrin's question and then managed to be even more personal than Zarrin talking about sex. "He hopes, and he frowns, and he will not ask, not even when he was a little boy. He'd stare and he'd want something so much I could see him shake with it, but he'd scowl and never say a word. The first time I guessed right and brought home the jumbo box of crayons, he held them to his chest and didn't use them for three days. You said you bought his art?"

"Yes." Zarrin's eager nod meant Zarrin was just as bad as she was. "Then I tried to give it to him because I loved it."

That took her by surprise, which Joe understood. She studied Zarrin again, as if reconsidering something. But her tone was dry. "Thoughtful of you to give him what was his."

Zarrin leaned in to whisper to her in the most beautifully shy voice. "I didn't know it was his when I did it. I only wanted to give him something amazing. Treasure for treasure."

Joe had never seen his mother so caught off guard. Her mouth opened, then closed. She wrinkled her forehead, then looked from Joe to Zarrin and back again. "So… you gave it to him because you loved it." She nodded. "Ah." She must have translated that into English from dragon. "You did it *because* it was hard to do?"

"It's how we…." Zarrin slid a look at Joe, apologetic and hungry. "I wanted him to like me."

"And does he?" His mom was fascinated now. Dragons had that effect.

Zarrin gave Joe that glance again, then let out a mournful sound. "We're friends."

"Friends!" Martin startled everyone by dropping his head to the counter and snort-laughing. Joe narrowed his eyes and ignored his stinging cheeks. Martin was right to laugh. This whole scene was some sort of joke.

"Martin." Jessie rolled her eyes. "You're so immature."

Martin raised his head to study the three of them. "I'm Joe's friend. But he doesn't sketch *me* on napkins whenever it's slow."

"Does he really?" Zarrin's delight was only matched by Joe's mother's.

She looked at Joe in astonishment. "You're doing portraits again?" Joe shook his head. Zarrin nodded. She faced Zarrin. "You know, he's very good at them, but he doesn't usually like to draw them. He has to know people to do that, and—" For the first time, she lowered her voice. "He's not as quick to let himself know people anymore. It's the dreamers who can get so hurt by the world that they need protecting. Do you understand? I tried, but I had to support us, and a mother can't always be there."

"I suppose not." Zarrin was quiet too. He stared at Joe. "I'm sorry I wasn't here either."

He'd said that before. One of these days, Joe was going to convince him he didn't have to apologize for having been a kid.

Joe's mom took another drink of her coffee. Her attitude had gone from barely civil to intensely satisfied. "What are you doing today, Zarrin? I was going to run some errands, but I'm glad I stopped in here first."

"Me too." Zarrin's tiny smile probably wasn't meant to be as endearing as it was. "I'm glad someone else is looking out for him aside from me, and Martin, and Ian Forrester."

Joe stiffened.

"Those dragon eyes see a lot more than most people realize." Joe's mother was getting smugger by the second. Then she leaned across the table, and Zarrin could probably smell the determination from her. "You know what I would really like to do?"

Zarrin leaned in too, intrigued. "What?"

She smiled, not unkindly, but not kindly either. "Go for a walk."

Zarrin licked his lips and inhaled. He very slowly sat back in his chair. His hands went wide on the table, and then he curled his fingers in, as if he needed to hold on to something as hard as he could and the tabletop was all he had left. "Would you… would you like to see the Preserve, Mrs. Andres?" His voice rasped. "I can show you, if you'd like."

Joe wanted to kiss him, right there in front everyone.

But he held still, and frowned as he watched his mom's smile get bigger. "I'd like that a lot, Zarrin. Thank you."

Zarrin jerked his head in a nod, although he was still gripping the table.

"Whenever you're done here," his mom allowed, gracious in victory. "Joe will be in town when you get back. He won't go anywhere."

"Mom," Joe protested in a slightly harder voice. "Don't tease him."

"Shh, treasure." Zarrin turned to Joe again at last, and gave him a warm, if shaken, smile. "You're being very good. I know you're upset, but please don't worry. Of course I'll show her. It's not losing anything, really, because I'll be gaining her too, won't I? She must be wonderful, because she raised you. She'll love it like you do."

He hit Joe right in the chest, then stroked his skin with pretty words, and returned his attention to Joe's mother now that he had Joe flustered and silent. "He's so very good. I have a lot to prove to him."

His mother lifted both eyebrows, but didn't deny that, or address the intimate way Zarrin said those things to her son right in front of her. She kept her eyes on Zarrin, who wasn't Russ, although he was a completely different kind of danger. "When I was a girl, there was a petition to open up the Preserve to tours. The papers were returned to us singed on the edges, and the issue was never raised again."

"I am not my parents, or my parent's parents." Zarrin blinked at her. "But Joe says I can do what other dragons can't, and let things go. He's wrong, though," Zarrin added, in a confessional tone. "In my heart, I haven't let anything go. But only in my heart."

"Joseph." Joe's mom's voice was strained. "I forgive you for not telling me about this. But Zarrin Xu? You had to choose this much trouble?" She looked at Zarrin and sighed. "Oh, don't give me those hurt eyes. You could kill me where I sit, and all I want to do right now is hug you and tell you everything is going to be okay. I can't help it. I'm a mother."

There was no word to describe the noise Zarrin made. "You want to hug me?" he asked, and the floor trembled.

His mother slapped a hand to her cup to hold the rattling china. "Zarrin, please." The tremor stopped. Zarrin's eyes widened. Joe's mother sat up and cleared her throat. Her hands only shook a little. "Well, I don't know about you, but I'm ready for that walk now."

That didn't sound like a good idea. It meant Zarrin was going to leave, and she would go with him, and who knew what the two of them would talk about together.

"Look at that frown." His mother got to her feet, and Joe immediately bent down so she could kiss his cheek. She made a fuss about straightening his apron and then gave a tsk when she spotted the love bite.

"Mom." Joe had no idea what he wanted to say.

But she patted his chest and then sniffled a bit before turning to Zarrin. "Really, Zarrin? A hickey?"

Zarrin went lofty. "I didn't ask him to display it for the world to see. He did that."

"Did he?" Joe's mom had a glint in her eye, but she spoke quietly. "There are less physical ways to announce you're dating. Social media, for example, is something the kids seem fond of."

"Should I do that? Bernard would like it, but I don't know what my parents would think." Zarrin put away his notepad and pen before getting to his feet. He seemed to realize something. "Marie would love it! Joe, you'd end up with so many friends!"

"This is the single greatest thing that could have happened this morning." Martin was both smug and loud. "And I am totally going to be Joe's first friend the moment this all happens."

"It's not, and shut up." Joe wasn't amused.

"You might as well, for your career." His mom patted his face, then addressed the others. "My coffee to go please, Martin. Zarrin, are you ready?"

Zarrin finished pulling his hat over his ears. "Yes. But, I should—"

"I'm fine." Joe didn't let him say another word about protecting him, or treasure, or people talking shit. Everything Zarrin said was something else his mother was going to interrogate him about once they were alone, and Zarrin didn't get it. "If I'm supposed to accept you when you say you're fine, Zarrin, then you have to do the same for me."

Zarrin's expression was absolutely mutinous, but he didn't say a word. He gave Joe a good, long glare, then transferred his attention to Joe's mother. "It will rain by tonight. We should go soon if you still want to."

The fact that Zarrin appeared to know the weather now was something Joe didn't have the energy to delve into at the moment. Anyway, his mom gave him one final pat before taking her cup from Martin and stepping back.

"I've always wanted to see the Preserve." She linked arms with Zarrin when he came closer, making him gape at her.

"I didn't realize so many people longed to see it," he commented.

"Well, now you know." Like a force of nature, Joe's mother led Zarrin away when Zarrin tried to approach Joe.

"Are you sure you aren't part wolf?" Zarrin sniped at her, in a huff even as he allowed himself to be drawn away.

"All women are part wolf, Zarrin Xu," Joe's mom informed him, with a laugh in her voice. Then they were out the door and gone.

Joe stared after them until his eyes were stinging.

"Now you have to meet his family," Jessie offered helpfully. "Ow! Martin, stop putting your hand over my mouth."

Joe ignored them both and collapsed into the chair his mother had left behind.

JOE FINISHED his shift, then went home to clean up and change clothes. There wasn't much else he could do to fill the hours while he waited to find out what happened with Zarrin and his mother. He told himself it could have gone worse. But his mom had been much faster than Joe about discovering Zarrin's family issues, which had softened her up. It also helped that Zarrin wasn't subtle around Joe.

Zarrin used to look at Joe as if he wanted to do something to him. Now he looked at him as though he was going to at the first available opportunity. Despite their shared embarrassment about it, his mom would like that. It meant there was no way Zarrin could go silent and play innocent if his girlfriend found out and started to spread rumors all over town.

Although it would have been better if Zarrin hadn't *said* anything about sex in front of his mom. Or, if he at least had mentioned anything about when he was planning to see Joe again. Joe, stupidly, had no way to contact Zarrin, short of driving out to the mansion.

They needed to talk. Joe needed to see Zarrin. Things were easier when Zarrin was there. When they were alone together, Joe didn't overthink things, or imagine Zarrin's family coming here and taking Zarrin away, and then feel so shaken he couldn't sit still.

That didn't mean they were anything more than two boys who liked each other. Joe was practical, no matter what else his mom had been trying to tell Zarrin. He wanted Zarrin to touch him, to fuck him and lie behind him and run his hands over his skin until the outside world was a distant memory. But that wasn't magic. Zarrin hadn't chosen Joe, and they weren't werewolves, and they weren't any other version of soul mates. Zarrin needed to know that Joe didn't expect anything.

To prove that, Joe left the house. He bundled up and walked the beach until the winds ripped his hair from its tie, and he could smell the approaching lightning. It began to rain on his way back, soaking his hair and sending rivulets down beneath his coat. His jeans absorbed every puddle, but the cold was distant until he was inside his apartment again, with the heater barely working.

He noted a text from his mother as he pulled his phone from his pocket. She wanted him to know she was alive and well and home again. He sent a brief answer, then shucked off his coat and jeans and headed to the shower.

He cranked the hot water all the way up and let that warm him. His mom was protective, but not nosy. If she hadn't told him anything, then she had a reason. His skin stung with the heat, and he felt scrubbed raw before he turned off the water and reached for a towel.

Sweatpants and a worn old shirt were all he could bear on his sensitized skin. He rolled on two pairs of socks to help him stay warm and then stood there, his hair still dripping, when he heard the knock at his door.

"Get in here," he ordered even before he recognized Zarrin's sopping wet form on his doorstep. Steam rose from the shoulders of his coat. His knitted hat was soaked. Zarrin raised his eyes to Joe's face, and Joe tugged him inside. He'd just gotten dry and warm and he didn't care. "You rode a Vespa in the freezing rain?" He reached for the damp towel he hadn't gotten to use on his hair yet, and draped it over Zarrin's head. "We need to exchange numbers so we don't have to do things like this."

Zarrin squawked indignantly yet nonetheless allowed Joe to unbutton his coat. It hit the floor as he plastered himself to Joe's chest. "Holding the phone isn't the same," he complained, and yanked his scarf off. It landed on top of his coat. Joe closed the door. He would have spent more time drying Zarrin's hair, but Zarrin lifted the towel to peek up at him. The rain was so cold next to his heat it was steaming, and yet Zarrin managed to seem chilled. "Anyway, your mom said…. I got the impression you were waiting for me to come back."

"Not through the rain on a scooter." Joe sounded grumpy but adoring, and Zarrin must have noticed, because his eyes were shining. "Come on. I don't want to damage the floor."

He shivered a little now that he was damp again, but picked up Zarrin's discarded clothing and carried it into the bathroom. The air in there was hot and heavy. Joe stuck everything at the bottom of the shower stall to drip-dry, then turned to find Zarrin right behind him.

Zarrin tossed his hat into the shower too, then focused on Joe. "Call me sweetie?"

Joe snagged a dry washcloth in order to continue drying Zarrin's hair. "You drove down here in weather you knew was going to be bad. You didn't have to do that."

"But"—Zarrin's hands crept up Joe's chest—"you were worrying, I could tell. And we haven't kissed in almost twenty-four hours."

Joe should have asked if Zarrin had really been counting the hours, but it seemed easier to duck his head and press a soft kiss to Zarrin's mouth. Then Zarrin curled his arms around his neck, and when Joe came up for air a long time later, Zarrin was against the tiled wall and panting into Joe's shoulder.

"I, um, was going to talk to you." Joe remembered that much. He leaned in to brush his lips along Zarrin's throat.

"It doesn't have to be 'sweetie,'" Zarrin murmured. "It can be anything. Now that there's a chance, I think I'll like it, dignity or not."

Joe paused, then slowly pulled back. "It would offend your dignity to have a pet name? But I can have one?"

"Did I give you a pet name?" Zarrin lifted his head and looked bewildered.

"Treas—" Joe exhaled before he could make a fool of himself. If that wasn't a pet name, then he had questions. "We need to talk."

Zarrin made an unhappy face but then nodded. "You sound like your mother." He picked up the abandoned washcloth from the edge of the sink and used it to squeeze water from Joe's hair. "She loves you a lot and was very kind to me. She let me collect stories about your childhood. They're mine now. Hers *and* mine," he amended, begrudgingly. "Turn your head."

Joe turned his head without thinking. Zarrin began to fluff dry his hair and then finger comb it. Joe's head was probably steaming, but it would dry faster. "Don't be angry, but she invited me to Christmas morning at her house."

Joe's every muscle tensed.

"I have no plans. It's not an event my family cares about." Zarrin swept Joe's hair from his face. "She looked the same as you do when I told her that. You're like her in a lot of ways." He dropped the washcloth in the sink and studied Joe, who hadn't managed a word. "When I asked what she wanted for a present, she laughed until she had tears in her eyes, and told me if I actually showed up, I might be worth the trouble of making a good dinner. I don't know what she means, but when I mentioned grilled cheese, she laughed some more."

"No one—in this town, anyway—has ever been interested in me enough to meet my mom, or go to her house for dinner, even when it isn't Christmas. That's what she means." Joe kept his voice level for the explanation, but different emotions flickered across Zarrin's face anyway.

"And her home is humble, because of money?" Zarrin guessed, because he did see a lot, even if it took him a while to understand it. "Which is the reason you commented on your apartment before I could, and another reason she is waiting to see what I'll do? The place you grew up in wasn't good enough for the one who said he loved you? How lonely you must have been."

"Well, I never expected to be his prom date." Joe could watch the glint in Zarrin's eyes for hours. "But it might have been nice to make out with my boyfriend in my own home, although it was a crap apartment near the harbor at the time."

"Boyfriend." Zarrin hissed. "He was never your boyfriend. If I had been here—"

"You would have been, like, *maybe* thirteen." Joe found it disturbingly easy to imagine a younger Zarrin leaving notes in his locker, or glaring at Russ in the halls. "And you would have automatically been one of the popular kids, and they never talked to me."

"You're very stupid about this," Zarrin informed him. "But I forgive you because you aren't dragon, and I wasn't here. But no, treasure, no, I would never have been able to ignore you. True, I would have been young, and silly, and not studious in the way teachers like, and your eye might have passed over me. But I would have noticed you."

"Stupid?" Joe scowled.

Zarrin curled a hand against the side of Joe's neck. "If my parents had let me attend the schools in town, I would have taken you to all the dances. I would have gone to your house and made out with you. There would've been no doubt in anyone's mind that you were mine."

Joe couldn't be blamed for the hoarse sound he made.

"What is it?" Zarrin peered into Joe's face. "Oh. You liked that?" He kissed a slow path beneath Joe's ear and then along his jaw, and sighed encouragingly when Joe wrapped his arms around him. "It wouldn't have been lonely." He brushed the words across Joe's lips. "I would have had you, and you would have had me."

"Yeah?" Joe stuttered over the question, like he really was a dumb kid who would have looked to a scrawny baby dragon for comfort when he'd been the most alone. It was a fantasy that could never have happened, but that didn't stop him from kissing Zarrin until they were both breathless. Zarrin dragged his hands down Joe's chest and then back up, taking Joe's shirt with them. He exhaled over Joe's damp skin, and everything was so hot and close.

Zarrin trailed kisses over Joe's carotid and then at the hollow of his throat. "Joseph, darling." He seemed to taste the words between each breath. "Joe, honey. Joseph, sweetheart."

"Treasure," Joe corrected, before dipping his head to find Zarrin's mouth again.

They bumped into the wall. Zarrin pushed a hand down past the waistband of Joe's sweats and hissed happily when he found bare skin. "Treasure," he agreed hotly, before wrapping his hand around Joe's cock. "My treasure," he murmured, the sound nearly drowned out by Joe's groan. Joe shoved at his sweats, then let Zarrin's hand close over his to slow him down, do it right. "You like that too?" Zarrin's surprise was beyond Joe at the moment. He panted against Zarrin's temple and then buried his nose in Zarrin's hair, which smelled like rain and redwoods.

Zarrin gripped hard at Joe's hip and turned his face to nip at his shoulder. Joe was half-dressed, towering over him, and Zarrin marked him with his teeth and pressed his hot hands all over Joe's skin. "*My* treasure," he said again, and rumbled with pleasure when Joe gave a weak moan.

"Zarrin," Joe complained, although he couldn't have said what he wanted until Zarrin read his scent and answered it.

Zarrin inhaled sharply, and then the room went hazy on his exhale. "Yes. Yes, Joe. Joseph. Treasure. Here, or wherever you want. Yes."

"Here," Joe grunted, although Zarrin had barely touched his cock and his legs were already getting shaky. "Wait." Not on the bathroom floor, not against the wall or the sink. "This isn't… I don't want… city hookup with you." Joe raised his head with effort, and got the full impact of what a jealous Zarrin looked like.

The dark gold of his skin shimmered as he rose in height, or that was a trick of the light, like flames across the scales Joe could never touch. Something lashed out behind him, the impression of a tail. He lowered his head to stare at Joe, and for a fraction of a second, his pupils were slits.

"Anonymous strangers do not get to have Joseph. They don't take my beautiful Joe in random *bathrooms* where they cannot take the time to love him." His rough, pained voice was nothing compared to how he grasped at Joe's skin to draw him closer. His hands opened and became slow and gentle. He ran his palms up Joe's back and then brought them to Joe's stomach. He held them over Joe's heart. "I don't want to frighten you. Please don't be frightened." Zarrin—Zarrin again, small and worried—kissed Joe's ear. "But you're precious. To be revered, even when fucked. Let me… let me…." He trailed off into more tiny, dotting kisses along Joe's neck and jawline.

Joe put a hand down to his cock. He leaned into Zarrin, and Zarrin held him up easily, magic and powerful and strangely determined not to let Joe fall.

"Not frightened." Joe wasn't afraid, and in a minute, Zarrin would probably find the scent of what Joe wanted, but Joe didn't wait this time. He turned his head so Zarrin's next kiss landed on his mouth, and then he pushed forward, pinning Zarrin to the wall.

Or pretended to. Zarrin was stronger than Joe would ever be. He was small and soft, but he was *strong*. Joe sucked a kiss at Zarrin's neck when Zarrin gasped for air and then tried out the words. "*Zarrin*." Not sweetie, not sweetheart or honey. "Zarrin." Because there was only the one for Joe. He was a little ashamed of how much he wanted what Zarrin kept offering. "Please."

Zarrin's growl got him harder than he'd ever been in his life. Joe huffed at him when golden hands splayed over his hips and yanked him forward. "Mine," Zarrin told him, as if he could smell how much Joe needed it. The tone was dragon, but human fingertips dragged across his navel and raised goose bumps. A soft mouth slid over his, making promises. "Take a step back, Joe, and I'll lead you there. Not here. You didn't want here. That's it. Shh, treasure. You don't have to worry. You asked, and I'll give it to you."

Joe lifted his arms to let Zarrin strip his shirt from him, and got a kiss for every step back he took. He felt drugged, slow with the heat, and horny, and stupid. His ass hit the bed, and then Zarrin was hot between his legs, kissing him, petting him, urging him onto his back.

Joe's sweats were pulled down. They dangled from one foot for a second; then they were gone. Joe had a moment of somewhat chilled nudity before Zarrin straddled him as he undressed himself. He smiled so happily when Joe curved his palms against his back that Joe smiled too. Zarrin's breathing hitched, and then he was down, spread out over Joe like he had to cover every inch of him with his body.

"This is how I imagined claiming you," Zarrin confessed, nuzzling at Joe's shoulder. His cock pressed into Joe's stomach. Joe had thought of this too, but never with sure knowledge that he was going to be fucked and kissed and then fucked again, that he would be called treasure, or that he would want it so much.

He moaned again, and bit his lip to stop it, and Zarrin spoke against his skin, his words mumbled. "You can ask. *Please* ask. You feel…."

"Zarrin." Joe bent his knees to bring Zarrin in tight against him and ran his hands down Zarrin's back until he reached his ass. Zarrin hissed in pleasure, but pushed himself up onto his hands and knees and then sat on Joe's thighs. Joe slid touches all over Zarrin's skin, watching the light hit every gleaming inch of him, and how he looked at Joe as if Joe was doing something wonderful.

He felt very large next to Zarrin, although he wasn't, really. But Zarrin was graceful, fire and air, and Joe was big hands, and salty skin, and coffee-stained fingernails. Joe tickled Zarrin's stomach and spread his fingers over Zarrin's ribs, and Zarrin grinned at him and expelled warm, shocked breaths, then shivered and tipped his head back.

Joe brought his hand up to Zarrin's throat and then ran his thumb over Zarrin's bottom lip. Zarrin darted out his tongue, and whatever he tasted made his eyes go almost black. He moved with no warning, pushing Joe's hand to the bed and then bending over him to tease him with a kiss that never came. He rolled his hips, and a hungry little whine escaped Joe's mouth before he stopped it.

"Do I get to call you mine again?" Zarrin asked while sucking bruises over Joe's tattoos. He lowered his head to bite softly at Joe's chest. "Mine," he murmured, with Joe panting and hot with embarrassment. "Pretty treasure laid out for me," Zarrin praised in his smoky voice, and later, Joe was going to die with how much he wanted it, and the noises he made. But every gasp earned him another rumble, like earthquakes, or the purrs of a giant cat, and Zarrin thrusting slowly against him.

Joe shouldn't have mentioned his hookups in the city. Zarrin was going to go out of his way to prove he was different, as though Joe didn't know that.

"Zar'in." Joe's tongue tripped him up on Zarrin's name every time. He sounded drunk, but Zarrin was marking him like a were. Joe shuddered because this wasn't a cheesy soap opera, and Zarrin didn't get to claim him, but then he said, "Yours?" like a *question*, and Zarrin answered with a gentle exhale near his armpit.

"Yours," Zarrin moaned, then slid down, without another word, to take Joe's cock in his mouth. He slurped and laughed, and Joe was going to kill him, but laughed too, because how was this happening? "This isn't what a strong dragon does," Zarrin apologized—*apologized*—while sucking messily on the head of Joe's cock like he couldn't get enough, so Joe tangled a hand in his hair to let him know it was good, and Zarrin pulled off long enough to call him beautiful, and Joe was going to go a little crazy here.

"Fuck, Zarrin, just fuck me." Joe got to boss a dragon around. Whatever they were, he got to do that, and gesture impatiently toward the drawer in the table by the bed, and watch while Zarrin stood up and idly stroked his dick as he searched for lube.

He picked up a condom with another flash of his real form, a golden, possessive dragon, but returned with it, his expression determined.

Joe's lips were numb from kisses, and he still wanted to draw that regally displeased face down to his until Zarrin wasn't frowning anymore. Instead he said, "Know about beings, Zarrin," and pushed the condom from Zarrin's hand.

Zarrin angled himself up haughtily to announce, "My boy is very bossy," but then came down on top of Joe again, and petted the inside of Joe's thighs in long, sweeping caresses. "But I can't deny him," he added, tone pleased and soft.

"Boy?" Joe pushed his shoulders against the pillows in anticipation when Zarrin slicked up his palm, and lifted his hips even before Zarrin touched his cock.

Joe swallowed just watching it. Zarrin's dick was already glistening. He thumbed Joe's foreskin and then slid his hand up and down his shaft, making things that much slicker. Joe kicked against the quilts, impatient, and Zarrin made room for himself between his legs. He pushed Joe's thighs up and kissed them and then up the crease to his hip.

Joe couldn't breathe. Zarrin was nosing flushed, damp skin and leaving slick imprints of his hands at Joe's inner thighs. He kept *looking* at Joe, inquiring, and the fact that he would have been this way with his dragon lovers made Joe scowl at him, and turn his head away so he would stop being so stupid.

Zarrin shushed him again. "Shh, treasure, don't do that. I'm here now, tell me. I can't please you if you don't tell me." He said that, but expertly teased Joe with his slippery fingers. Joe tensed, then fell back into the piles of quilts with a shuddery sigh of pleasure. He bent one knee to ask for more, and Zarrin mouthed his stomach, sparking small, distracting fires before giving him enough to make him grunt and curl his toes.

"Good," Joe told him, and put an arm over his eyes. He didn't know why he was upset about it. "You're *good* at this," he added, with something sharp in his voice.

Zarrin paused, then ran his tongue along Joe's hip. He took his fingers from Joe's ass and gripped tight at Joe's sides. Then he pulled Joe flush against him and exhaled over Joe's damp, stinging skin. "Yours now," he hissed, so vicious and pleased that Joe grabbed his hair and turned his head to watch Zarrin arrange him how he wanted.

He was so hot, always was, but especially like this, naked and sweaty, unsatisfied until Joe's legs were wrapped around him and Joe was wriggling closer. He took that for an answer, or he could smell Joe's desperation, and leaned up to pant over Joe's mouth as he lined up his cock with Joe's ass.

Joe's lips parted, and then he was shivering and hushed as Zarrin worked him open on his cock, slow but sure, inch by inch. Zarrin's strength was on display, muscles flexing under all that gold, but his eyes were incredible, steady on Joe's face. He eased Joe's thighs open and rolled his hips forward, and Joe thought of some dragon getting this when it should have been his. When Zarrin finally bottomed out, and Joe was so full of cock that his every nerve was sparkling, he whispered, "Mine," and felt Zarrin's rumble from the inside out. He jerked at the sensation, and then Zarrin did it again. Joe thought he could come just from that.

He trailed a hand down the elegant curve of Zarrin's spine, then grasped the back of Zarrin's thigh. His other hand curled tighter in the sleek strands of Zarrin's hair. Zarrin lifted his head, enough for Joe to see the antique gold of his eyes, and then he started to fuck him. He was slow and careful about that too, and growled approvingly when Joe closed his eyes and reached for his cock.

His knuckles brushed Zarrin's skin. He could feel Zarrin's breath, smell hints of smoke. If he looked, Zarrin would be watching him, learning. Joe shifted up, just a bit, and then they were pressed closer and Zarrin's grip on his thigh was bruising. He had one hand on the bed. Joe gasped and squeezed his cock, and Zarrin planted his other hand on the bed for leverage.

"Pretty," he said, mouthing the base of Joe's throat while steadily fucking Joe's brains out. "Pretty Joe darling," he murmured, rolling his hips, and Joe realized he was petting the back of Zarrin's neck and making soft, hungry noises. He begged without words, and got messy, openmouthed kisses at his chest, and then Zarrin rising to hold him by the hips.

Joe opened his eyes. Zarrin looked at him, the way he always had, but this time Joe's stomach tightened and he went still. Zarrin curled over him, fucking Joe hard enough to make his spine light up, but Joe couldn't move with that much admiration beaming down at him.

"Zar'in," Joe hiccupped the name, felt it tear out of him a second time when Zarrin shivered and groaned at the ceiling. "Rin." Joe managed the little name, shiny and new, and finally got Zarrin back down over him.

"Your Rin." Zarrin held Joe down by his hands, and Joe was blanketed in dragon, and the heat was safe, loving. The sounds of skin on skin and heavy breathing were nothing to the rumbling pushing him to the edge. Zarrin kissed him and pinned him and fucked deep, and Joe had nothing to hang on to. He locked his ankles behind Zarrin's ass, and swallowed, and panted for what he needed, and Zarrin whispered his name under his ear. He said how good Joe was, so very good, and Joe came with a loud, rasping moan.

He couldn't move his hands, and the orgasm dragged out of him, rough and overwhelming. He had to work himself on Zarrin's cock to get more, while Zarrin held him tight and called him good so many times Joe felt like he was floating.

When he finally fell back to the mattress to try to catch his breath, Zarrin let him go. He kissed Joe's closed eyes and panted against his mouth, and apologized for releasing him. He pulled out a moment later. Joe complained, a wordless sort of mumble, but then Zarrin breathed hard, and sprawled over him to come on his stomach.

After that, Joe was vaguely aware of soft touches to his face, and huffy murmuring into his hair. More come splashed onto him. He was starting to think that was a thing for Zarrin. He'd protest, but the part of him that hated to think about Zarrin with all his impersonal dragon lovers was soothed by it. It wasn't something Joe wanted to think about, but it was there, a warm glow of satisfaction to think of Zarrin's jizz all over him.

Zarrin splayed out on top of him with a series of contented rumbles. He seemed lighter, or maybe that was a tired Joe's imagination. He breathed heavily at Joe's neck for a while, then twitched and moved so his chin was on Joe's chest.

Joe cracked one eye, then two. Zarrin was staring at him. He was a mess, his hair spiked everywhere, but Joe probably looked worse.

"Yeah?" Joe asked. Zarrin was radiating possessive pride.

"So, so good," Zarrin praised him. "My treasure is the best treasure." He ran the backs of his fingers across Joe's cheekbones and smiled when Joe shivered. "Rin is a good name."

"It's not 'darling Joseph,'" Joe pointed out, warm and happy.

Zarrin inched forward to glare sternly into Joe's face. "It's a good name, treasure. I like it. I can be your Rin, and no one else's."

"Yeah," Joe agreed, unable to blink with Zarrin so fierce and so close.

"Yes." Zarrin nodded firmly, then breathed out and lowered his head to Joe's chest again.

"I'll need to shower again… stuff…," Joe argued, although his eyes wanted to stay closed. "Make food. Grilled cheese, if you want."

"Grilled cheese?" Zarrin sat up and then slid to his feet, leaving Joe to the cold air and the realization that his muscles were not ready for movement yet. Then Zarrin returned to peer at him. "Shower first?" Zarrin asked sweetly, and frowned when Joe shook his head.

"Kiss first," Joe decided aloud, and should have set the bedding on fire with his blushes for the way Zarrin beamed at him.

"Darling Joseph," Zarrin told him, as he slowly leaned in to give Joe what he'd asked for. "You are so very good for me."

JOE WAS going to have to do so much laundry. He'd pulled the top quilt from the bed and added it to his wet clothes from earlier before disappearing into the bathroom. When he emerged, Zarrin had gathered up his clothes for him, cleaned up, and gotten at least partially dressed, and was curled up on Joe's bed with the edition of Verne he'd left for Joe weeks ago.

He had tossed the book aside in order to follow Joe into the kitchen, and insisted on helping him prepare the food. Grilled cheese wasn't really a two-chef job, but Zarrin's version of helping involved lots of Zarrin insinuating himself under Joe's arm and telling Joe what a good cook he was, and then stopping to admire Joe's startled expressions.

The first two sandwiches were a bit singed as a result, but it turned out dragons didn't mind some charring on their grilled cheese. They also didn't mind doing the dishes, although Zarrin had only used a dishwasher before.

Joe watched him take way too long drying each dish, and sighed. They had to talk, but he was fed and clean and well-fucked, and getting warmer by the second. All he really wanted to do was sit in bed until he passed out.

He grabbed a sketch pad and a pencil and sat carefully on the edge of the bed. His mind was buzzing, but not with anything solid. The bed still smelled like sex.

"Was this yours?" Joe looked at the book while Zarrin puttered around the room, trying to locate a sock that had remained elusive.

"It was in the house." Zarrin shrugged. Joe's shirt was baggy on him, and he seemed to like making it fall off one shoulder. "It was mine—growing up, anyway, but it's older than I am. I think Mr. Verne might have met a dragon or two in his lifetime, or believed someone who had. He seems like the type to believe. Artists tend to be." Zarrin suddenly made a face. "Well, not Hemingway."

"I never read Hemingway." *A Farewell to Arms* had been assigned reading in high school, but Joe hadn't been interested in the "classics" when they didn't feature people like him. He'd failed the assignment, and ranted about it into Russ's shoulder while lying in his bed. Russ had told him it was easier to do what people said. Joe should have seen that as the red flag it was. "Or Verne," Joe added quickly, when Zarrin paused to sniff the air.

Zarrin gave up on his search for the sock and hopped onto the bed. "Don't mind me," he remarked innocently, and wriggled into a spot by the headboard and the wall before reaching for the book again.

"I tend to go to bed early on work nights. Sorry if this is boring." Joe still didn't make a move toward using his sketch pad. "You can go if you want. Borrow more clothes if you need them." It was freezing outside, and pouring down rain. They both knew Zarrin wasn't going anywhere. He stretched out so his feet reached Joe. "And I know you meant the book as a gift, but if it means something to you, you can keep it."

"Do you know there is a cat howling in your alley?" Zarrin asked, glancing up from the book. "I could hear it in the kitchen."

"Oh, him." Joe shook his head. "Yeah, I know. He lives out there, and we feed him at the shop, but he won't ever get close to anyone."

Zarrin slowly lowered the book. "May I try?"

"Try?" Joe blinked. "Try what? To grab him? You aren't hoarding stray cats, are you?"

He thought he was teasing, but Zarrin lifted his chin to a pissy angle, so Joe took that as a yes. He waved toward the door without another word and then watched as Zarrin slipped into Joe's hiking boots and then his coat, and went outside. He wanted to be in shock, but somehow he wasn't. Zarrin made friends with deer. He was almost a cartoon princess.

Joe got up and went to the door, trying to see through the rain with his apartment light and the bit of visible streetlight to help him. He had no clue if Zarrin could see in the dark, but he could hear him, a low, constant murmur from the direction of the dumpster outside the shop.

The sound stopped.

Joe squinted, and saw a flash of gold, and then Zarrin dashed up the stairs with a wet, furious cat in his arms. Stunned, Joe closed the door behind Zarrin and stared as Zarrin released a hissing animal into his apartment.

"This might make a mess, but you can bring your laundry to the house, if it's easier," Zarrin called out, while gently shooing the cat toward the bathroom. Joe heard a brief yowl and then nothing. He worried for a moment, then followed them.

The alley cat was being wiped down with a dirty towel and, quite possibly, enjoying it. Although Joe was willing to bet it wouldn't have liked it if he'd done it. Zarrin wasn't even scratched.

"How… how do you even get a stray cat to do that?" he wondered out loud, while Zarrin cooed at it and completely covered Joe's towel in fur and filth.

"I'm warm. Cats like warmth," Zarrin answered with a shrug, then stood up. He washed his hands in the sink while the cat stood there, bristling. "We should feed him before we name him. Come along, little one."

He sailed out of the bathroom, casual as anything, as if a moment later he wasn't stopping to hover outside the door and nervously wait for the cat to follow him. The cat sniffed the floor, and the space close to Joe—but not *too* close to Joe—and then, because he recognized Joe or because of some sort of dragon magic, he crept past Joe out of the bathroom. Zarrin moved on to the kitchen, chattering to the cat about what a nice, safe place this was, and what a good choice he'd made. The cat yowled once, and took his time following him, but follow him he did.

Joe turned all the way around to watch Zarrin put out a bowl of water and then a pile of paper towels.

"They like to dig when they pee. This doesn't mean the cat will use the paper towels, but you don't have any litter, so the towels will have to do." Zarrin glanced from Joe to the cat. "Pee in the kitchen, not on the carpet," he instructed the cat, then went to hang up Joe's coat. The shirt he'd borrowed from Joe was now wet, again, but Zarrin took it off as he returned to the bathroom. When he came back, he was naked.

He climbed into bed to stare at the cat from a distance, until the cat, spiked up and terrified, went into the kitchen to sniff around. "I think he knows your scent." Zarrin faced Joe with a suspicious expression. "Does *everyone* at the coffee shop feed him, or do *you*?"

Joe clenched his jaw when he felt his cheeks begin to sting.

Zarrin grinned. “You should have told me you wanted the cat. I would have gotten him for you sooner.”

“Zarrin.” Joe thought about telling him that people didn’t just adopt stray cats like this. But of course they did. Of course *Zarrin* did. If Joe wasn’t careful, Zarrin was going to leave fluffy toy mice and a food bowl and a litter box at his door. “You can’t make the cat stay here” was what he said instead. “He’s not used to it.”

“If you want to frown and not admit you like this cat, that’s fine, treasure, but don’t blame the cat for it. He’s probably been waiting for an invitation.” Zarrin leaned his head to one side. “Didn’t you want to go to bed?”

“There’s a stray cat in my apartment.” Joe got a wide-eyed stare for that. So he went to the bedroom and closed the door, at least keeping the cat from his artwork. Then he stalked over to the bed and sat on the edge. Zarrin immediately came up behind him to curl around his back. He rested his chin on Joe’s shoulder. For someone who hadn’t been hugged until a werewolf had taught him how, Zarrin was very good at them.

“He’s not going to stay.” Joe tried, one more time, to be reasonable. “If he wants out, I’m letting him out.”

“He’s not a prisoner. Who knew you were so dramatic?” Zarrin briefly nuzzled Joe’s ear. “What a worrier you are. So much concern behind those frowns…. You won’t love the cat more than me, will you?”

Joe made an absent scoffing noise, since Zarrin was more than a little dramatic himself, then stopped and stared at absolutely nothing. His heart was racing, but if Zarrin noticed, he didn’t comment.

The cat rubbed his cheek on the doorframe leading out from the kitchen and then started sniffing along the wall. Now that he was somewhat clean and dry, Joe noticed his fur had more white than gray, and his tail was incredibly fluffy, like a squirrel’s tail on a cat.

“How often do you feed him?” Zarrin asked quietly, and wrapped his legs around Joe’s waist. His arms went around Joe’s chest. “He trusts your scent. Not completely, not yet, but enough for him not to panic.”

“Yeah?” Joe asked, strained and helpless. He covered Zarrin’s arms with his.

Zarrin gave the side of his throat a tiny kiss. “Let’s leave him to get comfortable while we go to bed. It’s been a long day.”

It *had* been a long day, and Joe was getting used to falling asleep cocooned in Zarrin's warmth. But he didn't move. His pulse seemed unnaturally loud.

"He's a good cat, treasure," Zarrin reassured him, supportive and oblivious. He was so toasty that Joe leaned into him with a final, resigned sigh. He tipped his head to one side to give Zarrin more room, and slowly felt himself give in to Zarrin's calm murmuring about what kinds of cat food were the best.

The last thing he remembered before Zarrin laughed softly and tugged him down to the bed was a gray and white cat claiming Joe's apartment as his.

JOE WOKE to the sound of scratching, which was disorienting enough to make him reach for his phone to use the light. Then he remembered the cat. The apartment was dark, and the scratching was coming from around the kitchen.

He distractedly hoped the cat had used the paper towels, then froze as he was about to bury his face back in his pillow. He was abruptly wide awake because there was a cat in his house. He had a stray cat in his apartment because Zarrin had brought it in, as a gift, or because Zarrin couldn't stand to think of it out in the rain and alone.

Joe's heart kicked against his ribs, rebellious and stupid. His mom said it would change the world, but it felt more like it was determined to break itself.

He could make out the shape of Zarrin, the large, curled-up outline of dragon beneath the quilts, the long, elegant muzzle on the other pillow. Zarrin's tail was heavy and warm across Joe's knees.

It was strange to wake up next to a dragon. Joe wondered if he'd ever get used to it, or get the chance to. The one thing Zarrin had avoided talking about was his family, but he'd said enough for Joe to understand the situation. Sooner or later, Zarrin's family were either going to come here or send for him. They could be on their way already. They would take over everything—the town, the Preserve, Zarrin. They'd remind Zarrin of other dragons, and Zarrin might not agree with them, but in time he'd give in.

He could stand up to a town full of humans, but his parents, and generations of family history? Not for Joe.

Joe ignored the sharp twist in his chest. Zarrin wouldn't want to, but he couldn't resist that. He talked about Dìzhèn in worshipful tones. He'd never let her down.

Joe swallowed. He could hardly blame Zarrin. Zarrin had already done more for him than Russ ever had. He *wanted* to do so much, even with his nervous habit of biting his nails and the anxiety he couldn't really hide.

Joe was glad he hadn't let Zarrin promise anything, for both of them. Zarrin tried hard to be brave, and strong, but he was so soft. That's how Joe should have drawn him, sweet and smiling, or bundled up in Joe's bed to hide from the world.

He reached over to trace the ridge above Zarrin's eye and then held his palm beneath Zarrin's nostrils to feel his breath. Zarrin the dragon was so much bigger than Zarrin the man, but so much more delicate at the same time.

Joe hit a button on his phone to let the pale light wash over Zarrin's features. He distantly noted he had about twenty-five minutes until his alarm went off, but he wasn't going to lose this chance to get a long look at this version of Zarrin.

Zarrin's large eyes were currently closed, but they still took up most of his face, which was lean with a wicked jaw. He had tufts of feathery hair above his eyes, in such a dark shade of gold it might as well have been brown, and long eyelashes. Small, gleaming scales became larger at his neck, but even those weren't much bigger than Joe's palm. His one visible paw, resting daintily beneath his chin, had curved, metallic claws that dug into Joe's pillow without poking holes in it.

When Zarrin had been unconscious and drugged and flickering from human to dragon, Joe had distractedly noticed there was more of an Asian dragon about him than a European one, despite his mixed heritage. Zarrin was slender for the most part, except for the muscular strength in his legs and back. But the other side of his ancestry was evident in the small, spiky line of scales going down the length of his spine, and the two scars at his shoulder blades. Some dragons would have had wings there.

"That is very bright," Zarrin grumbled, startling him. Zarrin's voice as a dragon was still smoky, but lighter, which made no sense, since he was larger in size.

Joe moved the phone so it wasn't shining directly into Zarrin's face, and Zarrin opened his eyes.

His eyes were already beautiful, but when he was a dragon they were impossibly wide, incredibly deep, and a color only matched by the coins he'd left in Joe's tip jar. Joe had been waiting his entire life for a dragon to see him, but Zarrin looked at him this close, and he immediately glanced away. Zarrin saw too much sometimes, and Joe had never been very good at hiding what he wanted.

Zarrin inched back from him. "You don't… like me, like this?" he asked, in his strange, ethereal dragon voice. He closed his eyes and his eyelashes fell against his cheek.

"Like a dragon?" Joe frowned, confused. "I know you're a dragon. Anyway, I've seen you before, remember?" He didn't want Zarrin to think of the day of his attack, and he reached out to briefly touch one paw. The scales felt like shells, or smooth plates of stone. "This isn't my first time waking up next to you. It takes some getting used to, but it's not bad." Since Zarrin was holding still, Joe ran a touch along his cheekbone and then barely brushed the ridiculously soft fan of his eyelashes. Zarrin released a startled puff of breath. Joe dared a little more, and held his hand next to Zarrin's mouth. "You're smaller than your dad," he commented quietly. "Or that could be my memory of seeing him as a kid, making him seem huge. I remember your mom too. You look like her, right here." He traced the delicate shape of Zarrin's jaw and flinched when Zarrin pulled back.

"I didn't mean *that*." Zarrin buried his head beneath his pillow in one startling move and then mumbled, "I thought you knew. Oh, Joseph." He'd hidden under the pillows for Forrester too. At the time, Joe had thought it was lingering fear or embarrassment at being naked. But Zarrin wasn't especially bothered by nudity on its own.

Joe shut off his phone light in case that would help. "Zarrin?"

"You really can't tell?" Zarrin sighed. "You never saw any of us close up, did you?"

"Just the one time, when your family came to my school. But I was a kid." Joe sat up and caught a glimpse of Zarrin's muzzle sticking out. "Do you want me to turn on the light?"

"You should, but… no. No, if you don't mind." Zarrin breathed hard for a few seconds and then exhaled roughly. "Joe, dragons are… not human. We like human form, it feels good, and it's useful, but *this* is our real form. To you we seem… animal? You named reptiles after us. But we aren't either. We are magic. This is hard to explain. We aren't… the rules of the world, the social world of humans, they are not our rules. We might feel the same as humans, but our ties to magic are deeper, and stronger. What a human witch could do with all her strength, we can do without effort."

"Okay?" Joe wiped his face and tried to clear his thoughts. "I don't understand magic anyway, but I get enough. I mean, if Marie shifted to a wolf in front of us, we'd see it as it happened, right? But when you go from dragon to person, there's barely anything. One second you're on two legs, then you're on four."

"Yes." Zarrin huffed and then poked his head out. "The thing is…. What I thought you realized is that this is the body I was born with, and it is female. Or, well—" Zarrin made a sound that might have been a dragon cough while Joe blinked at him in the dark. "—it is what you might call, 'designated female.' It's why I'm small. Why I'm built along the same lines as my mother. You really didn't know? To other dragons, it's so clear."

Joe shook his head. He didn't think dragons had night vision, but maybe his blank confusion was in his scent. Zarrin made a quiet, distressed sound and pulled even farther away. He took his tail with him.

Joe reached out for it, but the outline of a dragon next to him became smaller, and paler, and the tail was gone.

Zarrin stayed buried beneath the protection of the pillows and quilts. "When I shift to look human, my body is this one. It has been this one since I was two, because it feels right, because it is *mine*."

Magic was something Joe had never understood, or wanted to. He realized dizzily that Zarrin was telling him dragons could shift gender and sex at will, which was something he'd never once considered. He wasn't sure anybody had.

Then he realized that most of them, like many humans, probably didn't want to or feel the need. But some did. *Zarrin* did. "Oh," Joe said out loud, and stared down at the Zarrin-shaped lump in his bedding. "But I saw you when you were little. You were dressed like—oh," he said again. Then he scowled. "Is this why you think your family is ashamed of you?"

"What?" Zarrin's surprised exclamation was muffled. Then the pillow moved, and Joe touched his phone to get the light back. Zarrin peeked at him. "No! This hardly matters to dragons. My parents are ashamed of me because I'm weak. I can barely protect my small hoard, and can't scare away the humans who hurt me. Would… I know what they say on TV, but would human parents really care?"

It wasn't Joe's job to explain the world to Zarrin, and yet Joe would, as gently as he knew how. "Yeah. Even with fairies and pixies and stuff around, yeah, Zarrin, some human parents don't understand. A lot of them are the same as Russ's parents, or Martin's mom. They—it scares them, the same way beings scare them. In Madera, or some town like Los Cerros, it might not matter as much, but here? We don't even get fairies here. Did—" Joe abruptly remembered something Addison Bernes had said, and shut his mouth.

Addison knew. The dragons must have announced the birth—hatching—of another baby *girl* all those years ago. Which meant most of the older people in town knew about Zarrin as well. Alice, his mother, even Mr. Marcus. And Addison had been the only one to say anything. Joe had no idea what to think about that information, but he had slightly kinder feelings toward Mr. Marcus than he'd had that morning.

He took a moment, then tried again. "Did TV convince you that I would care?"

He did care, although he wasn't sure about what yet. His mind was all over the place.

"Do you?" Zarrin countered. "Now that you know?"

Joe took another moment to stare at Zarrin in the faintly blue light, a boy with ruffled hair and worried eyes. He continued to speak in a secret, early morning hush. "Are you comfortable with… everything? How you are?" It felt like the dumbest question, but Zarrin nodded gravely. Joe nodded back, accepting that, then thought of another one. "Is this, uh, related to the scars on your back?"

He took Zarrin's puzzled silence to mean it wasn't.

Zarrin sat up and held the pillow to his chest. "The dragons of my mother's line have wings." He shrugged absently. "They're not useful for flying, not at their size, but they're distinctive. My sister and mother have them. I did, as well. They were removed."

"You got rid of them?" Joe tried to imagine Zarrin with tiny leathery wings. One more thing to think about in the predawn hours with his heart pounding like crazy.

"I didn't have much to do with it." The way Zarrin clutched Joe's pillow was making Joe anxious. He leaned over to take hold of one hand. Zarrin grasped it, then glanced away. "When I was hatching, although my egg cracked, I refused to come out. I *hid*. And then, so my parents tell me, when they finally coaxed me into trying to emerge, I cut my wings on the shell. Not enough to destroy them, but enough to leave scars. I grew, but the scarring meant my wings couldn't extend or move without pain. It was decided that I would live a happier life if they were gone. I wouldn't have to worry about them stretching as they grew." He pulled Joe's hand to his cheek, then sighed and let it go. "I wouldn't mind—it's not as though we can fly, but it's another reminder of what a failure I am. I was born weak and soft, and to them I always will be."

Joe could hear his teeth grinding together. His hands formed fists. "Fuck that." It burst from him, and Zarrin jumped. "They cut your wings. They cut off your *wings* and they hold it against you?" He thought he might be shaking.

Zarrin stared at him. "You're really angry," he commented.

Joe couldn't tell if he was amazed or afraid. He opened his hands and ran them down his thigh. He made his voice gentler.

"Come here." Joe tugged on the pillow Zarrin was clinging to, and Zarrin tossed it away to climb into his lap. Zarrin curled in close and put his face to Joe's neck. He took a huge, gulping breath. "I'm sorry," Joe grunted, which was as sensitive as he could get at the moment. "I'm glad you aren't in pain, at least, but I'm sorry I was—*am*—mad about it, and that scared you. If people think less of you because of something you did as a kid, then fuck them."

"Joseph." Zarrin said his name in a choked voice. And then, softer, "Joe, I wasn't scared."

"No, really," Joe went on, pissed in a way he hadn't been for a long time. "I don't care what a dragon is supposed to be. I like you. Nobody is who they were as a kid, and so what if you were timid? You're out in the world now."

Zarrin raised his head. His hair was all over the place again. "You look angry and you *smell* angry, and it's for wings you've never seen?

I tell you I'm not entirely what you think I am, and you're only quiet for a few minutes, then ask me if I'm comfortable?" His eyes took in everything about Joe, and he smiled as if he liked what he saw. "What else can I do but keep you forever?"

"So," Joe began again, after a while of hearing *forever* echo through the room. His heart was so loud Zarrin should have heard it. "From the age of two, huh?"

It wasn't his brightest moment, but it was early, and he hadn't had his coffee, and he'd recently realized he was in love, or something close to it. His spirit was a mess.

Zarrin studied him before answering. "Yes. It wasn't a matter of interests. Dragons in nearly every dragon culture don't divide activities by gender the way humans do. This was me. And as I grew older, I liked it more. I love my narrow hips and my shoulders and my jaw. I love my cock. Don't you? Isn't it nice?"

Joe bit his lip before he could ask if Zarrin's magic had let him choose his cock. Although, if it had, he agreed that it was very nice.

Zarrin passed a hand over himself. "This is me. And I like it, sometimes more than my dragon body, and not just because Dìzhèn built her home to intimidate humans—there are so many stairs. She was like me, you know. Or do you? I don't suppose you do. That's family history." He went on when Joe numbly shook his head. "Dìzhèn wasn't like me in the sense that her magic let her be herself. Instead, she used her magic to take on a male human body when dealing with humans. People of that time were more accepting of a male, even a Chinese one, than a woman. Although it would take considerable magic for a dragon to take a form unnatural to them. Even Dìzhèn might not have been able to without already having an inclination to—" Zarrin hummed thoughtfully. "Perhaps she *was* like me, and the family story is wrong. We'll never know, unless Alfie wrote it down somewhere."

"Dìzhèn was—" Joe would have said trans, but he wasn't certain if Zarrin would like the label. "Never mind. You're telling me your parents don't care that you're a boy? They're upset that you're soft? What about this? You and me? Would that bother them?"

"A dragon taking a boy, that is to say, a human or nondragon lover, is a time-honored tradition," Zarrin answered in a tone that implied Joe hadn't been paying attention. "The gender and sex of the boy—or the dragon—have never been an issue. Although, same-sex pairings *are* an issue these days because of the desire for dragon children. If one of them is human, well, children would be close to impossible. I mean, that amount of magic is more than what it must have taken to bind her magic to so much land in the first place."

Joe had had enough mind-blowing revelations for one morning. He tossed that idea right out, to be dealt with later, or never. Dragons were so *different*.

"So you, um, you're okay? With me?" His voice cracked as if he was going through puberty again.

"I am more than okay with you," Zarrin answered immediately. "And you don't mind too much that I am not a fierce dragon?"

"You know I don't." Joe smoothed Zarrin's ruffled hair while the cat began to make restless noises somewhere by the kitchen. There were too many other things for him to be concerned about this morning than giving in to his silly impulses about Zarrin's hair. Zarrin's hair had always been a distraction. "I remember you as a little boy." He deliberately didn't acknowledge the way Zarrin was staring at him. "Your hair was just like this, and you had on neat slacks and a striped sweater vest that you seemed to hate. You couldn't stop squirming. You probably wanted to go run through the trees, but your parents had made you come to some boring event at my school."

Zarrin parted his lips, but then seemed to rethink whatever he'd been going to say. He swallowed. "It must be frightening to not be as sure as we are."

"Frightening?" Joe frowned, because the one thing he was not was frightened of Zarrin. Their future, but not Zarrin himself. He took a deep breath. "What you asked before… I don't think I care. Maybe. I don't know." He'd never been in this situation before, but he couldn't think how it would change anything. "You're Zarrin, and I—you're Zarrin." Joe was stupidly in love with a dragon who was going to leave him. That was all he could think right now. Maybe the rest would matter later, but he didn't think so. "Did the other dragons you slept with care, or did you—" Obviously, Zarrin knew how to have sex in a human body. He knew it very well. But dragons must sleep with dragons as dragons too. Joe was an idiot.

Zarrin seemed to know what he meant, and cupped Joe's cheek. "Human bodies are designed for pleasure in a way ours aren't. Maybe that's why we choose human form more than any other. And it helps to appear human in a human world. But if you're asking if I prefer you to them, of course I do. You're Joseph, and you are so *good*. You're talented, and you're kind, and if you don't mind me saying so, very fuckable."

Joe snorted at that, despite the slow, easy, glowing feeling in his arms and legs, at odds with his jumpy, skittering nerves. He lowered his head to Zarrin's shoulder. "I didn't mean to make it about me, or to compare myself to your exes."

Zarrin made a quiet sound of amusement, or pleasure, and stroked the back of Joe's neck. "There is no comparison. I like it when you give yourself to me and want me to take charge of you. I like it a lot. I also liked the making out."

Obviously, Joe liked it a lot too. He groaned anyway, turned on, embarrassed, and painfully attached to one little dragon.

"If someone took you from me, I'd be very angry." Zarrin's tone was almost thoughtful. Then his hand stilled. "As angry as when I think about Russ. As angry as you were when I told you about my wings." His voice briefly hardened, and the air hummed with energy. Joe shivered, and Zarrin resumed petting him.

This was as close to being chosen by a dragon as Joe would ever get. Zarrin's family was going to take him away, or use their influence to get rid of Joe, or convince Zarrin it was best to find another dragon. Zarrin seemed to know it too, even if he wasn't going to say it.

But he deserved better.

"You're very good too," Joe told him, low and careful, as if the other dragons might somehow hear him. "Soft or not, Zarrin, without wings, you're good. You listen, and you try, and you let people you care about leave if it's what they want, even though it hurts you and dragons don't like to do it. A lot of people, humans and probably dragons too, give up when something hurts. That's when *they* run and hide. But you still try, and that makes you strong. Stronger than a homecoming king football hero, anyway. Caring is… caring is hard." His voice broke, and he couldn't have said why, except that Zarrin wasn't moving anymore. "You don't have to be fierce like they want. We don't need a scary dragon to fight for us, just someone good to be there. People like that." Joe swallowed. "*I* like that. I like this. I lo—" Joe shut his mouth with a snap. He closed his eyes. "I have to go to work."

Joe didn't want to raise his head, but the cat was prowling at the edge of his awareness, and any minute now, his alarm was going to go off. He spoke quickly. "If you want, you can stay here. You can sleep in or have another grilled cheese if you can remember how to make them." It wasn't a big gift, but Zarrin's sound of delight made his pulse speed up. "If you stay… if the cat stays too, make sure he doesn't tear up my stuff, or get into my studio, okay?" Joe listened to Zarrin's uneven breathing. "But you can go in there—if you want. You don't have to."

He tore himself away from Zarrin and rolled to his feet. The cold hit him now that he was so far from Zarrin, and he shuddered and went in search of a sweatshirt. He flipped on the kitchen light as he did, revealing spilled water, but no cat urine.

The cat ran to the front door.

Joe twisted his mouth but went to open it. He grimaced at the blast of chilly wet air. The rain and the wind hadn't stopped.

The cat sat on its ass and didn't move, at least not until Joe did. When Joe shut the door, the cat hopped away to a corner of the living room, where it stared at him.

"It's freezing out," Joe said at last, staring back. "That's why he won't go. I wouldn't go either in this weather."

"Oh, Joseph," Zarrin exclaimed sadly.

Joe slowly turned toward him. Zarrin had pulled the quilts over his shoulders, although his bare chest was still visible. He stared at Joe without blinking. In the brighter light, his eyes seemed almost liquid, pleading and warm. "I have to go to work." Joe had said that already.

Zarrin sniffled. "I know. Say good morning to Martin for me."

Joe shivered. His toes were frozen even in his socks. "You're going to stay? You'll be okay alone?"

"So worried and dramatic. I'll be in to see you in a few hours." Zarrin rolled his eyes playfully, although he continued to hide in the pile of Joe's quilts. Then he cleared his throat as if he was about to say something delicate. "Did it hurt to offer me your studio?"

Joe worked his jaw.

Zarrin scooted forward. "Did you offer it *because* it hurt? Oh, don't frown, Joseph." He rushed on before Joe could try to say anything. "Did you think I wouldn't want your treasure? Have I ever refused a gift from you?"

"A latte," Joe argued immediately, for no reason at all except it still stung. "A latte I made for you that Marie took."

Zarrin clapped his hands. "Darling jealous Joseph! Come here, and I'll show you what I would have done if I'd been there when you brought it."

With barely time to blink, Joe was back in his warm bed with Zarrin climbing over him and then wrapped around him. Zarrin kissed him softly, with sweet little murmurs of "thank you" and "such a good wooing gift" and "mine."

Zarrin moved against Joe in slow, torturous circles, teasing him while praising him, and waking Joe's body up with words like sparks and the hot press of him. Joe raised his hands above his head, and shivered for how Zarrin immediately slid his hands to his wrists to hold him.

Joe looked up, eyes wide, lips parted, and then gave a jolt when his alarm went off. He briefly shut his eyes and hated everything.

But the alarm was blaring, and the sound was making the cat huff in agitation.

"It's your treasure." Zarrin gently, if breathlessly, called Joe back to the moment. "I'm honored, if you still want me to see it. I'd never refuse a gift from you. I'm not *him*, and Marie is only a friend. Please believe me."

Joe looked away, and noticed the phone in the pile of bedding. He shut off the alarm before turning to Zarrin, and his throat locked up before he could say a word. He closed his eyes, and Zarrin pressed in closer.

"Did you know that dragons respond to need?" Zarrin asked, idly—or not, while nipping at Joe's tattoos and then rising up to lick at Joe's bottom lip. "You don't understand what that means yet, but you're my boy, mine. You'll be the very best for me, and I will give you everything." His bites were harder, for a moment. "I will fulfill my boy's every need. It will be my pleasure."

Joe's heart was going to burst from his chest. "Zarrin," he croaked, because Zarrin kept looking at him, he could feel it, and a dragon's gaze was no easy thing to bear. It saw even the things he wasn't going to admit to wanting.

"And now here I am," Zarrin continued, spread out over him, aroused, but kissing him gently. "You tell me I'm good and then offer me your treasure with your pretty lip trembling?" He lavished praise on

Joe's mouth, and breathed with him, and spread flames beneath his skin. "You waited, didn't you? You hoped and hurt and I made you angry, although I didn't know it. But now I'm here."

"Yes. *Now*," Joe said, without meaning to, and turned his face away.

Zarrin paused, then moved over Joe to put pressure around Joe's wrists again. "Now? Because you *did* wait? Because you know, don't you? It's the artists who see like Seers. You've known all along, but you won't admit it. You want it, and think it will hurt, so you say nothing. *Joe*." Zarrin purred his name, and Joe was so hard he felt feverish. Zarrin mouthed his throat, and held him down, and Joe couldn't think.

Zarrin's words sank into him. "I never thought I'd be the brave one, not like you. But I will be. You'll see. I'll prove it to you. I'll take such good care of you. You have to go to work, and I'll make sure you do, but first this. First this to remind you." He kissed along Joe's throat, and pulled Joe's unresisting hands down to keep them pinned against the mattress as he worked his way along Joe's body.

Joe was going to be late and have to open the shop in a rush, but he stayed where he was, his fingers curled into a quilt, although Zarrin finally released him. He slid his palms over Joe's thighs instead, and pulled Joe's sweats down to bite his hip bone. "Go to work and remember a dragon couldn't resist you." Zarrin groaned, and Joe felt it in his every nerve. "That I chose you because you are good. Joe," Zarrin panted into his skin. "You don't have to believe it yet, but say it. Please say it for me."

Joe heard himself whimper as Zarrin planted both hands on Joe's hips to keep him down. He tangled his hands in Zarrin's hair, which was like satin and gave him nothing to hold on to. He couldn't even tell why he bothered now. Zarrin had him seeing stars with a few words. So he exhaled a needy moan and then drew in air and said, "Rin," with his face still turned away. His jaw hurt as though it had been locked tight.

"Your Rin, and no one else's." Zarrin's growl rolled through Joe like the thunder outside, and then he took Joe's cock into his mouth and made the earth shake.

# CHAPTER 13

JOE SPENT the first few hours at the coffee shop off-balance, with that playing catch-up feeling that went along with showing up late to work. He hadn't been truly late, but Martin had been waiting outside the door when Joe dashed across the alley, and they'd had to do all the opening tasks in a rush.

Martin had taken one good look at Joe—hair in his face, mouth nearly bruised from kisses, wearing a sweatshirt that had obviously been thrown on moments before—and made a weird wheezing sound. Then he'd smiled one of the widest smiles Joe had ever seen and paused in the middle of arranging pastries to say, "You look so fucking happy."

A moment after that, he'd whispered, "I wish my mom could see it," and hurried to the front door to flick on the lights and let in an early customer.

Joe didn't think he looked happy. Happy shouldn't mean his heart racing, or going to the storage fridge three times because he kept forgetting the thing he was looking for, or flushing with heat when he had to borrow a hair tie from Jessie because Zarrin had taken his.

He was probably covered in love bites now as well, although most of them wouldn't be visible even if he removed his sweatshirt—something he had no intention of doing today. Customers were already giving him curious looks; he wasn't going to invite any more conversation about his love life.

Calling it a love life, even in his head, made him screw up the order for the office workers down the block, which he then had to run around to fix. He didn't have time to wonder if Zarrin was still in his apartment, if the cat was, or what Zarrin would think of the dragonfire painted on the walls of Joe's bedroom or the countless sketches of golden dragons.

But between orders, the itch of sweat down his back would remind him of Zarrin's hands on him. His thighs were stinging with the marks of Zarrin's teeth. All the quick splashing in the bathroom couldn't hide how he must smell like Zarrin, and sex. Maybe not to humans, but Zarrin would know. He'd done that on purpose.

Joe got hot again, and he determinedly focused on customers and not the dragon possibly in his apartment, who had begged Joe to claim him.

Joe reached for the steaming wand he had just used and hissed when it burned him. Not a bad burn. Nothing out of the ordinary that didn't happen to at least one of them every other day, but he glanced around guiltily anyway, and didn't like seeing both Martin and Helene wince in sympathy, because they'd been watching him.

Jessie, of all people, patted him on the shoulder and took over for him. "Sorry they're being weird about it."

Joe wasn't used to Jessie being calm or sensible, and couldn't help asking, "Weird about what?"

Jessie made a sound between a laugh and a scoff. "I've seen 'new relationship' face before. It's a lot like 'good dick' face, but cuter. I think it's weird because nobody expected it. I figured, even when you were in love, you'd frown. But, gosh, look at you."

She said "gosh" and "dick" in exactly the same tone. Joe turned to try to see his reflection in the shiny chrome of the espresso machine, and Jessie giggled. "Wow, okay. Good for Zarrin. You are *sprung*! Hey, Helene, did you get your second capp yet?" She left him reeling to make sure Helene's cappuccino was all right, then returned to the machine. "You can go do something else. I got this."

"Since when does Jessie 'got' anything?" Joe followed Martin into the back to ask, and Martin cackled at him.

"Since you explained why you didn't like her getting high at work." Martin filled Joe's arms with a bunch of milk cartons, then glanced significantly at the pitcher of iced tea cooling on a table. "I don't think you get how much she listens to you. People, um, like you, you know?" A bright pink blush spread through Martin's cheeks. "But we're genuinely happy for you. Even Helene. I know she gets all, 'the town needs this blah blah blah,' but you have this, um, not quite a bruise yet, with teeth marks, above your clavicle, and you're a mess today, and it's great."

"Great," Joe repeated flatly, with his heart loud in his ears. "Zarrin and I… we're not… we can't be—"

Martin's voice echoed out of the refrigerator. "Joe, you kind of already are. You know, like, how in high school, everything is scary, and you can't let yourself want things because they'll tease you, or beat the shit out of you, or kick you out of the house—I mean, figuratively?"

Joe stiffened.

Martin straightened up and used his foot to close the fridge doors. He studied Joe for a moment, then glanced at the iced tea again. "I think the coolest thing about growing up is realizing, shit, I'm not in high school anymore, and seeing that other stuff is possible. So, you guys are possible. Which is so cool when you aren't sure about yourself—I mean, for people who need to see things like that."

With that, Martin hurried out to the front.

Joe followed, mostly because all the milk in his arms was cold and heavy. His chest was tight and his stomach flipped anxiously, as if Zarrin were there in front of him. He wished he were. Things were easier when Zarrin was there, so damn certain of everything.

Maybe Zarrin had a right to be. Maybe, a small part of Joe whispered, Joe had a dragon boyfriend. It couldn't last, but at this moment, Joe had a boyfriend, and everyone knew it.

He set down the milk, then turned away and caught Jessie grinning at him, probably because Joe was smiling.

Wouldn't Zarrin love to know that? Joe's hand twitched toward his phone, although he still didn't know Zarrin's number.

He approached the register and then looked up into Addison's startled face. She stared at him, with her attention briefly falling to where Joe really must have a hickey starting to show, and then cleared her throat.

"Addison." Joe greeted her as levelly as he could, considering the one person in town to be openly hostile about Zarrin's human body was standing in front of him. "The usual?"

She opened her mouth, probably to answer, but the door opened and Joe saw a flash of red that made him go tense with instinctual alarm.

Addison twisted around to see what he was staring at and then froze. "Azar," she said, in strangled surprise and what sounded like panic. "Azar Xu is here."

*Red* was Joe's first real impression of Azar. He hadn't paid much attention to Azar as a kid, something he couldn't understand now, because she was striking. If Zarrin was old gold, his sister was red-gold, like flames.

She stopped in the doorway to brush droplets of water from her long, heavy coat, which was a fine coat for a place like Los Cerros, but not for Everlasting in December. She had no scarf or hat, or even an umbrella. Her hair was wet, and visibly steaming as it dried, hazy curls that added to the impression of fire, and danger. Even if she hadn't been dragon, she would have been someone to worry about, with her black heels with the soles as red as her nails. Her hair was dark and short, her eyebrows threaded with sharp precision. Her lips were the same shade as her nails, although Joe didn't think the color on her nails was paint.

Her scales extended farther than Zarrin's. He could see them beneath her shoulders, a hint of warmth at her chest, where her suit jacket came open. Small earrings of yellow-gold hung from her ears, and she had a thin watch around one wrist.

Her black suit looked like something from a magazine or the streets of New York, but her arrogant, displeased expression was all too familiar.

She shook more water from her coat and then lifted her chin to scan the coffee shop. Every human in her line of sight either froze or lowered their gaze.

The temperature seemed to rise. Which might have been her, or the growing tension as everyone realized a dragon was among them, a dragon who was very much not Zarrin.

Martin and Jessie stopped moving. Then Martin whispered, "This can't be good," and put a name to the knot of fear in Joe's chest.

He glanced at the door, but no other dragons came in with her. Not that they needed to, he supposed. Zarrin had said his sister worked for the family as a lawyer. That would have been intimidating enough even if she hadn't been dragon.

She looked at the other room, and the customers who had been calmly enjoying their drinks, and huffed. Smoke escaped with the sound, and Addison, as motionless as everyone else, murmured, "She's here for him."

Joe felt something seize in his chest.

Evidently not happy with what she saw in the other room, Azar took her time studying everyone at the counter or over by the milks and sugars. Forrester, in uniform, made her narrow her eyes, but then she focused on the register.

She didn't slink like Zarrin did. Her every step was punctuated by a precise click of her heels against the floor. Joe thought of claws, and suspected he was meant to.

She stopped several feet away and glanced up at the board and then at the tea display. "I assume you know how to properly prepare the tea you serve here. I want something hot. The Pearl Tea will do, at the correct temperature."

There was a kettle in the back for people who were particular about their tea. Martin tripped over his own feet in his haste to go get it ready for her.

Joe didn't have a strong memory of her. Which made no sense, unless she hadn't been this intimidating then. She watched Martin as he returned, with a flicker of interest for his nervous blushing, then seemed to forget him.

She had large gold eyes, not quite the same shape as Zarrin's, but close. Her skin, where it didn't hint at gleaming red-gold beneath the surface, was somewhere between apricot and cinnamon. She glanced around the room one more time before settling her attention on Forrester.

"A deputy?" She phrased it like a question, but Joe didn't think she was asking. "Perhaps you know more than your sheriff seemed to. You know who I am?" She paused while Forrester raised his head. "Do you know where my brother is?"

Forrester swallowed the coffee in his mouth, then widened his eyes to an almost comically stupid degree. "Your brother, ma'am?" he asked, forming each word slowly. "Is he missing?" Forrester took a notepad from a pocket in his coat. "Did you need to file a report?"

Every moment in high school where Forrester had never seemed to know the answer in class or the name of the jock getting in his face flashed before Joe's eyes, alongside the memory of Forrester in advanced classes and the Honor Society. Joe had known Forrester's oblivious idiot thing was an act, but he'd never had a reason to appreciate it before.

Azar didn't seem to care for it, or believe it. "You know who my brother is. How many dragons are there in Everlasting?"

"Two, that we know of," Martin mumbled. Even his ears were pink now. He'd pulled down a cup and saucer and they rattled in his trembling hands.

Forrester spoke up again. "Zarrin's missing? Well, you should come down to the station and—"

"I've been to the station," Azar interrupted without apology. "I arrived this morning and went to the house first. It was early but he wasn't home. I waited, and then I called him, but despite how he called me, at some point today, he must have turned off his phone. Considering that there was no sign of our housekeeper either, I decided to try finding him in town."

There was no way this was a visit from a concerned sister. She had to be here on legal business. But Joe wondered if she was worried about Zarrin anyway, underneath the imperious tone. If she was, it was a couple of days too late to show it.

Azar held Forrester's stare, and Forrester manfully stared back, although his dumb-small-town-cop routine wore thin the longer he did it.

"Your sheriff, with much hesitation, suggested I try this coffee shop." Azar gestured elegantly at the room. "But I don't see Zarrin."

"Where do you think he'd be?" Joe broke in, and went still as stone when Azar turned to him. He wet his mouth, and cleared his throat, and had a feeling he was scowling. "He's your brother," he pointed out a second later, in a rough, stupidly belligerent voice. "You ought to know. He's not in the hospital, if that bothers you."

"Of course he's not in the hospital." Azar swept a scornful look over him. "He'd heal before that ever became necessary."

Zarrin drugged out of his mind and only able to rest in Joe's bed wasn't an image Joe liked to remember, but he supposed Azar was right. Zarrin hadn't needed a hospital; he'd needed a place to feel safe and cared for. Joe was grateful he'd found one.

His silence seemed to pique Azar's interest. "You seem very certain of where he *isn't*."

Joe didn't think he'd given that much away, but then she glanced at Addison, who lowered her head, and he realized he was one of the few looking directly at Azar, and he was being openly rude.

He crossed his arms and ignored the prickle of sweat down his back that made him think of Zarrin. "I'm certain that your family has ignored us for years, and now you come back, and the first thing you do is ask for something. You should be asking what we need, shouldn't you?"

Azar raised her eyebrows. Then she blinked, and her surprise was gone, replaced with interest. She approached the counter, and Addison backed away. Jessie might have too. Martin seemed petrified over by the tea.

It was the first time Azar was remotely like her brother as she considered Joe's shoulders and his throat and then the lines of his face. "Hmm." She curved her lips in an appreciative smile. "I wondered why the sheriff would send me to this coffee shop."

"Martin." Joe's throat was dry. "Is her tea ready?"

"Uh, yeah, Joe." The cup and saucer clattered as Martin brought them over. Azar didn't so much as glance at them.

"I read the police report." She wasn't speaking loudly, so her voice probably didn't travel as far as Joe felt it did. It seemed to softly carry through the room. "It said those humans lured my brother with the scent of coffee." She paused. "Zarrin doesn't drink coffee."

"Lattes," Joe corrected her sharply, then took a breath. "He could have liked them for a while. How would you know?"

Azar's head went up. "Zarrin is always welcome to visit me. He chose to stay here alone." When Joe didn't bother saying anything to that, she narrowed her eyes. Then she clucked her tongue, the way Zarrin did, except without the fondness. "You're very defiant, aren't you? And handsome. Protective of him too. What was your name again?"

Her dragon eyes saw as much as Zarrin's, maybe more. But she was far less gentle about what she saw.

She continued without waiting for his answer. "Joe, wasn't it? How interesting. There was a Joseph in the report. My parents noted the name, intending to reward the one who'd found Zarrin."

Joe flinched from the memory of finding Zarrin.

Azar didn't react that he could see, but he could tell he'd given himself away. "How fortunate that you were there. That you were *allowed* to be there."

Her eyes weren't like Zarrin's at all. She looked straight at him, deliberately intimidating. Because she knew.

The knot in Joe's chest tightened. There was no way she didn't know. The house had let him onto the property for Zarrin. The fact that he'd found Zarrin in all those acres where he could have been. That Joe had even dared to go anywhere near the Preserve.

He'd just figured out his feelings for Zarrin, and she'd seen them in minutes. She was going to use them against him, or against Zarrin somehow. Joe was nothing to her, but Zarrin…. Someone so determined to learn how to cuddle should get the chance to.

Joe straightened as best as he could with his insides twisted up. Glaring at her was easy compared to that. "I don't want money. I'm happy to have helped him."

"He doesn't want money," she commented quietly, to no one in particular. Her eyes were steady on him. He had no reprieve, or chance to calm down. She darted out her tongue to scent the air the way Zarrin did, and Joe's heart kicked against his ribs. Her gaze dipped to his throat, to either the hickey Zarrin had left or the parts of his tattoos that were visible. She smiled again. "You don't need our gifts if you're already getting them. How unexpected of Zarrin to have found a toy."

Joe frowned harder in momentary confusion and then realized she thought what everyone thought, that he was Zarrin's plaything.

In a way, he was. But he jerked his head up like he would have done for anybody else in town, and snapped, "Are you asking if your brother and I are fucking?"

Addison made a strangled sound.

Azar rolled her eyes. "Of course you are. Zarrin has been dreaming of his special one since he was a child. Naturally he'd be drawn to the nearest brave human he could find in this town. And of course you agreed. There… aren't many who would refuse a dragon."

Joe felt like he'd been slapped. He'd known, deep down, despite Zarrin's words, that Joe wasn't his in the way Zarrin meant. But he'd hoped for something. Maybe he wasn't a fling, but he was a boyfriend. Not a One, not a mate, not a dragon's boy like Alfie. That was more than he'd ever been, and it should have been enough.

"Special one?" It slipped out in spite of everything Joe tried to tell himself.

Azar's smile actually softened, but the pity in it was so much worse than outright cruelty. "Zarrin is a romantic by nature. You shouldn't take him too seriously. He let his one fall through his fingers, but he won't do it again. He'll treat you well, I'm sure, but you were never going to last long." She even said it quietly, so it was possible only Martin and Jessie heard.

Joe lowered his gaze to the countertop. It was nothing he hadn't expected. Zarrin did believe in the idea of a dragon having a special someone, like werewolves did. He did make insanely unrealistic promises. Joe had warned him not to, for his own sake, and Zarrin had stopped. Joe was the idiot who'd been starting to believe him.

"Poor human." Azar crept closer. "I'm sorry. I really am. But I need to know where he is. I have to talk to him."

Joe clenched his hands. His voice was embarrassingly hoarse. "You could have done that a week ago, when he actually needed you." No wonder everyone had guessed he loved Zarrin. He was so obvious that he felt naked despite his sweatshirt. He raised his head anyway. "None of you seem to be good at being here when you're needed."

"You sound like him." Azar tipped her head to one side. "He likes to talk about this town, and her."

"You mean Dìzhèn?" Joe's throat was raw, but he could say the name if she couldn't. "Yeah, he mentioned you were all scared of her."

The wave of heat that hit him made him shudder. Christmas carols were coming from the speakers, which was something odd to focus on when he was burning up with the force of a dragon's fury. Azar appeared calm, but she wasn't. He guessed living in Dìzhèn's shadow *did* bother them.

"Really?" He still couldn't believe it. A rich dragon with all the power in the world, and she was afraid of someone long dead? "Every single one of you guys left the town that was supposed to be your treasure, because it had once belonged to someone else? That's the whole mystery of why Everlasting lost its dragons?" He didn't bother to lower his voice. "Instead of staying and leaving their own marks, they offer tribute and then run away. Some ferocious creatures you are."

"Her magic never transferred to—" Azar clicked her nails on the countertop one at a time. "Only dragons who can't build their own treasure guard someone else's."

"Like Zarrin?" Joe stepped forward. "Yeah, he's a romantic. But whatever else he is, he's dragon, and he's strong enough to do what none of you can manage. If you don't want what was Dìzhèn's, then let it go. If you do want it, then do your job and treasure it."

He pulled in a long breath that didn't steady his nerves or ease the pain in his chest.

He stared at the dragon in front of him, who was so different from Zarrin. She didn't lift her chin at the insult. She lowered it, and regarded Joe carefully. Joe could smell intense smoke, but there was no sign of any.

"Zarrin is a softhearted boy. Whatever he's been telling you—"

"Everyone in here knows the history of this town." Joe cut her off with a hot, reckless feeling behind his heart, like flames. "Everyone but you."

"Joe…," Martin warned him in a whisper. Addison was wide-eyed.

Joe shook his head. "No. This is what people wanted me to do, isn't it? I was supposed to ask the dragons what they wanted? Well, here's a true dragon." He locked eyes with Azar. "True dragon. Everything Zarrin thinks he should be, and all she's doing is asking me for something. Where is Zarrin?" Joe held up a hand and opened it to show it was empty. "Call him again and find out. I've got no hold on him, you said it yourself."

He closed his hand at the thought. When this was over, he'd have a handful of old coins and a set of colored pencils. He had nothing to lose, then. "Your family might think Zarrin is simple or something, but he's braver than you. He's probably out there in the Preserve again, maybe in the very place he was attacked. But he loves it, so he'll go. Every day—until your family takes him away." Joe took a moment to gauge her reaction, which was utter stillness. "For his own good, and not because you're all too intimidated to follow in your ancestor's footsteps? Or unable to?"

Joe exhaled heavily. "You do that. You protect Zarrin by taking him from the thing he loves, and make yourself feel good, trick yourself into thinking you're protecting him, that you care about him. But that isn't—" His voice broke. "That isn't how you treat treasure, and you know it."

Her gaze was unflinching. "And how do you treat treasure, Joe?"

Joe shut his mouth hard. He thought of the pride in Zarrin's eyes, Zarrin calling him pretty and good. He flushed to remember their kiss in the park and Zarrin's hand at his cheek. That had been real, even if it hadn't meant what Joe wanted it to.

He lowered his head to stare at Azar's red nails and her shiny watch of yellow-gold. "How would I know?" he admitted, quietly. "We both know I don't."

The crash of the door against the wall made Joe jump and sent Martin scrambling back. Joe had the fleeting, distracted thought that the door was designed so no one *could* slam it, and then he looked up to see a firestorm.

Black smoke flowed to the floor like waves of lava, with heat so intense the air was wavy. Zarrin, taller, dangerous in spite of his silly knitted hat and comfortable scarf, addressed the shop in a furious rumble. "*Who hurt Joe*?"

He met Joe's eyes for the briefest moment, intense and questioning, and then his attention slid from Joe to Azar.

"Zazzie?" he asked, his roar melting into confusion. The streams of smoke lessened, although they didn't change color. Zarrin glanced around the two rooms, then focused on his sister.

He was in his clothes from the day before, which were wrinkled from being hung up to dry in a bathroom. In one hand, he had a giant black-and-white umbrella he must have purchased at the drugstore. He hit a button to close it and then tossed it away.

He came forward, becoming smaller with each careful step, until he was Zarrin again, little Zarrin in his big coat. Knowing that he could do that whenever he wanted, even when still pissed off, was intimidating. Zarrin had never been deliberately intimidating before.

He narrowed his eyes and went right past his sister so he could stand in front of Joe. Then he tore off his gloves and let them fall to the floor.

"It's all right, Joseph," Zarrin said, as if his sister wasn't going to use this against him, and then reached across the counter for Joe's hand.

Joe didn't move, and glanced away before Zarrin could frown at him or flutter his hands in concern. "Your sister is here."

"I can see Zazzie." Zarrin's voice was low and intimate, soothing. "I can also see you. You're upset. You're *hurt*. I knew the moment I opened the door and saw you. Tell me."

Maybe the whole town couldn't hear Zarrin, but they could see him fussing over Joe. Joe raised his head. "Don't pretend you don't know what this means, Zarrin."

Zarrin took a breath and then another before a short, frustrated sound escaped him. "What… what do you think it means?"

"Zarrin," Azar interrupted sharply. "Don't confuse the poor human any more. We're not supposed to hurt them." Her firm tone wavered for a moment. "Remember? That was the first lesson. Never hurt what was Dìzhèn's."

"*Me* hurt him?" Zarrin faced his sister at last. "*You* upset him." Zarrin pointed at her, with his nervously bitten fingernails there for her to see, although she probably already knew about them. Zarrin seemed to realize it and put his hand down to the counter. "What are you doing here, Zazzie? If it's about those humans who—those humans, then you should be at the sheriff's station. Or the house." He stopped there, possibly remembering what she wasn't supposed to know about their housekeeper. "Have you been to the house?"

"Yes." She crossed her arms. "Where was Bernard? His room was…. Where is he?"

"He left." Zarrin raised his chin, and for a moment didn't seem to care that his sister took a step back at the news. "I haven't replaced him. In many ways, as you know, he is irreplaceable. So I am taking my time. But he's fine, Zazzie. He tells me so. Don't worry. I'm sorry. Please don't worry. Your tre—Bernard is fine."

"You know he isn't mine," Azar said, in a stream of words and smoke, then tightened her mouth. She uncrossed her arms, then didn't seem to know what to do with them. "He's gone?" She grasped at the air with her hands the way Zarrin did when anxious, and jerkily crossed her arms again. Once she paused and took a deep breath, it was as if someone else's voice had cracked at the mention of their housekeeper. "That is something to discuss later. Should we take this to the house?"

Zarrin looked at Joe and shook his head before Joe could say anything.

"All right." Azar studied Zarrin for a while. Zarrin didn't move and didn't say anything as she did, but if Joe were closer, he probably could have felt Zarrin trembling. Then Azar exhaled. "You look good."

"You sound surprised." Joe hadn't meant to say anything, but Zarrin was nervous, and no one should be so nervous around their family.

She hardly seemed to notice his comment anyway. She was focused on Zarrin. "Mom and Dad wanted to make sure you were doing okay."

Joe snorted. So did Martin, but it sounded more like a hysterical reaction.

Azar apparently felt that was also beneath her notice. "Obviously, they want to see you," she informed Zarrin. "They're both in New York, if you wanted to visit." She surprised Joe by lowering her chin to something less imperial, and speaking quieter. "I know you've always had an attachment to that house and the Preserve, Zarrin, but they can look after themselves for a while if you need to get away."

"You used to love the Preserve too, Zazzie," Zarrin answered, sad, or maybe nostalgic. "You would splash around in Fool's Creek no matter how cold the water was, and climb the boulders to the very top and play pirate queen, and—"

"Stop calling me Zazzie in front of—" Azar stopped herself before she could admit to caring what the humans thought of her. "Zarrin." She was calm again. "No one is saying you can't come back. After all—"

"After all, no one else in your family is going to come here?" Joe guessed.

"After all," Azar continued, still quiet, and so soft it was almost regretful. "The town is quiet and secluded, and Mom and Dad are aware you prefer it here."

Zarrin darted an embarrassed look at Joe, and Joe realized what Azar was really saying. Their parents were happy Zarrin liked it here, because it kept Zarrin out of sight.

"And it's best for everyone else to forget the son with no qualities to make them proud," Zarrin finished.

"Zarrin," Azar said, impossibly sad, and it was the realest Joe had seen her be. "You know I don't think that—"

Zarrin cut her off with a small shake of his head. "Thank them for their concern. I'm fine."

That was the Zarrin Joe should have painted, beautiful and brave. Joe reached over and took his hand. Zarrin tangled their fingers together and held on tight.

Azar had a strange, bittersweet expression on her face. "If they could see you now…."

Joe took his eyes off Zarrin's frozen, regal face to glare at her. "They could have. They didn't bother."

Zarrin squeezed his hand. "Joseph, it's okay," he said quietly. "I'm fine, truly, but thank you."

Joe studied him suspiciously but settled when Zarrin stroked his thumb over the back of his hand.

Azar observed that, of course she did, probably thinking Joe was an obedient plaything. But she didn't say anything about it. She tried a different angle. "I'm surprised to see you in town, Zarrin. My last visit we stayed at the house. Is this because—" She took a breath. "—Bernard is gone?"

"It's what we're supposed to be doing here, Zazzie." Zarrin continued to carefully pet Joe's hand, as if Joe were the one who was upset. But as if the act calmed him, Zarrin's tone stayed level.

She nodded, after a pause. "Dìzhèn's legacy is important. It shouldn't be forgotten."

"Dìzhèn's legacy doesn't fix cracks in the street or even stop poachers anymore." The sound of Addison's voice was so jarring that Joe did a double take. Azar turned around to study the older woman, and Addison immediately backed down. "If you don't mind me saying so."

As if that alone was enough for people to stop panicking at the Xu in their midst, someone else in the room hummed in agreement.

Zarrin gestured gracefully with his free hand. "If we aren't here to protect them or to live among them, then why are we here, Zazzie?"

"Zarrin, honestly." Azar looked back once at Addison and then spent a second staring daggers at someone else, possibly Forrester. She sighed at her brother. "If you care this much, I'm sure I can convince them to devote more money and energy to the town projects."

"It's not about the money." Zarrin hissed at her and tore his hand out of Joe's to wave it at him. "Don't you see? This town and the land around it are like Joe."

Joe's shoulders went so tense he knew he'd be sore tomorrow. He was under no illusions that everyone hadn't been watching this before, but now they were watching *him*.

Zarrin grabbed his hand again and stroked his arm as if in apology. "We protect it. It's our pleasure to do it. If it wasn't, then we should let it go. Not come back and go away again, or watch from a distance as if we have any right. It hurts them when we do that. We should claim them proudly, or release them."

Azar put a hand to her heart. "Release… release them?"

Zarrin's tone was chiding. "Dragons *can* release things, Zazzie. I've done it my whole life. I learned it early, when my wings were taken. It hurts, but it can be done, and should be, if it's the right thing to do. And I *know* you know what I mean."

"*Zarrin*." For a second, Joe thought Azar might faint.

Zarrin didn't take any pity on her. "Joseph has repeatedly told me they do not belong to us. He says over and over that he is not mine, that he can't be. He says that, because when I should have been here for him, I wasn't, and nothing will change that. But I can—I will—care for him anyway, even if someday I no longer get to be near him. You understand that. I know you do. I *have* to stay. It's the only way to convince him." Zarrin finally showed mercy to the anxious dragon in front of him and softened his voice. "We left them, Zazzie. Now we have to work twice as hard to make them trust us again."

"They hurt you!" Real anger made her voice rough, but made her less terrifying. She *was* upset about her brother. "Humans did that to you."

"A human saved me too." Zarrin pulled Joe's hand up and held it against his cheek. "He's treasure."

Azar slapped a hand to the counter and calmed herself, or at least found a surface calm. She was more like her brother than Joe had thought. She was also a volcano, but she deliberately kept her fires hidden.

She stared at their hands and then locked eyes with Zarrin. "You can't do that and not mean it, Zarrin. You can't make promises our parents won't let you keep. Think of what you'll do to the humans if you do. Think of what you'll do to him." She nodded toward Joe. "This boy loves you, Zazz."

The name made it all too easy to imagine the pair of them as children, as Zazz and Zazzie, running amok through the Preserve, going wild, where their parents couldn't see. Zarrin dreaming in his grotto, and Azar, the pirate queen. Joe should draw that too.

It was a nicer thing to think about than what Azar had just said, with everyone to hear.

Zarrin snapped his head up to look at him.

Joe swallowed dryly without speaking. There was no point in denying it, but he couldn't quite meet Zarrin's eye.

Then Zarrin said, almost to himself, "He frowns and he hopes, but he won't say a word."

Azar went on gently. "I'm glad you're here, Zarrin, because you've always loved Everlasting, and I know you will do your best. But you have to see reason. You're no Dìzhèn. None of us are."

Zarrin froze, as if he'd known that, but it still hurt.

"Good," Joe butted in rudely. "This town doesn't need Dìzhèn right now."

Azar sounded exasperated. "This part doesn't concern you."

Zarrin twitched, then rounded on his sister with his attention entirely focused on her. "This is Joe," he announced, in a tone that said she had missed something vital. "It's concerned him since before Dìzhèn was ever here." Zarrin raised his head, and the air seemed to sizzle. He was growing again, shadowed by his true form. "It concerns him, and everyone here, because we promised to look after them and we failed. We failed Dìzhèn too. Do you think this is what she wanted, us gone? Scattered?"

Zarrin rose up. "I'm staying here, Azar. In the house. In this town. It's mine by right, and only weak dragons would hide behind human law to deny that it's mine." Azar's eyes went wide. Zarrin didn't appear to notice. His voice was getting smokier. "Something happened—is happening, Zazzie. To the land and to me. I'm not *her*, but I can almost feel what she did to ensure the land and the town's survival. I care for it. I bled for it. It's *mine*. It was *my* magic that swept through the streets and shook them. I caused an earthquake, Zazzie, all by myself." Azar glanced to Joe, surprised or confused enough to look to the humans for answers. He didn't have one anyway. He was as shocked as she was.

Zarrin huffed, easily, almost casually sending billows of smoke to the floor. Smoke was supposed to rise, Joe thought, but this was smoke from dragonfire, and Zarrin was trying to tell them something.

"I'm stronger, Zazzie. Can't you feel it? The house answers to *me* now. It protects me, and what I care about. I can shake the entire coastline if I want." Zarrin huffed again. "Mom and Dad will be pleased to know that, until they realize what it means. If they left her treasure behind, then it belongs to the one who is here, who lives with it, no matter what any piece of paper says."

Azar stared at Zarrin, her lips slightly parted. Everyone else didn't seem to know whether to run away or stay and take their chances.

Joe realized, distantly, that Zarrin was still holding his hand.

"We are dragon," Zarrin insisted fiercely. "We are Dìzhèn's descendants. Not humans. We failed—I failed—but I'm still here. I'm trying. Which makes this mine, and I'll fight you, Azar. I will fight them for it too. And Dìzhèn's magic has chosen me… or might, or is about to, I can feel it. Although it's so much, Zazzie, almost too much." Zarrin was breathing hard, like he was scared, but his presence was everywhere in the shop. Old dragons, ancient dragons, had been that size, Joe thought dizzily, and kept his eyes on Zarrin. Zarrin was making his point. "*Dìzhèn* couldn't take me away from my treasure. It's mine now, and if I am too weak to protect it, I'll ask others to protect it for me. Humans, if necessary. It's theirs too. It's what *she* would have wanted."

Then he fell silent, and the great gold shadow over the room began to lift.

Zarrin was breathing hard. His hand was tight around Joe's, and shaking.

Zarrin caught his breath and then addressed his sister again. "Do you know what happened when I showed it to Joe? It welcomed him. I gave him that. I shared with him, and it felt good."

Azar stared at him without blinking. "And the others? The trappers, like the ones who hurt you?"

Zarrin bit his lip. "I showed Joe's mother too. She took me hiking. They can be trusted. They will love it like we do."

"You showed them both?" Azar considered their hands. Her expression was curious, but wary. "Did you show him the rest? All of your treasure?"

"Yes." The volcano was still present, but Zarrin bobbed his head like a shy kid.

His sister turned to Joe, weighing him without subtlety. "It's not riches. Not how you think. But that doesn't mean it isn't difficult to share it."

She didn't mean the redwoods or the family land. She meant Zarrin's hoard. Zarrin's treasure, aside from the Preserve and the town, his *personal* treasure, was the contents of his rooms. The feathers and rocks and seashells. The cats and whatever wounded animal he was currently tending to. The books on nature dating back a hundred years or more. A painting of the trees he loved. That was Zarrin's hoard. And he had shared it with Joe. Because he loved it, he shared it with him, the same way he'd shared the Preserve. He would have described every rock and leaf to Joe during that tour if he could have.

Azar tossed her head. "And you'd share more?" Her calm was only betrayed by the hand over her heart. "That's dangerous."

"I'm braver than they think I am." Zarrin wasn't calm, but he didn't have to be. He wanted her, or maybe everyone, to know he was emotionally involved in this.

His sister didn't seem to like that. "You'll endanger it, and yourself again. I don't want you hurt."

Zarrin startled Joe by snorting. Then he released his hand. "I didn't call you for you to tell me warnings I already knew." He waved off his own statement. If he was nervous, Joe couldn't see it anymore. He looked like the sort of dragon who could shake the entire coastline, exactly as he'd threatened. "How did you get here so quickly?"

"I was already on my way to see you," Azar informed him, before looking to Joe. "I was coming to see Zarrin, despite what you accused me of, human." She turned from both of them and frowned delicately at her tea waiting on the counter. "And now my tea has gone cold." She glanced up, and Martin fell over himself once more to serve her.

Her smile for that was pleased. Joe almost didn't like her again, but she didn't give him a chance to say anything before she looked right at him. "I know Zarrin is stronger than they think he is. I knew it when he made it clear he had no interest in any other dragons and then returned to Everlasting, although his treasure should have been long gone. He continued to believe, unlike the rest of us." She stopped abruptly, and then her distant, sad tone shifted into exhaustion. "I had a long flight and a longer drive, and I expected to at least see my—to see Bernard. I'm tired. Once I have my tea, can we go to the house, Zarrin? I can tell you want to be near your boy, but the rest hardly concerns everyone here. He can come with us, if you like. But I'm suddenly so very tired."

"I have work," Joe responded tightly, although the owner would hardly defy the dragons if they requested Joe go with them. Anyway, when it was all said and done, although he was glad Zarrin got to stay, she was still right. He glanced at Zarrin and spoke softly. "You can go."

Zarrin turned sharply toward him. "What?" His tone was extremely unhappy.

Joe wiped at his cheek and wished they were anywhere else. But the town would be full of rumors as it was. There was no hiding anything. At the very least, Joe wasn't anybody's secret anymore. It was not the pleasing thought it should have been.

He didn't meet Zarrin's eye. "You and your sister need to talk. You called her for a reason. So, you should go if you need to."

He wanted to go hide in the back and never come out. If Zarrin stayed in town, that was good. That was great for him. It was what he, and the town, wanted. And Joe would probably be his boy for a little longer. But as the sister kept reminding him, Zarrin wasn't for Joe.

Zarrin didn't leave. He stared at Joe for what felt like a very long time. "He still doesn't believe me." He licked his bottom lip and made a wounded sound. "Azar, please tell him why I called you."

Joe looked at Azar.

Azar drew herself up, suddenly formal again. "You called me—with no warning, with no greeting—and told me it was time to share the Preserve with the humans."

Joe bit his lip to keep from making a sound.

Azar went on, in a *slightly* pissed-off tone. "Since I was already in the car, I didn't waste time arguing or calling our parents. I came here to see if you had lost your mind or were under some sort of spell. Perhaps you are," she added, with a glance to Joe.

Joe put a hand to his stomach. "I didn't—"

"Joe didn't do anything!" Zarrin growled. "Is it so hard to believe I would risk everything for him? Look at him. Look at how good he is, and how much he needs me! Anyone would risk themselves for him, even cowards have tried!" He panted, and the room was quiet, except for the out of place songs of Christmas. "He doesn't believe me, Azar, and I need him to understand. This is the one gift I can give to equal a drink he brought to my door when he was so afraid."

"What?" Martin's voice was faint and far away.

Zarrin approached his sister. "He needs to know I appreciate his bravery. It doesn't have to be everything. At least not all at once." He grabbed at empty air, then dropped his hands deliberately to his sides. "I thought… from what his mother said, that the hike was good. Educational, she said. And Joe says you have to know something to love it. So shouldn't the people of Everlasting know their Preserve? Perhaps starting with the children?"

His tiny, uncertain ending after all that courage made Joe's heart pound.

Zarrin looked back at him. "He won't ask for it. He never asks. But he should have. I thought… this would make amends, for how we failed for so long."

"Treasure for treasure," Joe whispered.

"Huh?" Jessie wondered, from somewhere behind him.

"Treasure for treasure," Joe said, louder. He had to talk loudly to hear over the rush of his pulse. "It means Zarrin wants us to have something that has meaning to him. It means he's doing what even Dìzhèn couldn't."

"Joe!" Zarrin exclaimed, in a funny little voice, as if Joe was blaspheming.

Joe was dizzy and shook his head. "It means he's ours, right? Zarrin? Is that what this means? You're ours."

Zarrin twitched. He ducked his head, timid again, adorable in his hat. "If you don't mind."

Joe couldn't take his eyes off him, so golden and sweetly hopeful. "Martin," he asked without turning around. "Do you mind if Zarrin shares the Preserve with us? Do you mind if he becomes our dragon, instead of the memory of Dìzhèn?"

"Oh man. Oh fuck." Martin looked ready to collapse when Azar focused on him, but then he quickly shook his head no. "No. I mean, I'm cool with it, if we're really doing this. Jess?"

"I like Zarrin," she commented uncertainly. "Are we voting?"

"Yes," Martin whispered nervously. He was turning red now.

"Then yes," Jessie squeaked.

"An oral contract made before an officer of the law?" Forrester broke in, gruff and serious, and Azar's eyes left Martin. Forrester stared into his drink, which had probably gone cold. "Sounds fairly binding to me," he remarked, slowly, doing exactly what he'd done before. "But I'm not a lawyer, so I might be wrong."

Martin snorted in shocked amusement. Maybe he hadn't realized it was an act before.

Joe turned to Addison, who muttered under her breath. It might have been a yes. It wasn't a no. She would have shouted that.

Helene piped up from the other room. "He seems like a good boy."

Azar lifted both eyebrows. "*Zazz*."

Zarrin grumbled at her. "Well, are our parents dragon or human? It's mine. This makes it mine even more firmly. If our parents don't recognize that, then I will make them see it. *You* can make them see it."

"The land and the magic haven't actually accepted you yet. You don't know anything about any of this." Azar wasn't disagreeing, Joe noticed. Her arguments were more pointed and practical.

So Joe nodded. "He'll learn. It's what he does when something matters."

"*Treasure*," Zarrin exhaled, and turned to him. "I have learned, haven't I? Only promises I will keep." He crossed his heart. "I'm your Rin, aren't I? And you're my boy, my Joseph honey, my treasure, for as long as you want. Caring for you gives me such pleasure. Please don't ask me to stop."

There was no mistaking that. Joe wanted to say something, to contest the "Joseph honey," but all he did was open his mouth and then close it to keep staring at Zarrin.

Martin broke the silence. "Hey, Forrester, would that also be considered legally binding?"

"It's binding to dragons," Azar commented before Forrester could say anything. "Oh, Zazz, you had to choose a brave one? They're so much trouble."

"Joseph isn't trouble," Zarrin answered dreamily, while gazing up at Joe. "And if he was, I wouldn't care."

Joe was hot all over. "Zarrin, people don't say things like that."

Zarrin clucked his tongue. "I do."

"Dragons do," Azar added. She was very quiet. "I see. So you found him after all. Your treasure. You withheld part of the situation, Zarrin. Kind of important, don't you think? It will affect my negotiations with them."

Zarrin huffed distractedly at her. "I knew you wouldn't believe me. *He* didn't believe me, and I was in front of him." He sighed happily at Joe. "Do you really love me?"

“I—” Joe hadn’t ever said it in this way to anyone. And he wouldn’t, with half the town watching. “Rin,” he said instead, and burned up for that anyway.

“Isn’t he wonderful?” Zarrin beamed at Joe, at his sister, at Addison. “He was so worried I’d reject him. But he *wants* so very much. He needs me, and it called to me from the beginning. Joseph, you’re so *good.*”

Joe closed his eyes. “Zarrin, please.”

Zarrin apparently wasn’t ready to shut up. “But you’re so, so good, and you’re mine, and I will take care of you as I promised, and make up for when I wasn’t here. Treasure!” he exclaimed finally, in contentment, and the ground shook.

“Stop that,” Joe told him, in a voice so soft he was going to be embarrassed later. But the rumbling ended. He opened his eyes and found Zarrin pouting at him, which wasn’t fair.

“Say it, Joe, please.” Zarrin stuck out his bottom lip in a pout. The dragon who had only minutes before shown them what power he had at his fingertips. He had literally caused an earthquake, and now he was begging. “Joe, you don’t know how long I’ve waited.”

This was madness. Or magic. But the kind of magic that was right, because Azar smiled in her bittersweet way, and the others stared, but no one looked frightened or disgusted, not even Addison. Zarrin Xu, dragon, scion of Dìzhèn the great, was going to share the Preserve, for *him.*

All Joe had to do was say what he wanted. He took a deep breath, and kept his gaze on Zarrin. Zarrin made everything easier, somehow, warmed him and reminded him that it was safe. If he asked, Zarrin had promised to give it to him.

He thought about glancing down, but then at the last second, raised his chin. “I love you.”

“I love you too,” Zarrin answered, with his gaze hot and his voice rough.

Then the ground shook so hard the clean cups fell out of the dish rack and shattered on the floor.

# CHAPTER 14

ZARRIN PEERED into the window of a hair salon, startling one of the women inside. Their window display didn't have much for sale except hair products he didn't understand, so he sighed and moved on. It was Christmas Eve, and he was running out of ideas for what to buy Joe's mother. He knew he'd get it right sooner or later—he was much better at gift giving once he knew the person—but he'd hoped he would have figured it out by now.

He straightened his coat and left a hand on his bag as he walked down the street full of people searching for last-minute gifts like he was. He held his umbrella high, and tried not to be annoyed at the spoke that was bent at an angle from when he'd dropped it on the coffee shop floor. Joe insisted the umbrella was still usable and to throw it away was wasteful.

But the spoke would have to be fixed. It was too distracting.

Zarrin tore his attention from it in order to nod to some of the humans he passed. Most didn't nod back, but some did, which was pleasing. He'd put in effort for their holiday, with a green-and-red scarf from Bernard and a new, strangely conical hat, meant to look like Santa's.

The package from Bernard had arrived yesterday, with a wrapped gift of a scarf for Joseph and a note Zarrin had nearly memorized.

*Merry Christmas, Golden Boy. Glad to hear everything worked out. I had a feeling it would. That's not elf magic. That's me knowing you, and how determined you can be. Although the earthquake was a surprise. Good job there, but maybe try not to rattle the neighborhood every time you get a smile from that boy of yours.*

*Speaking of, I can't wait to really meet him, which might be sooner than we thought I'd visit. Something is up, I think, and I'm starting to get a nervous feeling when I think of the house in someone else's care. I need to see the old girl.*

*Which reminds me, say hello to your sister for me. Wish her a Merry Christmas too, if you feel like it. She might listen to you.*

*I have to say, I'm surprised to hear she stayed with you, even if only for a few days. I was beginning to think she'd forgotten where the house was. If it's not too late, try to get her to spend the holiday with you. She shouldn't be alone, and she might prefer the place without me in it.*

*Don't make that face, Golden Boy. I'd rather you both enjoyed yourselves instead of trying to please your parents. You learned what power, and love, can be, and so can she. I'd tell her myself, but I don't think hotshot corporate lawyer and heiress Azar Xu would spare the time for me.*

*But then, what do I know? I'm just a foolish elf, already fed up with human nonsense, missing my trees and my house. (Don't growl. It's my house too.)*

*I miss you. Of course I do. I need to see my dragons soon.*

*Love,*

*Bernard*

*P.S. Wear the hat for the holiday. Your dragon dignity can take it.*

Zarrin didn't see what would possibly offend his dignity about the hat. The bell on the end made a sweet tinkling sound, and the blinking lights around the white brim were very festive. He'd never understood what colored lights had to do with the meaning of the holiday, but they did brighten things up.

It had snowed the night before, and today it was back to misting rain. The streets were lined with gray ice and some mud, and yet the lights in so many shop windows made it all look lovely.

His town was good, so good.

He took in the sight of it with a pleased sigh and continued on his way.

Bernard would be happy at his progress when he returned, and perhaps if Zarrin followed through with the information Zazzie had given him for a Christmas present, Zarrin would find restorers and electricians and painters and gardeners to help around the house, so Bernard could relax more. The present was very thoughtful and supportive of Zazzie. Bernard shouldn't be so hard on her. Not every dragon found it easy to hold their treasure, and Bernard had confused her from the moment they'd met.

Something would have to be done about them.

But in the meantime, Zarrin had plans and other concerns.

He had parked his scooter in front of Joe's apartment but was making a slow trip through town for one last look at the shops. He'd also needed to stop off at the post office to get today's mail, which had included Marie's version of a Christmas card.

The postcard had a picture of a nearly naked human man on the front, wearing a hat not unlike Zarrin's, but positioned over his crotch. The front said *JINGLE THESE BELLS.* On the back she'd written, *Is he yours yet? Did you put that poor boy out of his misery and finally claim him? I need to know!* with an e-mail address at the bottom.

That made him smile, while also vexing him almost as much as finding the right present for Joe's mother.

Zarrin liked to think he had claimed Joe. He had declared his love for him in front of witnesses, including Zazzie. He'd offered to share the Preserve with him and the others in town—in small groups, at first, although the legal aspects and logistics were all something he'd have to figure out with his sister's help. He had until spring to work out the details anyway.

He had fucked Joe more than once in the past few days, and held him close while he slept, and lured him up to the house with movies and popcorn and kisses so Joe would feel more and more comfortable in Zarrin's lair.

Joe had assured him that he didn't need to visit the coffee shop every day if he didn't want to. That boyfriends visited, of course, but Zarrin didn't need to drive all the way into town in bad weather to make Joe feel better.

And perhaps that was the source of Zarrin's unease. The use of "boyfriends" was human, and forgivable. Joe had never been allowed to say that word with the other one whose name Zarrin preferred to forget, so Zarrin could tolerate *boyfriends*. But there was something about the way Joe said it, as if he didn't quite understand what he actually was.

Marie was very wise. She knew about broken hearts. If she was telling him that Joe needed more, she was probably right.

Zarrin chewed on his lip as he considered this problem. As much as Joe would love the paper and charcoal Zarrin had gotten him as a present for tomorrow, Zarrin didn't think they would remove whatever Joe's remaining doubts were.

He also didn't think—though he would enjoy it—that fucking Joe somewhere public would work either, with or without a full moon to help. For one, Joseph didn't like being the focus of attention, and two, they weren't wolves, after all. Zarrin had a town to take care of, and humans would not be reassured if Zarrin took Joe against the counter of the coffee shop.

The idea was pleasant, however. He considered it as he crossed the street at the light so he could walk through the park. There were times when Joe didn't look at him and silently beg for Zarrin to take charge of him, times when they fell onto his bed and Joe rode him, or kissed him and turned Zarrin over onto his stomach and swept his hands up Zarrin's back as if he thought Zarrin's golden-brown skin was beautiful. Then there had been nights of Joe's face to the pillow and his hips in Zarrin's hands and Zarrin's cock driving low, grateful sounds from him, or Joe trembling in his shower barely able to stand, while Zarrin cleaned him and petted him and ignored Joe's hard, leaking cock until he was sure Joe understood how wonderful he was.

And afterward, with Zarrin still swallowing the taste of him, Zarrin got to snuggle in close and practice his cuddling. He was glad Marie had taught him how. Joe needed someone's arms around him. He needed it so much that Zarrin nearly couldn't wait to see him again, to drag Joe to the mansion with him so they could spend the evening together, with nowhere to go in the early hours of morning.

He would get to hold his treasure all night. That was the best present Joe could have gotten him.

Not that Joe would consider it a gift. Zarrin was pretty sure if he mentioned it in those terms, Joe would frown at him in confusion.

"It's tricky, isn't it?" Zarrin stopped and looked up to the statue of Dìzhèn. "Loving a human. Caring for them. Or was Alfie not difficult?" Zarrin tilted the umbrella up to let the mist hit his face. Dìzhèn regarded him steadily, not about to answer such a personal question. "I suppose it's like watching over the town. I have a lot to learn."

Pools of rainwater slipped down Dìzhèn's back, making her curving scales seem to ripple with motion, like a cat stretching before it settled down for a nap. Zarrin had never thought that someone as powerful as Dìzhèn might have struggled to learn about the town too, but of course she'd been from another culture, was another creature entirely than the ones she'd chosen for her own. It had to have been difficult, which must have been why she'd taken whatever drastic step she had to bind so much land and so many people to her magic.

But she'd had help. Alfie's help. *Human* help.

Ah, Zarrin should have realized that sooner. What she must have thought of him, so confused, ashamed to even look at her, when all the while she'd known Joe was waiting for him, and that learning to listen to Joe would teach him so much about everything else.

He bowed his head to her, although he still had questions, and then swung the umbrella back over his head to protect his new hat. He wanted to know if she had recognized Alfie as her own the first moment she saw him, or if it had taken longer, or why her house had chosen Zarrin now and yet the magic wasn't fully his. If—when—his parents came here for him, he would need that magic to convince them. She wouldn't answer, though. Her expression was too sleepily amused for that.

He felt almost human at the realization. He was looking to the dragons for answers, and there were no dragons to help him.

*There are no dragons.* That's what Joe's teenage graffiti had said. It sounded like a challenge, but now Zarrin wondered if it was. *There are no dragons.* Joe had written it in paint, with his magic. He might as well have written it with all the hopes he'd set aside.

"Did he know he was asking for me?" Zarrin wondered, although he had no reason to suspect Dìzhèn knew anything. Her eyes, bright with water, were almost luminous. Zarrin took a deep breath and felt his eyes prickle with tears as well.

Joe, darling Joseph, must have been in a lot of pain to come so close to demanding what he wanted. Enough pain for him to deface the sign in the hope that someone would notice.

Deep down, he'd known Zarrin was meant to be his. And yet now he called them *boyfriends*.

"So I haven't given him everything," Zarrin realized aloud. "Not yet."

He nodded respectfully to Dìzhèn once more, then continued on his slow path to Everlasting Cuppa. This was his treasure, and therefore a problem only he could solve.

The gray sky above made it difficult to guess the hour, but Zarrin had taken his time so he could show up at the coffee shop as Joe's shift ended. Joe had a short shift today, and no work tomorrow, which meant more wonderful hours together. Zarrin had planned a dinner of frozen pizza and some snacks, and all kinds of interesting movies were on TV tonight if Joe wanted to watch any. Then, in the morning, they were going to Joe's mother's house to exchange presents.

Zarrin moved a little faster once the shop was in sight, then stopped when Ian Forrester came out of the entrance. He was in uniform and clutching a paper cup, and nodded distractedly when he saw Zarrin.

"Wait!" Zarrin hurried forward while digging into his bag. He held out a package as he reached Forrester, and had no idea why the man stared at it as if it might be poison. It was a simple book, wrapped in brown paper with a stick-on bow on the top. Zarrin wiggled it until Forrester took it. "You were very helpful to me even when the rest of the people at the station were frightened of me. Thank you."

Forrester, as Joe called him, and not Ian, opened and closed his mouth as if he wanted to argue, then thought better of it. "That's my job," he said faintly, at last. Zarrin didn't believe a word of it. Forrester was a strange sort of person, hidden, in many ways. But he showed his feelings despite that.

Zarrin smiled at him. "And because you once said something that meant a lot to Joe, and I haven't forgotten."

That made Forrester stare for a long time, until he seemed to notice the mist was slowly soaking his hair as well as the paper around his present. The sky was overcast, but his chestnut curls shined in the limited light. A murder of crows perched across the street flew closer, and landed above him on the roof of the coffee shop.

"I wasn't brave then," Forrester said at last, and pulled the gift to his chest. "But I should have been."

"You can be brave now. That's something I've learned." Zarrin nodded at him, then leaned in closer to offer him the shelter of the umbrella. "Did you know—" Zarrin glanced at the gift, a book he had specially ordered for this moment. "—that Martin loves graphic novels?"

He met Forrester's stare and held it.

Ian Forrester had very blue eyes, inhumanly so, but when he had glasses on, most people might not have noticed. He cleared his throat and stowed the book under his jacket, where it would stay dry. "Happy holiday, Mr. Xu," he said formally, then inclined his head. "Joe's inside, pretending he isn't waiting for you."

With that, he walked away.

Zarrin watched him go. The people in Zarrin's town would be seen to. Perhaps not as Dìzhèn would have done it, but in a way that was still good.

Zarrin nearly bounced through the door in his excitement, and barely remembered to close his umbrella and remove his gloves. Forrester, who seemed to understand Joe, had summed up the situation all too well.

Joe had spent a very long time pretending he wasn't waiting for Zarrin. Zarrin didn't think he should have to anymore.

His treasure was leaning against the counter, speaking with the older woman Zarrin had seen a few times before, the one with skin a few shades darker than his. She wore brown pants and what looked like a man's shirt underneath her puffy, practical, all-weather jacket. Joe must like her. He smiled at her the way he did with customers he was fond of.

He was such a beautiful boy. Zarrin sighed to see him, content and evidently warm enough to have removed his outer shirt. The shop wasn't all that busy, which might have been why it was just Martin and Joe and Jessie, and why Joe had the time to chat.

Although his chat had ended. Zarrin looked back from making sure Jessie and Martin were nearby, and found Joe alone and turned away from the entrance. He wiped down the counter and set a pitcher aside to be washed, probably helping the other two with some of their closing duties since they only had another hour or so before they also got to leave. Joe was so thoughtful, and there was something so appealing about how he stretched as he leaned over to get something.

"You gonna stare at that boy like that, you should back it up." The voice in his ear startled him into jumping. The woman Joe had been talking to a moment ago was at his side, watching him with dark eyes.

"I plan on fucking him later," Zarrin told her, because *obviously*. "If he would like that," he added, because of course Joe had a choice.

"Oh, there's no doubt about that in anyone's mind." The woman was nearly as dry as Bernard. "But that wasn't how you were staring at him—for once." She shook her head. "You want to go to the boy, then go to him while you can."

She walked off while Zarrin blinked after her in amazement. He slowly turned to Joe, then moved forward without another moment's pause.

Jessie stopped at the edge of the counter as he came closer, and Martin darted out of his way, his eyes wide. Joe turned around right as Zarrin reached him.

"Zarrin?" he said, with the beginnings of a smile, and Zarrin couldn't take it any longer. He slid his arms around Joe's chest and held him close. Joe smelled like a lot of peppermint today, but also coffee and sweat, and faintly of Zarrin. The scent beneath that was strange, like relief and happiness together, like he wanted this hug more than even Zarrin had.

"Hello, Joseph." Zarrin regretted the umbrella that kept him from stroking Joe's back with both hands, but he buried his face in Joe's shoulder, and that would do. He didn't want to think about what might have happened if he'd let his parents convince him to never return here, or to choose a dragon in spite of his heart. It made him shudder and grab Joe's shirt. "I missed you."

"It's only been a few hours," Joe pointed out, although his scent stayed the same, and he curled one arm around Zarrin's waist.

Zarrin made a noise. "It's been years," he corrected, and his words must have been muffled, because Joe didn't seem to understand them.

"Are you going to be like this in front of my mom tomorrow?" Joe asked, as if he weren't warm and calm when Zarrin was near.

Zarrin raised his head, and Joe's attention briefly strayed up to his hat before returning to his face.

"Depends," Zarrin announced, "on whether you need me to or not."

"You know, you aren't supposed to be behind the counter, Zarrin." Jessie was so sensible these days. "But that is a cute hat."

"Bernard gave it to me." Zarrin tried to tip his head to look at her, but also didn't want to take his eyes off Joe. "And I dare anyone to try to take me away from Joe now."

Joe was watching him intently. "Is everything okay?" His gaze went to the hat again. Then he frowned. "Bernard? Nothing from your parents?"

"Marie sent me something." Zarrin placed a small kiss to the hollow of Joe's throat. The tension in Joe's shoulders at the mention of Marie was subtle but unmistakable. Zarrin understood it now, after seeing Mads and Russ together. "A card," Zarrin explained with another kiss. "She asked if you were mine yet. She's hoping you are."

"Yours?" Joe echoed, and stiffened even more, with a glance to his coworkers.

"She means mated," Zarrin told him, with a significant look.

Joe drew his eyebrows together. Then he glanced away. "You don't have to do this, Zarrin. That isn't something I need."

Zarrin actually took a step back in shock at the first lie he'd ever heard Joe tell.

"Did you want your tea before we go?" Joe appeared to think Zarrin had given up when Zarrin stepped away from him. He cleared his throat. "I have to stop by my apartment first, for clothes and presents. See if the cat is there."

"The cat," as Joe called him, since he hadn't named him yet, sometimes appeared beneath the stairs to Joe's door and would enter the apartment with a little prompting. He usually, but not always, stayed the night when he did, and then he'd leave in the morning to sit outside the coffee shop's back door and wait for Joe to feed him.

Normally, Zarrin found both the cat and his Joseph endearingly shy with each other, but not today. He narrowed his eyes at Joe while Joe prepared his drink and then immediately forgave Joe's stubbornness, because Joe was going to give him the tea and a straw, with that cautious, hopeful frown.

Zarrin considered him while reaching in his bag. He pulled out his presents for Jessie and Martin, and handed them over. "For you. I hope you like them. You've both been wonderful to me, and to him."

Joe shot him a startled look, which Zarrin chose to ignore. He focused on Jessie's squeals over her makeup set—baffling to Zarrin but with very shiny colors—and Martin's absolutely shocked silence for the small framed sketch Joe had done of part of the bay, in which Joe had only colored in the remarkable blue of the water that particular day.

Martin stared at Zarrin and then at Joe before taking the painting with him into the back of the shop.

Joe's art had that effect on the right people.

Zarrin glanced at Joe, now tense and quiet, possibly embarrassed. He hadn't known Zarrin was going to give the picture away when Zarrin had asked to have that one. But Martin had earned it, and he would treasure it, and he seemed to be growing fond of the color blue.

He turned to Jessie. "Would it be all right if I took Joe from you now? That could be your present to me," he added, with a grin, and twitched in surprise when Jessie lunged at him to hug him.

After a startled pause, he patted her shoulder, and she let him go only to turn around and hug Joe. "You guys are the best!" she announced to everyone in the shop, which made Zarrin first wonder what Joe had given her for a present, and then if she was ever going to release him.

Thankfully, she stepped back before Zarrin had to intervene to get her hands off his treasure. Joe needed more hugs. But witnessing someone else in Joe's arms was very trying, especially when Zarrin had to finish claiming him.

"Don't worry about Martin. He's fine. He's just not used to feelings. That's the problem when you don't get high as much anymore." Jessie laughed to herself—if she was high at the moment, Zarrin would not have been surprised. It had such a weird effect on humans, but at least it made her happy.

"Merry Christmas," Zarrin told her, and paused when Joe held out his tea for him. Zarrin was not currently interested in sweet tea, but Joe offered gifts so carefully Zarrin had to accept it. "Thank you, Joseph," he said gravely, and had a sip. "You can wish Martin a happy holiday if you want, before we go. I don't mind waiting a little longer."

Joe gave him a funny look for the emphasis Zarrin put in the words, but Zarrin didn't care. With another puzzled frown, Joe took off his apron and then went to the back. Martin was, as Zarrin understood human relationships, Joe's best friend, even if Joe was probably as afraid to use that term as he was to name the cat.

Zarrin slowly followed him, sipping from his tea as he went. He'd never been in the Employees Only area before. The big metal sinks and the giant dishwasher were something to explore another day, when he wasn't anxious, or when he didn't go still for the sight of Martin curled against Joe.

Martin immediately hopped away as if he hadn't been squeezing Joe in a tight, emotional hug. Joe blinked at Zarrin in surprise. Zarrin had no idea what about him at the moment could be surprising.

He watched a cloud of his own smoke escape to the ceiling, and then he had another drink of tea and left the cup on a countertop. The plastic was slightly dented, but Zarrin couldn't be blamed for that.

"Joseph," he said clearly, with a hint of further smoke. "I was wrong. I am tired of waiting."

"Waiting?" Joe's expression was lost. "You want to go now?"

"Joseph." Zarrin pronounced it sharply, the opposite of how he'd pronounced it the night before in his bed, with Joe beneath him. "My special one." Or when he'd whispered it over and over to Joe as he'd washed his beautiful body. "My boy. My one. My treasure. My mate."

"I should go." Martin crept past Zarrin and dashed out the door, as if Zarrin were angry with him, when he wasn't. The touching was something he could live with, but not while Joe was denying the obvious.

"Are you still so afraid you can't admit that?" Zarrin asked, and felt his shoulders droop. "Didn't Zazzie tell you? Didn't Marie? Didn't your mother ever talk to you about humans and true love? How everyone feels it differently, but you can't pretend it isn't there once you've found it?"

"Zarrin." Joe frowned at him and glanced to the door, but the others were either busy or giving them privacy. "I… told you how I feel about you."

He had. Zarrin nodded and let the pleasure from that memory wash over him. "And that is more than enough for me." Zarrin clucked his tongue. "But it isn't for you."

Joe lowered his gaze to the floor and scrubbed at his cheek. "I'm not a kid, Zarrin. I don't need a fantasy."

"Fantasy?" Zarrin gaped at him for a moment, and then jutted out his chin and swept forward. "Dragons aren't werewolves." He stopped when Joe looked up. "Clearly, we aren't. But like weres, we have similar concepts to explain the things we don't understand. Our magic is stronger, but we are rare. This thing, when it happens, isn't as common for us as it is with them. Perhaps we are afraid of it or don't want to hope for it, so we have no name for it." He held Joe's stare, because that, at least, should sound familiar to Joe. "But it happens. We know when it does. Some of us more than others, certainly more than dumb werewolves on TV."

"Zarrin—" Whatever Joe meant to say, he forgot when Zarrin curled around him again. His scent had a shiver, not like fear, and not quite desire.

"You found me." Zarrin drew in a shaky breath, cold and afraid all over again whenever he remembered that day. Joe trembled too, so Zarrin put a hand to his chest. Calming his treasure calmed him. "Out of all the people in this town, *you* came out, and *you* found me."

"Yes." Not even Joe could deny that.

"The house let you. The Preserve let you. That wasn't Dìzhèn's magic then, Joe. It was mine. You were safe. You were mine." Zarrin kissed a patch of Joe's bare skin.

"Yeah," Joe agreed again, with a change in his voice.

Zarrin pushed closer. "I was safe with you. Safe enough to rest and heal." The peaceful scent was returning, the right scent, the *good* scent of Joe when Zarrin was near and Joe was happy. "I bought your painting when I didn't know it was yours."

Joe began to breathe hard. "I know I—the things we want as children don't make sense, Zarrin. Just because I—"

"Saw me," Zarrin finished for him, and the shop seemed to get hushed, and very far away. "You saw me from the stage, and you stared at me, and I didn't know what it was then, but I could feel how much you needed me. To be your friend. To choose you."

Joe's heartbeat was frantic under his hand.

"Do you believe me now, treasure?" Zarrin hid his face in Joe's shoulder and held him so tightly Joe should have protested. "When you saw me, you were so young, and so was I. I was squirming to get away, to get to you, and they said—" His voice broke, shamefully, but Joe wouldn't care. "They said I was dreaming. That I was imagining it. That you were just a human boy and I was a child, so I couldn't know that it was you, that you were mine." Zarrin took a shaky breath. "I *was* a child. I couldn't fight them more, or remember the details of who you were. I came back, but I couldn't find you. You wanted me to choose you and I wasn't here."

"Shh." Joe pulled away the Santa hat and ran a hand through Zarrin's hair. "Zarrin, don't be upset."

"I wasn't here." Zarrin closed his eyes. "And he was. And he hurt you. He took what was mine and he hurt it, because I wasn't brave enough."

Joe's hand stopped at the back of his neck.

"I was too young. I lost the specifics of you." Zarrin lifted his head so he could see Joe's worried, hopeful face. "But I recognized you, from time to time. Glimpses of you as I passed through town, as you waited. Like you waited on that stage and stared at me. You stared at me so hard. All I could remember was that expression. Yearning, although I didn't know that word then." He dropped his head again and sighed. "That's why I had no interest in the other dragons, or anyone else I was allowed to see. It's why I came here again, even though I knew no one believed me, not even Zazzie. She thought you'd be long gone by now."

"I did leave." Joe's voice was hoarse. "I came back."

"Yes." Zarrin was eternally grateful. "And somehow, Bernard knew. However elves use magic, I guess. He sent me to this coffee shop, and I knew you the moment you raised your head and stared at me. If you say you still don't believe, I—" He curled his hand over Joe's heart, and listened for an argument, but there was none. "I've waited almost my whole life for you, treasure. You could at least admit you've done the same."

"I'm not magic." Joe's argument was very soft, as if he wished he were.

"Silly boy. You've got magic in your blood and in your fingers." Zarrin rose up to whisper in his ear. "Your paint. Your pencils. When you were in high school, when you were in pain, and I wasn't here, what did you do?"

He'd spray-painted the sign at the edge of the Preserve, which they both knew. Zarrin saved him from admitting it a second time. "You called out for our attention. Because we weren't there? Or because *I* wasn't?"

The silence went on so long, Zarrin began to notice the distant Christmas carols again. Then Joe said, "You," in a raspy voice, and Zarrin felt as if he might die from one simple word. His heart, his mind, his fire, couldn't take it.

"Again, please, treasure." He barely heard himself.

"You." Joe was gruff. "Because you weren't there, and somehow I thought… you should be."

"I'll make it up to you." Zarrin dropped the umbrella so he could cling to Joe's shoulders. His legs seemed unable to support him. "Mine. You admit you're mine! Oh, ask me, treasure. Anything you want, and it's yours. I won't go again."

"Yeah?" Joe's quiet question was painful, but Zarrin didn't mind anymore. Joe understood. He believed.

"Yeah," Zarrin answered the way Joe would have, and wished they were anywhere else so he could lie on top of Joe and feel secure in having his treasure at last. "I challenged Dìzhèn for you. My sister. My family. Whatever happens, here I am." He peeked up. "Do you mind?"

"What?" Joe looked stunned. He blinked a few times, handsome and befuddled, so Zarrin pulled him down to kiss his parted lips and then his pretty cheek. "I was so mad at you, and you're happy?"

"I've been trying to claim you, as Marie suggested, for months now." Zarrin leaned up for another kiss. This one was longer, and slower, as Joe started to come out of his daze. "But werewolves are not dragons, or humans, and I couldn't figure out how. But it wasn't the how." He stopped for kiss number three, and bit softly at Joe's bottom lip until Joe groaned. "You weren't ready. You didn't understand."

"Yeah?" The sweetly trusting way Joe said that when he was aroused was one of Zarrin's favorite things about his treasure.

"And now you do." Zarrin was so pleased he kissed Joe again, hard enough to make Joe pant and then lick his lips when it was over. "So now I'll tell you that you are my treasure, and you will say—"

"Yes," Joe exhaled, and followed Zarrin's mouth. Zarrin came forward a few steps, grasping Joe's shirt, then pushing it up. They bumped into the refrigerator, and Zarrin kissed Joe in apology for the roughness, in case of any bruises. But Joe's mouth was so tempting. One kiss became another, and Zarrin's hands on Joe's skin, and his words at Joe's throat.

"Yours." Zarrin ran his teeth over the vein to make Joe tremble and then sucked a bruise there. "Mine."

"Um…," Jessie interrupted from the doorway. "Wow. I just need some milk, though."

Zarrin took handfuls of Joe's shirt and glanced blindly around at the hooks on the wall by the back door. "Your coat, Joe?" he wondered, then wished he hadn't. But he had to be responsible where his treasure was concerned. He led Joe away from the fridge, and stopped long enough for Jessie to hand him his umbrella. Then he folded Joe's coat over his arm and stepped outside.

The rain had gotten more intense, and Zarrin had been too distracted to notice. He was soaked in moments, and cold enough to feel it, and then Joe stepped forward and took the umbrella from his hand to open it and hold it over his head. Some rain had wet Joe's shoulders and his hair, and water dripped down onto his thin T-shirt.

Zarrin raised his eyes. Joe was shivering, and he couldn't have that. He unfolded Joe's coat, which, now that he got a good look at it, seemed much too light. He draped it around him anyway, although he didn't think it was going to stay on Joe long enough for it to do any good.

He had to touch Joe's face. "So good, treasure," Zarrin said, with the rain drowning out everything else, and Joe close enough for Zarrin's heat to warm him. Joe shook, a brief shudder of need, and stared at Zarrin with so much longing it made Zarrin's fire rise.

Zarrin trembled, because he was dragon, but he couldn't possibly be worthy of such a look. He was soft and weak again, and then Joe asked, "Rin?" and Zarrin remembered he was Dìzhèn's heir, and the one Joe had been waiting for, and he could never fail Joe, never.

"Your Rin, and no one else's," Zarrin promised, and took his hand to pull him toward his apartment. The cat was underneath the steps, waiting to be let in, but Zarrin stopped at the foot of the stairs and found Joe close behind him. "Joseph?" he asked in return, because claiming *must* work both ways, and he needed to hear it too.

Joe frowned and then leaned down to press their foreheads together. "Yours," he breathed, in a whisper, then made a hopeful little sound when Zarrin took his face in his hands.

"And I will give you everything," Zarrin promised, and felt the power of the earth itself in him when Joe closed his eyes and nodded.

R. COOPER lives among the redwoods of northern California in a tiny house she refers to as her Writer's Retreat. She has two cats, overthinks almost everything, and has more books than bookshelves. Someone once said her stories stick up for the damaged ones, and that is the greatest compliment she's ever gotten. She loves mutual pining, fairy tales, and slightly broken everyday heroes with lonely hearts. If you want to contact her or to merely observe a shy nerd in her natural habitat, feel free to visit her LiveJournal or Tumblr.

E-mail: RisCoops@gmail.com
Website: r-cooper.livejournal.com
Tumblr: sweetfirebird.tumblr.com

Some Kind of
MAGIC

R. Cooper

A Being(s) in Love Story

Being a police detective is hard. Add the complication of being a werewolf subject to human prejudice, and you might say Ray Branigan has his work cut out for him. He's hot on the trail of a killer when he realizes he needs help.

Enter Cal Parker, the beautiful half-fairy Ray's secretly been in love with for years—secretly, because while werewolves mate for life, fairies… don't. Ray needs Cal's expertise, but it isn't easy to concentrate with his mate walking around half-naked trying to publicly seduce him. By the time Ray identifies the killer—and sorts out a few prejudices of his own—it may be too late for Cal.

A Boy and His
DRAGON
R. Cooper

A Being(s) in Love Story

Arthur MacArthur needs a job, and not just for the money. Before he dropped out of school to support his younger sister, he loved being a research assistant at the university. But working for a dragon, one of the rarest and least understood magical beings, has unforeseen complications. While Arthur may be the only applicant who isn't afraid of Philbert Jones in his dragon form, the instant attraction he feels for his new employer is beyond disconcerting.

Bertie is a brilliant historian, but he can't find his own notes without help—his house is a hoard of books and antiques, hence the need for an assistant. Setting the mess to rights is a dream come true for Arthur, who once aspired to be an archivist. But making sense of Bertie's interest in him is another matter. After all, dragons collect treasure, and Arthur is anything but extraordinary.

www.dreamspinnerpress.com

A Beginner's Guide to
WOOING YOUR MATE
R. Cooper

A Being(s) in Love Story

Zeki Janowitz has returned to his hometown of Wolf's Paw to start his wizarding career. Unfortunately, Wolf's Paw, a werewolf refuge, follows centuries of tradition and shuns human magic and a very human Zeki. He knows he's in for a struggle, but a part of him has always belonged in the mountain town, or rather belonged to Theo Greenleaf. Years away at school haven't lessened Zeki's crush on the quiet werewolf. When town gossip informs him Theo still suffers from his mate's rejection and does not date, it does little to ease Zeki's embarrassing feelings. He decides now's the time to get the man he's always wanted.

Werewolves usually don't recover from losing their mates, and Theo barely pulled through by focusing on his love of baking. It's a daily struggle, and Zeki's return to Wolf's Paw shatters his peace. Theo doesn't know what to think when Zeki attempts to woo him, talking about his wizarding business and settling in town for good. It's like Zeki doesn't have a clue how his words years before left Theo a shell of a werewolf.

Beginners in love, Theo and Zeki must seduce each other with a bit of heavenly baking and magic.

www.dreamspinnerpress.com

R. Cooper

LITTLE
Wolf

A Being(s) in Love Story

On the run from his old-blood werewolf family, Tim Dirus finds himself in Wolf's Paw, one of the last surviving refuges from the days when werewolves were hunted by humans and one of the last places Tim wants to be. Kept away from other wolves by his uncle, Tim knows almost nothing about his own kind except that alpha werewolves only want to control and dominate a scrawny wolf like him.

Tim isn't in Wolf's Paw an hour before he draws the attention of Sheriff Nathaniel Neri, the alphaest alpha in a town full of alphas. Powerful, intimidating, and the most beautiful wolf Tim has ever seen, Nathaniel makes Tim feel safe for reasons Tim doesn't understand. For five years he's lived on the run, in fear of his family and other wolves. Everything about Wolf's Paw is contrary to what he thought he knew, and he is terrified. Fearing his mate will run, Sheriff Nathaniel must calm his little wolf and show him he's more than a match for this big, bad alpha.

www.dreamspinnerpress.com

THE Firebird
and OTHER STORIES
R. Cooper

Being(s) in Love Stories

Magical creatures known as beings emerged from hiding amid the destruction of the First World War. Since then they've lived on the margins of the human world as misunderstood objects of fear and desire. Some are beautiful, others fearsome and powerful. Yet for all their magic and strength, they are as vulnerable as anyone when it comes to matters of the heart.

A firebird in 1930s Paris is drawn to a writer with a haunted past. Upon returning from fighting in the Pacific, a jaguar shifter finds a third-gender human on his doorstep. Early rock 'n' roll DJ Hyacinth the fairy shocks his listeners with his admiration for his quiet assistant. During the AIDS crisis, a gruff, leather-wearing troll dreams of a settled life with a mixed-species elf across the bar. An imp, who remembers only too well how cruel the world can be, tells himself he's content to stay behind the scenes—if only his chaotic, impish magic would stop getting in the way. And a shy human tending his poisonous and carnivorous plants is convinced no one will ever want him, certainly not the handsome werewolf grieving for a lost mate. Human or being, all must overcome fear to reach for love.

CPSIA information can be obtained
at www.ICGtesting.com
Printed in the USA
BVOW08s0822271216
471915BV00013B/77/P